Praise for *When a Stranger Comes to Town*

"There are 19 wildly varied stories in this collection from...Mystery Writers of America, and each one packs a punch of plot and character, bound so tightly in the short story format that their power can be explosive... *When a Stranger Comes to Town* will give you the very best of what crime fiction should deliver. Means, opportunity, and obsession—right?"

—New York Journal of Books

"Mystery enthusiasts will be hard-pressed to find a story they don't like."

—Library Journal, starred review

"Exceptional... This is the best kind of anthology, consistently excellent and inventive."

—Publishers Weekly, starred review

"A top-drawer, themed anthology... Excellent stories about strangers, fear, and usually, murder."

—Mystery Scene Magazine

"This collection offers the best of both worlds: expert storycraft from genre stars (Unger, Michael Connelly, and Steve Hamilton, among them) and standout entries from some new faces in crime fiction."

—Booklist

"Even with [Mystery Writers of America's] stellar reputation, *When a Stranger Comes to Town* is special.... Each author provides a twist or two not only in the plot, but also in what constitutes a 'stranger.'"

—Bookreporter

WHEN A STRANGER COMES TO TOWN

WHEN A STRANGER

COMES TO TOWN

A COLLECTION OF STORIES FROM
CRIME FICTION'S TOP AUTHORS

EDITED BY MICHAEL KORYTA

S.A. COSBY • AMANDA WITT • ALAFAIR BURKE

SMITA HARISH JAIN • MICHAEL CONNELLY

JACQUELINE FREIMOR • JOE R. LANSDALE

EMILYA NAYMARK • LISA UNGER

BRYON QUERTERMOUS • TILIA KLEBENOV JACOBS

LORI ROY • PAUL A. BARRA • MICHAEL KORYTA

ELAINE TOGNERI • JONATHAN STONE

STEVE HAMILTON • TINA deBELLEGARDE • JOE HILL

HANOVER
SQUARE
PRESS

HANOVER
SQUARE
PRESS™

Recycling programs
for this product may
not exist in your area.

ISBN-13: 978-1-335-42581-2

When a Stranger Comes to Town

First published in 2021. This edition published in 2022.
Copyright © 2021 by Mystery Writers of America, Inc.

Introduction
Copyright © 2021 by Michael Koryta

Solomon Wept
Copyright © 2021 by S.A. Cosby

Relative Stranger
Copyright © 2021 by Amanda Witt

Seat 2C
Copyright © 2021 by Alafair Burke

Kohinoor
Copyright © 2021 by Smita Harish Jain

Avalon
Copyright © 2021 by Michael Connelly

Here's to New Friends
Copyright © 2021 by Jacqueline Freimor

Room for One More
Copyright © 2021 by Joe R. Lansdale

Hanover Square Press
22 Adelaide St. West, 41st Floor
Toronto, Ontario M5H 4E3, Canada
HanoverSqPress.com
BookClubbish.com

Printed in U.S.A.

CONTENTS

INTRODUCTION

When the opportunity to serve as guest editor of the Mystery Writers of America's latest anthology came along, I had one goal for it: give the writers as much room as possible. I wanted to see all of the talent in this genre push in different directions, try some new things, and have some fun. But what theme would allow for that?

I thought then of a quote that has been misattributed to half the famous writers in history, most frequently to Leo Tolstoy. I'm still not sure who first said it, frankly, and that seems positively ideal for a mystery collection! The quote is: "All great literature is one of two stories; a man goes on a journey or a stranger comes to town."

A stranger comes to town. I liked that. I liked how broad it was. The stranger could be the hero or the villain. The town could be welcoming or hostile. It certainly allowed the writers plenty of room to have fun, and maybe stretch in some new directions.

I'm not sure how much fun they had writing the

gems that you're about to discover—based on the kvetching I heard about deadlines, which remarkably always seem to be a new discovery to writers—but *I* certainly had an enormous amount of fun reading them.

We range from the wickedest of visits-gone-bad (I'm thinking of Joe Lansdale's dark tale here) to the beautiful and emotional (looking at you, Lisa Unger!) and the spooky and surreal (thanks, Joe Hill!). I could go on about everyone's contribution—S.A. Cosby delivered a particularly delightful read, and, bless him, did it *ahead of deadline!*—but when you're talking about short stories, spoilers are all too easy to offer, and I refuse to rob the reader of the experience.

I'd be remiss, however, not to point out the breadth and depth of the genre's talent at this moment. When the judging committee forwarded to me their selections as winners for this collection, I was awestruck by the quality and excited by how many of these writers were new to me. One of the goals of MWA has always been to nurture and support new voices, and we have some terrific ones here. Of course, you're going to enjoy the likes of Michael Connelly and Alafair Burke and Lori Roy and Steve Hamilton showing off their pro chops and reminding you why they've amassed so many Edgar Award nominations, but please, please don't skim in search of the names you know; look for the names you might *not* know. I'm certain that from the minute the GPS instructs our protagonist to "exit now" in Emilya Naymark's lovely chiller, you'll be willing to take the ride with her. Emilya was a new name to me. Think I'm going to be looking for her work in the future? Absolutely.

The same goes for Smita Harish Jain, who takes us on a journey of morality—and morality policing—in

Mumbai. And you probably have heard of Bryon Quertermous by now, but if you're new to his work, you'll understand why I'm a fan after you read this opening:

> Howard told me three things before he died:
> 1. His last name was also Howard
> 2. The love of his life was a Ukrainian chat girl named Elsa
> 3. He was psychic

There are nineteen dark treats ahead for you, and my job is to shut up and get out of your way so you can get on to the main event. I know you'll enjoy the show. It was a privilege to be involved with this project, an appreciated chance to see new and different work from some of my longtime favorites, and a chance to be introduced to some I know I'll be reading for years to come.

Onward, then. Somewhere in these pages, an inebriated woman in need is about to slide into a most unusual cab in the desert, a man is saving his 2C boarding pass in the spirit of true love, and a boat called the *Double Tap* is running at 20 knots toward a place called Sheepshead Bay. I think they're all headed for trouble, personally. Turn the page and tell me if I'm wrong.

Michael Koryta

SOLOMON WEPT

BY S.A. COSBY

Parrish parked the car in the far corner of the gravel parking lot and killed the engine but it didn't die. It sputtered and coughed for a full minute before it went silent. She pulled down the visor and checked her makeup in the mirror. The wig was one hundred percent human hair that spilled down her back to the crack of her ass. The heavy rouge and dark lipstick gave her a mysterious look. She'd applied too much foundation on purpose. Her natural amber complexion was now close to olive. She got out of the car into the sultry night air. Beads of sweat appeared as if by magic at the base of her neck and on her chest. Her low-cut skintight red shirt offered scant relief. She grabbed her purse and hurried toward the bar. Her high heels crunching the gravel with every step. Just before she went inside she checked her purse. She knew the gun was in there but she wanted to see it again with her own eyes.

Calling the place a "bar" was a bit of a misnomer. It was more like a juke joint with bar-like aspirations.

A bluesy tune was playing on a crackling sound system. She didn't see a jukebox so it must have been the bartender's choice. She went to a booth in the back just past an ancient pool table with netted pockets. A sign above the bar informed patrons that it was a dollar a game and they kept the balls behind the bar. The few patrons in attendance didn't seem to have an interest in billiards. Parrish slipped into the booth and pulled out her phone. It was a burner with just enough minutes to last her through the weekend. Just enough minutes so she could text Jim and Tammy and tell them she had made it into town and was waiting for them at Deacon's out on Route 630. She'd gotten their real names from Curtis a week ago. She'd been out a year and it had taken her almost that long to find him. He'd left the pimp game and was cutting hair in a little nowhere town called Mathews County and dealing on the side. He'd had to switch careers rather abruptly. That's what happened when you were a pimp and one of your girls stabbed a date who was the son of a Richmond city councilman. They'd given Parrish a five-year sentence for stabbing the white boy. She'd tried to tell her public defender the boy had tried to choke the shit out of her and stick a flashlight up her ass but he didn't want to hear it. Neither had the judge.

Good behavior and overcrowding had gotten her out after eighteen months.

Her cell phone vibrated.

We are on our way, the text message said. Parrish sent back a text that indicated she couldn't wait to meet them. Pressing Send made her skin crawl. She got up and went to the bar.

"Hey, darling. What can I get you?" the bartender asked. He didn't try to pretend he wasn't giving her the once-over.

"Jameson on the rocks," Parrish said.

"You want to start a tab?"

"No," she said and pulled a five out of her purse. The bartender poured her drink and slid the glass over to her. She downed it and went back to the booth.

At first Curtis had pretended he didn't know who he'd sold her baby to or where they had gone. He'd belittled her. He'd insulted her. He'd laughed at her. He'd tried all the old tricks that had worked when he had been Silky C and she had been on his first string. None of that had bothered her. He didn't know it but the dynamic between them had changed irrevocably. She wasn't afraid of him anymore. He was just an old wannabe player standing in the middle of a small kitchenette in a raggedy trailer, heating up some grease to fry some fish, trying to make her feel bad about shit he'd made her do.

"I just want my baby, Curtis."

"I told you I don't remember nothing about them motherfuckers. You need to get on back down the road, trick," he'd said. Parrish had felt the dam inside her break.

"You sold my fucking baby! You ain't had no right to do that shit!" she'd yelled.

"Bitch, I did that boy a favor. He better off with them white people than with your junkie whore ass," Curtis had said. She'd gotten in his face then and that was when he had slapped her. A sharp backhand shot that snapped her head back and made her stumble. Back in the day she would have gone and hid for an hour. She would have spent that time trying to come up with a way to get back in his good graces.

That was then. This was now.

He'd had the audacity to turn his back on her. Like he was still the man. What a joke. He'd never been the man and she wasn't the scared little girl that he'd pimped out of a motel room on Chamberlin Avenue. She'd snatched the pan of grease from the stove.

"You still hit like a bitch," she'd said. When he turned she had tossed the bubbling oil in his incredulous face with a forehand shot that would have made Serena Williams proud. Once he'd gone down, she'd cracked him on the head with the frying pan. He'd sprawled across the cheap linoleum, whimpering like a newborn calf. Parrish had found some duct tape and tied his skinny frame to one of the mismatched chairs in his kitchen. At first he'd held on to the lie about who had bought her son. Then she'd gotten the paring knife and a bottle of rubbing alcohol from the bathroom. They had greatly improved his recall. White couple who said their names were Jim and Tammy. They lived in Blue Line County, North Carolina. They were rich and kinky and they didn't mind buying a mixed-race baby who would probably be able to pass for white out the back of a strip club.

Parrish motioned at the bartender. He brought her another Jameson and she handed him another five. She downed this one as quickly as the first.

After Curtis had told her everything, he'd begged her not to kill him. Right up until the moment she'd dropped the knife on the floor she thought she would. She'd held the knife to his throat as he blubbered and apologized before cursing and screaming at her. Telling her she wasn't shit. That she'd always be a "hoe." That was when she realized she didn't have to kill him. He was in the boonies barely eking out a living hustling rednecks for Oxys and Percs. For Silky C this was a living death. She'd ransacked the metal rectangle he called a home. She'd found the gun, $1500 in cash, a few dozen pills and the keys to the multicolored Oldsmobile Delta 88 he drove. She'd left him there among his tears and regrets.

Parrish's phone vibrated again.

Here. What are you? the text said. Parrish stared at the screen. Another text came through.

Sorry where are you.

She sent one back saying she was in the booth in the back.

It had only taken her a week to find their ad on Craigslist. All she had to do was narrow the search field down to Charlotte and surrounding areas. Curtis had told her what they liked the most. MW4W. AA. A man and a woman seeking a Black girl for adult fun. They even had their pictures in their ad. A thick-neck blond guy and a tight-faced brunette with more plastic than a Barbie doll. She'd searched ads with the keywords *Jim and Tammy*. They had been the second ad on the Blue Line subpage. They traded pics for a week. Finally, they had made a date. She'd talked to them on the phone. They'd been open and excited. They'd told her about themselves. How they were down for some fun. How they were church leaders. The "Jim and Tammy" thing was an in-joke.

They talked about their kids. The older ones who were grown and off spreading the gospel or their legs in the big bad world. And the little one. Their baby boy.

Their baby.

Parrish saw the front door open. A shaft of light from the pole lamp in the parking lot sliced through the cigarette smoke in the bar. A couple came through the doorway. A short, thick-necked man and tall, tight-faced brunette. Parrish bit down on the inside of her cheek and made herself smile. She waved them over. They both lit up like a Christmas tree when they saw her.

"Well, hello," Jim said. Parrish got up and hugged him and kissed him on the cheek. Tammy came around and gave her an awkward half hug and kissed her on the cheek. They slipped into the booth, Jim on one side, and Tammy and Parrish on the other.

"It's so nice to finally meet in person?" Tammy said. She ended the sentence with an interrogative inflection that set Parrish's teeth on edge. Jim was staring at her like a starving man staring at a slow-moving rabbit.

Just get to the house. Just get to the house. Just get to the house, Parrish thought. Her plan, if she could even call it that, was to get to the house, find her son, flash the gun and leave. That was it. She didn't have a backup plan and she hadn't thought about what would happen after she got her boy back. None of that really mattered. She just wanted to hold her son. He was six months old when she went inside. A beautiful ball of laughter and squeals that filled her with joy every time she looked at him. When Curtis had found out she was pregnant he'd told her to get rid of it but she kept putting it off until it was too late. He didn't care if he was the father or not but a pregnant hooker was a niche market. Curtis wasn't Dominic's father. Contrary to popular belief, sex workers were not mindless bags of meat without emotions who didn't try and take precautions. Dominic's father was not a date or a client or a john. He had started out as a friend and had evolved into a lover. She'd kept him a secret from Curtis. Not because Curtis would have hurt him but because he would have killed Curtis. Tony worked for Shade Sinclair, kingpin of the Carolinas. Dominic's father was a mountain of a man who never raised his hand to her. When she had gotten a letter from her girl Hope telling her Tony had been killed in a drug deal gone bad, she thought that was the worst pain she could ever feel. Until she'd gotten the letter from Curtis telling her he'd sold her son.

"What ya drinking?" Jim asked. He grinned so wide she could swear he had sixty-four teeth. Parrish smiled back.

"Jameson on the rocks," she said. She felt a hand on her thigh. She turned her head and Tammy was smiling too. The skin around her eyes was as tight as a rich man's pockets. Parrish thought Tammy needed to cut back on the Botox.

"Barkeep, three Jameson on the rocks!" Jim yelled. Parrish thought Jim looked just the kind of guy that would call a bartender "barkeep." She didn't hate these people. They might have bought a baby illegally but they didn't know they had stolen her son. She didn't really like them though. Their phoniness was like the rot from roadkill that's been roasting in the sun for a few days. She could almost taste it. She was just a kink for them. An "exotic" Nubian princess they could share.

Well, you do plan on pulling a gun on them, so maybe don't judge them too harshly, a voice in her head intoned.

The bartender brought over a round of drinks. Then another. And another. By the time they had settled up, Jim was red-faced and drooling just a bit. He tossed Tammy the keys and leaned against the passenger side of their Lexus.

"Why don't you girls give each other a kiss," he slurred. Tammy turned to Parrish and moved a lock of hair out of her face. Parrish closed her eyes as Tammy's tongue pushed into her mouth.

"Yeah. That's nice. I like that," Jim said. His breath was coming in ragged staccato bursts.

Just get to the house, Parrish thought.

* * *

The house was a mansion. A tan brick and rough-hewn stone monstrosity that could hold every house Parrish had ever lived in stacked on top of each other with room to spare. Jim and Tammy's house sat at the end of a nearly mile-long driveway covered with white peastones and lined with Leyland cypresses. She'd insisted on driving the car she'd stolen from Curtis. She parked it behind the Lexus. She checked her purse again and then got out. The couple wrapped their arms around her as they all climbed the stone steps to the front door.

The foyer of Jim and Tammy's house was a cavernous expanse with gray marble flooring. Jim playfully squeezed Tammy's and Parrish's backsides.

"Let's get some more drinks," he said. He went to a tall armoire in the corner of the living room. He took out a heavy glass decanter and three whiskey glasses. Tammy kicked off her heels and came up behind Parrish.

"I'm gonna suck your clit like it's a pacifier," she whispered in her ear. Parrish moaned just enough to make Tammy chuckle. She took in the rest of the house; an ornate spiral staircase was to her left. Straight ahead was a hallway that led to the rest of the darkened house. Jim walked toward her on spaghetti legs.

If I was gonna fuck him he probably couldn't get it up, Parrish thought. As if he'd telepathically received her bon mot, Jim tripped, stumbled and dropped the tray of glasses and liquor. The crash was thunderous. The excellent acoustics in the house turned the echoes into a symphony.

"Goddammit!" Jim yelled.

"Jim, the baby," Tammy said. A brittleness to her

tone told Parrish this wasn't an unusual occurrence with good old Jim.

Then she heard it. As sharp and as clear as Gabriel's horn.

A child's cry. A child crying, awakened from his sleep and afraid. Her baby boy. Her Dominic.

"You fucking woke him up again," Tammy said.

"Well, go put him back to sleep. I'll… I'll clean this up," Jim said. He shambled off into the darkness. Tammy smoothed back her hair and smiled at Parrish. It was like she was putting on a mask.

"Excuse me for a minute. I'll be right back," she said. Parrish watched her stomp up the stairs. She heard Jim crashing around in the back of the house and before she knew it, her feet were moving and she was climbing the stairs. When she reached the landing, she heard Tammy's voice coming from the last room on the left.

"You better stop that fucking crying. You better lay your ass down. I'm not playing with you, ya little crack baby," Tammy said. A pain grabbed Parrish's guts and squeezed them in an iron grip. Saliva filled her mouth as she walked closer and closer to the open door. She heard a sound like the clap of bare hands and the cries of the baby, her Dominic, stopped with a frightening suddenness.

Tammy was standing above his bed with her hand raised. The room was a baby boy's fantasy. It was filled with so many toys Parrish could barely see the floor. All manner of cartoon characters populated the walls in framed posters. Tammy was standing at an angle that afforded Parrish a view of the toddler's tiny face. She locked eyes with him and she knew that this was not a rare occurrence either. Tammy noticed her and turned to face her.

"Kids. They need discipline," Tammy said.

"Yeah," Parrish said.

She reached inside her purse and pulled out the gun. A six-shot revolver. A .32 or maybe a .38. She wasn't sure. She aimed it at Tammy.

"What are you—" Tammy started to say but Parrish shot her in the throat. Her last words with that interrogative intonation reverberated in Parrish's head. Dominic started crying again as Tammy crumpled to the floor. Hard footsteps pounded up the stairs. Parrish stepped out of the room just as Jim hit the landing.

"What the fuck was that?" Jim asked.

"This," Parrish said. She shot him in the stomach. He stumbled backward but caught himself and started to advance on her. She shot him again and this time he dropped like a wet sheet falling off a clothesline. Parrish went back into the room and stepped over Tammy.

"Hey. Hey shhh it's okay. I gotcha now. Mama got you," she cooed at the boy. He was having none of it. He screamed and screamed even as she hugged him to her chest. Tammy's last words floated up from the lake of her memories. She could see her eyes stretched as wide as the Botox would allow.

What are you.

Parrish had to drive around Blue Line County for thirty minutes before she found the sheriff's office. All the driving had put Dominic to sleep. He was curled up in his blanket in the passenger's seat with his plump thumb in his mouth. An unruly mop of blackish-brown curls on top of his head. A gift from his daddy.

Parrish parked the car in the parking spot farthest from the door of the sheriff's office. The area around the sheriff's office was the only place she'd seen in the whole county with sidewalks and streetlamps. To the west was the town grocery store and pharmacy. To the east was the courthouse and what she assumed was the fire station. Parrish leaned over the center console and kissed Dominic on the forehead.

She got out the car and left the keys in the ignition. She started walking east. She had traded her heels for a pair of Tammy's workout athletic shoes. They were snug but they were better than heels. She walked until she passed the grocery store and the sidewalk ran out. She saw a sign up ahead that said the interstate was five miles if she turned right on Route 609. She pulled out her burner. She dialed 911.

"Blue Line Sheriff's Office," the female voice said.

"There's a little boy asleep in a car in your parking lot. He needs a good home. He needs a good mama," she said. Before the dispatcher could ask any questions, she ended the call and dropped the phone. Parrish stomped on it and started walking again. She thought she might start to cry but all her tears seemed to have gotten lost on the way to her eyes.

* * * * *

RELATIVE STRANGER

BY AMANDA WITT

When the doorbell rang, Glory Crockett was up to her elbows in flour and Crisco. She took five seconds to finish crimping the edges of the last piecrust, shot a glance at the oven timer—one minute and thirty-eight seconds, and the pies wouldn't quite be done even then—and headed for the front door, snatching up a dish towel to wipe her hands as she went.

The floor gave off a hollow echo underfoot; the house was old, a shingle-sided farmhouse plunked down alone in a quarter section of wheat and cotton fields. Owen's grandparents had modernized periodically, but time had a way of passing. The kitchen boasted white-painted aluminum cabinets, and the dishwasher was a portable that had to be pulled in from the mudroom and hooked with a hose to the kitchen faucet. The bedrooms were small, the walls thin, and skunks kept wriggling into the crawl space and setting up housekeeping there.

But Glory loved the place; she loved everything

about it. For one, it held generations of Crockett family history. For another, it was bought and paid for. She and Owen were one hundred percent debt-free.

They'd made some upgrades—brought the electrical and plumbing up to code, installed ceiling fans. Glory tipped up her face as she passed beneath one, its breeze fluttering her dark hair and, more to the point, drying the sweat on her brow.

This was the thing that stunned their town friends, even more than did their lack of internet or cell phone coverage: the Crocketts didn't have central air. And it did get hot in North Texas; there was a reason the Wichita Falls bicycle race was called the *Hotter'N Hell Hundred*.

But the Crocketts had more means of relief than any other generation who'd lived on their farm. They had the ceiling fans, and plug-in box fans and a couple of loud rattly window units if they got really desperate. And they had screen doors to catch the breeze, and strategically planted trees, and old-fashioned window shades pulled down tight on whichever side of the house currently faced the Texas sun.

At the moment the sun was in the west, so the living room was dark save for watery blue light filtering in through three narrow vertical windows in the front door.

Through those windows Glory could see a man standing on her front step. He was looking back toward the gravel road, his face in profile, and for a split second Glory thought it was her husband.

One of the boys must have locked the storm door— they did that sometimes, locking each other out, grinning through various windows before slipping out the mudroom door to round the house and pounce. As for why Owen would be home this time of day, well, there could be any number of reasons—tractor trouble, fences down, what have you. And Owen never grabbed what he needed from the barn or tractor shed without swinging by the house to say hey. He and Glory might be cresting their thirties and raising four kids, but they still had a spark.

Glory pushed her hair out of her face and smiled, was still smiling as she reached for the doorknob.

The man on the step turned and looked straight at her. Glory's heart gave a startled thud; her cheeks flushed hot.

She and Owen had been married fourteen years. She knew every angle of his face, every scar on his body, every expression, gesture, posture, mood. How could she possibly have confused him, even for a heartbeat, with a stranger?

For this was a stranger, a man she'd never seen before in her life. Glory was sure of that, just as she was sure he wasn't actually looking at her—the reflective window film worked like a one-way mirror.

But he certainly appeared to be looking at her, and he certainly bore a resemblance to Owen, though not as strong as that first glance had suggested. They both had deep-set blue eyes and thick dark blond hair, and their general build was the same, but this stranger was older, or at least had lived a harder life. He might once have been better looking than Owen; he had that air of conscious charm that formerly handsome men so often wore. Formerly handsome men, and grifters. Used-car salesmen and the like.

The stranger raised one hand to his forehead, shielding his eyes as if that might help him see through the window and into the house. "Glory?" he said.

He knew her name.

Maybe that should have been reassuring, but Glory's

mouth went dry. She wanted to turn the dead bolt, then run back through the house to slam and lock the other outside door, too. But that was silly—this man clearly wasn't some random stranger, but an unmet relative of Owen's, and anyway, the kids were outside somewhere, and Glory wasn't about to lock herself in and her boys out, not ever, but especially not with a stranger on the front stoop.

In the kitchen, the oven timer began to beep. She pulled open the solid door.

"There you are," the man said easily, smiling at her through the screen of the storm door. "Owen told me to come on inside." He was wearing jeans, boots and a lightweight chambray button-down over a T-shirt— the clothes of a workingman, although now, without the distorting blue tint of the windows, Glory saw that his flesh was pale.

The stranger glanced off to his left, toward the barn. "Owen said he'd be right on in. Said you'd give us some ice tea before we head back out."

Glory leaned way over, near the screen, giving her-self a line of sight. She still couldn't see the outbuild-ings, but sure enough, Owen's battered pickup sat on the sandy pull-around, half-hidden by the silvery pro-pane tank and the giant lantana bush, where he always parked when he needed something from the barn.

The sight sent relief tingling through her veins, fol-lowed by annoyed embarrassment. Glory was a per-fectly capable woman, and not the nervous sort. It was that brief moment of misidentification that had unnerved her, she thought, that visceral sense of solid ground turning to quicksand beneath her feet. She still hadn't quite regained her footing.

And so she hesitated one moment more. "What's Owen doing?" she said.

"Looking for something to jury-rig the tractor." The man grinned. "Actually, to jury-rig the hell-forsaken motherless son of a waffle iron, if you want to know the truth."

Glory smiled. "Owen's a master of creative cussing," she said, slinging the dish towel over her shoulder to free both hands, and the man stepped back as she un-latched the storm door and pushed it open.

"And he always was good with a wrench," the stranger said, moving past Glory into the house, so close she could feel the heat of his body intensified by the heat he'd absorbed while standing on her concrete stoop in the sun. He felt hot and he smelled hot, but he also gave off a faint smell of something else, something unpleasant—not sweat, dirt and machine oil, a combi-nation with which Glory was intimately familiar, but something sharper and uglier.

"Owen can fix anything," she agreed absently—try-ing to identify that odor: sharp, foully organic, like he somehow was sweating ammonia—and in fact, Owen could. Like many small farmers, he scorned modern equipment in favor of old machines that could be fixed with baling wire and a can-do attitude. New machines, with their proprietary this and that, their computerized motherboards, their high-tech electronics, required a phone call to the dealer, diagnostic software, specially ordered parts, an appointment with a certified repair tech. And in the meantime, fields sat fallow or crops rotted unharvested.

In the kitchen, the oven timer continued its relent-less beeping.

"Sounds like you're busy," the stranger said, glanc-ing around the dimly lit room as he moved toward the kitchen. "Don't let me keep you."

"It's the pies," Glory said, and because she was hoping Owen would hurry on to the house, because she didn't want to sit through a glass of tea and piece of pie alone with this too-charming stranger who smelled of—chemicals? Cat pee? She kept her hand on the storm door longer than strictly necessary, holding it open even as she began turning away.

Something on the white outer door frame caught her eye.

A thick smear, glistening in the sun. Red. Not orange-red like the mud in the nearby Red River, not flaming red like the strawberries she'd given the boys with lunch, not red like any other naturally occurring substance in the whole wide world.

Glory was a farmwife with a husband and four boys. She was not unduly flustered by blood, either animal or human. But her mind ran the calculation: *wet blood. Hot dry day.*

That meant the blood was newly deposited, and by a stranger behaving with painstaking casualness, a stranger who had not said, "Hey, Owen told me to come on in and get a bandage because I caught my hand on barbwire," nothing like that.

Instinctively Glory leaned into the still-closing door, moving toward the outside and her husband. They were out in the middle of nowhere—half a mile from the nearest neighbor—but Owen kept a varmint rifle behind the seat in his truck, a .22 for skunks and snakes, and maybe Glory was being stupid, maybe this was nothing, but the stranger smelled like evil and Glory had children to protect.

Her foot was raised to step outside; her heart pounded so hard it hurt. She was a breath away from freedom when, from inside the house, came a sound she heard dozens of times each day: the unmistakable screech of the mudroom screen door swinging open.

Owen? She hoped it was Owen. Dear God, please let it be her husband. The stranger was watching her, a faint smile on his face.

If it was yet another strange man, if there were two of them—

"Mom!" Eric called. Her middle boy, ten years old. "Mom, the timer's going off!"

"I'll get it!" Glory called, thinking, *Go back outside, Eric, go back outside—*

The mudroom screen slammed shut. *Please be outside—*

"I can do it," Eric said from the kitchen, and the beeping stopped. "Do you want me to take the pies out?"

Glory moved her hand and let the storm door swing closed.

"Now, this is nice," the stranger said, surveying the kitchen. He inhaled deeply, appreciatively.

Over by the oven, Eric looked smaller than usual. He was staring at the stranger with round eyes, and Glory didn't know if he was startled in general by the sudden appearance of a stranger in their kitchen, or startled by this stranger in particular, or wasn't startled at all but was picking up on his mother's tension.

Glory cleared her throat. "Eric," she said carefully, "this is—"

She didn't know his name. She had let this stranger into her house without even knowing his name.

She looked at him standing there between her and her son, big and threateningly amiable, smiling like he knew some secret malevolent joke.

"What's your name?" she said bluntly. She was going to get him out of her house, and then even if everything turned out to be fine—which it wouldn't,

according to the hollowness at the pit of her stomach—
she was going to pass his name along to the sheriff.

"Well now, that's the funny thing," the stranger said,
looking at Eric. "I'm Owen Crockett, same as your
dad."

Pieces fell into place. They didn't make things
any better, but they gave a little context. "Your dad's
cousin," Glory said to her son. Had Eric heard those
stories? And would he remember if he had?

"First cousin once removed," the stranger corrected,
a bitter edge sliding through the thick charm. "Heavy
on the *removed*."

Outside the kitchen window, boyish laughter rang
out. The stranger leaned over the sink and reached for
the blue gingham curtain, twitched it to one side.

Glory shut her eyes. She'd hoped the twins and Little O would stay away, playing by the river or explor-
ing the derelict house down the road, building forts in
the hayloft, traipsing around the pasture in search of
arrowheads. Out of sight, out of reach. She'd hoped at
least some of her children might be safe.

When she opened her eyes, Eric was looking at
her. He was the only boy who took after Glory—dark-
haired, dark-eyed—and likewise the two of them often
were on the same wavelength. He looked at her, and she
looked back, and she knew that he knew she was afraid.

Maybe Eric could get to the phone. It was a land-
line, old-fashioned copper wire, unreliable nowadays because the phone company wanted everyone to
switch to fiber-optic, even in areas where fiber-optic
hadn't come. If the phone worked, and if Eric could get
through to the sheriff, and if the sheriff happened to be
way out in this part of Wilbarger County...

Too many ifs.

But what else could they do? Glory's mind felt paralyzed, like a rabbit in a spotlight, unable to do anything but keep up a constant static hum, saying again and again the mantra she'd been repeating ever since she spotted the blood: *Please, God, let Owen be okay.*

Meanwhile the other Owen stood gazing out the window at Glory's other boys, a calculating expression on his face. Calculating, and something else.

Hot. His eyes were hot.

Glory felt the hair rise on the back of her neck.

She cut her eyes at Eric, then at the other Owen, then back to Eric. She didn't dare do more than that, couldn't convey anything to her son other than a general warning, didn't even know what else she might hope to convey.

Eric apparently thought she communicated something.

He straightened up and squared his narrow shoulders. "Pleased to meet you, sir," he said. "I'm Eric Delaney Crockett."

The stranger with his father's name lingered at the window a moment longer, the tip of his tongue moistening his lips, before turning away with evident reluctance. "Say again?"

"Eric Delaney Crockett." The boy took a step forward, and Glory saw his throat move as he swallowed nervously. "Pleased to meet you."

When he stuck out his hand, Glory's heart broke a little. Eric was distracting this man from his brothers because he thought Glory wanted him to.

The other Owen stared at Eric a long moment, blinking rapidly. *Drugs*, Glory thought belatedly. *That smell, the dilated pupils. Maybe meth.*

Then he laughed, confirming her guess with blackened molars. "It's a treat to meet such a well-brought-up young man," he said, and reached for Eric's outstretched hand.

Glory shuddered, praying that this Owen's fingers weren't sticky with her Owen's blood. Of course, even if his hands were pristinely clean, she didn't want him touching her boy. But she couldn't intervene. She couldn't escalate. She couldn't openly acknowledge what was happening, because maybe he hadn't seen her notice the blood, maybe if she acted casual there would be a chance to somehow get the upper hand. A chance to get her boys all safely away. A chance to check on Owen.

Glory cast her gaze wildly about, searching for an idea or a weapon. The knives were out of reach, her rolling pin was only an empty beer bottle, the buttermilk was no help, and—

"You must be the middle kid," the other Owen said, gesturing at the window.

Eric nodded. Clint and Cody—fraternal twins—were twelve; Eric was ten; Little Owen was six. But Eric didn't explain any of that, and Glory was glad. She was going to get rid of this man, and when he was gone she didn't want him thinking about her boys, tasting their names, counting their years. She didn't want a single detail about them taking up residence in his mind.

"Me, I was the oldest kid in my family." The man shifted from foot to foot, scratching vigorously at one arm. "And the youngest. And the middle-est." He laughed, then turned mockingly serious. "An only child is everyone all rolled into one. Would you like to be an only, do you think?"

Glory's jaw clenched.

"I think I'd miss my brothers," Eric said evenly. Glory couldn't tell if he'd registered the man's words as any sort of threat, but he clearly wasn't finding this other Owen appealing. He stood with his back pressed against the oven door, hot though it was. His dark hair stuck to his head in sweaty curls.

"Well, sure," Other Owen said, scratching at his other arm. "Onlies can get lonely. I was born less than a week before your dad, did you know that?"

"So at least you had a cousin," Eric said.

"Once removed," Other Owen said, darkly. "The removing part sucks."

Juvenile detention, Glory knew. Jails, treatment centers, prison, halfway houses. Crimes of violence, crimes of opportunity. Assault. Blackmail. Perjury. Petty theft. Drugs. You name it, the other Owen Crockett had done it.

"He's a one-man crime spree," Owen had said with a sigh, filling out an affidavit for their lawyer. "At least people around here know he's not me."

At the time Glory had never met the man; she wished she could still say the same. "Why do you have the same name?" Eric asked.

"That's a good question." Other Owen rocked back on his heels and shot a glance at Glory. "Supposedly my folks didn't get word out soon enough. So your grandparents stole my name." The harsh words rang out sharply, like a plate dropped on the linoleum floor.

"I'm thinking I should get it back again," he continued. "Maybe merge the two, you know?" He brought his two hands together, squeezed like he was choking someone.

Glory, appalled, was speechless.

Eric's face went thoughtful. "Lots of people in the world have the same name," he offered. "Especially in Iran. In Iran the government has a list, and you're only allowed to give your kids names on that list."

The Crocketts had befriended a Persian immigrant

at church, a man who delighted in explaining to the boys how very alike—and very different—Iran and North Texas were.

"They hunt falcons in Iran," Eric said. "That's okay there."

Other Owen didn't answer. Instead he raised his head and sniffed the air. "You better deal with those pies," he said. "They're starting to burn." Glory moved toward the oven, toward her son.

"Where's Dad?" Eric said, not quite in an undertone.

"In the barn," Glory murmured. In the barn, hopefully still alive.

"How about you go call the other kids," Other Owen said, and gestured with a wide emphatic motion that knocked the saltshaker off the counter. "I want to meet the whole family."

Glory took a deep breath. "Go on," she told Eric. "Find your brothers." *Go and keep on going*, she thought, wishing for telepathy. *Take the truck. Get help. Don't look back.*

"Not him." Other Owen put his hands on Eric's shoulders. "You."

Glory forced her eyes away from those hands on her boy.

"Sure." With effort she kept her tone easy. "Just let me get these pies out first." She opened the oven door, filling the already hot kitchen with more heat and the scent of cinnamon apple.

Eric whistled, shrill in the small room, piercing Glory's jangled nerves.

"Can you do that?" he asked. He pulled away from Other Owen and wrested a chair out from under the kitchen table, banging it loudly against the table leg. "Some people can't whistle. Mom can't. But I can." He sat down and whistled again, waving one hand like a conductor as he shaped the distinctive first eight notes of Beethoven's Fifth.

Other Owen looked at Glory. She managed a shrug. "We don't get many visitors," she said. "Be glad we don't have a piano."

She removed the pies from the oven as slowly as she dared, while with varying degrees of accuracy Eric whistled Beethoven's Fifth again and again.

Hot pies could be weaponized. If Other Owen weren't standing so close to Eric, Glory would throw a hot pie in his face.

Eric changed tunes, producing a high wavering siren. "I can do that, too. We have mockingbirds, and sometimes they answer me." He made the siren noise again, even more loudly.

Glory moved the two pies from the stove top to the counter. Slowly, she slid the other two pies onto the oven rack. She tore strips of foil and laid them along the edges of the crusts. She closed the door. She opened the door, adjusted the foil, closed the door again. She set the timer. She retrieved the saltshaker from the floor. She canceled the timer and set it again. All the while, Eric whistled.

Other Owen frowned. "Get all the boys in here," he told Glory, dropping all pretense of charm. "Do it now."

With one last look at her son, Glory crossed through the mudroom and pushed open the screen door. Her yard, so peaceful and familiar, looked strangely out of joint. The clothesline sagged dispiritedly, one short end dangling in the dust. Beneath the fruitless mulberry an array of toy soldiers lay abandoned, dying on a battle-field of sand. Near the three-sided tractor shed a pair of angry kites plunged and screeched, defending their nest, and from here Glory could see, as she hadn't be-fore, that one door to Owen's truck hung ajar.

She could no longer hear her other boys—she hoped they'd caught Eric's signal, prayed they'd realize he meant it, that he wasn't just fooling around.

Da-da-da-dum. Go to the barn.

Owen had gone through a phase of calling the kids that way, claiming that whistling a code was easier than shouting. But the habit had faded, as so many family phases did; Glory didn't dare hope the boys would actually pay attention now.

If they did, she prayed they wouldn't be scarred for life. A scene flashed through her mind—the boys going to the barn, finding their father's bloodied and lifeless body, running screaming to the house. Straight to the drug-desperate man who watched them with hot eyes.

"You going to call those boys, or just let flies in?"

Glory moistened her dry lips. "Little O!"

Beethoven's Fifth rang out again behind her.

"Clint!"

The siren.

Glory was opening her mouth to call Cody when the sound of a chair juddering across the kitchen floor stopped her.

"That's enough, kid," Other Owen said. "Zip it."

Glory shot an uncertain look over her shoulder. What was he doing? She didn't want to leave Eric alone with him a second longer than necessary, but if she could catch the eye of the other boys, wave them away while pretending to call them—

Clint came around the corner of the house. Wildly, Glory shooed him off. "Clint!" she shouted, as loudly as if he were miles away.

He frowned at her. "Dude," he said. "I'm right here."

"Don't call me *dude*," Glory said automatically.

Her older twin stopped at the base of the concrete stoop—twelve years old, sure of himself, and so vulnerable it made Glory's teeth hurt. Clint drew the eye. He was a lovely child, angelic in appearance in a way his three brothers were not. Glory knew with sick certainty that it was his innocent beauty Other Owen had been eyeing.

"Hey." Clint looked past her shoulder and jerked his chin up in greeting. "Who're you?"

Glory felt the man standing behind her before she turned her head. Felt him and smelled him, the meth seeping out of his pores, his rotting teeth.

"The pretty one's not as polite as his brother," Other Owen said. He'd brought Eric along with him, one large hand gripping the back of the boy's neck.

"Where's the other one?" he said. "The little one."

Glory's heart filled her throat. She stepped off the stoop and stared at Clint, willing him to let it pass, to just this once refrain from correcting misinformation. To let Cody's existence pass unremarked.

Clint gave a one-shouldered shrug. "Last I saw he was feeding the fish." He looked at Glory. "You told him to stop giving them so much oatmeal, so he started digging worms behind the barn. I told him too much food was too much food, but he wouldn't listen."

"What fish?" Other Owen asked.

"Goldfish." Clint pointed at the concrete watering trough beside the barn. Its outer wall showed dark where water had overflowed, as it did when one of the boys fell in.

"Get inside the house," Other Owen told Clint. "We're going to have a little party."

Clint took a few steps backward. "I need to look for Little O."

Other Owen moved toward him, still gripping Eric by the nape of the neck. "No, you don't. You're going to come with me. In fact—"

He glanced at Owen's pickup. The keys would be dangling in the ignition, Glory knew. "Don't even think it," she said. "You're not taking my children anywhere."

Other Owen stared at her, squinting, his pupils dilated even in the blazing sun. "Who's going to stop me?" He sounded honestly baffled.

"I am," Glory said, and he laughed outright.

"You're just a little thing," he said, fondly amused. "And you've been dithering around for twenty minutes."

Glory had never been less amused in her life. "I will kill you before I let you take my sons."

Clint blinked at his mother, impressed, but Other Owen didn't seem to even hear her words. Instead, his face lit up with a thought. "Once we're away from here, I can show identification. Prove they're mine. Heck, maybe they *are* mine, in some parallel universe. The two blond ones look like they'd be mine."

A chill ran through Glory despite the sweltering heat. Psychosis, drugs, dead brain cells, evil—whatever twisted thing worked in this man, there was no reasoning with it. He was a loose cannon.

Something moved at the corner of the house. It might be nothing—wind in the myrtle bushes, a mockingbird. Glory didn't look.

Instead she shifted, and the man's eyes followed her, and Eric—watching Glory's face with utter focus, as if for some cue—yelped in sudden pain.

"You're hurting him!" Clint said, pointing at the hand around his brother's neck.

Other Owen looked down as if he'd forgotten Eric's existence. When he looked back up at Glory, his expression had turned thoughtful.

"You can keep the littlest," he said. "I'll only take these two. You and Owen can always make—"

Something flitted across his face, a memory, a darkness—*Don't say it*, Glory thought, and her stomach turned over and filled her mouth with bitter saliva. *Don't say you killed my husband. Don't say we can't make more.*

Sunlight flashed. From behind the man Cody raised a gleaming shovel, brought it down hard.

The blow fell with a sickening thud. Other Owen looked surprised; he staggered, but he didn't fall.

Glory lunged, yanking Eric away, pushing him behind her. Other Owen surged forward, grappling with her, reaching for her boy. His breath was hot on her face; his hands were everywhere.

Glory cocked back a fist and punched him hard in the nose. His head jerked to one side. Blood ran streaming down his face, into his teeth.

His eyes went suddenly blank with fury and he roared, grabbing Glory hard by the upper arm, slinging her around and out of his way. She hit the side of the house, her shoulder reverberating with pain, and turned to see Clint plowing forward, bulling his head into Other Owen's stomach. The man stumbled backward into Cody and all three went down in a heap, the shovel clanging to the ground as Cody lost his grip on it.

"Get off my boys!" Glory yelled, and kicked Other Owen hard in the ribs.

Clint wrapped his arms around the man's legs. Cody squirmed out from the bottom of the pile and flung himself down on the man's chest. Together the two boys might have been half Other Owen's weight. Glory circled, trying to find an opening for another kick, but the boys were everywhere, arms and legs flailing.

"Tie him up!" Clint yelled. "O! Where's O? Tie him up!"

"First we have to roll him over!" Cody shouted. "Roll him, then hog-tie him!"

They wrestled with their father all the time, but Owen would never hurt them. This Owen had no such qualms. He grabbed Cody around the jaw and wrenched him off, then kicked free of Clint and got to his feet as Little O came banging out the front door, cowboy hat on his head, a length of cut clothesline trailing behind him.

Glory shoved Other Owen hard from behind, putting all her weight into it. He staggered—and so did she—and he spat a mouthful of blood and lunged toward the nearest boy.

"Get away from him!" Glory yelled at her sons. If he got hold of one of them, they'd be right back where they started—a hostage, a standoff. "Run!"

The boys didn't run, but they danced out of arm's reach, forming a half circle behind their mother as she snatched up the shovel, held it threateningly.

"I'm gonna take that away and beat you bloody with it," Other Owen said, wiping his mouth with the back of his hand.

"Get the .22," she said to the boys, not looking at them. "Get it out of Dad's truck."

"They already did."

The voice came from behind her. Glory didn't look—she couldn't take her attention from the threat to her sons—but her chest filled with light and her eyes filled with tears. "Owen?" she said, blinking hard.

"I'm okay." He moved up beside her, rifle pointed. "Put your hands on top of your head and sit down."

"They attacked me," the other Owen said. His face turned pitiful, his voice aggrieved. "I came to meet your family, Owen, and—"

"Sit." Owen's tone brooked no argument.

"Cross-legged," Eric suggested. "So he can't get up very fast."

The other Owen looked at his cousin. "You aren't going to shoot me. You wouldn't do that. Anyway that baby gun wouldn't do much."

"It kills feral pigs," said Cody. "If you get them right in the eye."

"And snakes," said Clint. "Blows the heads right off rattlers."

"A .22 can actually be worse than a bigger bullet because it might not go straight through you," Eric explained. "It ricochets around inside the body and turns your organs to mush."

The other Owen lowered himself to the ground and laced his fingers together on top of his head. Bloody, dusty, drug-addled and prematurely aged, still he looked heartbreakingly like Glory's husband. After a moment's hesitation, he bent his knees and crossed his legs.

"You're not very good at that," Eric observed, eyeing him critically. The other Owen spat blood into the dirt, didn't reply.

For a moment the family stood silent, catching their breath as the hot summer afternoon settled peaceably around them. In the shade near the house a turtle trundled along. In the distance, a cow lowed.

"Well, that's that," Clint said, and dusted his hands. "Mission accomplished, even if it didn't go exactly like we planned."

Cody snorted. "That's because our plan sucked."

"We didn't have time to make a better one. And, anyway, it worked."

"I could have hit him harder," Cody said musingly. "Only I didn't want to kill him."

Little O pressed against Glory's leg. "Can I tie him up now?"

"No," she said. "I don't want you getting too close. He might grab you."

"But that's my job. Tying him up is my job."

Clint broke in before Glory could answer. "O, did you call the sheriff?"

Little Owen nodded, looking up at his mother. "That was my other job," he said. "Get the clothesline to tie him up, and call the sheriff. And I did. I climbed in your bedroom window and I called. He said he'd hurry."

"You did great." Glory pulled him tight against her. "You all did great. I am so proud of every one of you."

"I made him look the other way," Eric said, spreading his arms expansively. "When I saw Clint and Cody in the yard, I went over to the kitchen table so he'd look at me and not at them. And I whistled. I sent them to the barn."

"We found Dad out there," Cody said. "We woke him up, but he was sort of wobbly. He couldn't really stand. So we left him the rifle, in case the guy managed to get back there again."

"I wanted to keep the rifle," Clint conceded. "But Cody thought somebody might get hit in the cross fire. So we let Dad keep it."

"And I got a shovel from the tractor shed." Cody shook his head. "Those stupid kites wouldn't shut up. I really thought they were going to give me away."

"Then I drew his attention so Cody could flank him," Clint said. The sun gilded his long eyelashes, kissed his flushed cheeks. "I was the bait."

Glory's heart constricted.

"It was good that you lured him outside, Mom," Clint went on. "We were going to do it in the house, but the floor's so loud. We were worried about that."

Lured him.

Glory opened her mouth to say she hadn't lured him, that she hadn't done much of anything to save her boys, really. Except raise them. But they were chattering too much for her to get a word in.

"I could have been quiet enough inside," Cody said. "But I could whack him better outside. Inside, the walls might have gotten in the way." He frowned. "But I should have whacked him harder. Mom, don't you think I could have whacked him harder without killing him?"

On the ground, the other Owen stared blankly at Glory's noisy, jubilant family. Her men. Her own Owen breathed a tired laugh, and—finally—Glory felt confident enough of her sons' safety to glance up at her husband.

"You're soaking wet," she said, dropping the shovel and putting a hand on his arm.

"That's how they woke me. I think you probably lost a few goldfish." One side of his face was badly swollen and discolored, and blood sheeted thinly from a cut on his scalp.

"We need to put pressure on that," Glory said.

"Can't." Owen gestured with the barrel of the rifle. "I've got to keep Owen here in line."

"Give the gun to Cody."

"Cody might accidentally-on-purpose shoot him."

"Well, at least I could hit him a little harder," Cody said, picking up the shovel.

"No," Owen said, softly but with something in his voice that made all four boys straighten with respect.

And the other Owen, too. Eyes glazed, alone in the circle, emotions shifting like shadows across his face, he stared at Glory's husband.

She pictured them—two cousins very much alike, boys with the same name and almost the same birthday. Playing together, fishing, building forts, unwrapping Christmas presents, laughing at the table during Sunday dinners. Stepping onto divergent paths through months and choices and years that eventually, part and parcel, led them far apart and then, full circle, to this moment at their family's farm—one standing with a gun in his hands, the other sitting in the dirt at his feet.

The other Owen's gaze sharpened. "Owen, you better tend to that," he said. No charm, no menace, no mockery. Just genuine concern. "You're bleeding something fierce."

"Lean over," Glory said to her husband. "Let me reach."

Owen did, and Glory pulled the dish towel from her shoulder. It smelled like apples and cinnamon.

Inside the house, the oven timer rang.

* * * * *

SEAT 2C

BY ALAFAIR BURKE

The man in the booth at the facility entrance stared into the screen of an iPad, his brow furrowed, seemingly oblivious to the quiet hum of her Tesla or the sound of the car window rolling down.

"Good evening," she finally said.

He tried stepping backward on instinct, but had no room to maneuver within his one-butt work space.

"Sorry. I didn't mean to scare you. Don't worry. I made sure to pull the car up at least six feet away from you."

This man, with a round, ruddy face and a belly that pulled at the buttons of his uniform, was literally the first human being she had seen face-to-face in ten days.

"I recognize your voice," he said. "You're the one who called?"

She nodded. "I thought maybe the whole place would be locked down like everything else." She gazed through the security gate in front of her and saw no evidence of other employees. "You're holding up okay? It can't be easy to work a shift all alone."

"Just happy to have a paycheck. And tell you the truth, sitting in this booth by myself is a perfect gig for me. Social distancing is my natural habitat. Only sacrifice is having to read off this thing." He wiggled his iPad. "Bookstores are all closed, and no way I'm ordering them from you know who. Found a way to buy ebooks from an indie, so I'm good."

She was usually the type of person who would have been tapping the steering wheel impatiently after a few seconds of unnecessary chatter, but she found herself not wanting to leave. Fear of what was waiting for her next, yes, but also…it was nice to talk.

"I swore I'd never give up my beloved hardbacks," she said. "But I love to travel. Well—I *used to*, back when things were normal. It was much easier to pack a little tablet with all my beach reading than to lug a ton of books."

He pressed a button in his booth and the metal gate began to slide open. She raised her voice to be heard above the mechanical grind.

"Do you know where I go for unit 78? It's my son's," she added quickly. She had never been a skilled liar.

"Oh no. I hope he's okay? He didn't catch it, did he? You'd need to stay away from him, your being—" His lips remained parted, but he didn't finish the sentence.

Old, he meant to say. Old enough to be one of those people who might actually die if struck by this mysterious illness that was little more than a cold to someone half her age. "Not to worry. He's perfectly healthy, as am I. But he was cross-country when all this started, so won't be flying home." That part of the story was actually true. He and his wife were at their house in Hilton Head when this madness began, and were choosing to stay put for now. "He's got some of my old papers in there. Thought I'd use all this downtime to go through them."

It was a more elaborate cover story than necessary. She had already learned when she called earlier that all she needed was the unit number and a key. He spelled out the two turns she'd need to take to find the unit she was looking for.

"Have a good night," he said, as she shifted the car back into Drive. "And thanks for even bothering to ask how I'm holding up. Most of the people who've come around the last few days have been jackasses. I saw one guy unload an entire pickup truck full of toilet paper and every kind of disinfectant. I was tempted to rat him out to the local news. At least I know whose stuff to steal if this keeps up."

She made her way through the security gate, maneuvered the two turns within the maze of identical green corrugated-metal garage doors, and stopped in front of the one marked 78.

She stepped out of the car and watched her fingers tremble as she raised the key to the stainless-steel disc lock. She had no idea what to expect once she rolled open the door, but the details no longer mattered. She knew the truth already, as obvious to her as the deep lines and mottling she now noticed on the back of her hand. *Had she looked this old when she met him?*

Until five months ago, Marilyn Frost had only been in love once, with her beloved husband of thirty-seven years, Thomas Hunter Frost III. They met when she was a young travel agent, chosen by her agency to be one of the first guests to experience the soft opening of a new resort in Anguilla, the latest Frost luxury property and the chain's very first in the Caribbean. A member of the Frost family, the firstborn son and heir apparent,

Thomas, kicked off the Friday cocktail-hour ribbon-cutting ceremony with a champagne toast on the marble sunset deck overlooking Meads Bay. By the time she showed up to the reception desk for her Monday morning checkout, he was waiting there to escort her on the hotel's private charter boat to the airport in St. Maarten.

"I hope you like to fly," he had said before giving her one final hug at the boarding gate.

"I'd make a pretty crummy travel agent if I didn't."

"Good. Because I live in Philadelphia, and you live in Kansas City, so we'll be logging a lot of miles."

"You have better places to be than with me in Kansas City."

"Eventually, maybe. After we get married."

She thought it was a joke, a bittersweet way to mark the end of a magical weekend. They were married on that same marble deck as the sun went down exactly one year later, and then returned on that same date another thirty-seven times to celebrate each anniversary, staying each time in the same hotel villa, flying always in their favorite first-class seats, 2A and C, window for him, aisle for her, on the only direct flight from Philly. Then, when Thomas got the news that there would likely be no thirty-eighth, they flew there together one last time to stay and to wait.

He nearly made it. Just two weeks shy. Instead, she commemorated the date alone, scattering his ashes in the Atlantic Ocean, knowing she was lucky to have had their time together.

Still, the following year, she kept up the tradition, and every year since. The airlines wouldn't allow her to book a seat for the purpose of keeping it unoccupied, so she opted for Thomas's spot in 2A. She always flew into St. Maarten the Friday morning before their anniversary. She kept the same meal schedule they had favored as a couple: Mexican food Friday night after sundown, a decadent Saturday lunch at the elegant French restaurant down the beach, Saturday dinner at "home" in the villa and Sunday by the pool. And she always took one solo trip by boat to the reefs where she thought of Thomas as a permanent part of the ocean's life cycle.

So committed was she to this annual rite that their son, Tommy, had asked if Frost Hotels could feature her "widow weekends" in the company's in-room travel magazine. She agreed on the condition that she write the article herself and, of course, choose the most flattering photographs. She had donated her modest freelance fee to Anguilla's animal rescue organization in memory of Thomas. He always told her she was an excellent writer.

Five months ago, on the Friday before anniversary number forty-two, she sipped a pre-takeoff mimosa. Despite feeling a bit goofy about it, she raised her flute to the still-unoccupied Seat 2C and snapped a photo of her private toast. She emailed it to Tricia, the company's social media manager.

Playing up the family-business angle of a globally respected chain of luxury hotels, every member of the Frost family had become a persona on the Frost Hotel Instagram page. To brand loyalists, she was known as "Mama Marilyn." She initially hated the moniker, picturing a grandmotherly type with a white bun, cat-eye glasses and orthopedic shoes. But Marilyn Frost was not your typical seventy-year-old. She power walked twenty miles a week, worked with a private trainer and Pilates coach in her home gym, and treated monthly facials and root color as a second religion. Her social media content included suggested workouts for seniors and her annual summer reading list.

Five minutes later, she received a text from Tricia. Love it! Have a perfect trip. But what our followers would REALLY love is a photo of Mama herself. Pretty please?

Marilyn had smiled to herself. She checked to make sure no one was paying her any mind before holding up her phone for a quick selfie, posing with her champagne glass and boarding pass in her free hand. Another text round with Tricia, and the photo was posted with the caption, Bon Voyage, Mama Marilyn! #lovelastsforever #42ndanniversary #ThomasFrostIIIalwaysinourhearts.

She had powered down her phone and powered up an ebook when a final passenger boarded at the last minute, stopping in the aisle at her row to stow his roller bag in the overhead compartment. "I'm afraid you've got company," he said, glancing at the cell phone and magazine occupying Seat 2C. "The flight from Detroit was late. I nearly missed the connection."

"Oh, of course. I'm sorry." She gathered up her belongings and placed them in the seatback.

Snapping on his seat belt, he mentioned that he felt overdressed. While most of the passengers were in casual travel clothes, destined for vacation, he wore a jacket, tie and dress pants.

"I take it you're not heading for the beach like the rest of us?"

"I am, in a way, but not for fun in the sun." He was a geologist, flying to St. Maarten to advise the government after recent earthquakes in Puerto Rico had affected several other Caribbean countries. Officials on the Dutch side of the island had made a last-minute decision to bring in outside consultants to conduct an independent assessment to avoid any impression that the risk assessment was tainted by concerns for the tourism industry.

"You know? It didn't dawn on me until now that I don't have the foggiest idea what a geologist actually does."

"You're not alone. Someone asks me what I do for a living? It's a surefire conversation-stopper."

But not for the two of them. He talked about his work and all the travel it required. When he asked about her, she said she and her husband had "retired" from the "travel industry." She even told him about her yearly anniversary trips, but omitted the bit about owning the resort where she stayed. And, yes, she did know St. Maarten well enough to recommend the best French restaurant.

Halfway through the flight, as their meal service was cleared, he apologized for being so chatty. "So much of my work is computer modeling and writing reports. I tend to get a little too talkative when I'm around other human beings."

Even though Marilyn was usually the person who wore noise-canceling AirPods to ensure a silent flight, she assured him that she was enjoying their exchange.

"So I noticed your tablet when I was putting my bag up top. What book have I kept you from reading?"

"A Mary Higgins Clark novel. I thought I had read them all, but apparently I missed one. I've been saving it for this trip."

"I also consider myself a completist when it comes to writers. I've got the new Harry Bosch book preordered to automatically download this Tuesday."

"Ah, so you like them hard-boiled."

"All the way. Green yolks and cracked shells."

And off they went again on yet another topic, falling silent only when the wheels touched down.

"Well, thank you," he said, "for the company. I can't

remember the last time I enjoyed a flight so much. I'm Patrick, by the way. Nice to meet you."

"Marilyn."

They shook hands, but here was the thing about an airplane: you couldn't really say goodbye quite yet. He helped her retrieve her carry-on. They walked off the plane as a pair. Lined up for immigration together. They went to separate counters for passport inspection, but then merged right back into the same hallway that led to the exit. *Bread and butter*, as Thomas used to say.

Then, at last, it was time to go their separate ways. He was heading to a local taxi. She had the hotel's charter boat waiting for her at a dock across the street from the airport. "Good luck with your…geology-ing."

"And enjoy your time in Anguilla." He pronounced it Ang-wee-la, like most people did.

"Anguilla," she corrected, "rhymes with *vanilla*."

On her fourth day on the island, she returned to her villa from a morning water aerobics class to find the red message light blinking on the hotel telephone.

"Good morning, Mrs. Frost." She immediately recognized the voice at the front desk as Stephanie's. She'd worked at the resort for a quarter of a century, now as a manager, and would never feel comfortable calling Marilyn by her first name. "I got a call this morning from someone asking for a Marilyn. He described you to a T, but I wasn't going to put the call through when he didn't even have your full name. He left me his number, though. Patrick Miller?"

He answered on the second ring. "I'm so glad you called." She thought she heard the crackle of a PA on the other end of the line. "So, I just got to the airport. My flight leaves in ninety minutes."

"Oh, you'll be fine. Not to worry." She had it on good authority that the warning for tourists to arrive three hours early was to drum up business for the airport bar.

"Yeah, but… I find myself not wanting to leave. It's beautiful here. And warm and sunny and…beautiful. I hope this isn't weird, but…would you want to have lunch?"

"With you?"

"Oh wow. Yes, that is what I was proposing."

"As in—"

"As in…lunch. I hear Anguilla is worth the day trip." He pronounced it correctly this time. "And, yes, as in a date. I should probably make that clear before bailing on this flight."

Her silence was brief, but her thoughts were racing. She had of course noticed that he was handsome—trim with a strong jaw, salt-and-pepper hair and green eyes behind his tortoiseshell glasses. But she had noticed in a "what a nice-looking young man" kind of way, and now here they were.

"I'm very flattered, Patrick, but you should know I am much older than I look. *Much.* Proudly so, in fact." How many times had she been told she could pass for fifty?

"Well, I certainly don't believe you're old."

"My *son* is thirty-nine."

"Then it's a good thing that I'm considerably older than that."

As she would learn over lunch, he turned out to be fifty-two, giving them an eighteen-year age gap. He courted her long-distance, FaceTiming and texting from airports and hotels, and visiting her whenever possible. Tommy didn't approve, but she told him that she deserved to keep living her life. "He's going to want to marry you, Mom. Just watch." She replied that she should be so lucky.

He had proposed on Valentine's Day, surprising her with an unannounced visit, his duck confit and a bottle of Burgundy waiting at a candlelit dining table. After a chocolate soufflé, he dropped to one knee and handed her a shallow, rectangular gift box.

"I knew you'd want to pick out your own ring," he said. Sometimes she thought he understood her even better than Thomas ever had. "But I wanted to give you something to show how sure I am that I want to spend the rest of my life with you. Marilyn, will you marry me?"

She untied the white silk bow and lifted the top from the box. Inside was a framed slip of paper.

A boarding pass dated four months earlier, Philadelphia to St. Maarten. Seat 2C.

"How do you even have this?" She felt a lump in her throat larger than any ring he possibly could have chosen.

"I kept it because I knew that flight would change my life forever."

They agreed to keep things simple. A judge friend of hers would marry them in a private exchange of vows with Tommy as the (reluctant) witness. The plan was for him to relocate his consulting office from Detroit to Philadelphia and to search for projects that wouldn't require so much work in the field. They had already moved the bulk of his things into storage until they found him a proper office space. And at her son's insistence, a prenuptial agreement had been drafted. Patrick, to no surprise, had no reluctance to agree to it. They were all ready to say "I do."

And then, faster than anyone could have expected, the entire world changed. It was that virus she'd first heard about right after the New Year, the one from the seafood market in China. By the beginning of March, what seemed like a tragedy from the other side of the globe felt like a real possibility at home. When she attended the monthly Women of Philly lunch, all the ladies greeted one another with silly elbow taps instead of the usual hugs and kisses. Within ten days of that, Americans around the globe rushed to airports in search of last-minute flights home, terrified that routes would be canceled and they would be unable to return. They stood in crammed waiting areas, sharing pens with bare hands to complete customs forms, knowing that every second gathered together increased their risk of infection. From the airports, they dispersed domestically, no one bothering to screen them for exposure or monitor their temperatures.

One of those panicked passengers was Patrick, who flew back from Copenhagen, then headed directly to his home in Detroit to self-quarantine voluntary for the two-week recommended period.

"Come to Philly," she had pleaded. "If you get sick, I'm an excellent caretaker."

He said he'd never forgive himself if he exposed her. He implored her to shelter in place. The implications were clear. He was young and healthy. She? She was old.

She made it to Night Ten, completely alone at home, before she got weird.

One through nine, she envisioned as a mini staycation, reading the entire paper front to back, working out a little longer and stretching a bit deeper than usual. She streamed binge-worthy television shows with abandon and finished a novel every thirty-six hours.

But then it was Night Ten. In another world, she and Patrick would have been married the previous weekend.

Like everyone, she was restless. Claustrophobic. Longing for something as simple as a meal in a restaurant. How many times had she been annoyed by the volume at the adjacent table? By Night Ten, she could imagine nothing lovelier than the screeching sounds of an over-served bachelorette party.

If she couldn't enjoy her fabulously curated life, she could at least plan a special outing when life finally returned to normal. *What would Patrick love?*

She opened Google and searched for "best French restaurants in US." She had a lazy tendency to favor the Frost resorts, including for dining options. She was comforted by a list of familiar culinary giants: Le Bernardin, Daniel, French Laundry, Jean-Georges. She scrolled down farther and saw mention of a newer restaurant in Atlanta, called simply Lyon. Promising. Clean, simple, sophisticated.

She opened the Tripadvisor website to check for customer reviews, already picturing the weekend getaway she would spring upon Patrick once the world began to turn again.

An average of 4.86 stars, the second highest–rated dining establishment in Atlanta. Four dollar signs, naturally. She clicked to pull up an array of photographs posted by the amateur reviewers. She had learned from experience that some highly rated restaurants did not have an ambience suitable for a seventy-year-old woman. She had no interest in spending her first celebratory meal after the Apocalypse seated family-style at a picnic table, drinking hooch from a mason jar.

White linens. Soaring ceilings. She could picture them there.

She was about to close the web page when a photograph caught her eye. A shot down the length of the bar, bustling but refined. At the back corner, facing the camera, a handsome man in a sports jacket with salt-and-pepper hair, holding a wineglass, leaning in toward his companion. She zoomed in. It was Patrick.

The photo could have been taken anytime, but it was posted two weeks ago, when Patrick was still in Copenhagen.

It's amazing how different a person appears if you actually give him a hard look.

She pulled up his LinkedIn profile. Nice head-shot. University of Michigan, undergrad and masters. Founder and CEO of Miller GeoTech for a decade. But where were the jobs in between? She still knew nothing about geology, but she knew that you didn't start an independent consulting firm from scratch.

She googled "Miller GeoTech." There was a website, sure, but what did it really contain? The same head-shot as the LinkedIn profile. Gobbledygook about the services provided. A phone number she recognized as his cell. And not a mailing address in sight.

What did she really know about her fiancé?

One thing. One thing she knew for sure. He had been rescheduling a flight one night while she was sleeping, and she woke up to the sound of his voice, giving the customer service agent a password.

Twenty-eight minutes on hold to get a human being. No one was flying on airplanes anymore, but everyone was calling. All those canceled conferences, reunions, weddings and dreams.

When Marilyn finally got a real person's voice, she decided at the last second to narrow the scope of her request. Asking for a full summary of an entire travel history might trigger a red flag, especially since she couldn't exactly pose as a customer named Patrick.

But one trip in particular? She could pull that off.

The rep was named Darla and wanted to know how she could help this evening.

"Hi, Darla. I know you're helping a million people through this mess right now, but I'm trying to get our tax stuff together and I need help tracking down a receipt for one of my husband's flights last year?"

"I heard that even the IRS deadline got pushed. And they say only death and taxes are certain, so where does that leave us now?"

Marilyn sighed. "I'm running out of ways to stay busy, so I'm doing it anyway."

She could tell Darla was relieved to have a caller who wasn't screaming at her while she feared the loss of her job. Marilyn recited the confirmation number from the framed boarding pass that she kept on her nightstand, because that's how much it meant to her.

"Passenger name and either the Miles Plus account number or phone number?"

Marilyn realized Patrick could have multiple phone numbers, so she read the frequent flier information from the boarding pass.

"Oh—" A pause. "Your husband's got a security pin for phone inquiries. He may need to call back himself unless you happen to have it?"

When she and Thomas saw *Rain Man*, he said she was just like Dustin Hoffman's character. 82, 82, 82. 246 toothpicks. She wasn't quite that gifted with numbers, but could immediately memorize a string of digits because she automatically envisioned them on a ten-key pad from all the data entry she had done as a travel agent.

"It's 3515," she said. A V-shape.

"Yep. I've got it right here. You want me to send that to the email address we've got on file?"

"Can you send it to me instead? If I need to track him down for it, who knows how long that could take."

"I know exactly what you mean. We girls just knock it out, don't we?"

"Oh, and I think that might have been the trip when he had to change his return flight, so there may be an extra charge for that, too."

She heard taps on Darla's keyboard. "Nope. He flew the original itinerary."

A minute later, Marilyn had what she had asked for, Patrick's proof of payment for his spot in Seat 2C, purchased four months before he ever boarded.

As she tugged on the storage unit's rolling gate, she wondered again how he had found her. Had he stumbled upon a mention of Mama Marilyn in a Frost publicity campaign? Maybe it was last year's *Time* profile, featuring enduring family-controlled businesses. Or had he been planning this ever since Thomas's half-page obituary appeared in the *New York Times*?

However it happened, once she was on his radar, what an easy mark she had been. A complete stranger could know four months in advance what flight she would be taking on a specific Friday morning. He'd even know her seat number and affinity for mystery novels.

Just as he had looked different to her when she took a more scrutinizing look, so, too, did his belongings. Water rings on tabletops. Worn edges on the arms of the wingback chairs.

Who was the woman with him at the restaurant in Atlanta? Another potential fiancée, one without a son who would insist on a prenup? Or perhaps she was supposed to be next, after he'd taken as much from Marilyn as she would give.

She stood before his desk. Thomas's desk had been

grand, worthy of a lion. This one felt like a cheap imitation.

She opened the top drawer to find a paperback book, *Geology for Dummies*. Reaching behind it, she pulled out a stack of papers, some connected with paper clips, all bound together with a rubber band. The paper clips were attached to blue index cards containing names, dates and other notations.

She slipped off the rubber band to get a better look at the white rectangular sheets of paper clipped to the blue cards. Boarding passes. So many boarding passes. Flights going back at least three years. And notes on every passenger who had ever sat next to him.

The sound of her own laughter bounced off the corrugated steel walls, and for one second, she forgot she was alone.

* * * * *

KOHINOOR

BY SMITA HARISH JAIN

Govandi Road Jail stood broken and decrepit on a dirt field inside the "Gas Chamber of Mumbai." The pollution from the garbage incinerators at the nearby Deonar landfill, the largest dumping ground in the city, coated the buildings inside the prison with black soot and filled the air with the smell of rotting food and burning rubber.

I stood outside the prison's massive iron gates, waiting for the warden to arrive. Several meters away, three young men—I guessed them to be in their early twenties—sat under a neem tree and shared a Gold Spot. They passed the bottle of orange soda around, until one of them waved it off and reclined under the shade of the giant tree, a temporary respite from the searing August heat of the city.

They were joined a few minutes later by two more men, who had just emerged from the prison compound.

"Then what, Vikas?" the one lying in the shade of the neem asked.

Vikas checked the sheaf of papers in his hand. "You have Shetty today at 7 p.m. Don't be late."

"Shetty is easy. I don't even have to ask anymore," the man said, puffing out his small chest and waggling his eyebrows.

"They're all easy," Vikas said. "One by one, we'll take care of them. Amit, you keep the schedule." He handed the papers to the other young man who had come through the prison gates with him.

Amit pocketed them and motioned the others to get up. The three friends rose to their feet, and all five mounted Maruti scooters and left in a cloud of dust.

Before I could make any sense of their conversation, I heard my name. "Mr. Dhawan?"

I turned to see the warden, a large woman dressed in a dark olive uniform and combat boots. Together we walked to Jali Mulaqat, the visiting cage for undertrials, where those waiting to move from the prison to the courts were housed. She described the many structures we passed along the way, sounding more like a real estate agent than a prison official.

"In these buildings, we keep our serious offenders, those imprisoned for murder, cheating, rape," she said and directed my eyes to a row of five brick barracks with standing seam steel roofs. "No one has ever escaped from there."

She continued her tour, taking me past outdoor toilets, a small grassy maidan, and a crude gym consisting of several mismatched barbells and a treadmill that was plugged into nothing. She gave me tidbits about each area that she hoped would make it into my article, until, finally, we arrived at the cage.

Inside, women sat in large groups, sharing their problems and proclaiming their innocence. Some were just girls, and busied themselves chasing cockroaches or pulling lice out of each other's hair. I searched the crowded space for Kohinoor, and found her in a corner of the cage, listening to the occasional caws of an Indian ringneck perched in a peepul tree outside the Jali.

"Miss?" I started, not sure exactly how to address a dance bar girl.

"Sunil*ji*, you have come." She greeted me with the familiarity of a fast friend. Despite the closeness in our ages, she added the honorific *ji* to acknowledge the difference in our stations.

I bobbled my head from side to side, a classic Indian gesture which can mean yes, no and maybe—sometimes, all three at the same time. I felt like a teenager seeing a naked woman for the first time, even though she was covered from head to toe in traditional women's prison garb, a white sari with blue borders. Still, she took my breath away.

"Kohinoor...*ji*," I said, adding the honorific as an afterthought. It wasn't necessary for someone like her, but in her presence, I was merely a disciple.

Kohinoor had hit the Mumbai dance bar scene just one year ago, and instantly became the subject of every male conversation and fantasy. No one knew where she came from, and no one cared. That was just part of her allure. I didn't even know if Kohinoor was her real name. It didn't matter. It was the name that had made her famous.

She motioned me to the floor space directly beneath us, and we lowered ourselves onto the slab of cold, gray cement. I turned to the first crisp page of my new notebook and waited for her story.

"They all come," Kohinoor started. "The thugs and the *taporis*, the ministers and the Bollywood heroes. In the dance bars, everyone is the same."

I wanted to tell her that I understood, that I, too, had been one of them; but this was her story, not mine.

"The dance bar is a place where people come to be entertained," she said in clear self-defense. "It is not the purveyor of evil that the morality police will have you believe."

Mumbai's morality police had gained tremendous ground in the past five years. Self-professed custodians of Indian culture and tradition, they took it upon themselves to save India from what they termed, "the encroaching moral depravity of the West." They openly threatened young couples holding hands in the park, loudly chastised female college students drinking in bars and even inflicted violence on restaurant owners advertising Valentine's Day specials.

In the last election, the candidates running on a morality platform had won in landslide victories all over the state of Maharashtra. "We must create boundaries for our women, if we are to succeed as a nation," Deputy Home Minister Ram Shetty had shouted from his pulpit at the morality rally organized by his supporters. "We must give them decent work to do, and not allow them to sell their bodies to drunks and degenerates." Then, addressing the dance bar activists who had come, many of them the bar girls themselves, he declared, "It is more dignified to take your life than to live with immorality."

Once in office, Shetty and his cronies in the Mumbai city and Maharashtra state governments had organized themselves into the Ring of Morality, and enacted legislation that closed down the thriving dance bar industry. A mainstay of Mumbai's nightlife, dance bars had been part of the city's entertainment offerings for over forty years. The move by the ministers was historic and left approximately seventy-five thousand bar dancers in the state unemployed; the majority of those were in Mumbai.

"They blame us for corrupting others, but where is the responsibility of those who come to us?" Kohinoor asked. "We must show everyone, Sunilji, or the truth shall surely lie rotting."

Only days after Kohinoor had been incarcerated for threatening the lives of the Ring's members, blaming them for the death of her younger sister, she called me and offered to tell me her side of the story.

"I brought her to Mumbai." Kohinoor spoke softly. "I couldn't let her stay with our parents in Tandur. They would have sold her to the highest bidder. A virgin requires less of a dowry, you know."

Tejal was only thirteen when she started dancing in the bars. The bar ban took effect only a few months later and Tejal, lost for money, turned to prostitution. When she learned she had become pregnant by a client who had then abandoned her, she could not face the shame of telling her sister. Instead, Tejal swallowed a mostly full bottle of DDT insecticide she and her sister kept at their flat in Harmony House. When Kohinoor found Tejal, she was having violent convulsions, which turned into paralysis. A few minutes later, Kohinoor held her dead sister in her arms.

The death of a thirteen-year-old girl by her own hands riveted the city. The papers, including the *Mumbai Times* where I worked, called Tejal "the first casualty" of the Morality Ring's war on indecency and vulgarity, and made Kohinoor the face of the anti-ban rebellion.

"This is a morality of convenience," Kohinoor said, her tone a combination of grief and defiance, anger and sadness.

She rubbed her wrists and cried quietly. I had read

once that bar dancers cut themselves every time they
lose a love, either by choice or otherwise. A quick
glance told me that Kohinoor had loved only once.
Tejal, I thought.

"Kohinoorji, what will you do if the High Court
does not overturn the ban?"

The Dance Bar Workers' Union had put forward an
appeal of the bar ban immediately, and now, nearly six
months after the passage of the ban, the Bombay High
Court was scheduled to consider it. Kohinoor wanted
the truth out there before the trial.

"We will continue to fight the bar ban and, one day,
it will be lifted," Kohinoor said, confidence gleaming
in her eyes. "Only this time, we will fight the morality police with morality."

I assumed she meant that by leading a good life, by
showing that the bar workers were decent people, just
like anyone else, they would convince the High Court
to overturn the ban.

I'd soon find out that that wasn't what she meant
at all.

The first time I saw Kohinoor was at the Maharajah Dance Bar in Wadavali. Some college friends and
I had heard about the sexy village girl who had moves
that would put any Bollywood item to shame, and we
had to see for ourselves.

The drive to the notorious nightspot took us out
of our predictable, middle-class existence to a world
known only to the initiated. We headed down the Eastern Express Highway, through Kanjurmarg and Ghatkopar, and watched the Mumbai we knew fade into VD
clinics, prostitutes and the best dance bars in the city.

Not sure what to expect, we dressed in our temple best and tight double underwear for good measure.

We parked in Nirman Colony in Ghatkopar East and walked the rest of the way. We passed a row of shops hawking everything from sexual aids to rosary beads, before reaching a tin door with a sign for Seema's Restaurant. The entrance to the Maharajah wouldn't be visible until we stepped inside.

At the door, we were greeted by an East Indian man, judging from his speech—*o*'s drawn out into *aw*'s—probably a Bengali. He was small-framed but still managed to look fierce, a wad of *paan* lodged in his cheek, the red juice from the betel leaf coating his lower lip. He slurped up the tart liquid before welcoming us.

"Hellaw, sirs. Good evening, sirs." In the distance, we could hear a tune from the latest Hrithik Roshan film.

A quick exchange of money for passes, and we moved into the dark hallway, slapping each other to celebrate our coup: we had gotten in.

The large room at the other end was awash in bright lights strobing from the ceiling and floor, the unnatural colors more suited to a children's cartoon than to a target of the morality police. In every corner, security guards in half-sleeve shirts that accented their biceps stood akimbo, watching everyone's movements. On the stage, a woman shimmied in place to a popular classic film song from the eighties. Her feet never moved; only her hips swayed in a half-hearted attempt to keep time with the music. I wondered who was more bored, me or her?

"What rubbish dancers. *Chee!*" my friend Manish said.

"I hope those others can dance," Babu said, indicating the row of women sitting in chairs at the back of the stage, waiting their turn. They all looked out of shape—midriffs pouring out from under too-tight costumes, flabby arms barely fitting inside their blouses, faces full of baby fat. If they were providing the evening's entertainment, we had doubled our underwear for nothing.

"*Arre*, why are they wearing saris and *ghagaras*? My sister wears those," I said, adding to our disappointment. These weren't the skimpy outfits we had hoped for; merely traditional garments covered in sequins.

"Yah, *yaar*, I can't see anything good," Manish complained. He downed his Johnnie Walker and motioned to a waiter to get him another one.

An announcer gave details about each dancer as she took the stage. Nothing an ardent fan could use to find the girls once they left the safety of the bar, just their stage name, city of origin and a carefully chosen tidbit: "Shefali is from Bangalore and enjoys eating warm *moongaphalees* on the beach."

"Kumkum was first-pass in school in Pipad."

"Divya comes from a long line of Kashmiri entertainers. Her mother and aunties were also bar dancers."

I checked the time. Kohinoor always danced at midnight. I ordered another Kingfisher and settled in for the long wait.

The parade of dancers over the next hour and a half did little to hold my interest. Others felt differently. I watched as a handful of men walked up to the prettier dancers and pulled ten- and twenty-rupee notes from a stack in their hands, raining them down on the dancer of their choice in an act known as scratching. They were careful not to touch the dancers, with so many security guards watching. Other men invited a girl to come to their tables and, in exchange for letting them hold her hand, the girl made an easy fifty rupees or even a hundred rupees. If she sat down and talked, maybe gave them her name, her number—both assuredly fake—she could make even more money.

The combination of the men's becoming enamored of their favorite dancer, coming in nightly to see them, and the free-flowing booze in these establishments allowed bar dancers to make upward of two hundred thousand a month for their "dancing." The story of Abdul Karim Telgi's dropping ten million rupees on a bar dancer in a single night is now the stuff of envy and aspiration among many regular bar customers. That men would spend their hard-earned money on a bar dancer instead of on their wives and children was just one of the many reasons Ram Shetty and his cronies gave for the urgency of shutting down these "dens of wickedness," as they called them.

By the time the last of the second-string dancers had exited the stage, the crowd had become lulled into an easy, alcohol-induced stupor, many of them forgetting their reasons for coming. I hadn't forgotten, and nudged my friends to wake up.

The lights dimmed, the music slowed and time seemed to stop. Smoke released from a noisy apparatus on the floor behind the stage, and when it cleared, the most sublime creature stood in its place, striking a pose straight out of the *Kama Sutra*.

The crowd erupted, their cheers drowning out the music coming from the large speakers flanking the stage. Men lined up to shower Kohinoor with bills. Some came prepared with their notes already strung into garlands; others patted themselves, frantically looking for even more cash, any excuse to be near her longer. Hundred-rupee bills, five hundred–rupee bills. If they held the deeds to their houses, I wouldn't have been surprised to see them scratched over her. Anything less for this goddess would be an insult, even a

risk that the offender may be removed from her presence, never allowed to worship her again. No one was
willing to take that risk.

Kohinoor moved slowly with the music and, as it
sped up, so did she. She wore a fitted sequined mini-
skirt in electric red—the color of a bride on her wed-
ding night—the bra top held in place by crisscross,
beaded straps in the same color. With her every move,
she matched the flash of the strobes, until the bar manager turned down the lights and her movements became
the strobes, the dim lights reflecting off the glitter on
her costume.

We sat mesmerized by the spectacle, clutching our
drinks because we needed to hold on to something or
fall to our knees. Light and sound and motion swirled
around us, enveloped us, in the form of this devi, Rati,
the goddess of love.

When the stage was no longer big enough to contain
her, she danced around the room, the music struggling
to keep up, until it became irrelevant. She moved in a
blur, and the room filled with her. When it was over,
she glistened onstage, and the rest of us panted in our
spots. The silence lasted for only seconds, before the
bar guards swept the rupee notes off the stage and the
floor. The rest of us collapsed into our seats, remembering to breathe and trying to lock away the memory
of what we had just experienced.

I returned to the Maharajah for the first time since
that night to learn more about the dancer that had cap-
tured Mumbai—first as an enigma, then as an icon,
now as a martyr.

The route I took to get there hadn't changed, but
the bar itself had transformed into a three-star pub.
The narrow passageway that once separated the cho-

sen from the hopefuls had been expanded and lit, its
walls now displaying oversize pictures of Limca bottles and Bollywood starlets. I couldn't help noticing the
skimpiness of the outfits on the actresses—much less
than any dancer had worn before the ban. The stage
had been replaced by a polished oak bar and oak-and-
wicker stools. The strobe lights remained in their tracks
on the ceiling and floor, but were turned off.

When I called to let Manmohan Singh, the owner,
know that I was coming to talk to him about Kohinoor,
he cleared his schedule. "Anything to help my Kabutar," he said, calling her by his pet name for her, Pigeon.
He used to have the hottest bar dancer in Mumbai, and
she had made him a wealthy man.

"*Arre*, they are *bekaar*, only, these rubbish politicians!" He needed little provocation to complain. "They
shut down the dance bars, but still they are taking their
haftas. Every week, they come, asking for their cut.
Fifty thousand rupees per month, just to give us permits…for parking, pest control, playing music—one
for live music and one for recorded. For everything.
Such a *dhanda*, a racket. If we don't pay the *haftas*,
they delay our permits or cancel them. Then we have
to pay more to get them back and, without our dancers, we are barely making enough. What bloody rot!"

He stopped for air, then asked, "How is my Kabutar?"

I told him she seemed to be holding up well, but
left out the part about her living conditions. Since he
couldn't do anything about them anyway, there was no
reason to upset him further.

We were joined by three women dressed as wait-
resses. Singh made the introductions, then left. I motioned them to sit with me and offered to buy them
the drinks they now served. Everyone I met from the

dance bars was eager to talk, eager to get the bar ban repealed, eager to return to their former lives. Their ardor wouldn't be enough to take on the morality police, but I didn't know what would be.

"There were so many bars, and to close them all down at once, what else was there for us to do?" the first waitress, Rosy, said.

I asked them about their lives since the ban. Two had turned to the flesh trade, it being the only place they could make the kind of money they had made as bar dancers. The third danced at a five-star hotel on Peddar Road and sometimes at private parties.

"Customers are there, you know?" the second one, Sarita, added. "If I don't send money home, then how will my parents survive? My father is sick and my mother is old. They have come to expect the money. They even bought a satellite dish. I can't quit. Shetty Sahib does not understand this. He has always had a satellite dish."

"My daughter goes to an English-medium school. I can't take her out. What will she do? Become like me?" Rosy asked. Then, as if feeling the need to defend herself, she said, "I made fifteen thousand rupees per month when I danced. That is more than my parents can make in one year. Why else did I come to Mumbai?"

The stark nature of their world was becoming disturbingly clear: without the dance bars, it was either prostitution or destitution.

"Shetty Sahib and Jalan Sahib think all our money goes into drinking or having parties. But so much of the money is needed for our work, you know," Meera the hotel dancer said. "Costumes are there, and rent and makeup and props. What can I do with waitress pay? It is only one hundred to two hundred rupees per day."

I brought her back to her current line of dancing,

asking how parties differed from dancing at the Maharajah or at the five-star hotel.

"There we can do the same things, but because it is in someone's house, it is called dancing and not prostitution." She looked at the other two and bobbled her head. "We are careful and always use condoms," she added proudly, as if she had broken the code.

"My parents don't know what I do," Rosy said. "They think I am a maid to a rich family. I have to tell them that, or they will be shamed in their village. Maybe they know. We don't talk about it." She looked away.

"What can I do, it's a *majboori, na*? A weakness. I have to get my sister married, so she doesn't end up like Tejal," Satellite Dish said.

"*Arre*, Tejal was stupid, only. She could have made a lot of money—she was a virgin. She could have sold it for at least two lakhs."

"That's two years' rent in Harmony House," Sarita said.

"That much money will pay for the rest of my daughter's tuition till the tenth standard," Rosy added.

"I could buy two really nice saris at Benzer's," Meera said. "So sweet I would look, *na*?"

"Idiot girl. She thought she was in love!" Rosy came back, as if that possibility for a bar dancer was just a pipe dream. "Tejal could dance, but inside, she was still a villager. She played games with the man, telling him she did only some things, not all things. She didn't give him what he wanted, so he took it. She could have made so much money."

The shame wasn't in her rape; it was in her not profiting from it. Not one of the three women mentioned Tejal's suicide.

I had heard enough. I thanked the girls for talking to

me and headed over to Harmony House, where Kohinoor and her sister used to live, and where some other bar girls made their homes.

Inside, many of the flats kept their doors open. Music blared, and girls in various stages of undress sprawled on the floor, eating samosas and *chikkis* and giggling about the new man in their lives. In other flats, large groups sat in front of a TV, watching *Love U Zindagi* or *Pratigya* or some other Indian serial. There seemed to be no secrets in Harmony House.

I sat inside the flat of Tejal's neighbors, four former bar dancers named Begum, Chimka, Reena and Reshmi. Just one mention of Kohinoor's name and of the article I was writing granted me easy access to the girls. None asked for anonymity, since none had ever danced under their real names.

"Mostly I was dancing, but sometimes, to make extra, I let men drive me home." Begum examined her nails, freshly painted in a flaming orange, while talking to me. She looked up and continued. "I made 1.5 lakhs in a single month. That is not money I can make being a maidservant to some rich woman." She scoffed, then added with a self-satisfied smirk, "I have my own maidservant."

"It's not prostitution if all they do is discharge on you, is it, Sunilji?" Chimka asked, convinced she had set firm boundaries.

"Did you try to find work?" I asked Reena.

"When the ban happened, all the money stopped, just like that." She snapped her fingers. "I tried to find domestic work, but getting a full-time servant's job is impossible unless you know someone. They don't trust just anyone in their house, near their children. And who did I know? Huh? No one. We are not convent-educated rich girls. It is dancing or selling ourselves or thieving," she explained.

The fourth woman, Reshmi, joined our conversation. "I'm not a prostitute like the others. I get paid to travel with men—rich men, powerful men. They give me clothes and jewelry." Reshmi held up her hands and made the gold bangles on her wrists chime. "One Crime Branch inspector makes me pretend I am his wife at parties, and for that he pays me forty thousand rupees, minimum. There is one client, he lets me keep my clothes. Even sweets are there."

She stopped for a minute to let me write down her words. Then, she continued.

"I have been everywhere—Delhi, Goa, Jaipur. I have stayed in only fancy places, five stars. I am not angry with the morality police. I want to touch their feet. They have made me even richer. You can close the dance bars, but you cannot change men," she said with all her twenty-three years of wisdom.

"Why didn't Tejal do this escort business?" I asked, thinking that may have saved her life.

"Tejal didn't know English, only Marathi, and even that was simple Marathi. She looked like a Mumbai girl, but acted like a village girl. You can't make a wife out of that," Reshmi said.

"Ay, your Hindi is also just *Bumbai-ya* Hindi, but you get clients," one of the girls teased her.

"That's because with her, they don't want any talking," another said, and fell backward on the bed, laughing.

I left them in their new reality, at least their version of it, and headed to my car. When I was almost out of the building, I thought I heard Manmohan Singh's voice coming from behind an open door. He must have come to Harmony House just before my arrival. I heard two more voices coming from the same flat. They spoke in whispers.

"How much longer do we do this, Singhji? So dirty it is with these old women."

"Kabutar said only one more week, then we finish them," Singh replied.

"Still one more week?" a different voice said.

"We have to wait until the High Court is getting ready to vote, Amit. If we come out too early, they will conveniently forget everything."

I pulled myself closer to the wall outside the open door.

"Vikas, who is left?" Amit asked.

"It is only Mrs. Bhatt and Mrs. Jalan. Then we are done."

"This week, you have two visits scheduled at Jalan's and one at Bhatt's. Patel and Gankar are finished," Singh's voice came in. "That will make five of the seven Ring members complete. That should be enough."

I heard them get up to leave and moved quickly past the open door. Vikas and Amit nodded to each other and said, "*Phir milenge*. We'll meet later." Vikas moved toward the staircase leading out, and Amit stepped back inside the flat and closed the door.

I stood there for several seconds and let their words settle. It sounded like they were planning to carry out Kohinoor's threats against the home minister and his cronies. I remembered these same men outside the prison yesterday, and the schedule they were discussing. Had they just come from seeing her? Had she given them the schedule for killing the ministers? Or was this about something else?

I thought about calling the police but didn't have anything concrete to give them. I didn't know when

Vikas and Amit would strike, or how. I wasn't even sure what their plan was.

.I had to see Kohinoor again.

"Sunilji!" she greeted me. "Thank you for coming back."

What choice do I have after what I heard at Harmony House? I thought.

"You are seeming troubled today, is it?" she asked, as if we weren't standing in a large, metal cage in the middle of a prison compound, with fifty or so women and young girls hanging on our every word.

"Kohinoor…ji." I stumbled over the honorific, no longer feeling like it applied. "Will you tell me who are Vikas and Amit?" I didn't feel like wasting any more time.

Kohinoor smiled. "Vikas and Amit? They are co-workers…former coworkers from the Maharajah."

Her response sounded scripted, rehearsed, as if she already knew about my run-ins with them—at the prison the day before, with the open door at Harmony House. Kohinoor had invited me to tell her story, but I felt like she was writing it, and I was merely one of the characters.

"Tell me, do you know what they do at the houses of the deputy home minister and the other Ring members?"

"I imagine they must have found work there. After all, we all have had to."

I thought about asking her what type of work they were doing, but assumed she wouldn't tell me.

"You know, Kohinoor," I said, "there are options."

She turned to watch the Indian ringnecks in the tree behind the Jali Mulaqat.

I continued anyway. "There are NGOs set up to help

migrants, to teach them a new trade. You could learn how to—"

Before I could finish my thought, she turned to me and smiled. I was amusing her. "How to what, Sunilji? Make candles or bead jewelry?"

I could see that she was trying not to laugh in my face. After the money she had made as a dancer, dipping cotton wicks into colored waxes wasn't going to do anything for her.

"It may not give you the same money as dancing in a bar, but it would give you legitimacy."

"There was nothing illegitimate about what we were doing before," she countered. "Only because of the Morality Ring do we have to justify our actions." She lowered her head and wiped away a tear.

I didn't know how to ask my next question. She had threatened to kill the home minister and his cabinet. Even if she didn't do it herself, had she arranged for her friends to do it? In the undertrial section of Govandi Road Jail, the purgatory between a lifetime of imprisonment and a future of freedom, I knew she couldn't, wouldn't answer truthfully. I would have to find my own answers at the ministers' houses.

All the members of the Ring of Morality lived in Pooja Colony in Juhu. Home to Bollywood royalty, wealthy industrialists and old money, the beach area was one of the ritziest in the city. A far cry from my drives lately, through poverty, construction and filth, the drive to Juhu took me along Marine Drive—the glitter of the Queen's Necklace on full display—and the delicious smells coming from the bhel poori and *pav bhaji* stalls along the beach.

I had rung Ram Shetty's office earlier in the day to ask for an interview about the upcoming High Court deliberation on repealing the bar ban. He scoffed at the possibility that his bar ban would be overturned, but granted me an audience with him anyway. He even offered to invite some of the other members of the Morality Ring to join us. They would welcome the chance to put their rationale for the ban before the public again, he assured me.

"Are you concerned, sirs, that with the death of the bar dancer Tejal, the High Court will say the cost of the ban is too high?" I asked the assembled ministers and government leaders.

"She was a morally corrupt girl," Shetty responded for the group. "How can we mourn her loss?"

Sachin Jalan, the finance minister, chimed in. "If our daughters did what those bar girls did, we would tell them to drink DDT also." The man seated next to Jalan patted him on the back, and the others nodded.

Piyush Bhatt followed up with, "Let them make their living on the streets. They are already unclean."

Mrs. Bhatt whimpered, then, realizing we had all heard her, covered her mouth with her sari and ran out of the room. Some of the other wives glared at her retreating form and made an effort not to look at each other.

"Sirs, have there been threats?" I asked, wondering about the strange reaction of the police commissioner's wife.

They laughed heartily. "Who can touch us?" one of them asked, incredulous.

I looked at their wives pacing in small lines in the corner, alternately biting their fingernails and bunching up the *paloos* of their saris in their fists, and wondered: *Who could touch them?*

"Madam, I will come back Thursday, is it?" a male voice said from the kitchen.

I turned to see the young man named Vikas holding two balled-up cloth bags in his hands.

Mrs. Shetty, realizing he was addressing her, stumbled on her response. "What? Yes. Of course, of course. Thursday." She bobbled her head.

Vikas nodded and strolled to the door. He looked at me as he pulled it shut; a slight smile tugged at the corners of his mouth.

"That one boy brings vegetables from the market on Tuesday and Thursday," Mrs. Shetty explained to me, without my asking. "He goes from our house to the Patels."

Mrs. Patel glared at her and turned away.

I jotted down Mrs. Shetty's words, not sure what this had to do with the story I was writing.

"Yes," Minister Patel confirmed. "Vikas comes two times a week with groceries. Dinesh comes once a week with clothes from the tailor."

Mr. Gankar said, "My wife also has weekly deliveries from the tailor. Sometimes Dinesh brings them, sometimes Amit. How many clothes these women are needing, is it? I haven't even seen them all!" He laughed at the frivolousness of his wife, and the other politicians joined him. Their wives looked at them with nervous smiles, nodding in agreement with whatever their husbands were saying.

It was then that Mrs. Bhatt came back into the room, still visibly shaken. The other wives joined her, and the five of them moved away from their husbands.

I watched them cower in the corner of the room, and Kohinoor and Manmohan Singh's plan became clear in my mind. Did it matter that the whole thing was orchestrated by Kohinoor? Would I even include her role in my story?

That night, Manmohan Singh came to my flat. He

held a large manila envelope, stuffed full. I sent the pictures to my publisher and waited for the morning paper to be delivered.

When the story broke about the wives of the Morality Ministers paying gigolos for sex, the High Court had the recourse it needed to overturn the ban. Their husbands, unable to live with the public's reproach, hanged themselves. Ram Shetty's words had come back to haunt him: "It is more dignified to take your life than to live with immorality."

The Maharajah Dance Bar Grand Reopening happened within a week of the High Court's decision. I sat in the VIP section, a guest of Manmohan Singh, and waited for midnight to come.

"And now, for the star of our show, the one, the only, Payal!" the announcer said. "Payal is a student from Goa, who is studying commerce, and hopes to open her own dance bar one day."

The lights dimmed, the music started and I got up to leave. I wanted to ask Manmohan Singh what had happened to Kohinoor but doubted he would tell me, if he even knew.

* * * * *

AVALON

BY MICHAEL CONNELLY

Searcy always watched the first Express come in. He'd take his morning coffee up in the break room and sit at the table by the window. There was a view straight down the pier and if he leaned toward the glass he could take in the whole horseshoe of the harbor going all the way over to the casino. There was even a set of binoculars on the windowsill if needed.

Searcy's own office was a converted cell on the first floor and was, therefore, windowless.

He was at the table, coffee in the mug he'd brought up from his desk, reading the transcript of his grand jury testimony on the Gallagher case when the 7:10 came in from Long Beach. He set the prep work for the trial aside and trained his observation skills on the passengers disembarking and walking down the pier to the island.

It was usually too early for tourists. Mostly it was workers, craftsmen and domestics coming over to do a job. In early, then back to the mainland on the 4:10

return. Sometimes it brought people in who were hard to read. He called them the strangers. Watching the strangers was an exercise. It kept his skills sharp.

A few of the arriving passengers he recognized. Housekeepers that worked up at the Mount Ada or the Zane Grey or other hotels. There were also men carrying toolboxes or pulling equipment on two-wheeled luggage haulers. One man had a collapsible table saw on a two-wheeler. He was a carpenter Searcy knew was putting in a new floor at a house up on Falls Canyon by the high school.

There were also a few tourists who made the early trip to get a whole day in. They were revealed by their cameras and Jimmy Buffett shirts.

One man caught Searcy's eye because he wasn't dressed like a tourist or a craftsman. He carried no bag of any sort as he made his way down the pier with seeming purpose. He wore dark pants and a blue button-down shirt beneath a green windbreaker he had unzipped after the biting winds from the crossing were no longer an issue. Searcy wondered if he was a gambler who mistakenly thought the casino was a gaming house. There were a few of them every day.

And then Searcy's mild curiosity about the man in the green windbreaker changed in one moment.

There was a tourist walking next to the man. He was made obvious by his shorts, black socks and the camera hanging from a strap around his neck. The tourist was walking with his eyes up, staring at the cathedral-like mountain that rose behind the town. It was a beautiful sight, especially to the first timers to the island. The tourist wanted a photo and removed the cap from his camera without taking his eyes from the vista he hoped to capture for posterity.

He fumbled the cap and it dropped to the pier's wood

planking and started to roll on its side. It was heading to the edge and a twenty-foot drop to the water below. But the man in the windbreaker made a move, leaning down without missing a stride and swiftly grabbing the cap before it could go over the edge. He did it fluidly. Like a shortstop scooping up an infield dribbler and tossing it to first base, the man in the windbreaker flipped the lens cap back to its owner, who caught it easily and then thanked him. But by then the man in the green windbreaker had moved on.

All of that was mildly interesting to Searcy—one stranger doing a nice turn for another—until he saw the front right flap of the windbreaker flip open while the man was scooping up the lens cap. That was when Searcy saw the gun tucked into the waistband of the man's pants.

Searcy left the transcript and coffee table and immediately moved from the break room down the stairs and to the dayroom. Mary Emmet, the substation clerk and dispatcher, was at her desk and Randy Ahern, a uniformed deputy, was at the shared desk filling out a report. Matt Rose, the other deputy on duty, was out in the field. Searcy took a two-way out of the charging station and grabbed the key to his golf cart off the hook. That drew Emmet's attention.

"Heading out?"

"Got a nine-twenty-five off the boat. I'm going to check him out."

Searcy clipped the radio to his belt.

"Suspicious person?" Ahern asked. "You need help?"

"I'll let you know," Searcy said.

He went out the front door of the substation and unlocked the bicycle lock on the golf cart assigned to him. He looked around for the man in the green windbreaker and didn't see him at first. He then saw the courtesy cart from the Zane Grey on Crescent heading into the roundabout. Searcy could see the green jacket. He backed out and followed.

The Zane Grey cart took the first right off the roundabout onto Casino Way. Searcy hung back so as to not be noticed following. He knew where they were going anyway. They cruised past the Tuna Club and then the Catalina Yacht Club before taking the left onto Chimes Tower Road. In three minutes the cart pulled into the adobe-style hotel's parking lot. Searcy slowed to a stop and watched from afar as the man in the green windbreaker got out of the cart and went through the doors into the lobby.

Searcy thought about what to do. The man in the windbreaker had not acted suspiciously other than the fact he was carrying a firearm. He could be one of the few people in California with a concealed-carry permit. Maybe he was retired law enforcement. He had that demeanor in his purposeful walk. But he carried no bag. That made him a day-tripper—a day-tripper carrying a gun. Searcy's instincts told him that this was more than a 925.

Emmet's voice came up on the rover asking for a status check. Searcy radioed back that all was good and that he was still engaged. He watched the Zane Grey for another five minutes, in case the stranger came out, and then drove into the front cart lot when he did not.

The lobby and front desk area of the boutique hotel was the former living room of the famed writer who had lived on the island. The man behind the desk was Jerry Daniels, a born and raised islander Searcy had known since he first came to the substation as its sole detective five years earlier.

"Nick," he said with a smile. "How are you?"

"Doing good," Searcy said.

He moved closer to the front desk. It was chest high and he leaned over the top to speak confidentially.

"You just had a check-in?" he asked. "The man in the green windbreaker?"

"Uh, yeah," Daniels said. "Mr. Christov."

"Christov? What was the first name?"

"Uh, Maxwell."

"Can I see the registration form he filled out?"

Searcy expected no pushback from Daniels when he asked the question. No talk of search warrants or protections of civil liberties. Avalon was a small town on a small island. Only an hour by Express ferry from the mainland but a world away in civilities. The locals went along to get along. That meant they cooperated with the lone investigator assigned to the LA County Sheriff's Department substation.

Daniels handed Searcy a one-page printout of the registration form. Searcy studied it and saw that Christov had paid in cash. There was no credit card information, but he had listed an address on Fairfax Avenue in Los Angeles.

"Did you check his ID?" Searcy asked.

"He showed it to me—it's required," Daniels said. "But I don't remember what—"

"Did you check the address against what he put down here?"

"Yes, I did that."

"Okay, and he's staying two nights? Did his luggage come separately?"

"No, there was no luggage. And the first night was last night. He had to pay for last night to get into a room this early. So he's technically only staying one night."

"Was it a reservation or did he just show up?"

"No reservation but I think he called from the

boat—somebody did—and asked if we had anything available."

"He say anything about what he's doing here?"

"Uh, no. I mean, I didn't ask. A lot of people come here, you know, to just lay low. I don't really ask them their business."

Searcy heard his name come up on the radio.

"Just a second," he said to Daniels.

He turned away from the counter and responded on the radio.

"Go ahead."

It was Emmet. She told Searcy that Deputy Ahern was requesting an investigator at the Trading Post on Metropole. Searcy said he would be there in fifteen minutes. He clipped the radio back on his belt and returned to the front desk.

"Which room is Christov in?" he asked Daniels.

"He took the Purple Sage suite," Daniels said. "Harbor view. It's all we had available."

"Okay, you've got my cell number, right?"

"In my phone, yeah."

"If he goes out, text or call me, okay?"

"Uh, sure. You going to tell me what's going on?"

"Hopefully, nothing."

Searcy turned away. Daniels called after him.

"Hey, I thought the Gallagher trial has started," he said. "Aren't you supposed to be overland for that?"

"Just jury selection this week. I'll go over Sunday, testify Monday, maybe Tuesday."

"Must be exciting. Big case and all."

"Well, big around here, I guess."

"Only murder I remember ever happening. Unless you count Natalie Wood as a murder."

"Not officially. Anyway, I gotta go. Somebody needs me at the Trading Post."

"Okay, I'll call ya—if I see him go out."

"Thanks."

Searcy took the golf cart back down to the basin. Along the way he used the radio to ask Emmet to run a wants and warrants check on the name Maxwell Christov. It came back negative. Searcy knew he would do a deeper dive on the name later, when he got back to the sub. He turned onto Metropole and a half block up was the Trading Post. One of the other sheriffs' carts was parked outside.

The Trading Post was a shop that sold tourist knick-knacks and T-shirts in the front and basic convenience store items in the back. Inside, Searcy found Ahern with the store's manager, Todd Helvin. They were waiting silently. Ahern had only been working on the island for eight months and had not established many relationships.

Catalina was always seen in the department as an R and R posting—that was R and R as in redemption and recovery. An assignment to the substation in Avalon usually followed an on-the-job injury or a scandal or an internal political fuckup. Searcy had been assigned to Catalina five years earlier while recovering from injuries incurred while making an arrest in a domestic dispute. While he had gotten into a wrestling match with the husband, the wife came up behind him and stabbed him in the back.

Searcy knew Ahern had come in from the jail division, where scandal was always rife, usually from use-of-force complaints. Over the five years Searcy had been at the substation several jail deputies had been rotated in and out of Avalon for R and R reasons. But Searcy had not yet gotten the story about Ahern because the stories were basically all the same and didn't really concern him.

What did concern him was that Ahern had brought his jail persona with him to the island. In the jail, everybody was accused of something and the high majority were most likely guilty of the offense and rightfully behind bars. Jail deputies had to walk with a don't-fuck-with-me bearing and menace. More than once Searcy had seen him employing that persona with islanders and tourists. It wasn't a good look and it didn't go over well with the locals. Searcy was aware that many of the islanders referred to Deputy Ahern as Deputy A-hole.

"What've we got?" Searcy said as he approached the two men.

"Shoplifting," Ahern said. "He's got it on video."

Searcy paused in midstep for a moment. A shoplifting report hardly needed a detective.

"What was taken?" he asked.

"A can of beer," Ahern said.

"Are you fucking kidding me, Ahern?"

"Hold on, hold on. It's not what was taken, okay? It's who took it. Show him, Mr. Helvin."

Helvin led Searcy behind the checkout counter where there was a screen quadded into feeds from four surveillance cameras. Three of the cameras were located over the front door, checkout counter and the rear of the store where the cold case lined the back wall. The feeds were live and Ahern could be seen on the third camera checking his phone.

Helvin pointed to the fourth feed where it was obvious the camera was located inside the cold case. It was actually a walk-in refrigerator that allowed Helvin to stock the cold cases from behind.

"He didn't see this camera," Helvin said. "They never do."

"Go ahead and play it," Searcy said.

Helvin rewound the playback almost an hour and

started playing it. On the playback, Helvin was busy checking out a customer when a boy of about sixteen entered the store, backpack over his shoulders, and proceeded to the cold cases in the back. He wore a hoodie and baggy cargo pants. He went to one of the cold cases and opened the door. His eyes followed his right hand as he reached up to the top shelf to grab an orange juice container. At the same time his left hand reached to a lower shelf and grabbed a can of beer. As he turned away from the case to his right he slipped the can into an open side pocket of his backpack.

The maneuver was clearly seen on the feed from inside the case. On the camera feed from outside the case, the sleight of hand was unseen. The kid was good. He just hadn't scoped the fourth camera.

"You know who that is, right?" Helvin said.

"Ricky Galt," Searcy said. "The city manager's son."

"That's fucked-up," Ahern said. "Kid needs a beer on his way to school."

"I didn't see it until after he bought the orange juice and left," Helvin said. "After he was gone I started thinking. I'm down a six-pack or two a week on Bud and that kid comes in, gets orange juice five mornings a week. So I look at the cameras and…called you guys."

Ahern came over to the other side of the counter and looked at Searcy.

"What are you going to do?" he asked.

"Go up to the school," Searcy said. "Yank him out of class, scare him."

"That's it?"

"What would you want me to do? Haul him down to the sub, have his dad come in?"

"Well, not much lesson in what you're going to do."

Searcy looked at Helvin.

"You want him to come sweep the store out after school every day?" he asked.

"I might lose more beer that way," Helvin said.

Searcy nodded. He had thought so. He looked back at Ahern.

"I'll handle it," he said. "You can get back out there."

"Roger that," Ahern said.

He walked out of the store, leaving Searcy and Helvin.

"A-hole," Helvin said.

Searcy didn't respond.

"I hear that a bunch of people are going across next week to watch the trial," Helvin said.

"I figured they would," Searcy said.

"And you know Ricky Galt was in the same class with Jamie Gallagher, right?"

"I know."

"Maybe that's where all this started. The drinking, I mean. Something like that…go easy on him."

Searcy was annoyed by Helvin's last remark. If he wanted to go easy on the young thief he should have handled the incident on his own and not called in the sheriff's department.

But he said nothing about that.

"Is it possible to get a copy of that fourth camera feed?" he asked instead.

Searcy took the cart up Sumner Avenue, then passed by city hall and the office of the city manager, before cutting over to Falls Canyon Road. At the high school he followed procedure and went to the security office where he asked John Bozak, head of security, to take Ricky Galt out of class for an interview.

That process took nearly twenty minutes and then Bozak set them up in a small office alone. No introductions were needed. Searcy had interviewed the kid once before. It was the morning Jamie Gallagher's nude body was found floating in the harbor.

"You missed the fourth camera," Searcy said.

"What?" Galt said.

Searcy opened the video app on his phone and started to play back the surveillance footage Helvin had emailed him. He slid the phone across the desk so Galt could watch it. The edges of his ears got red as he did so.

"That's fucked-up," he said.

"Yeah," Searcy said. "You gotta stop doing that."

"I will."

"The stealing *and* the drinking."

"One time, what's the—"

"Mr. Helvin says he's been coming up light at least a six-pack a week."

"One can a day, what's the big deal."

"Come on, Ricky. You're sixteen years old, drinking on your way to school. You've got a problem and there are ways to deal with it. Do your parents know?"

"No, and they don't have to."

"If you do something about it."

"I said I'll stop."

"You might need help stopping. Most alcoholics do."

"I'm not an alcoholic, okay? I just…don't like thinking about what happened to her. With everybody talking about the trial and his lawyer trying to act like he's the victim and she was the bad person…like she rowed out to his big fucking yacht uninvited."

"Look, what you are going through is totally understandable. I have some of that too, and I have to go testify against the guy next week. You're just not going about it the right way. Talk to your parents. Tell them you need to see a counselor. It will then be a private thing and you can talk about Jamie and the drinking and everything. It will help. You do that and this little thing goes away."

Searcy held up his phone with the video feed cued up and ready to play again—to the kid's parents if necessary.

"Okay, okay, I'll tell them," Galt said.

"Good," Searcy said. "Shoot me a text and let me know."

Searcy knocked his fist down twice on the wood desktop like a gavel—end of discussion.

Sitting in the cart outside the school, Searcy called the Zane Grey and talked to Daniels.

"How's our guy?"

"What guy?"

"The guy in the green windbreaker—Christov."

"Oh, I don't know. Still in his room, I guess. At least I haven't seen him."

"Okay, let me know when he makes a move."

Searcy drove back down to the basin, passing by city hall again.

Only Emmet was in the sub. She told him that Ahern and Rose were out and about on routine patrol. Searcy sequestered himself in his windowless office and opened up the search window on the National Crime Information Center. He put in the name Maxwell Christov and the Fairfax Avenue address he had to go with it. Through the federal database he would get a nationwide search of criminal records and warrants. The search Emmet had conducted for him earlier had only a local reach.

The kickback from the search was immediate. His running the name had drawn an FBI flag and a request to contact an agent named Alex Cohen at the Las Vegas field office. Searcy made the call and was immediately put through to Cohen.

"Deputy Searcy, I was just about to give you a call," Cohen said.

"Why is that?" Searcy said.

"Because like you, I got the alert when you put the name Maxwell Christov into the NCIC database. It says you are LA County Sheriff's Department. Can I ask where you work and where you encountered Christov?"

"I'm a detective assigned to the Avalon substation. I encountered Christov here this morning. Who is he to you?"

"You encountered him how?"

"I observed him acting suspiciously."

Searcy had decided not to give up the gun unless this agent started giving up information.

"Where is Avalon located?" Cohen asked. "Is it South LA?"

"Close," Searcy said. "There is an Avalon Boulevard in South County but the town of Avalon is on Catalina. An island. We're twenty-five miles off the coast. About four thousand people live here full-time and a million tourists come visit each year."

"I've heard of Catalina and I don't need the tourism pitch. Christov is there?"

"Got off a boat this morning."

"And you found that suspicious?"

"That's not what I thought was suspicious. But I'm not going to tell you what that was until you start to fill in some—"

"I'm assigned to an organized crime task force here in Vegas. Does that make it clear enough for you?"

"Okay, this guy is OC. He still might be a tourist over here."

"Did you confront him, speak to him?"

"Agent Cohen, I get that he's OC, but you don't put an NCIC flag on every person with ties to organized crime. What's so special about this guy?"

There was a long pause while Cohen apparently decided whether to engage further.

"What is the name of your supervisor?" Cohen finally asked.

"I'm pretty autonomous out here," Searcy said. "But I report to a lieutenant at the Hall of Justice. His name is Turner, but if you think calling him is going to—"

"Maxwell Christov is an alias used by a contract killer. If it's the same Maxwell Christov, then he is most likely on your little island to kill someone."

That hit Searcy like a jolt, and he was embarrassed that he had danced the local/federal tango with this guy.

"It's him," Searcy said. "He caught my eye because he was carrying a gun when he got off the boat."

"Do you know where he is right now?" Cohen asked urgently.

"He checked into a hotel this morning. The Zane Grey. I have someone there who's supposed to let me know if he leaves. And I think I might know who his target is."

"Who?"

"Me."

"What are you talking about?"

"I arrested a man last year for murder. The trial goes next week and I'm a witness. The main witness."

"What was the case?"

"We have yachts from all over the world come in here all the time. There was a sixteen-year-old girl—a local kid. She went to a party on this guy's sixty-five-foot boat. She got roofied and raped. Her body was found floating in the harbor. It took the homicide unit three hours to get their shit together and get out here on a helicopter. Meantime, I traced her movements to the boat and went out there to secure evidence. I talked to the guy and arrested him when he made incriminating statements. I wasn't expecting it and wasn't recording. At trial it will be my word against his."

"And if you're not there to testify…"

"Exactly."

"What's the defendant's name?"

"Rory Stanfield. He's thirty-two years old. He supposedly made his money in software. I don't know of any connection to Las Vegas."

"Doesn't need to be one. Christov—we think his real name is Eric Reece—is an equal opportunity killer. Not associated with any organization though many have hired him. Anybody who can get to him can hire him."

Searcy felt his body heat rising. He glanced through the open door of his office into the front room. Ahern and Rose were still out on patrol. Only Emmet was out there and she would put up no resistance to an intruder with a gun.

"What should I do?" he asked.

"I need to hang up and get the Los Angeles FO moving on this," Cohen said. "I'll head them your way. You sit tight and take all precautions. If you can, see if he is still at the hotel. My guess? He's probably waiting until darkness. If we get out there earlier, we'll take him at the hotel. You live on the island or commute?"

"I live here."

"Wife? Kids?"

"No, alone."

"He probably knows all of that and is waiting for darkness. We have some time."

"All right."

"Let me go and I'll get back to you as soon as I set things in motion. You're armed, right?"

"Yes."

"Good."

Cohen disconnected and Searcy was left in his office by himself, thinking about how a stranger had come into town to kill him.

"Mary?" he called.

"I'm here," Emmet responded from the dayroom.

"Call Ahern and Rose in. No delays."

"Something up?"

"Just do it."

He would keep the two deputies close while the FBI mustered. Searcy knew he had to inform Lieutenant Turner of what was going on, but he called the Zane Grey first.

"Daniels, it's Searcy, is Christov still in his room?"

"Far as I know. I haven't seen him."

"I'm going to see if he answers. Put me through."

"You sure?"

"Just do it."

Searcy knew that the call could serve to spook Christov and let him know he had aroused suspicion, but he would bluff his way out of the call.

There was no answer. After twelve rings he hung up, then called the Grey's main number again.

"He didn't answer."

"Well, hmm, you want me to check his cart?"

"What cart?"

"I told you. He rented the Riders of the Purple Sage suite. It comes with use of a private golf cart. I gave him the key when he checked in."

"Damn it, you didn't tell me that. Yes, go check and see. I'll wait."

Searcy could hear Daniels put the phone down on the desk. It was a long forty seconds before he came back.

"It's gone," Daniels said. "He not here."

Searcy knew the Zane Grey was known for its colorful golf carts.

"What's the cart look like?" he quickly asked.

"It's got a yellow body and the roof is blue-and-white stripes like a beach towel," Daniels said.

"Okay, if he comes back call me. But be discreet. This guy's a killer."

"What?"

"You heard me."

Searcy disconnected. He leaned back in his chair so he could pull the gun off his belt. He checked the action and returned it to the formfitting holster. He had to think a moment to recall when he had last fired the weapon. It was seven months earlier at the academy for annual qualifying.

He got up and went out into the dayroom. Ahern and Rose were nowhere in sight. He looked at Emmet.

"Did you call those guys in?" he asked.

"I put out the calls," Emmet said. "Rose is coming in from Descanso and Ahern hasn't responded."

"Try him again."

Emmet picked up the radio mike on her desk and put out the call to Ahern. Searcy paced in front of her desk while they waited for Ahern to respond.

He didn't.

"Keep trying," Searcy said. "I'm going up to the break room for coffee."

Searcy bounded up the stairs, but he wasn't going for coffee. He wanted to get to the window that gave him a full view of the harbor and business district.

He was at the spot less than a minute when he spotted the golf cart from the Zane Grey. From the angle of his second-floor position, it was easy to pick up the blue-and-white-striped roof. The cart was parked illegally alongside the seawall on the south side of the pier.

He grabbed the pair of binoculars that had sat on the windowsill since his first days at the sub and scanned the crowds of tourists on and around the pier.

People were lining up to board the 2:10 Express going back to Long Beach. There were people fishing, posing for photos. He was looking for the green windbreaker but didn't see it.

He heard steps behind him and turned to see Rose enter the break room. He was in uniform with his short sleeves tailored to the middle of his impressive biceps.

"Searcy, what's going on?" he asked.

"Need you here," Searcy said as he turned back to the window and raised the binoculars to his eyes again. "Where's Ahern?"

"I don't know. Mary can't raise him."

Just then Searcy thought he caught a glimpse of the green windbreaker. A man had just moved across the five-foot boarding bridge onto the Express and then disappeared from view behind the boat's cabin structure. It had happened so quickly Searcy wasn't sure what he saw. Had it been the stranger? Was Christov or whatever his name was leaving without his kill?

This didn't make sense.

They were then joined in the break room by Mary Emmet.

"I can't get Ahern on the radio," she said. "I'm getting worried."

It hit Searcy then. He may have had it wrong. He turned to Rose.

"Rose…you transferred in from jail division, right?" he asked.

"Right," Rose said. "Why?"

"Did you know Ahern there?"

"No. We had some overlap but I didn't know him in there."

"But you talked to him when he got here, right? Shared experience, all of that."

"Yeah, we talked. What's going on?"

"What happened? Why'd they send him out here?"

Rose glanced at Emmet and then back at Searcy.

"Uh…" he began. "He didn't really—"

"Mary," Searcy interrupted. "Go back down and keep trying the radio."

Emmet looked at the two men. It was clear she knew she was being dismissed so they could talk.

"Go," Searcy said.

"Okay," Emmet said. "But I don't think his radio is working."

She left the room and went down the stairs. Searcy looked at Rose.

"It's important," he said. "No bullshit—what did he tell you happened?"

"He just said he fucked up the wrong guy."

"He had to have said more. You didn't ask? Who was the wrong guy?"

"He didn't say, like, a name but he said it was up at Wayside. This kid came in to do a bullet on a probation violation. He had a smart mouth and his old man was getting money in to him so he could buy up protection. He mouthed off to Ahern—kept calling him A-hole—and he got tired of it. One day at yard time he diverted the kid's protection and he went out there naked. A couple of bangers set on him and fucked him up good. Lesson learned except he got brain damage. Permanent brain damage and one of the bangers said it was Ahern who put them up to it."

It was the kind of story Searcy had heard coming out of the jail for years.

"So they didn't fire him," Searcy said. "Instead they sent him out here."

"I guess till things sort of blew over," Rose said.

"Except they didn't," Searcy said.

Searcy left the break room and went down the steps. Emmet was standing behind her desk in the dayroom.

"Nothing," she said. "He's not answering."

"Run the locator on his cart," Searcy said.

Emmet sat down and pulled up an app on her computer. All the sheriff's carts were LoJacked with GPS. After a few moments she got a location.

"Avalon Canyon Road. By Sky Summit. Why would he go up there?"

Searcy and Rose rode up together. Up past the high school, the city hall and the golf course. At the top there was an open view off the back of the island with the misty Pacific seemingly going on forever. They first saw Ahern's cart parked in the rough off the side of the road. They followed a hiking trail and fifty yards in they found his body. He was face down in the rocks, two entry wounds in the back of his head. It looked like maybe he had been forced to his knees before he took the shots.

Rose got dizzy and had to drop to a knee with one hand on the ground for balance.

"If you're going to puke, move away from the crime scene," Searcy said.

"I'm not going to puke," Rose insisted. "I knew the guy, all right?"

Searcy pulled his phone. He called Cohen at the FBI first.

"I was wrong about the target," he said. "It was somebody else. Divert your helicopter and everything else to the harbor in Long Beach. Your hitter is on the Express that left here a half hour ago. It'll dock over there in twenty."

"Got it," Cohen said. "We'll redirect."

"Let me know if you get him."

"Absolutely."

Searcy disconnected and then called in the murder to his own department. They told him a homicide team would be on the way shortly.

* * * * *

HERE'S TO NEW FRIENDS

BY JACQUELINE FREIMOR

I've been watching him watch her for almost fifteen minutes, and I know he'll make his move as soon as the train pulls out of the station. He: late thirties, big head with glossy black hair; she: maybe twenty, a rabbity strawberry blonde.

As for me, I'm in my midfifties, tanned and quite bald, but I'm not in this story yet; I'm an observer, as both my profession and my avocation have trained me to be.

Sure enough, as soon as we start moving, he rises from his window seat, squeezes past my knees and heads to the aisle. The first red flag.

"Excuse me?" he says, his voice deep and smooth. She's sitting in our row at the window on the other side of the train, hunched down, attached to her phone by earbuds. There's an open book in her lap. Her body language clearly states *Leave me alone*, but he's decided to ignore it.

Red flag #2.

"Excuse me?" he says again. "Miss?"

She looks up warily and plucks out the earbuds. "Yes?"

His formfitting tank top and thin jogging pants show well-defined arm muscles and a lean physique. He bounces a little on the balls of his feet like a boxer and points to the aisle seat next to her. "Do you mind if I sit here? I'm at the window there—" he gestures vaguely "—and it's making me claustrophobic."

Red flags #3, too much information and #4, false information. Claustrophobic at the window? Not likely.

The train from Union Station to Newport News this evening has a number of empty seats. And yet he's chosen the one next to her—red flag #5.

Honestly, how many warnings does she need? But she has no doubt been brought up to be polite, which is another way of saying she's been trained to be prey. If I were her father, I would have made sure she understood the possible consequences of that kind of passivity.

"No problem," she says, but she shrinks into herself even further. She puts her earbuds back in and looks down at her book.

He pulls his phone from his pocket and sits, manspreading into the aisle on one side and into her space on the other. A tattooed tiger snarls on his biceps.

He stares at his screen, pretending to read, then scrolls down with a spatulate thumb and grins. He chuckles. "Aw," he says and then repeats himself: "Aw." He angles his body toward her. "Sorry to interrupt, but do you like animal videos? You have to see this."

Completely fatuous. Who doesn't like watching a half-drowned baby squirrel being nursed back to health? A one-armed spider monkey befriended by a cat? You'd have to be a sociopath not to respond.

Reluctantly, she detaches her earbuds once more,

lips compressed into a thin smile that looks more like a grimace. I can see her entire body sigh. So can he, I know. He just doesn't care.

"Sure. I like them," she says flatly.

He holds up his phone and leans toward her. Whatever they're watching is engrossing. They both laugh, and little by little, she leans toward him, too. She's softening. She closes her book and puts it in the mesh pocket of the seatback in front of her.

I'm impressed. He's a quick worker, having accomplished steps one through five of the Request Assistance Scenario—identify the target, enlist her help, invade her space, establish a common interest and get her to mirror you—in record time.

After that, he's got her. He introduces himself—Tony, like Tony the Tiger, ha, ha, ha—and quickly establishes that her name is Megan, she's a student at George Washington University, and she's joining friends in Virginia Beach for spring break. They don't know she's coming. She didn't have enough money for the trip, but her parents surprised her with cash for her birthday, which was just last week.

I keep listening and watch them out of the corner of my eye. Here's his opening. "Hey, happy birthday!" Tony says. "Let me buy you a drink."

Megan reddens. "No, no, you don't have to."

"I know I don't have to. I want to."

"No, that's okay. Really."

"Come on. We have to celebrate."

He stands and crooks his finger, and after a moment, she stands, too, grabs her backpack and hoists it over her shoulder. Slick. He's established a pattern in which his wishes override her objections.

Tony steps into the aisle and retreats a foot or two, gesturing for Megan to precede him.

After a moment's reflection, I find that I, too, have developed a powerful thirst and, grabbing my newspaper, follow him following her as we lurch toward the café car.

Once we arrive, we line up at the counter—Tony tall, broad, meaty; Megan short, thin, insubstantial. Now that I'm close to her, I see she has pale orange eyelashes and a charming overbite. She's wearing black leggings and a too-big GWU sweatshirt into which, I can tell, she likes to disappear.

"May I help you, sir?" says the blue-aproned attendant, whose nameplate identifies her as Trisha.

Tony points first to himself and then to Megan. "Champagne for two."

The attendant says, "I'm sorry, we don't carry Champagne. But we do have a lovely California Chardonnay."

"That's fine," Tony says without consulting Megan. It's clear from the look on her face that she's never had Chardonnay. Maybe she doesn't even know what it is.

Trisha says, "I'll have to see the young woman's ID."

In full blush now, Megan fumbles in her backpack and pulls out a card. Trisha gives it a cursory glance. "Thank you."

When Trisha turns her back and does a deep-knee bend to retrieve the wine from the half-size refrigerator, Tony glances at Megan's ID, and, heads together, they laugh softly. They keep their voices down, so I'm only guessing they're murmuring about Megan's fake ID, which she may even have procured specifically for this spring break. Now the two of them share a secret. They're Bonnie and Clyde, bucking an unfair system. Next on the checklist: he's going to get her drunk.

It never ceases to amaze me how unsuspecting young women can be, despite daily reminders of the world's dangers. In any city you visit in the United

States, you'll see flyers headlined *Missing* taped to storefronts and telephone poles. Even in Town Center, near my home in Virginia Beach, a few still broadcast the search for an Old Dominion student who disappeared eight years ago. Hasn't Megan seen flyers like these? Or does she think nothing like that could ever happen to her?

Involving myself in this kind of scenario was not on my agenda when I boarded the train, but now I think I'm going to tell Megan Tony's not the good person he's pretending to be. I'll take the opportunity when—if—he goes to the lavatory. Until then, I can only wait.

Trisha sets a half bottle of wine and two plastic glasses on the counter, deftly peels the foil, inserts a corkscrew and pops out the cork. As she pours, Tony pulls cash—of course—from his pocket, licks his thumb and counts out the bills. "Keep the change."

"Thank you, sir. Enjoy."

"Thank you," he says. Megan nods.

Tony picks up the glasses and slides onto the blue vinyl seat of the nearest booth. Megan sits across the table from him. He hands her a glass and lifts his in a toast. "Here's to you. Happy birthday."

She clicks her cup against his. "Thank you."

"And here's to new friends."

"To new friends," she echoes.

Over the next sixty minutes, I sit in the booth across from theirs, sipping ginger ale and pretending to read my newspaper. The café is doing a brisk business in beverages, sandwiches and microwavable pizza, and a steady stream of people pass. They provide cover for me while I track the progress Tony is making with Megan.

Both are now leaning their backs on the window,

their legs on the seats. His are outstretched in front of him, crossed at hairy ankles; hers are bent at the knee, sneakers flat on the vinyl.

From this angle, I can see him only in profile, as he's looking straight at her and making her the focus of all his attention. She looks mostly at him and occasionally turns her head to stare into space—in my direction, but without seeing me.

One half bottle of wine has turned into two, and Megan's doing most of the drinking, especially since Tony's also bought pretzels to make her thirsty. Tony himself takes small sips and keeps topping up her glass.

I can hear snatches of their conversation whenever the flow of passengers thins. I learn she's from Roanoke and majoring in art history at GW, and he lives in Newport News, where he's a software developer. This is almost certainly a lie. Had she said she was studying computer science, he would have said he owned an art gallery or was a Realtor. They make small talk about movies and TV shows and what they like to do in their spare time, etc. I turn the page of my paper and wait, sensing a shift in the atmosphere.

Tony ostentatiously clears his throat. "So, first spring break, huh?" he says. "Excited?"

"Yes!" she says.

"You're going to have a great time. But you know this train doesn't go all the way to Virginia Beach, right? You have to transfer to a bus at Newport News."

"I know." But she sounds uncertain.

He laughs. "Don't worry. I'll make sure you get on the bus."

She picks up a pretzel and nibbles on it. "Thank you. That's so nice of you."

Here it is. He's going in for the kill.

"Wait a minute," Tony says, and actually smacks

himself on the forehead. "My car's at the station in Newport News. I can give you a lift."

Her eyes widen. "To Virginia Beach? But isn't that, like, two hours from there?"

He shrugs. "Nah. It's an hour fifteen. An hour, if you drive like me." He grins.

She shakes her head. "I can't ask you to do that. It'd be totally out of your way."

He shrugs again. "Not really. Plus, my girlfriend lives at the Beach. It'll be great to go meet her for a drink."

"But—"

He lifts a finger to shush her and picks up his phone. "I won't take no for an answer." He stabs at the screen, scrolls down and taps a number. He lifts the cell to his ear and winks at Megan. She smiles faintly.

"Hey, baby," Tony says. "How you doin'?" He waits a beat. "Great. Yeah, listen. I'm going to be out your way tonight. Want to—?" He laughs. "That's what I was going to say. How about—" he looks at his watch "—11:00?" He waits. "You got it. See you then."

He hangs up and smiles at Megan. "See? It's all good. I'll drop you at your friends' house and go meet my honey after."

She hesitates, then gulps her wine. "I guess that'd be okay. I mean, as long as you don't mind."

He raises his glass to her. "Not at all. Anything for a friend."

She heard what he wanted her to hear. He's already taken. He has no designs on her.

They're just friends.

Nicely done, Tony. Very nicely done.

I give them a few minutes to return to their seats before following suit. When I sit down, they're talk-

ing quietly, apparently about Tony's nonexistent girlfriend. I put my newspaper in my briefcase, then lean
back and close my eyes. If I'd had lingering doubts
about Tony's plans for Megan, they're long gone. It's
time for me to step in.

My chance arrives when Tony finally stops prat-
tling and says, "Excuse me for a minute. I have to use
the facilities."

"Sure," Megan says. I hope she doesn't take the opportunity to visit the restroom herself.

I hold my breath. I hear the sound of soft footfalls
and feel a slight whoosh of air as he moves past me. I
wait a beat, open my eyes and turn my head to see Tony
hesitate at the lavatory—it must be occupied—and then
open the connecting door between cars. When it slides
shut with a bang, I hurry into Tony's seat, warmed by
his body.

Megan rears back in alarm. "What—?"

"I'm sorry to frighten you," I say in a low voice, "but
this is important. I'm a psychologist, and I've been listening to your conversation with this man. I feel obliged
to warn you. His intentions toward you are not good.
He's not going to drive you to Virginia Beach. He's
going to abduct you and...force himself on you. I'm
sorry," I say again. "I know it's a lot to take in."

Her eyes are wide with shock and fear, her freckles
standing out against her white skin. "What? What are
you talking about?"

I scan the car for Tony. I hope there's a long line for
the lavatory.

Quickly, I repeat what I've just said and pull a business card from my wallet. "Here. I have a practice in
Virginia Beach. I specialize in sexual deviance."

She takes the card and stares at it—James McIntyre,

PsyD, and my office address—and then at me. She's
trembling.

"When we stop at Newport News," I continue, "get
on the bus to Virginia Beach. You can't miss it. It'll
be waiting at the station. Whatever you do, do *not* get
into a car with Tony. Do you understand?"

She nods mutely. Then, in a small voice, "How do
you know—?"

"I have patients with this paraphilia who have described exactly this scenario. There's no time to explain."

"Paraphilia?"

"It's—never mind. I know you have no reason to
believe me, but please. Don't get in the car."

Quickly, I stand up and reclaim my seat across the
aisle. Just in time. The sliding door opens, and Tony
saunters in. I glance at Megan and see her stuff my
business card into the front pocket of her backpack,
pull the hood of her sweatshirt up and curl up against
the window, her face mostly hidden.

"So listen, I—" Tony says when he reaches our row.
He stops when he sees Megan. She murmurs something
unintelligible, as though half-asleep.

"Whoops! Sorry," Tony whispers. He takes out his
phone and gently eases himself into his seat. He gives
Megan a long, hard look and then turns to his screen.
She's fooled him; he thinks she's sleeping.

Good girl.

The remainder of the trip is uneventful. Megan
sleeps, or at least pretends to, and Tony also nods off.
I feel the need to stay alert, even though there's nothing else I can do. The rest is up to Megan.

The conductor announces we'll be arriving at Newport News in just a few minutes. Passengers traveling

through to Virginia Beach must transfer to the Amtrak Thruway Motorcoach waiting at the station.

Tony awakens, yawns hugely and nudges Megan. "Hey, Sleeping Beauty," he says. "We're almost there."

She starts and sits up. "What? Oh." She turns her head to look at me, then past me and back at Tony. There's a large red mark on her cheek where it was mashed against the window.

"Are you okay?" he says.

"Mm-hmm. Just tired. And my head hurts. You got me drunk." She says this with just enough flirtatiousness for him to think she's teasing, but I can see a flicker of anger in her eyes. Again she looks at me and then away.

"Guilty." He laughs. "But that's spring break, right?"

"Uh-huh."

With a shriek of the hydraulic brakes, the train pulls into Newport News, and the gathering of belongings obviates further conversation. A pulse beats in my throat, and I realize I'm nervous. I think I know what Megan's going to do, but will she be strong enough to go through with it?

Tony and Megan detrain first and stop midway between the tracks and the bus idling in front of the station house. The night air is chilly, blustery, bracing, and as I walk past them, I see Megan's long red hair blown into wild shapes that look like the flames of a bonfire. I take a seat on the bus and watch their silent interaction under the bluish glare of the parking lot lights. Is she refusing his offer?

She's refusing, all right. At first, her body language is submissive—crossed arms and legs, slumping to make herself even smaller than she is—and his is puzzled, then cajoling. He's pleading with her, arms outstretched, palms up, but as she gradually unwinds herself and stands her ground, his posture becomes more aggressive and threatening. He spreads his feet apart and puts his hands on his hips. Then he reaches out and grabs her wrist. Even through the thick window glass, I can hear her scream, and she tries to yank her arm away. He won't let go. Then, before I or any of the other men around can intervene, he sneers and shoves her backward, releasing her. She staggers but doesn't fall. She races around him toward the bus.

"You're not *that* hot, bitch," he bellows after her, so loudly that I can hear every word. "Fuck it! Fuck you! Fuck YOU!"

"Hey!" says the burly bus driver, lurching from his seat and lumbering down the steps and onto the pavement. "What's going on?"

I watch from the window. "I have to get on the bus," I hear Megan say through the open door. "Please. I have a ticket."

The bus driver points to Tony, who's now backing away with his hands raised. "Is this guy giving you any trouble?"

"I'm okay."

"Go ahead, honey," he says, and moves to let her pass.

Tony's still retreating. "Sorry," I hear him call out. "Sorry."

The bus driver shakes his head in disgust. "Get outta here before I call the police."

Tony doesn't need another warning. He turns, hurries into the darkest recesses of the parking lot and disappears.

When I turn away from the window, I see Megan making her way down the aisle, rubbing her wrist. When she sees me, she drops into the seat next to mine. She's shaking.

"So you were right," she says. The corners of her mouth are turning down as though she's going to cry and, sure enough, one tear drops, then two.

I reach into my pocket and pull out a package of Kleenex. "Here."

"Thanks." She plucks out a tissue and hands the package back. She scrubs at her face, and when she looks up again, she's gotten herself under control. "I mean, I tried to be nice about it. I just told him I changed my mind and wanted to take the bus. I didn't mention you or tell him what you said—" good "—but it didn't matter. He went crazy anyway."

I take a deep breath. "If he really was a nice guy offering to help you, your turning down a ride wouldn't have set him off. That little display—" I nod at the window "—shows you he cared too much about the outcome."

"I guess," she says dully.

"Look," I say kindly, "you've had a shock. But Tony's gone. He can't hurt you. And we'll be in Virginia Beach before you know it."

"Okay." She gives me a watery smile. "Thanks."

We spend the short trip chatting. I'm happy to see Megan relax as we increase the distance between her and the train station. By tacit agreement, we don't discuss what happened. Megan seems to want to put it all behind her as quickly as possible. Which is fine with me.

By the time the bus deposits us at the small shelter at Nineteenth and Pacific, it's almost 10:00, and it's even colder by the ocean than it was in Newport News. The other passengers are either being picked up or walking to their cars. As usual, there are no cabs. Megan sets her backpack on the pavement and looks around anxiously.

It's crucial I get this part right.

"Well, good night, Megan," I say casually. "Despite everything, I enjoyed talking to you. I hope you have a lovely vacation."

Her voice wobbles. "Thank you. I enjoyed talking to you, too."

I start to walk away. I go ten steps, then twenty, with bated breath. Can it be that I've misread her?

"Dr. McIntyre?"

I exhale. No, I haven't. I stop and turn. "Yes?"

She huddles inside her sweatshirt. "Do you know where I can get a taxi?"

I act taken aback. "You don't have anyone meeting you?"

She shakes her head. "My friends don't know I'm coming. It's a surprise."

I let a note of impatience creep into my voice. "Well, can't you call and ask them to pick you up?"

"They don't have a car." She bites her lip.

I walk back toward her. "What's the address?"

She picks up her backpack and unzips the front pocket. She pulls out a piece of paper and shows it to me. Her friends' house is five blocks from where we're standing.

I furrow my brow. "Hmm. That's a good two, three miles away. You can't walk it. You'll freeze."

She gazes at the deserted streets and looks forlorn. "Oh, no." This is it. It's important that it be her idea.

I look at my watch. "I hate to leave you here all by yourself, but I have to get home. My wife is expecting me."

The words "all by yourself" and "wife" do the trick. Megan puts her hand on my arm. "Please, Dr. McIntyre. Is your car around here? Could you give me a lift?"

I pretend to ponder this, then say, "Sure. I'm just around the corner."

Relief washes over her face. She slings her backpack on her shoulder. The unzipped front pocket gapes, and I see my business card. I make a mental note to retrieve it. Afterward.

"Thank you so much," Megan says, when we're snug and warm inside my car. "I hope this isn't taking you out of your way."

Having successfully activated the Provide Assistance Scenario, I now activate the automatic door locks and smile. "Not at all. What are friends for?"

* * * * *

ROOM FOR ONE MORE

BY JOE R. LANSDALE

Cars had whizzed by him all day, but none had stopped, all had ignored the hitchhike gesture of his thumb.

On the edge of the town, Jackson paused at the city limit sign, leaned against it. He was feeling the long walk. He shifted his pack a little. Catching a ride these days was harder and harder. No one wanted to stop for a stranger. Especially now that it was night and the moon was thin.

Not stopping for strangers was good thinking on their part. If they stopped, he was going to rob them. He didn't have any real wish to kill them. He wasn't a serial killer. He had the numbers to identify as one, but all of his murders were for a financial reason, not to satisfy some kind of need beyond commerce, some kind of sexual deviancy, though he was not averse to taking advantage of certain situations.

His job was simple. Stealing enough to live through the day, until he got the big score. He was uncertain what the big score was, but felt he would know it when he saw it, and to get to the big score, sometimes, on the subject of murder, you had to be flexible.

Jackson had the kind of face that was hard to remember. Still, spend too much time with someone, women especially, and they seemed too inquisitive, looked you over like they were picking a lobster for lunch. They'd probably remember too much. The little dark mole above his right eye, the cut on the left side of his lip that had left a white scar. His mother had a good throwing arm.

You had to judge murder on a case-by-case basis, though lately, his judgment had mostly led to homicide. In the end, it was more certain. Take no chances. Leave no witnesses. Keep going until he figured out the big score, and then once he had it, he'd stop robbing and killing. It wasn't that he felt any moral conundrum about it, but after a while, you had to figure the odds. You could only throw good dice for so long, and eventually it would have to be snake eyes. So quitting was on the agenda. He thought he might even get married, settle down. Provided he had that big score. Something to live on for the rest of his life. Diamonds maybe. Gold bullion. Jackson had a lot of dreams.

He looked out at the lights of the town. The town that said on its sign that its population was twelve hundred and six. At least one of that number, maybe more, were going to wake up tomorrow minus some goods. If he could do it without confrontation, steal something and get out. If he was confronted, well then, they may not wake up in the morning, and someone would need to subtract some numbers from that sign.

Jackson shifted the pack again, and started walking toward the lights.

* * *

By the time Jackson reached town, many of the lights that belonged to houses were out. Most of the town's occupants had tucked in for the night. There were some town lights, spotted here and there. The place wasn't exactly the Great White Way.

He watched for cop cars, didn't see any. When he reached the heart of town, he stuck to the shadows, alleys behind buildings. Some cop saw him, he might be spending the night in jail for vagrancy, or some such. Thing to do was hole up a while, wait until it was late, then pick a house that looked rich enough to have money, jewels, something he could steal and carry out effortlessly. Later, when he made it to a city, he could locate a fence for what he had stolen.

Jackson found a place behind a dumpster, next to a curb. He removed his pack, sat on the curb in the shadow of the dumpster, took a granola bar out of his pack and slowly munched on it.

There were lights beyond the alley, and they were soft and golden, belonged to Main Street, or whatever it was called; the street that ran through the center of town. After he finished his granola bar, he eased out from behind the dumpster, sat where there was a better view of the street. He could only see a portion of it, the part that ran by a theater. It was letting out, and he watched people ease outside, laughing, talking.

He couldn't remember the last time he had been to the movies. The happiness he saw amongst the crowd irritated him. Ten minutes later he was still sitting in the shadows. The theater had completely emptied out. The marquee lights were on, but the lights that had glowed through the glass doors, revealing the concession stand and a cardboard cutout for a forthcoming movie, were dimmed.

After a few minutes, a young woman came walking down the street. Jackson liked the way she looked, way she walked, way her dress swung around her legs, way her heels clicked on concrete.

A long black car with a man driving, a woman in the passenger seat, slowed next to her and stopped. The passenger window went down, and Jackson heard the woman in the car offer the young woman a ride, but she declined.

The woman walked faster, and then she was out of sight behind a building. After a few seconds, the car turned and went along the street next to the dumpster.

Jackson stepped back behind the dumpster and watched it pass, rolling slowly up the street and out of sight.

He needed to wait a while longer. To be certain the town had settled.

Nesting behind the dumpster again, he leaned against a tree that grew up next to the curb and bordered a business building of some sort, closed his eyes and fell asleep. The long day and the long walk had depleted him.

When he awoke, he felt refreshed and eager. He checked his watch in the glow of his penlight.

Two a.m.

He put the penlight away. It was time to locate a house and make his move.

Jackson followed the route of the long black car that had passed him, and then took a turn on a residential street with magnificent houses on either side. The rich section. There were lights in a few of the houses still, and there were streetlights, but overall it was shadowy, and now that there were fewer lights, he could see the partial moon again, a cold scimitar in the sky.

A dog barked. Jackson paused, determined it was a street over and started walking again. He stopped when he saw the black car he had seen earlier. It was parked in a driveway leading to a closed garage. Must be nice to have so many cars you could leave one in the driveway, another, perhaps two, in the garage. Jackson's guess was the ones in the garage, they would be really nice. The one in the driveway was nice enough, but it was probably the couple's around-town car. He thought if he got through with his theft, he might hot-wire the car, ride off in that until he got to the next town, better yet a full-blown city to find that fence. He'd be there before the owners woke up. If they did. It depended on how things went. He felt for the knife in his pocket. It was there. It was the sort that he could pull quick, pop open. It was as sharp as a comedian's wit.

The car, the house and garage were fancy looking. There were trees in the yard, and a big oak grew up beside the house, and next to that a fence bordered the neighbors. On the other side of the house there wasn't a tree, but there was more fencing, and from where he stood, he could see along the edge of the house and spot more fence at the back.

The house was three stories, and the top story had a balcony. The ground floor had a long porch and an indented entrance, and then a doorway with colored glass in panels about head height. There was a porch light on, but it was a light so thin, you got the feeling it didn't really mean it.

Jackson tried to catch sight of any kind of camera, or security light that might pop on when he stepped into the yard. If that popped on, he would feel like a nightclub act about to start up. Most likely, no one would notice him. Not this time of night, but the idea of it didn't appeal to him.

Jackson didn't see any cameras, but he walked along the sidewalk, and went into the yard through the trees that grew there, paused, decided the oak might be the best way to go. Might be an alarm at the door, but if he climbed the oak, went through the window, he could be inside quiet as a mute mouse in tennis shoes. If it turned out to be a bedroom, he might change his plans. Or, he might change their dreams, wreck their plans for tomorrow.

Still, there might be an easier way. A way he could go inside and then sneak about without ever having awakened them. With just a knife, someone inside might give him some trouble. They might have a gun.

Best plan was in and out with goods in his pack. He'd decide on the car after that.

Easing across the yard, no burglar lights came on. When he came to the oak, he considered, then went around it, slipped behind the house, and worked his way to the other side, where the garage was. There was a window there, and he leaned forward and looked in. The garage was the size of some houses he had lived in. He could see the shape of two cars and, though he couldn't tell what make and model, their sizes were impressive.

Jack slipped off his pack, pulled a crowbar out of it and gently slipped it under the window, cranked up. There was a popping sound, and then the window slid up effortlessly. Replacing the crowbar, he dropped his pack inside, and climbed after it. He crouched for a moment, then took out his penlight, snapped it on, flashed it around.

The cars were indeed nice. A Beamer, and a sleek new red Cadillac about the size of a yacht.

Jackson felt he had hit the jackpot, and his excitement raced through him. He took a deep breath, slipped on his pack and, guided by the penlight, crossed to the door across the way. He touched the knob, tried it.

The door was not locked. Jackson turned out the penlight, and entered the house.

Creeping along a hallway, he clicked on the penlight again. He entered a large room. There was a TV about the size of a theater screen, lots of chairs, and there was even a platform in front of it where someone might make a speech or sing a song. The room could easily hold twenty, maybe thirty guests.

As Jackson turned, the penlight beam fell on a shape. A young woman, beautiful, well-dressed, with shiny hair and a face white as a ghost in the penlight beam.

"Oh, hi," she said.

Jackson dropped the light, grabbed her, threw her down on the floor.

"Like it rough, huh?" she said, and giggled.

"What are you? Crazy?"

"Depends on who you ask."

"Don't scream, bitch, or I'll kill you. This may be your house, but I'm the master now."

"Oh, baby. This isn't our house."

Jackson sensed too late that someone was behind him. Then he felt a sharp pain in the back of his head, and the dark of the room became darker.

When Jackson awoke, he was tied, feet and hands, his pack had been removed, and he was sitting in a chair in the front row of the home theater. The lights were on, but the light was soft, the color of fresh butter, and with the dark curtains drawn, the room had a cozy feel about it.

For a moment.

The girl and a man had pulled up chairs and were sitting in front of him, watching him. The man was as handsome as the woman was pretty. She was dressed as if for a night on the town. Little black dress, a string of pearls, high heels. The man wore a nice suit with a bright blue tie with red checks in it. His shoes were shiny enough you could use them to signal a ship offshore.

"Hey, there, sleepyhead," said the young woman.

"Thought I might have hit you too hard," said the man. "Karate chop. Nah, not really. I don't know karate, but I did hit you with the side of my hand, hard as I could. I've had some practice with that, if not professional training. Know what I mean?"

Jackson didn't.

"I'm Doll," said the woman, "and this is Guy. That's not really our names, but we like it, don't we, Guy?"

"We do."

"Look," Jackson said. "I shouldn't have come in. I was looking for a place to sleep. Thought no one was home."

"Oh, I don't believe that," Guy said. "Do you, Doll?"

Doll shook her head, clicked her tongue. "That's a windy, dear. You are telling us a windy."

"Just let me go, and I'm out of here. Out of your house, out of your lives."

"Didn't I say," she said. "This isn't our house."

"Yeah," Guy said, "but it's nice, right? I mean, if this isn't nice, what is? Way we like to work, is we come into a town, small one, look for some place with privacy, and if it's nice, like this, well, all the better. And we want someone to be home."

"You tried to get that girl in your car," Jackson said. "I saw that."

"You did? I'll be damned. Hear that, Doll? He saw us."

"She was so delectable," Doll said. "But she was smart, didn't get in. And it doesn't matter you saw us or not."

"Here's the thing, and I think you have the right to know," Guy said. "And this should be clear by now, as Doll has told you twice. But I'm one for clarification."

"Oh, God, is he. He doesn't care, you know, darling. He just likes to hear himself talk."

Guy reached out and patted Doll's knee. "Now, now. Don't be mean."

"Sorry. Just thought she'd have better clothes. It put me on edge. That closet, for all their money, looks like something from the children's department, and her with cash to spare. And that jewelry. Costume mostly. There was money in the safe, though. Oh. Go on, darling, tell him what you want to tell him. I'm just being nasty."

"No. You're right, Doll. I'm just hearing myself talk. I've said all I need to say, really."

"You can steal it all," Jackson said. "I'm not competition."

"Don't interrupt," Doll said. "Daddy is talking."

She smiled, reached out and touched a finger to Jackson's lips. "Shhhhh."

Guy leaned in close. "We're not here just for items to steal. Items to bleed are very important to us."

Jackson let Guy's words bang around inside his head for a moment.

"We like to find a nice house and some nice people, and turn it and them to not so nice."

"We're in the papers," Doll said. "You've heard of us, I bet. The Midnight Ramblers. Sometimes the Break-in Killers. I like the Midnight Ramblers. The other sounds so basic and crude."

"All we had to do was park right out front. It's late. No one will notice. We picked the lock, found the owners upstairs. Nice-looking young couple. Soon we'll be gone from here. But you won't. And what a mystery that will create when you join them."

Guy stood up and moved his chair.

Jackson had a straight view of the stage in front of the TV, the one that had been empty when he broke in, the one that had been filled while he was unconscious. The one with two nude and well-dissected bodies on it. It was wet and red up there.

"You'll be staying here with them," said Guy. "I mean, there's room up there for one more."

"No. I'm one of you," Jackson said.

"Isn't that sweet?" Doll said.

"Just a big sack of sugar, baby," Guy said, and Jackson noted there was a tiny bit of drool running from the corner of his mouth, like a man about to eat a slice of hot apple pie.

"I am going to keep your penlight," Doll said. "Is that okay? Of course it is."

Jackson said nothing. He could hardly breathe.

"Ain't life just full of surprises?" Guy said, bent down and unzipped a leather bag at Jackson's feet. It was filled with shiny sharp objects.

Guy removed a meat cleaver from the pile, held it up. The light winked off of it. Doll pulled a long knitting needle from the bag.

"I like to start with the toes and slowly work my way up to the head," Guy said. "Sometimes, our objects of desire don't last that long. But we're learning better and better how to make them last so as to make it last. You know, do it right."

"I like to poke," Doll said, making a jabbing motion with the knitting needle.

"By the way," Guy said, leaning in close to Jackson's sweat-popped face. "Just so you don't have false hopes. This is really going to hurt."

* * * * *

EXIT NOW

BY EMILYA NAYMARK

Part I

Fergle

"Exit now," the GPS lady commanded.

Fergle peered at the hazy highway, swerving as he did. His GPS lady had an Irish accent and reminded him of his aunt Maura, who also loved issuing directions.

The exit caromed around the bend and he took it, the GPS lady satisfied to silence. Still miles from the ocean, the air already had a fresh, marine tang to it—iodine and seaweed. He turned his face into the breeze and inhaled deeply. He needed this.

"Exit now," the GPS Aunt Maura said, and Fergle obliged, finding himself on a narrow two-lane road. As if passing through a veil, the air shifted from white-bright to silver, and the sky dropped low and heavy over the beach bungalows and pizza shops either side of him.

"You sure?" he asked, but the GPS lady was not in the business of answering questions, same as Aunt Maura when she didn't want to talk. Like when he was three and kept asking when he could go home, please, and if she would rub his back and sing to him the way his mother used to.

No more going home for him now, not ever. Another family lived in the house where he grew up, and Maura occupied space in a nursing home. The last time he'd visited her, which was yesterday, she had screeched in horror and crab walked along the wall until she found her closet and locked herself inside.

"Maybe she was looking for the toilet," the dementia ward nurse said, patting his arm, but he knew better. The simple truth was Maura reacted the same way everyone did the first time they saw him—with fear. Six foot seven, big-boned, heavy-browed, with a face that looked chopped rather than chiseled, Fergle's outward appearance inspired fear.

A sign caught his eye: "Efficiency rooms to let. By week or month." Fergle crunched into the dilapidated parking lot and unfolded his bulk from behind the wheel. He'd been here before, twenty-some years ago. Not at the motel, but at Old Town Beach, Maine, though he remembered absolutely nothing from that first visit, not even the accident that left him with a broken cheekbone, clavicle and arm. He'd been only a toddler when his mother took him on one of her spontaneous road trips. Yet something of that primordial junket remained in his cells, and a shiver shook him, traveling from the top of his beige hair to his slabby feet.

His phone buzzed, and he put it away without answering. It had been buzzing ever since he walked out of his office building, weighty duffel bag in hand, broken glass and dented metal glinting underneath an emptied display case behind him.

The late afternoon cooled; the town still groggy from winter, even though it was mid-June. Fergle paid for the first night with cash, collected a brass key and entered a small, stuffy, stained room. He threw his backpack onto the bed, opened the window and ducked back out through the doorway.

He'd stay a week. Or two. It wasn't like he had a job anymore, not after taking the thing occupying half his trunk right now. Even six months ago, being unemployed (never mind under what circumstances) would have distressed him. He loved designing toys, had even majored in just that at university. Lately, however, the toys he built felt a lie, a promise to children the world would not keep.

The phone clamored again; he powered it off. A walk to the beach. A dip in the cold ocean. That's the thing. At the boardwalk, he passed a tent, and a man as tall and burly as he eyed him, then said, "You here for the job?"

Fergle paused in bewilderment, and only then noticed the half-built carnival rides, the flaccid tents, the boxes of cables and duct tape.

"Sure," he said, because he was a curious person, and why not.

"All right, fill this out." The man pushed a clipboard toward him, form attached. Missing his front teeth, the man was a leathery burgundy color, and had a flattened nose that spoke of past violence.

"Axl?" The man grinned at Fergle's form.

Fergle grinned back. "That's me."

The man held out his hand, his crooked and flattened fingers rough against Fergle's office-smooth ones. "I'm

Del. You can start now," he said. "Three hundred a week and you get a discount on the grub."

"Sure beans," said Fergle, because he enjoyed building things, and he figured if he weren't assembling rides or manning booths, he'd be wandering the hard sand, alone with his thoughts and the phone in his pocket with its thirty-two messages and twenty-seven missed calls.

He spent the rest of the afternoon helping with setup and the early evening running the cotton candy machine. The hour before closing found him at the Wild West shooting gallery, taking sticky tickets and cash, handing out plush animals, all while the tiny manager offered frequent nips from the whiskey bottle she kept under the counter. He accepted, the alcohol wrapping him in cheerful gauze.

"Thank you for that," he said. "The next bottle is on me."

She waved his words away with a shy smile, her hand fluttering to cover her mouth.

After the lights shut and the motors quieted, Fergle raised his face to the moon. He'd been working such long hours for the toy company—eighty, ninety hours a week—that he couldn't remember the last time he'd been outside like this, cool air on his skin while still alert, awake. Fried dough and onions, body spray, spilled beer and cigar smoke shimmied on the night breezes.

He didn't want to return to his little efficiency room with its stingy window and thin mattress, and instead strolled through the hushed fairground toward the trucks and tents where the permanent carnival workers were winding down for the night. Their radios and phones emitted classic rock, reggaeton and hip-hop as the ocean rose and fell behind them like a benevolent beast.

He meandered the grounds toward his motel, feeling so light, so hollow, so *empty*, he wanted to cry, but that reaction made no sense, so he quashed it. He soon found himself facing yet another set of trailers partially obscured by what, even under the moonlight and in his exhausted state, looked like a very unstable billboard wall, thirty feet long, twelve high, acting as a barrier between the two camps. Posters, ads and graffiti announced fireworks past and future as well as concerts and revival meetings. Layers and layers.

Someone was shouting behind that wall, then a thud, and the wood shook as something body-sized smashed against it. Fergle paused. He was drunk. He was tired. This was not his circus, not his monkey.

A grunt behind the wall and the body-sized thing slammed against the wall again. He marched to the corner and peered around the wall's edge.

The man who'd signed him up earlier (what was his name? Something like a computer) held a young boy immobilized against the plywood with one jumbo hand on his neck, punching him in the face with the other. The boy's head snapped back with every punch, thudding against the wood.

"Hey!" Fergle stepped forward, his hands closing into fists and his shoulders hunching forward. Usually that's all he needed to do. He hadn't had to fight anybody since sixth grade.

The man (his name was Del, that's it) dropped his hands and faced him, squaring his shoulders. "Not your problem, man," Del said, echoing Fergle's thoughts of a minute ago.

"Are you okay?" Fergle asked the boy, who clearly

was not. His face bulged in the nose and cheek, blood like a bib over his shirt. But the boy nodded.

Del shrugged. "Kids," he said. "You got any?"

Fergle shook his head.

"Wait till you got one," Del said. "They'll drive you crazy. This one—" he raised his hand and the boy ducked, slid sideways along the wall "—is a dummy. Won't talk, won't listen. What'm I supposed to do?"

The boy scuttled away into shadow, and Fergle followed, having a vague idea of bringing the child to the police. He trailed him to the beach where the boy sat down cross-legged, hunched, thin arms around his knees. He shied away when Fergle lowered himself to the sand but didn't run.

"Are you okay?" Fergle repeated. Up close, Fergle saw the boy was older than he first thought, fourteen or fifteen, but slight, small for his age.

The boy shrugged.

"Here." Fergle took two twenties from his wallet. It was money he could hardly spare. "You can come with me if you want." He extended the cash, and the boy stared at him with rounded, bruised eyes.

A heat suffused Fergle's neck and he said, "No, I mean, if you want to go someplace else. I don't want anything." He looked away. "I just want to make sure you're okay. Do you have anybody? Can I take you someplace else?"

The boy shook his head, then scooted over and grabbed the cash from Fergle's hand. "Just stay out of his way for a while, okay?"

The boy tucked the money away but kept staring at him, his poor, swollen face simultaneously hopeful and cautious. Looking at him hurt Fergle, so he turned away, wishing he could do more. And then he knew exactly what he could do.

He rose, shook sand off his legs and said, "Come on. I have something for you." He walked a few paces, paused, and the boy was right there behind him, close, yet out of reach.

"What's your name?" Fergle asked.

The boy crouched and used his index finger to scrawl a name in the sand. *Billy.*

The drone was a prototype, one of a kind so far. But it was perfect. Fergle had designed it over a year ago, drawing it by hand until he saw how every part would work. He'd gone to his manager with the idea and received approval to proceed. He'd called it The Imagidrone. The idea was simple—children played by building things, assembling, disassembling. The Imagidrone contained hundreds of configurations. It could look like a pirate ship, flying against the moon. Or an elephant. A house, a fire truck, an eagle, a centaur. It could be folded into a kite, a swan, a shark, a tulip. There were preprogrammed designs, and a flick of keys and switches would transform the drone. But Fergle's favorite setting was the free-form one.

Fergle sat on a plastic chair by his car and watched Billy press this and that as the drone bulged in one direction, then another, spluttered to the sky, plummeted, only to stop a foot from gravel, hovering.

"It's like origami," Fergle said. "You can take one piece of paper and fold it into anything."

The boy made a soft, stuttering sound, and it took Fergle a moment to realize he was laughing.

The Imagidrone won awards, and was going into mass production over the summer, ready for the Christmas rush. It had won Fergle's manager a six-figure bonus and massive promotion.

Fergle still wasn't clear how the manager's name, and not his, appeared on all the documents.

The manager's name on the patent.

And it was the manager, now director of the entire division, who was interviewed in the trade publications.

The boy turned the drone off and put it into its box. He hugged the box and looked at Fergle, uncertain.

"It's yours," Fergle said. "Go on. Make something nice."

After the boy vanished, Fergle creaked to his feet and put his hand into his pocket.

His room key was gone. Wasn't in his pockets, nor in his boots. He looked everywhere, even under the car. He turned on his phone just long enough to call the motel office, but nobody answered.

The moon had set, and the single streetlight cast a glow so feeble that when a figure darkened the alley between office and motel, he could only be sure it was someone tall, wide and most likely male. He yelled out a "Hey," but the person dissolved into the alley without answering.

The motel office door was unlocked, and he entered, pinged a little brass bell, heard no response and proceeded to poke around. Ten minutes later he was no closer to locating a spare and was about to crash on the office couch when he noticed another, inner door. Knocking on that one produced no results, but when he put his ear to the wood, he heard voices. Laughter, low music, rustling and thumping told him a party raged beyond.

Feeling a surge of hope mixed with frustration, he put his shoulder to the door, and it popped open, revealing a red-lit room that seemed much too large due to the unusual number of mirrors it contained.

At first, he wasn't sure what he was seeing, but all

at once his brain clicked into gear. The two dozen or so people before him were naked (more or less), horizontal (for the most part) and quite happy. He had to bend his head to the side to figure out what the threesome on the red vinyl sectional were engaged in and was impressed with their agility once he did.

Only when his eyes locked with those of a woman lounging back in a strappy contraption, and she sat up, her face going from bleary pleasure to tight fury, did he register he was intruding. He lowered his head and ducked out, marching toward his car and climbing into the backseat.

Unable to stretch out, he had to open the back door and prop his feet on the plastic chair. He slept like that, two-thirds of him in his car, legs sticking out, the evening's events fusing into a single fun house movie inside his brain.

Part II

Melissa

Melissa Fraser blotted her lipstick, slathered more concealer under her exhausted eyes and sipped her double espresso. The pull to check if the message was still on her phone overwhelmed her, but she restrained herself because just at that moment her husband hustled into their kitchen, his tie cinched around his bulbous head like a string around a balloon.

She smiled and gave him her cheek to peck because that's what they did, every morning, weekday and weekend, no matter what. His dependability and sunny disposition were two of his best qualities, and she appreciated them deeply. Days like today she needed a bit of sunshine.

"Early meeting this morning?" he asked, grabbing a banana from the bowl and car keys from the counter.

"Just want to get some paperwork done," she answered. "I haven't reviewed the carnival docs yet."

He smiled, checked his phone, tucked it away and nodded his goodbye.

"Go get 'em, tiger," he said, just as he always did, and she hoped that meant he hadn't received the message. He paused at the door, and her heart thumped hard inside her chest. "I'll be home late, hon," he said. "I've got three kids for tutoring."

"SATs?" she asked.

He nodded again, winked and shut the door behind him, leaving her alone in the large, bright, clean kitchen. It was sweet, really, how he believed his tutoring high school math for forty bucks an hour paid for the stainless-steel smart oven and fridge, the state-of-the-art wine cooler, not to mention the very good wine inside. She could see how he might have, years ago, his salary as math professor being higher than hers as mayor. But now? Not for the first time she questioned his innocence, and, as always, pushed the thought away. Her husband was the King of Denial, as the chief of police told her on many occasions.

The thought of one such occasion—from last night—caused the coffee to turn acrid in her throat, sour in her stomach. She flipped her phone over and brought up the message, then zoomed into the attached pictures. If she wasn't so queasy, she'd appreciate that she looked damn good in them. She worked hard to maintain her appearance, and between Pilates, yoga and regular Botox, at forty-six she could have passed for ten years younger, in bright sunlight no less.

A wave of nausea overcame her, and she ran to the bathroom where she upchucked the morning's coffee and last night's wine. As she brushed her teeth once more and reapplied lipstick, she checked her phone again. The photos were still there. The message was still there, demanding twenty thousand dollars in cash or else.

She had the money. That wasn't the point. The point was those photographs and the way everything lived on nowadays forever and ever in some ineffable cloud. The point was that whoever sent those pictures might ask for more later, might dig around for real dirt.

Last night had been hazier than usual. Could be because she'd started earlier—her husband had gone to the carnival and came back pale and ill from the sausage and peppers he shouldn't have eaten, and went straight to bed, gifting her a two-hour head start. Or maybe it was the little pill the chief of police had placed on her tongue (with his tongue) as she leaned forward to smooth his hair.

The memory hit her like an electric shock as she got into her car. There'd been a stranger in the room last night. Usually she liked to close her eyes, but something, a noise, alerted her and she saw him. A big lunk of a man, dangerous looking, obviously a bad actor. She stomped on the accelerator and zoomed into town, parking in front of the village hall before 8 a.m.

Once in her office, she made herself a K-Cup, black, and opened the folder with the carnival's papers. Then paused and checked the photos on her phone for the umpteenth time. She forced herself to look at each one—pixel by pixel. There. Her finger was so sweaty she had to dry her hand with a tissue, but when she zoomed in, she saw a reflection in one of the mirrors.

The guy, it was the guy, the stranger, his phone and ham hands obstructing his face, but his build and height unmistakable, even with the dim lighting. Sure enough, he was wearing the carnival's red T-shirt. She could even see part of the word *STAFF* reflected in the mirror.

A half hour later, she sat back and rubbed her temples. None of the forty-seven driver's licenses in the carnival's documents folder belonged to the goon.

A knock startled her, and she jerked, overturning the mug at her elbow, sending lukewarm coffee all over her desk and onto her rose-gold dress. She sprang to her feet, her eyes narrowing at the man in her doorway.

"I'm sorry, Melissa," Del said.

Melissa Fraser prided herself on her open-door policy. She believed it was one of those things that got her reelected term after term, and it was a great sound bite. But she could have howled for forgetting to lock herself in this morning.

"Have a seat, Del," she said, ripping tissues from the dispenser to dab her ruined dress.

"I heard dish detergent and vinegar—" Del started, but she aimed a glare of such vitriol in his direction he stopped.

"Close the door," she said.

He got up, sauntered to the door, shut it, then sat down again.

She abandoned her dress, and unlocked the bottom drawer in her desk, tugging out a small yellow envelope. The envelope contained the results of last week's raid, or at least as much of the contraband the police chief's man could stash before vouchering the rest.

"Whatcha got there?" Del leaned forward, his lips stretching apart to reveal black gaps.

"Percs, Molly, Oxy in here—" she pointed to the envelope, then removed a second, white one and placed it on top "—dope in here."

Del honest to God smacked his lips.

"Twelve thou," she said.

"Oh, come on. I only got a week," he said, but the excitement in his voice was unmistakable. She was giving him a very good price.

"Fine," she said and reached for the envelopes. "I have someone else lined up for these, anyway."

He placed his paw over the packets. "Nah. It's okay. I got the cash."

She tried not to grimace as he counted bills off the roll he withdrew from some unsavory depths in his jeans. The cash would be split between her and the chief of police, a smidge going to the detective who led the raid. Over the next few nights, arrests would be made at the carnival and these same illegal substances confiscated. They wouldn't arrest the dealers—no reason to burn those bridges. But they'd recover a good chunk of the drugs. Those would be sold to a dealer out in the suburbs, and she might take her math whiz hubby on a Mediterranean cruise this summer. It would make him happy, and she liked making him happy. Cycle of life.

"Oh," she said, lightly, as if it didn't matter, "did you by any chance sign on new people last night?"

"Yeah, five of 'em." A cautious question in his voice.

"You have their driver's licenses?"

He grimaced and shook his head. "Tomorrow. Too much going on last night."

She stared at him until he broke eye contact, settling on her spider plant instead. "Well, do you have pictures of them at least?"

He shrugged. "I might."

Oh, the slowness with which he extracted his phone and began scrolling, zooming, bringing the phone close to his face, squinting, grunting, snuffling. Was there no end to the annoying noises that man could generate? No. She did not want an answer.

"Here's one. That's Henry." He turned the phone

over and showed her a pockmarked, slim man in his forties. Del waited until she nodded and flicked to the next picture. "Frank." No, this one was an African American, youngish, with pink hair. He flicked forward again. "Axl."

Adrenaline sent blood to her face. The intruder from last night. No doubt. Tall, big-boned, sandy hair and potato face. The man was standing over a cotton candy machine, lit blue and red from below like a horror movie villain. Which he was. Her blackmailer.

She paid no heed to the next two pictures, and sat back in her chair, affecting a calmness she didn't feel. "Fine, but bring copies of their licenses tomorrow."

He nodded, stood. "Sure thing."

"One moment." He paused. "That Axl."

He raised an eyebrow.

"He reminds me of somebody." She bent to her desk again and pretended to riffle through file folders, pulling one out and shuffling through its papers. "Right." She shut the folder and stood. She wasn't as tall as Del, but she'd had a lifetime to practice authority. That's why people listened to her. That's how she had the life she had. Which she had no intention of losing. "He's a perp, Del. I knew I recognized him. He tried to muscle in on our business a few months ago. We ran him off but looks like he's back."

Del looked confused. She'd never done more than sell him drugs before and she realized she was being much too oblique.

"What I'm saying, Del, is you need to watch out for this man. He's going to interfere."

Del knit his brows. "So—"

Jesus, she could almost hear the rusty gears grind in his brain. "Get rid of him, Del."

"Oh."

"You do that, and I'll give you back the twelve thou."

A sly look came over him. "It's risky."

"Oh, please. Just threaten him or something. Tell him to get lost. Tell him if he meddles with us, you'll cut his legs off."

He blanched.

"So, we're good, right? Once I know he's gone, you get the twelve thou back."

"We're good," he said.

She gave him her mightiest unblinking stare, the one where she lowered her face just an inch and let her eyebrows form a strict line.

"I'll see you tomorrow," Del said, his shoulders slumped, and his strut less exuberant as he left.

She closed her door with a thump and locked it. Screw the open-friggin'-door policy today. She needed a moment.

Part III

Fergle

The cinder block missed him by bare inches, whooshing along his arm and landing with a subdued but hefty thud onto the sand at his feet. The only reason it missed him at all was because he'd heard a whistle—one of those "hey, look here" kind of whistles—and he'd turned toward it, letting the cinder block fall through air rather than through his muscles and bones.

Fergle stepped away from the billboard wall and looked up. Nothing. He peered in the whistle's direction. Nothing. Unsettled and pukish from the fried chicken and fries he had for dinner, he walked back into the heat of the carnival and resumed his place at the cotton candy machine. Sleeping in his car last night had left him tired and sore, and by the time he cornered the motel manager and got a replacement room key, he needed to head back to the carnival. And yet the sheer transformation of his life excited him, made even the exhaustion interesting.

Loud. The fair was loud. Screams and laughter, rides and the motors that powered them, classic rock over the PA, all fusing into a throbbing alloy of sound.

He spun pink and blue clouds of sugar and handed the hot, sweet masses to children, to adults and, twice, to a teddy bear behind which a child hid. It took a half hour, but the carnival calmed him. Something about his uncomplicated task, the joy in the faces around him and the sensory stimulation eased his tension. The wall from which the cinder block fell was unsteady. He'd seen that last night, noticed the weak spots without even trying, his engineer's mind picking up on the splintered and bowed trusses. Nobody was trying to kill him. That was a crazy thought.

And so, when he got pushed from behind and half fell onto the cotton candy drum, he was unprepared, his defenses sluggish. He righted himself, burning his hand, and only after snapping it away from the biting metal realized something was wrong. The muscles in his side spasmed, then pulsed with pain, and he looked down at the same time as a little boy said, "Mister, you're bleeding."

All noise fell away and a forceful surge of illness gripped him, bending him. His stomach convulsed, sending his dinner up and out, where it landed at his feet.

"Ewww," said the boy.

"Oh," said his mother.

"Excuse me," said Fergle because Aunt Maura brought him up to be polite. He lurched sideways, hand pressed tight against his obliques, his breathing shallow and panicked.

His idea at that moment was to walk back to his efficiency unit. He wasn't thinking clearly, shock forcing him to seek a locked, safe room. By the time he reached the far end of the fairgrounds, logic prevailed, and he understood he needed an ambulance.

As he stopped and tried to withdraw his phone with his bloodied hand, someone jumped him from behind, sending him sprawling on the dusty, pebbly ground, the rip in his side screaming red-hot. The person straddled him. Through the haze of panic and pain, Fergle felt the man's thigh muscles stretch and his hips angle forward. Fergle's body knew (without it being verbalized in his brain), that this meant the man was raising his arm, and when the arm came down, he'd be dead, and so he bucked and twisted in an instant, teeth slicing through his bottom lip, unseating his attacker.

For a shocked second Fergle lay in the dust, staring at the opponent who was already climbing to his knees. It was Del. The dogged violence in Del's face jarred him, and he wondered if the man really planned on killing him over last night's altercation.

But then his animal brain took over, and he rose, screamed (because pushing his right leg back involved moving his outraged oblique muscles) and kicked Del square in the balls. His booted foot connected with an immensely satisfying crunch, and Del collapsed facedown.

Fergle ran.

The little shantytown was just ahead and Fergle made for it, trying to decide if he'd hide in a trailer, a Porta-John or—

He didn't have time to decide because a knife whizzed into his back and stuck. He didn't scream.

That would have required taking a deep breath and doing so was impossible. Fortunately, not screaming meant he heard that "look here" whistle again, but all he saw was the wobbly billboard wall and a slim shadow at the other end.

Maura used to say his head thought things before he knew he thought them. And that's what happened now, his body swerving to the left as he staggered along the length of the wall. Reaching the far end, he looked back and saw Del huffing toward him on bowed legs, another knife glinting in an upraised hand.

Fergle squinted at the supports, finding the one he'd noticed last night, the one with the sag in it from the wall's weight. He threw his whole body against it.

It shuddered, but held.

Del was now fifty feet away.

Fergle wrenched at the support and felt small hands pulling alongside his. Then one of those hands raised a hammer and smashed into the wood.

As the carnival raged and an early firework shot into the purple sky, Del threw the second knife, the wall juddered once more and collapsed to the ground in a cloud of dirt and sand, taking Del with it.

Fergle weakened and plopped into the dust, his breathing louder in his ears than even the crash.

He watched, dumbfounded, as Del's boy pulled a sheet of plywood off his father's torso and head, then another one off his legs. Billy knelt and flipped his father onto his back. This took effort, and the boy grew white with determination. He then unsnapped Del's wallet and key chains, removing them from one pocket, yanked his phone from another pocket. He gestured for Fergle to come closer, and when he wobbled over, Billy pointed to his, Fergle's pockets. Fergle did not move.

Billy stepped close and carefully, maintaining eye

contact, withdrew Fergle's room and car keys. He then stuffed them into Del's pocket.

Fergle couldn't remember the first time his life twisted upside down. In any case, fate or his drunk mother, or the slick highway had altered it on his behalf. He'd had no say in it then.

But now? He dug his phone out of his pocket, dropped it and ground his boot heel into it until it cracked, and ground some more. Billy watched, then picked up the pieces and stuffed them into his father's sullied jeans.

Billy next lifted a remote control from his waistband and the Imagidrone dove from the sky. The boy had made extensive use of the freeform setting. The Imagidrone looked like a medieval mace, and it smashed into Del's face in a fountain of blood and gore. It got stuck for a few seconds, but the boy maneuvered it out, and it flew up, then slammed down again. And again. And again, until Del's head was hamburger meat and glistening bone. When he finished with the head, the boy turned to his father's hands.

Afterward, Billy's cheeks, nose, chin, shirt and jeans black with blood, he held Del's truck keys in his palm, extended them to Fergle.

Billy waited, looking at Fergle with a question in his battered eyes.

Breathing was hard. Thinking was hard. But just as his aunt always said, Fergle had thought his thoughts before he knew them.

"Do me a favor." He shifted so his back was toward the boy. "Take this out, would you?"

He'd spent his childhood shell-shocked, blindingly lonesome, and as an adult tried to bring magic into children's lives to make up for reality. But brutal realities breed brutal magic, he saw that now. He considered going to the police. He imagined Billy in a foster home, or in a home for delinquent youth. Unloved. Beaten for being small, strange, mute. He felt, in Billy's body language, a tentative trust. The boy had humanity in him yet. When he'd pulled his father's knife out of Fergle's back, his touch was light, gentle, and he'd pressed against the wound with a small, cool hand until the blood slowed.

Fergle asked the boy to unlock Del's phone for him before Billy rushed to his trailer to gather his and his father's things. They'd go west. They'd sell the truck for cash, buy something else. It was a big country. There were other carnivals they could join, smaller ones, wait things out. Fergle would figure it out. One thing he knew for sure, he had a chance to improve someone's life. And what kind of person would he be if he didn't take it?

As he peered at the dead man's phone, ten photographs popped up and his finger froze over the screen. There was the red-lit, mirrored room from last night. There was the woman who'd seen him, her head thrown back in ecstatic joy, eyes shut.

Fergle blinked, thought, and erased each picture. He then entered a coordinate into the GPS.

Seven hours later, with the sun rising behind them, and Fergle drifting in and out of sleep as the boy drove, the new GPS lady said, *"Exit now."*

And they did.

Epilogue
Melissa

Melissa Fraser, mayor of Old Town Beach, Maine, stood in front of the new tombstone and smiled as the local reporter took her photo. The stranger had blown into town almost a year ago on a bad wind, and sent her world spinning for a few days. But she didn't get to where she was by cowering in corners every time a bully tried to take advantage of her. No, not her.

The murder had caused a great commotion at first, but she took control and swore up and down that Old Town Beach was, and always would be, the perfect family-friendly vacation spot and a wonderful place to live. Within hours of the grisly discovery under the fallen wall, cops broke into Del Baciano's trailer, where they discovered a stash of heroin in a white envelope and an assortment of pills in a yellow one. Del, his son, his truck and most of his belongings were gone.

As far as she knew, he hadn't been found yet, despite being on the most wanted list for all the municipalities in the country. And what of the stranger? Her instincts had been right all along. After that night, not a single new threat came her way, though she'd worried for months, and still had an occasional nightmare.

They were never able to identify the murder victim. The name he gave on his job application was false, and he paid for his room with cash.

Melissa patted the tombstone she'd funded with her own money. She hadn't really meant for Del to butcher the man, and wasn't sure how her request could have been so misinterpreted. Still, though, the interloper had threatened her very life.

On the other hand, theirs was not a town to throw a stranger into a pauper's grave (Did they even have pauper's graves anymore? She didn't know.) or to cremate his body without a soul to mourn him. No, they were a kind, friendly, welcoming town. Where the good de-

served to be remembered, and wannabe villains fore-
warned.

She'd come up with the epitaph herself, and was
quite proud of it.

> **THIS STRANGER CAME TO TOWN**
> **AND A WALL FELL ON HIM.**
> **IT HAPPENS.**

* * * * *

A SIX-LETTER WORD FOR NEIGHBOR

BY LISA UNGER

I.

The moving truck comes first. I'm having coffee on the porch, doing the crossword in the morning paper, when the large vehicle lumbers up the street, rattling the manhole cover and scaring the birds from the branches of the oak trees that line Marbury Lane.

I try to ignore the racket, focus on the clues. But the truck's progress is distracting, a halting stop-go, stop-go. I finally put down the puzzle. The truck slows, gears grinding, then picks up speed for a few yards, finally coming to a noisy stop at the house next to mine.

Great. New neighbors.

Number 235 has been pleasantly empty for the last year since its owners left it to foreclosure. The property, a run-down Craftsman with a postcard-sized front lawn, is a study in what happens when a place is abandoned. Nature takes back what belonged to it all along, reaching out with her green-brown fingers, pushing through boards and concrete. The mailbox tilts, paint peels, eaves sag. The grass is as tall as a toddler. Weeds spring up between the slats of the porch. Birds nest in the gutters, flit through the trees. Squirrels run amok.

The family who used to live there, a youngish couple, with two dark-haired skinny boys and a mangy brown dog, weren't exactly ideal neighbors. Their name escapes me—something with a lot of consonants. Even though we barely spoke, just a cordial nod at the mailbox or a wave as one of the boys rode by on his bike, I got the sense that they didn't like each other much, any of them. Unhappiness has a frequency, doesn't it? Or maybe it was the late-night screaming fights that sometimes spilled out onto the lawn, or the fact that the dog was left out so long in the yard in all weather that he sometimes barked endlessly in his misery that clued me in. There were no parties or sleepovers, no after-dinner strolls around the block. Lots of slammed doors, once a shriek so loud it woke me from sleep. I wasn't disappointed to watch them slip from the house in the night, carrying suitcases and loading up the car with boxes.

They left the dog.

Now he lies at my feet, floppy ears tented in mild curiosity at the noise, at the direction of my attention. I have no idea what his name was before they left him. I call him Scout; he seems to like it. The vet said he was about four years old when I took him in. He was malnourished, dirty, never registered, maybe never vaccinated. All taken care of now. He rarely leaves my side, howls in despair when I have to go out. Which, lucky for both of us, is rarely.

"Someone moving in," I tell him. I rub at his ear with my bare toes—which he loves. He issues a huff, rolls onto his side and closes his eyes again.

"That's what I think, too."

The truck sits, two men in its cab, one of them on the phone. I watch a moment, return to my puzzle. What's a four-letter word for nuisance? *Pest*, I think. I'm confident enough to write it in.

"New neighbors?"

Can a person not do the crossword in peace?

Ralph, my neighbor from the other side, stands at the border of our lawns.

"Looks like it," I say easily. I do try to keep my equanimity.

"Maybe you'll get a cat out of the deal." He guffaws at his own joke. He is a big guy, tall, muscular, with a thick, lustrous head of dark hair, a full beard. Men do that now, don't they? Grow these long beards. Today he wears a flannel shirt and jeans. Is he going for a lumberjack look?

I glance at my watch. Yes, I still have one.

"Aren't you running late for work?" I ask. Hint. Hint.

He clicks his tongue and Scout gets up and runs for him. Ralph kneels and rubs the dog down vigorously. Scout wags his whole body, practically vibrates with pleasure. That's the difference between Scout and me; he still likes people, despite how they've treated him.

"What a good boy!" Ralph makes that funny voice that people do when they talk to animals and children. "How's it going, buddy?"

Together they amble back to the porch. I think Ralph has quite a few years on me, but I *feel* older. Like I'm the grouchy old lady, and he's the affable youngster. He has a problem with boundaries. A lot of people seem to. Or maybe it's just that they have trouble reading cues. Like they don't get that some people would rather be left alone. Ralph sits in the chair beside me, wicker creaking.

"Crossword?"

"I *was* working on it, yes."

I look down at the page, my scrawl in the little squares. Almost there, just a few more clues. I'm fidgety. Won't be happy till it's solved.

"Any coffee left? No school today. I'm free as a bird."

Perfect.

"Help yourself."

He rises. "Freshen you up?"

"Why not? Thanks."

He takes my cup and disappears through my front door like he owns the place. In fact, he does. He's my landlord as well as my neighbor. He inherited this house from his parents; they passed not long after he bought the house next door to be close to them as they aged and he thought about settling down, starting a family maybe. Life's funny.

Seems to me like teachers—at least Ralph, high school math—are the recipients of many days off. It's always a half day, or a long weekend, or a half day in anticipation of a long weekend. And over the summer, he's around all the time. At least he's handy. And not too nosy. I don't mind him really.

"Heard anything about who might be moving in?" he asks when he returns.

"I make it a point not to hear anything."

"Right," he said. "You've always got your nose in a book."

"I'm a book reviewer."

"So that makes sense, then."

I give him a look and he offers me a smile, something patient and kind. Scout gets up and settles between Ralph's feet and the chair.

"Well, I heard that it's just a guy, not a family," said Ralph. "And that he's—a little weird. Off."

"Where'd you hear that?"

"From the Realtor, Sandy. You know, my ex." His voice pulls a little tight. Yes, I know his ex. Big hair, tight suits, high heels, vacant smile and an overly bright voice. She had this obnoxious cackling laugh that I don't know how he could stand. Good riddance, I say. But I'm sensitive enough to see he's not over it.

I peer over my glasses at Ralph. "Well, then, he should fit right in."

"Antisocial."

"Sorry?"

"Six down. 'Prefers the company of one.'"

I look at my puzzle. "Huh." So it is. He sits, drinking his coffee, while I finish, the pencil scratching pleasantly on the newsprint.

II.

Later from my kitchen window as I do the dishes, I watch our new neighbor arrive. He pulls up in a white van as the movers are still carrying items—boxes, a couch, a desk, bookshelves, a dining room table. All of it old, heavy antiques and ornate pieces, brocade chairs with clawed feet, a landscape painting in a gold leaf frame. Not your usual particleboard-put-it-together-with-an-Allen-wrench junk. Interesting. But the place must be a mess inside. I haven't seen anyone come in to fix it up. Wouldn't he have had the walls painted or the floors done before moving all that stuff in? Well. What do I know?

He strolls up the walkway, his stride light and quick, dressed in a pressed white shirt and khakis, thick black glasses, sensible brown shoes. Then he stands on the porch, taps at one of the slats with a toe, then glances up, inspecting. He has the wiry build of a runner or a dockworker, slim but strong. I watch, drying and redrying the glass in my hand. There's something about him, something strange and familiar all at once. What is it?

He stands, hands on his hips as the movers carry in next a parade of mannequins, bodies stiff, limbs helter-skelter. Glossy hair, blank faces. One wearing a sequined cocktail dress, one clad in leather. One in a pair of overalls. Okay. Ralph said the guy was a little off.

As I'm pondering our new arrival, he turns to see me watching. Slowly, I raise a hand in greeting. He stares. Maybe he can't see me—a glare on the window, or his eyesight is poor. Finally he turns and walks inside.

What's a six-letter word for puzzling and mysterious?

Enigma.

III.

I don't see him again for a while, not that I'm looking for him. The next day, a team of landscapers descend, mowing the grass and pulling all the weeds and dead plants, replacing them with young, bright green shrubbery, some perennials up the walk. They trim away brown branches, clean out the gutters, rake up the detritus of years of neglect. The racket is enormous, and I take to wearing my noise-canceling headphones to drown out the incessant roar of lawn mowers, Weedwackers and chain saws. By the end of the day, the house looks like a man who's just shaved his beard— bare, awkward, raw. All flaws bright and angry. But better. Fresh. Revealed.

A day later, the painters come in a bright blue van. A man and a woman in matching jumpsuits haul buckets of paint, tarps, ladders, rollers. They open lids, revealing thick, glossy tubs of magic. They apply it with fat rollers. A transformation. By the end of the week, they've painted the little house a dove gray, shutters bright white, the front door a shiny fire-engine red. It is tidy and cheerful. I didn't realize how bad the place looked. Its decay has been incremental, falling to pieces day by day, as do we all unless we fight the creep.

I watch all this from my attic window as I work. This week I'm reviewing a book about lies. Well, better said about *liars*. The author posits that we all lie, all the time. We lie to help, to hurt, to protect, to inflate, to soothe. Men, she claims, lie more than women. Extroverts lie more than introverts. She also declares that there are about a million little tells. She does a good job of making her case. She's convincing that with a little practice we might all become "lie spotters," easily determining who is being truthful and who is not. I'm skeptical. I know all about lies and liars, how slippery, how tricky, how we're often complicit, seeing what we want to see until it's far too late, even then doubting ourselves. Still, I've given the author the review she deserves in a major paper, the kind of thing that might make a career. I don't write bad reviews. If I hate a book, I'll beg off. I'm a writer after all. I know how much words can hurt, how they can slice like razor blades, go deep, leave scars.

There's a heavy knock at the door, and Scout rouses his fluffy self from slumber to career down the two flights of stairs, barking like a maniac. It's early evening Friday, so it must be Ralph. We have a ritual— when he's not dating someone. And he's been single for a couple of months now. Though I know he's had women back to the house a couple times, late, after he's been to the bar with his buddies. Anyway, on Friday nights he brings a bottle of wine. I order a pizza and we watch a horror movie—the schlockier the better. Sometimes science fiction. Even better science fiction horror. *Killer Klowns from Outer Space*, *Night of the Creeps*, *Piranha*, *Eight Legged Freaks*, *Cat People*, *Creature from the Black Lagoon*. There are some decent recent additions to the genre: *Sharknado*, for one. I can't handle the news, the real stories of murder and mayhem, violence and destruction. Zombies, genetic experiments gone wrong, giant spiders taking over the world, *that* I can manage.

I don't bother following Scout down. The door is open and Ralph will come in, leash up the dog and take him around the block. I give my review a last proof, then send it on to my editor. I have a few other deadlines looming, but I suppose I'm done for the night.

Downstairs, Ralph and Scout are returning, both of them looking breathless and happy as if they've had a little jog. I fill Scout's bowls with food and water, call the pizza place and order our large everything-on-it pie, while Ralph decants the wine. Looks like an overly nice bottle of cabernet. We're usually in the fifteen to twenty-dollar range. This particular bottle of Caymus I know approaches a hundred.

"Are we celebrating?" I ask.

"Why not?" he says cryptically.

We take our glasses out to the porch. The air is growing cool, and the leaves are just beginning to turn. Soon they'll litter the lawn and Ralph will hire the neighborhood kids to come rake his and mine.

"Met the new neighbor," he says, the wicker chair creaking beneath his weight. The wineglass looks small in his big bear claw hand.

"Oh?"

"Quiet guy," says Ralph, glancing over at the house, which seems empty. The van is gone. "Not overly friendly. I brought a pie."

"That was very neighborly of you." I haven't considered doing anything but spy from my attic windows, three portals from which I can see his house, Ralph's, the teenager's bedroom across the street—a wild young redhead named Sabrina, who is going to get herself into trouble if she's not careful, sneaking out at all hours.

"I thought so."

"And."

"He says he restores antiques—furniture, art, clocks, what have you."

The furniture makes sense now. But I wouldn't think there would be much of a demand for his profession in this throwaway world we live in.

"He's setting up a workshop in the basement apparently. Says he apologizes in advance for any noise."

"Is antique restoring a noisy business?"

"I wouldn't think so. But what do I know? I'm just a high school math teacher."

There's something uncharacteristically dark about him tonight, something heavy.

"What's eating you?"

He rubs at his temples with a thumb and forefinger, blows out a breath. "Long week."

"Want to talk about it?"

He stares at the house with its fresh paint and new greenery. "Seems that Sandy's interest in the new neighbor isn't strictly professional. She's doing more than selling him a house."

"Oh."

I didn't know what he saw in her in the first place, other than a toned, compact body, and a serviceable prettiness which won't stand the test of time. To me, she seemed vacant, dull, all hair dye and gel manicure. She didn't even know what "Soylent Green" was.

"You can do better," I say.

He gives me a grateful smile, with real crinkles around his eyes—which apparently, according to the book I just read, cannot be faked. We clink glasses.

"Thanks," he says. The heaviness lifts, but just a little. Does he really like her? Or does he just not want to watch anyone else have her? That's too deep for us. I wouldn't dare ask.

"What about you?" he says into the early-evening hush. Mourning doves hoot softly from the nest in the oak on my lawn. "Left the house this week?"

"Yes," I say. "I went to the store on Tuesday. Took Scout to the park on Thursday." Scout lifts his head at the mention of the park, his spiritual home, then drops it again between his paws and looks at me accusingly.

Huh. What do you know? That author was right. We lie all the time, easily, without really even thinking about it. I haven't been to the store or the park.

"Good," he says, obviously not schooled as I am now in the art of deception. "Good for you."

He reaches for the folded-up newspaper on the little table between us and looks at my completed crossword puzzle. "You have all the answers, don't you?" he says.

No. I don't. Not by a long shot.

"Some," I say. "At least when it comes to puzzles."

When the pizza comes, we go inside and decide on a classic, 1988's *Maniac Cop*. We turn out the lights, me on the couch, him in the recliner, each with our television trays. We laugh uproariously, cringe and moan at the joyful schlock of bad moviemaking, and make obnoxious comments like teenagers—polishing off the pie and the bottle.

It's getting late when the beam of headlights strobes through the dark living room. We both watch as the white van pulls in next door, the garage door opening and swallowing the vehicle. Ralph gets up and walks out onto the porch. Scout and I follow. As we stand there, we hear a cackle of laughter that carries impossibly loudly through the night. It's unmistakably Sandy. I hope. Because, *God*, let there not be two women who laugh like that.

Ralph goes back inside without a word and clears our plates. In the kitchen, we watch the garage door close without anyone emerging. A moment later a light inside goes on. Ralph loads the dishes in the dishwasher, takes the pizza box and wine bottle.

"I'll put these in the recycling," he says, walking toward the door.

I want to say something to make him feel better. But I've never been good at that. Life sucks and sometimes we have no choice but to slog through. That's the advice I have to give on most things. It's not a popular sentiment. These days people like magical thinking— manifestation, and law of attraction and all of that.

I leash up the dog and follow him out to the street so that Scout can have his final pee. The dog sniffs every inch of ground, pulling this way and that, trying to find the precisely perfect spot. Finally, he finds it.

"Thanks for a great night," Ralph says, dropping the box and bottle in our shared recycling bin.

"I think I got the better end of the deal. That was a nice bottle of wine."

"No way," he says. "When I'm with you, I always get the better end of the deal."

The lie of flattery. That's one of the most common. "Sweet," I say. "Not true but sweet."

"Good night, Jay."

Jay, short for Jayne—which, really Mom and Dad, you couldn't do better than *that*?

Ralph tips an imaginary hat to me and walks toward home. Scout pushes his weight into my leg in that comforting way that he does, his flesh and fur hot against my bare skin.

What's a ten-letter word for the thing no one wants when he's looking for love?

Friendship.

IV.

The next day, my head aches a little as I put the finishing touches on an article I'm writing for a travel magazine about "packing hacks." Which is ironic because I haven't left my own house in weeks, haven't traveled anywhere farther than the doctor in over two years. A weekend getaway, that dreamy tropical holiday, a European excursion—might as well be a trip to Mars. Still, thanks to my research and should I be so moved, I could pack a suitcase like nobody's business now—rolling clothes, storing items in shoes, leaving behind soap and shampoo (unless you're camping—and why would you do that?—the hotel will have this), wearing my heaviest item. I could go on. But I only have three thousand words for this one, and I think I have it covered. My personal favorite packing hack? Stay home. There's nothing out there that you don't carry inside you.

I send the article off to my editor with the satisfying electronic swoosh of sent mail.

When I'm done I enter the new neighbor's name into my search bar. His website is the first thing to pop up. Carlton Wilson, antiques restorer. I click on the link to find a serviceable site without much flourish. His name appears in a crisp black type across the top of the page, under which there's an epigraph.

A beloved thing can have a new life. I can turn back time.

There are a few before-and-after pictures—a wing-back chair, an armoire, a grandfather clock. There's an address in the city, an email and a phone number.

I scroll down through the other listings: a few mentions in trade magazines, a couple of social media posts from delighted customers. Looking at nana's old secretary! It's new again! Thank you, Mr. Wilson! There's a grainy picture of him from a trade show in Chicago, where he looks pale and uncomfortable—shoulders hiked, a frown wrinkling his brow—in a group shot of other antiques restorers from around the county, all nominees for an industry award.

I dig in the bottom drawer of my desk and pull out a maroon leather box. I flip it open and stare at the pocket watch ensconced in the soft interior, remove it and hold its comforting golden heft in the palm of my hand.

I'm a minimalist. I purge. I think the stuff we own can become a kind of bondage, lashing us to lives we don't really want. But this is something that belonged to my dad, and his dad before him. And before him, my great-grandfather who was a historian of some note. It was a gift from the publisher of his seminal work on the American Civil War.

I am an orphan. A twenty-nine-year old orphan. Not a *tragedy exactly*. Not like I was ten or five when my parents had the car accident that killed them both. They weren't *young exactly*—late fifties. Though that's the sentiment I heard most often—*They were so young. There wasn't enough time.* Probably everyone feels that way, though, when they lose someone. Of course, the truth is that there isn't enough time. Period.

I pop open the lid of the watch and look at the ornate hands and black roman numerals on its white face. Inside, my grandfather's initials, HRM. The watch stopped at 12:02 some day or night in the distant past. To be honest, time has stopped for me since they died. Just over two years now. I can't seem to—*just move on.*

Dr. Black says that there is no set time to grieve. That there is no one way to heal. I'm sure he's right.

A beloved thing can have a new life. I can turn back time.

Something mystical about that, isn't there? The cryptic message hanging over a wizard's door in an enchanted forest.

Maybe I could ask my new neighbor to restore this watch. Having it fixed would be an excuse to connect with my brother, from whom I'm estranged. We weren't close before my parents died, and their loss severed whatever fragile bond we shared. He's older, was gone off to college before I turned ten. I was the "surprise" baby. I always thought of myself as an only child. He was the rebel, always in trouble. When he was around, there was always lots of yelling.

Dr. Black wonders in that shrinky way he has if I could try to repair the relationship. Or maybe establish it, since there wasn't much to us before. Christmas is around the corner. This might be the perfect gift, at the perfect time.

At my feet Scout is having a bad dream, his legs twitching as he emits a soft whine. I put my bare sole on the doughy down of his belly and rub.

"You're okay, buddy. We're okay."

He quiets.

What's a four-letter word for the belief that things can get better?

Hope.

V.

I am not afraid to leave the house. It's not that. That's agoraphobia and it's a psychological condition. Or maybe a neurological one. A brain event, something that a person can't control. I reviewed a book about it once; the author herself was an agoraphobic. It was a self-portrait, and a clear-eyed, eloquent examination of the condition and its various treatments. Quite well-done, though it did drone on. I found myself thinking: *Just go outside, already! It's fine!*

Personally, I just don't *like* to leave the house. The truth is I don't like people that much and they seem to be everywhere. Always looking, chatting, trying to make conversation or sell you something. They judge you, think they know something about you. Sometimes I wish I was invisible, a ghost, so that I could go about my business and not be seen at all, by anyone.

Let's unpack that, Dr. Black would surely say. *Let's get deeper.*

Let's not.

I gird myself and leash up Scout. I check myself in the mirror—nothing in my teeth. My wild dark curls are as tamed by a brush as they're likely to get. No unwanted hairs needing to be plucked. I put on my glasses and the blue of my eyes seems magnified. A touch of lip gloss so that, pale as I am, I don't look like a corpse. Okay. Fine. That's as good as it's going to get.

Scout is happy for our errand and his step is bouncy as we walk up the street. Of course, he has to mark every tree. And then hunt for the perfect place to poop, back and forth, back and forth. Okay, *this* is it. I clean up after him, putting the little baggie in the bin. We go inside so that I can wash my hands and pick up the plate of cookies I baked—chocolate chip of course, my mom's recipe. Then we head next door.

I'm pretty sure my new neighbor is home. The van is in the driveway. I haven't seen him leave today. It's early, but not too early—11:30 on a Saturday. At the gate to the walkway, Scout digs in, he sits down on the sidewalk and pulls back. I almost drop my plate of cookies.

"What?"

He issues an unhappy whine, does this little shifting thing with his haunches.

"No," I say. "I'm not taking you back there. Just a visit."

I tug. He's not a big dog. But he's stubborn and has a gift for making his body impossibly heavy.

"Okay, fine."

I let go of his leash and watch as he walks back to my house, and settles on the porch steps, watching me with sad eyes. I don't worry about Scout running off or chasing squirrels into the road. He's not that kind of guy.

I walk up the path to my neighbor's porch, noticing that things look tidy, if a bit sparse. Fresh shoots of green grow already where the hedges have been trimmed back. Weeds that were pushing up through the pavers and porch have been pulled. Fresh paint, its odor still lingering, gives everything a hopeful aura. A fresh start. That's a good thing. I feel optimistic, as I hold my plate of cookies, and use my free hand to ring the bell. Its chimes echo behind the door.

I wait. No answer. No sound of movement from inside.

It *is* Saturday. Maybe he's still sleeping. Late night with Sandy perhaps. Should I ring again? This is an example of a thing I don't know. Simple rules of engagement that others seem to have mastered but which elude me. How many times do you ring a stranger's bell on a Saturday morning? If he doesn't answer do I leave the cookies? Come back later? I look over to my own house. From this angle, I can't see Scout. I know he's there, waiting. A little buzz of anxiety—forget about the watch. My brother doesn't want anything to do with me. And the cookies—the guy is probably allergic to whatever. The desire to run back home is powerful. I'm about to make a break for it when the door swings open.

He's even smaller than he looked from a distance. Maybe an inch shorter than I am. Dressed in that same crisp combo I saw him wearing the other night—button-down white oxford, pressed khakis, sensible brown shoes. He pushes up his glasses.

"Good morning. Can I help you?"

"I'm Jay," I say. "Your neighbor."

The flicker of a smile as he steps forward. "Nice to meet you."

I thrust the plate at him awkwardly. "I brought some cookies. To welcome you."

He reaches for them. His eyes are hazel flecked with green, his face all hard angles. He clears his throat, flushes a little. Oh, okay. He's an awkward person like me. There are a lot of us. Don't judge. We just don't do a great job of handling the everyday encounters.

"Thank you," he says. "That was very kind."

"I—uh—heard you were an antiques restorer." I don't like that word—restorer. It doesn't feel right on the tongue. Surely there's a better one. I'll have to think on it.

"That's right," he says.

I take the box from my pocket and open it to show him the watch.

All his focus goes there. "Ah," he says. "Come in."

I walk through the door into the foyer. The walls are all freshly painted, floors scrubbed clean. He puts the plate of cookies on a thin console table that stands under a mirror. I catch sight of myself; my gray dress looks like a muumuu. I looked okay in my own mirror, but in his I am a wreck, hair wild, dress too big, glasses dominating my face. I press down on my curls. Damn them. They're so fluffy.

"May I?" He extends a hand.

"Of course."

I hand him the box, and he takes the watch out, holds it up to the light, turns it this way and that. He pops open the lid. He holds it tenderly in his palm, leaning in close as if it's telling him a secret.

"This is a Patek Philippe for Tiffany and Company, key wind, late 1800s," he says, looking at me quizzically. "It's very valuable."

"It's been in my family for a long time," I say. "It's stopped working."

The watch has stopped working. My family has stopped working, so to speak.

He regards me with an expression I can't read. "Have you wound it?"

"I wasn't sure how. Or if I should. I didn't want to break it."

I am aware of a distant knocking sound, something from downstairs in the basement. I hear something similar in my own house when the water heater kicks on. But no. It's a bit more erratic.

"Patek Philippe is one of the holy trinity of watch-makers in the world. If you want one new, you have to apply. They decide whether or not you deserve one. Who was the original owner?"

"My great-grandfather was an author and a historian. This was a gift from his publisher."

He presses up on his glasses again, nodding. Then back to the watch, which he's looking at like other men might regard a beautiful girl. "Do you have the original certificates?"

"Yes," I say. "I think so. Somewhere in my parents' files."

Which are all in boxes in the attic closet. I could start digging. But what else would I find? The detritus of their lives—diaries with abrupt endings, and to-do lists that never got completed, love letters. My artwork, math tests, my brother's old trophies. Time stopped.

"Do you plan to sell it?" he asks, placing it gingerly back in its box. "You could go to auction with this piece. Patek Philippe is buying back significant pieces for their Geneva museum."

"I don't plan to sell it, no," I say. "My parents are gone. This is really all I have of them."

Something travels across his face, something sad. "I see. I'm sorry."

I wave him off. Pity I don't need.

"Can you fix it?" I ask, maybe too crisply.

"Yes," he says. "Of course."

That knocking again. It seems rude to ask about it, as if his stomach was rumbling. Best to just ignore it. Old houses make noises, right?

"It probably just needs cleaning, winding and a little

love. I'll polish it, and do some research for you. Just so you know exactly what you have here."

"That would be wonderful," I say. "How much?"

I do all right. But I'm a writer. I always have to ask what things cost.

Something lovely happens to his face when he smiles. It lights him up, turns him boyish and sweet. The angles soften. My heart flutters a little. "My rate is a plate of chocolate chip cookies."

"No," I say with a little laugh. "Really."

"Really," he says. "The engineering on a Patek Philippe is magnificent, truly unsurpassed. Do you know that it takes over a thousand people to make a single one of their watches, that it might take nine months to a year to complete a timepiece?"

He pops open the back and shows me. The innards gleam, a lovely glitter of copper and gold, tiny little pieces fit together perfectly. A delicate little machine. "Every single lever, gear, wheel is crafted by the hands of an expert. If it's truly broken, we can discuss that. But it looks as if it has been cared for. It will take me an hour tops to figure out what, if anything, is wrong."

I experience an unexpected surge of joy that it might not be broken beyond repair. That perhaps it's just neglect or ignorance. *Did* I ever try to wind it? That, with a little love, time will begin again. Or time-telling, anyway. Timekeeping?

"Come by tomorrow afternoon?" he says.

"I will," I say, a tiny bit breathless. He locks me with those eyes, and I find I don't mind his stare. He's someone who sees beneath the tarnished outer shell to the gears turning inside. "I can't thank you enough."

What's a five-letter word for when an expected act of kindness is like a ray of light through the murk?

Grace.

VI.

Scout and I must have fallen asleep on the couch watching television. He sits up from his place on my feet, ears tented. We were watching one of the late-night shows and now it's local news, the screen flickering white and blue into the darkness of the room. Scout leaps to his feet, and rushes barking toward the door. Someone's knocking. It's nearly midnight. I stay frozen. Who would come by so late? I'm groggy, disoriented from what must have been a deep sleep.

Knocking again, louder. Scout sits and starts to whine with excitement. I hear the key in the door and listen as it opens.

"Jay?"

He has a key. I should really ask for it. He shouldn't really just walk in here at all hours, should he? Landlord or not.

I sit up. Ralph is petting Scout, who is wagging his tail enthusiastically, whining with excitement and delight, rubbing himself against Ralph's legs. What does he see in the guy, really? He's not *that* great. Dogs.

"Ralph," I say, sitting up. "You scared me."

"I tried to call," he says, still by the door, looking embarrassed. "I'm sorry. I was worried."

I would ask him why he should be worried about me. But I know the answer. Let's just say that the last two years since my parents died have not been easy. And I have made some questionable choices. And Ralph, well, he's had a front row seat. If not for him, I might not be here. So I guess he's more than just the landlord.

Still.

"Does he need to go out?"

I nod. Ralph puts the leash on Scout, and they exit through the front door. I rush to the powder room, brush my hair, tidy myself up a little. But in the mirror I look as startled and disheveled as the subject of a mug shot. Oh, well. Ralph has seen me at my worst. This is probably an improvement.

"Everything okay?" Ralph asks when he returns with the dog.

"Sure," I say.

"I called you today," he said. "And yesterday."

"Did you?"

"Where's your phone?"

I look around. "I'm not sure." It could be anywhere. Probably up in my attic office. I never call anyone and the only person who ever calls me is Ralph. Most of the communication with editors occurs over email. People don't want to talk these days. Conversations are messy and complicated, require too much presence and effort. They take time and energy. Better just to send off your missive and wait for a crafted reply.

"Want some tea?" I ask him.

"Sure."

He looks tired, dark circles under his eyes. A little paler than usual, not his normal rosy-cheeked self. His beard is a little ratty; I wish he'd shave it off. A little thinner maybe? He's a beefy guy, big through the shoulders, tall, with hands like meat hooks. But he looks deflated somehow.

"Something going on with you?" I ask, as I put the kettle on the stove.

He waves a hand at me. "It's probably nothing."

He takes a seat at my kitchen table and I get the teapot, tea and cups from the cabinets.

"This isn't about Sandy," I say.

He's not lovesick, is he? Over the cackling Realtor?

"So I tried to call her a couple of times. No answer, right? Her phone goes straight to voice mail. Which is weird. She's a Realtor after all. She *has* to answer her phone."

"Maybe she's blocking you." The teakettle whistles and I take it from the stove.

"Yeah, okay," he says with a shrug. "Maybe. But I went to her place. And her car is not there. There are a couple days' worth of papers on her porch."

"You tried to call her," I said. "She didn't answer. So you went to her house?"

I pour the hot water in the pot and the pleasant scent of peppermint wafts up.

"Right," he says. "It's not like I'm stalking her or anything. I was just—"

"Worried?" I offer.

Ralph might have an issue with boundaries. It's come up before in his relationships with women.

"Yeah," he says. "Anyway, I reached out to a mutual friend. You know Kate? She hasn't heard from Sandy either. Which is weird, because normally they talk a lot."

"So she doesn't answer your calls. You go to her house. And then you start calling her friends?"

He hangs his head, gives a little nod.

"Maybe she's just on vacation, Ralph," I say. "People do that."

"I guess. I just have a weird feeling."

"Okay."

"So, I called the cops."

"You did?"

"Yeah, and a detective came out to see me, asked a few questions. And this is where it gets weird. Turns out that Sandy had a restraining order taken out against *me*. Can you believe that?"

I pour us each a cup and walk over to join him at the table.

"Why would she do that?" I ask gently.

"I don't know," he says. He looks truly mystified. "I mean, yeah, maybe I've called too much. She said that she didn't want to talk to me anymore. But I thought if I just kept trying, right? I think we shared something special. And, once, just one time, I did turn up at an open house with flowers."

"Okay."

"But when she asked me to leave, I left."

He nods his thanks for the tea, blows on it to cool it a bit.

"I mean," he goes on, "I waited outside in my car, to be sure she got out of there okay. It gets dark early these days, and there she is, in an empty house, strangers coming and going."

"You waited outside her place of work in your car. After she told you to leave."

He looks at me. His eyes dark and heavily lashed. They're so sad, I have to avert mine. "Was that wrong?" he asks.

"Ralph." I put my hand on his hand.

He shrugs, looks down. "I guess I just have a hard time knowing when to let go."

I draw in and release a breath, choose my words carefully. "When a woman takes out a restraining order on you, it's *past* time."

His hand is cold, the nails bitten to the quick.

"I can't stop thinking about her. What if she was the one?"

"She wasn't."

"How do you know?"

"Because 'the one' loves you back."

He nods, some of the color returning to his cheeks. We finish the tea in an easy silence. We are both broken pieces. Maybe that's why we fit together. The clock over the sink tells me it's midnight.

"I'm still worried about her," he says softly. "Where is she?"

"I think the point here, Ralph," I say as gently as I can, "is that it's none of your business."

Scout sighs underneath the table. Ralph sighs, too. "I guess you're right."

What's a six-letter word for when the truth hurts? *Always.*

VII.

I stop by Carlton Wilson's house the next afternoon, like he told me to. I wait until three because noon seemed too early and four too late. But when I knock on the door, there's no answer. His van is in the driveway. I ring the bell. Wait. Then I ring it one more time. But the house is dark and no one comes. I feel a little rush of panic. I left a very valuable watch with him. Why? Because he was nice to me. I've made this mistake before. That watch is the only thing I have left of my family; it's my bridge back to my brother.

I wait a little longer, my heart thumping. Then I return home.

An hour later, I go back. This time when I knock on the door and no one answers, I try the knob. It's unlocked and the door swings open. I step inside.

I stand in the foyer where I stood yesterday. There's a living room to the right, with a couple of the pieces I saw carried in predictably arranged. The couch and two wingback chairs facing each other, with a polished, claw-foot coffee table in between. No photos. The landscape hangs over the fireplace. To the left, a dining room. Big, heavy—looks like rosewood?—table, with six velvety blue chairs.

"Hello? Mr. Wilson? Sorry to trouble you."

Nothing.

I shouldn't be in here. I know that.

The kitchen is bare and spotless. From the window I can see the fence that separates my property from his, my house beyond that.

A back door leads to the yard where I found Scout after the family left in the night. His howling had woken me in the early morning. I did just what I did today, pushed in and walked through the house. Scout was chained out in the far corner, no food, no water, not even a doghouse. He was so skinny and shivering, but he still stood up and wagged his tail when he saw me. I took off his chain and picked him up—he was so light, trembling—and carried him to my car, took him straight to the vet.

"Keeping him?" the pretty young vet tech had asked, after he'd had a checkup, been given his shots, bathed, deloused.

"Yes," I said.

"Good. Because I think he needs you."

I needed him, too.

"Excuse me?"

I spin to find Carlton Wilson standing in the doorway to his kitchen, his face pinched in a scowl. "Can I help you?"

I am embarrassed. Of course, I shouldn't be in here.

"I'm sorry," I say, trying for a smile. "The door was open. I'm just here for my watch."

His scowl deepens. "Your watch?"

My heart is thudding uncomfortably. "The pocket

watch I brought to you yesterday. You said you could fix it."

He shakes his head. "I'm sorry—who are you? I have no idea what you're talking about."

Panic is a bird in the cage of my chest.

"I brought you a plate of cookies. And the watch. You said you could look at it and see why it had stopped. I'm Jay. Your neighbor from next door."

Something like recognition crosses his face. Maybe he's a stoner. Or there's something wrong with him, his memory. It's coming back to him now.

"Miss, I think you should leave. You must be…mistaken." Was he going to say "crazy"? "We've never met."

"No," I say. Heat has rushed to my cheeks. Tears to my eyes. "Not without the watch. It belonged to my father. I need it back."

He stands aside from the kitchen door. And I keep my place.

"Please go, miss." His face, grim behind his thick black glasses. "I don't have your watch. I've never seen you before."

I have no choice. I walk past him, shaking, and exit through the front door. He closes the door behind me and I stand on the porch for a moment, buffeted by great gusts of emotion.

I go back to my house, where Scout greets me manically, sensing my despair. I am crying as I search for my phone, Scout at my heels. When I find it in my attic office, I see about five calls from Ralph. But I have my own problems right now.

I call the police. Scout rests his head in my lap as I weep. My watch, my parents, my brother. All lost. Because of me, my stupidity, my mistakes. All my fault. We wait for the cops.

There is no word for the depth of my sadness.

VIII.

When the cop comes, he seems too young, too small to help. His dark blue uniform is wearing him. The gun at his waist looks so big and plastic that it can only be a toy. His features are narrow, his eyes a darting stormy gray. His lips are thin. But he listens to the story I have to tell him. Then, he calmly suggests we go next door.

I stand beside him on the porch while he knocks.

"He's in there," I say.

He nods and knocks again, harder. "There's a bell," I say.

But then I hear footfalls, and Carlton Wilson swings open the door. He rolls his eyes when he sees us.

"Can I help you, Officer?"

"Ms. Byrne here says she brought you a watch for repair yesterday. And that today you would not return it."

"No," he says. "Incorrect. I have never seen this woman before. She did not bring me a watch. I don't have anything that belongs to her. She's mistaken."

"She seems quite certain." The young cop looks at me, and I am grateful. I can tell he believes me.

"I don't want to be rude," says Wilson, stepping out onto the porch and closing the door behind him. "But it's my understanding that Miss Byrne suffers from some confusion. That she has a history of—"

My whole body goes stiff. What does he know about me? Who told him? Oh, right. The cackling Realtor.

"A history of?" the cop prompts. His nameplate reads Merle.

"Mental illness."

The words are like a Taser. I feel like someone has stolen all my breath.

"There was a car accident," he goes on. "A couple of years ago. She hasn't been right since."

"Who told you that?" I ask, my voice just a rasp.

"Is that true?" asks the cop.

I find I don't have words. They've escaped me. I *was* in an accident. The one that killed my parents. It's true that things haven't been right since—all kinds of things. But I'm not crazy. I did have and bring him my dad's watch. He's trying to steal it. I can see the glimmer of dishonesty in his eyes.

"I brought him my watch," I manage, though my voice is quavering pitifully. I clear my throat. "I just want it back. And my cookies. I want my cookies back, too."

"Cookies," says the cop with a frown.

"I brought him a plate of cookies to welcome him to the neighborhood. I take it back. He's *not* welcome to the neighborhood."

Wilson shakes his head and raises his eyebrows at the cop, who has the courtesy to avert his eyes. He's not going to treat me like the crazy lady from next door. He's reserving judgment. Which is all we can ask sometimes.

"Do you mind if we come in and look around?" asks the cop.

"When I was here yesterday, I heard a suspicious knocking in his basement," I say.

Wilson shakes his head again. "You weren't *here* yesterday. And, yes, I do mind if you look around. If you'd like to search my house, please come back with a warrant."

The cop regards him, cool and level, then offers a

careful nod. "Miss Byrne, let's go fill out a report about your stolen watch. That's the first step."

"You *don't* believe her," says my terrible neighbor. "I mean you can see. She's—"

"I'll stop you there," says Merle the cop, lifting a hand. "Miss Byrne says she brought you a watch to fix. You said she didn't. We'll just do this the right way. File a report and open an investigation."

"An *investigation*?" he blusters. "This is a joke."

"No, sir. Not at all."

Wilson blows out a breath. "Fine," he says. "Whatever. Don't come back here without a warrant."

"Understood," says the cop evenly.

Wilson goes back inside and slams the door on us.

Tears threaten again as we leave. By the time we're back at the house, I am ugly crying. I cry the whole time Officer Merle and I fill out the report, sobbing and stuttering like a little kid. He is patient, takes all the details. When he leaves in his cruiser, I feel a crush of hopelessness so total, I just want to get into bed. But I feed Scout and clean his water bowl, walk him around the block. Because you have to take care of your friends, even when things are awful.

In the powder room mirror, I look at myself. *Do* I look like a crazy lady? My fingers find the scar on the side of my head. I pull down the collar of my shirt. There's a scar on my throat, on my shoulder. It was a bad accident. I shouldn't have survived it. Sometimes I wish I hadn't.

It's not an hour before Ralph is at the door.

"What happened?" he says, coming in without knocking. His face is pulled tight with worry. "Mrs. Miller from across the street called, said the police were here."

I've since calmed myself, but the sight of him calls the tears back. I tell him everything—about the watch, about my brother. He already knows most of it—my parents, the accident, the long, wobbly road I have taken back. Forward? He's the only one really. When I'm done, the look on his face is so sad. We are on the couch. He has a heavy arm around my shoulders.

"I wanted to fix it for my brother," I said. "I wanted a reason to call him."

He pulls me in and I rest my head on his shoulder. "You don't need a reason to call your brother, Jay. I'm sure he'd just be happy to hear your voice."

"He hates me."

"No," he says softly. "No."

But he doesn't know. How could he?

He makes dinner, heating up chicken soup he made and froze a couple of weeks ago, boils some fresh noodles, heats up some rolls he finds in my fridge that I don't remember buying. It's good. I feel better. When was the last time I ate? I don't remember.

We do the only thing we can do. We google Carlton Wilson.

We sit at the kitchen table with my laptop, Ralph at the keyboard.

We visit Wilson's website, which I've already seen. The few comments online. A business listing with a five-star rating. I'm about to go lie down. Forget about Carlton Wilson, about the watch he stole. Exhaustion tugs at my muscles. Then, something else. An old news story from 2015, buried deep on the third page of links.

Local Businessman Questioned in the Disappearance of Cleveland Wife and Mother of Two. A grainy image of Carlton Wilson, antiques restorer, and one of a woman with light blond hair and a wistful smile, stare back at us from the screen. Ralph starts reading aloud.

"'Police brought thirty-nine-year-old Carlton Wilson in for questioning in the disappearance of Gayle Marin who has been missing since late last week.'" He makes himself sound like a newscaster, voice deep and measured. "'Friends say that Marin argued with Wilson over an heirloom piece of jewelry which she claims she left with him for cleaning and restoration. Mr. Wilson states that while she visited his shop and inquired about his services, she did not leave her grandmother's emerald brooch in his care.'"

Ralph looks at me. "So he's done this before."

My breath is shallow, heart racing again.

He continues reading. "'Marin, wife and mother of two, was quite distraught, according to friends, because the item had significant financial and sentimental value and had filed a report with police. She had plans to confront him again.'"

Ralph's face has gone dark. "I knew this guy was a weirdo."

I lean into him, try to read over his shoulder but I'm not wearing my glasses. I can see a little but the smaller type is blurry.

"What else does the article say?" I press.

He looks back at the screen. "'Wilson was released and is not, according to police, a suspect in Ms. Marin's disappearance at this time.'"

"Did they ever find her?"

Ralph taps on the keyboard, then shakes his head. "It doesn't look like it. Here's an article about her a year later, talking about how the case has not been solved. Nothing about the brooch. This was almost six years ago, now."

Ralph stares at the screen.

"This woman," says Ralph. "Do you think she looks a little like Sandy?"

"Sandy?" I say. "You still can't reach her?"

Oh, great. We're back to this.

"No, I can't," he says. "She's missing."

The word sends a little jolt of alarm through me. "Missing? Like *officially*."

"Well, no," says Ralph. "But no one seems to know where she is."

Or they just won't tell you because you're *stalking* her, I think but don't say.

I lean in to get a closer look just to be polite. But, yeah, she does look a little like Sandy. Same feathery hair and light coloring, same brightly vacant expression on her face. We both glance up when we hear the garage rattle open next door. Ralph rises quickly and turns out the kitchen light, plunging us into semidarkness. We watch as the white van pulls out and backs out of the driveway, then slowly rolls up the street and out of sight. We both sit there a moment. Scout starts whining, not sure what the hell we're doing, just sitting there in the dark, looking out the window.

"Are you thinking what I'm thinking?" asks Ralph.

What's an eight-letter word for when a terrible idea seems like a brilliant one?

Delusion.

IX.

We clumsily climb over the back fence. An owl hoots disapprovingly from the trees. And Scout, still at home, can be heard distantly howling his outrage at being left behind. The night is dark and moonless, the neighborhood quiet.

"He's not going to leave the door open again," I say as we approach the back of the house. I have butterflies in my stomach, sweaty palms. This is stupid. "What about cameras? Everyone has cameras now, don't they?"

"Shh," says Ralph.

No sensor lights come on as we climb onto the back deck. I don't spot the seeing eye of a doorbell or security camera. Good. Well, we won't be able to get in, anyway. We'll have to slink back home and go through the proper channels to get my watch back. Ralph tips up a flowerpot by the door and produces a key.

"This was here when Sandy was showing the place. Her lockbox was broken and we found this when we were trying to get in."

Maybe Wilson, like any smart new homeowner with something to hide, has changed the locks. Nope. The key slips in, Ralph turns it, and the door pushes silently open. We listen. No beeping alarm.

I have to be honest. Since the accident, my memory isn't the best. I lose things. Items. Words. Time, occasionally. Processing is sometimes slow. I have to focus on conversations, casual encounters, in a way that other people probably don't. I miss cues. But I'm not crazy. I had a watch. I brought it to my new neighbor, Carlton Wilson, antiques restorer, and I think he stole it. Or is trying to steal it. He probably thought I was an easy mark. Sandy must have told him I was crazy. We never liked each other.

"Did you tell Sandy about my accident?" I ask Ralph as we step into the kitchen. The room is all shadows.

"What?" he whispers.

"He knew that I was in an accident," I say softly. "He would only know if Sandy told him. Sandy would only know if *you* told *her*."

He stops and looks at me. "I might have mentioned it. We were getting closer. Is it a secret?"

"I guess not," I say. "It's just that I don't want people thinking I'm crazy."

"No one thinks that."

"He implied it."

"He's a *thief*," says Ralph. "Maybe worse."

We go upstairs first, walk room through empty room. There is a stack of sealed boxes in one. In another, there are some old pieces—a desk, some chairs in various states of disrepair, an armoire. There's a king bed that looks like it has been recently slept in dominating the small master bedroom. I rifle through the dresser—socks, underwear, T-shirts. Everything orderly, folded neatly. Ralph takes the walk-in closet.

"Check this out."

I turn to see with a jangle of alarm that Ralph is holding a gun. A small revolver, flat black with what looks like an ivory-plated handle. It's hard to see in the dark.

"Whoa," I say, holding up a hand. It suddenly occurs to me how wrong this is. We broke into this guy's house and we're going through his things. He could come back at any moment. And then what would we do? How would we explain ourselves?

"What does an antiques restorer need with a gun?" muses Ralph.

"What does anyone need with a gun?" I say. "Put it back."

"Not likely. I'm keeping this until we get out of here."

"You don't even know how to use it."

"Point and pull the trigger, right?" He looks at it. It's dwarfed in his big hand. There's something about his goofy smile that makes me remember another moment. Something long gone. I grasp at the memory and it slips away.

I put my hand on his arm. "This was a mistake. Let's go."

He shakes his head, sticks the gun in his pocket.

"Not without that watch." But there's more to this, isn't there? Addled as I am, even I can see it. This is about Sandy.

Downstairs, we go through drawers in the kitchen. Through the side bar in the dining room. There's not much here. Not many places to hide things. The high energy of our errand abandons us. I'm about to suggest again that we leave before he comes back—which could be any minute. That's when I hear it. The knocking from the basement.

"There it is," I say.

"What?"

"The sound from downstairs."

"The basement?" he says, cocking his head as if to listen better. "I don't hear anything."

How does he not hear that? I follow the sound and find myself in the hallway, in front of the door that leads to the basement. On the white door, there is a newly installed lock. A dead bolt that needs a key.

"I hear it," he says, putting his ear to the door. "I think. Could be the water heater."

He tries the door but it's locked. We freeze when we hear the sound of an engine, a pair of headlights lighting the foyer from the road. But then the vehicle passes. Anxiety is a pulse in my veins. We should go. He's going to come back. We should just call the police again. But then Ralph reaches up onto the molding above the door and comes back with a key. He looks at it triumphantly.

"It's down there," he says. "It has to be."

Before I can stop him, he easily unlocks the door,

opens it. The darkness swallows him. I hear him creaking down the stairs.

Wait, I want to say. I've suddenly come to my senses. *This is a bad idea. And if he comes back there's no exit from down there. We'll be trapped.*

But he's already downstairs, and this is my fault. So I follow.

There's only one word for when you know something is going to end badly but you do it anyway.

Stupid.

X.

The basement smells of damp and mold, of course. It's pitch-black and I feel along the walls for a light switch. I can hear Ralph stumbling and breathing up ahead of me. When the light comes on, I am momentarily blinded. Slowly, the things around me come into focus.

What did I think we might find down here?

Sandy bound and gagged on a table? Locked in a box? A horror movie torture chamber complete with metal trays of sharp tools designed to inflict pain?

Guess what? It's filled with antiques: a towering armoire; some paintings under tarps; a wingback chair; a grandfather clock; some old desks; a mid-century modern coffee table. The knocking is louder now, and Ralph makes his way toward the sound. And I stand frozen, blood rushing in my ears.

I was driving the car the night my parents died. It wasn't anyone's fault. It wasn't that I'd been drinking or that I'd been texting, or even distracted. I'd taken the train home that night after work, to take my parents to dinner. We were celebrating my dad's birthday, which had been the week before. My brother was supposed to meet us at our favorite childhood Chinese restaurant, The East Winds. It was kind of a silly family tradition—big plates of egg rolls and flaming pupu platters. Fortune cookies instead of cake. But my brother never showed up, and the meal was less fun because my mom was worried. Until she got a text: Sorry. Got hung up at work. Can't make it. Then she was mad. My dad tried to make light of it. But I could tell he was disappointed.

It was cold. My dad had two glasses of wine, when he usually only had one. So I offered to drive. There'd been a light rain so the roads were slick. And then as I made a blind turn, a deer came bounding from the side of the road. I slammed on the brakes and the car went into a spin. That's the last thing I remember. Everything after that is a total blank. A black hole in my memory that swallowed my parents and everything I was while they were alive. I missed their funerals, languishing in a coma, my own prognosis uncertain.

Just an accident.

No one's fault, not even the poor deer who was doing what deer do. No reason. No crime. No need to hunt for justice or exact revenge. Just the mundane brutality of being alive. If I am honest, that's been one of the hardest things. That there's no one to blame.

Ralph stands before a closed door. The knocking is coming from behind it. He swings it open. A rusty old water heater, clicking and banging in the dark. He stands there watching.

I make my way through the maze of the basement, winding through passages created by old furniture and tall boxes. When I come to the back corner, I find a work space. A long table, a stool, shelves of tools, and rows and rows of all manner of watches and clocks, wristwatches, pocket watches, travel clocks, a cuckoo clock. Tiny faces. Little analog numbers. Each of them ticking. A muted cacophony, the sound of time passing.

And there on the work space, my father's watch, polished and sitting in its box. I lift it. It's alive. I can feel the gears moving, a delicate energy against the skin of my palm, watch the second hand make its measured journey. It gleams and fills my heart with a joyful longing. What if I *could* turn it back? Back to the hours before my parents died. *Let's stay in*, I'd say. And they'd agree because they always did whatever I wanted. But no. The watch keeps ticking. Always forward. Never back. I breathe my relief, that I haven't lost this piece of them.

Ralph comes up behind me.

"You found it," he says. "That little fucker. He *was* trying to steal it."

I nod, unable to trust my voice. He puts a strong arm around me, squeezes. I lean into him.

"Let's get you home," Ralph says.

That's when we hear the door open and slam closed upstairs, and heavy fast footfalls heading our way.

What's a seven-letter word for no way out?

Trapped.

XI.

We are frozen, listening. But the footfalls seem to grow fainter as if they're heading upstairs. The door to the basement doesn't open, and no one comes down.

"He went up," said Ralph. "Let's get out of here and call the police."

We move quickly, quietly back through the maze of boxes and furniture, and pause at the bottom step. The door, which we left open, is closed. Ralph runs up to try the knob. It's locked.

"I know you're down there," comes a voice from

the other side of the door. "I saw you on my security camera."

So there *was* a camera. I knew it! I move into Ralph, and he holds on to me tight.

"Call the police," Ralph shouts. "We found the watch. You're a liar and a thief. We know about the missing woman in Cleveland, the emerald brooch."

Wow, way to blow your wad.

There's silence from above, then the sound of footfalls fading. Ralph takes out the gun.

"What are you going to do with that?" I ask, incredulous.

Ralph pulls me back into the shadow of the staircase, looks at the gun in his hand uncertainly. "Defend us if I have to. What if this guy's, like, a serial killer or something? He killed that woman in Cleveland. Maybe he killed Sandy. What if he would have killed *you* if you hadn't let it go about the watch?"

Is this really happening? Maybe I am a crazy person and this is all just a hallucination. I really hope so. Is it my imagination or do I hear Scout howling? Who will take care of him if I go to jail? Or worse?

But it's not Scout. It's a siren which draws closer, grows louder. We wait, both of us with ragged breath, clinging to each other.

"This was a bad idea," said Ralph.

"Yeah."

"But at least we got the watch."

A moment later there's shouting upstairs, then the basement door swings open.

"Police!" A commanding voice from the top of the stairs.

Ralph sticks the gun in his pocket and we move into the light slowly with our hands up.

Officer Merle is standing at the top of the stairs

with his gun drawn. He looks less commanding than he does scared and young.

"Good news, Officer Merle," I say. "I found my watch."

He looks relieved to lower his gun and holster it. As we climb the stairs, I can see that his hands are shaking. He backs up to let us exit the basement. Carlton Wilson sits on the staircase, fuming, his nostrils wide, eyes dark.

"Ms. Byrne, did you break into this house with this man?" asks Officer Merle, nodding to Ralph.

"It was my idea, Officer," says Ralph. "We just wanted to retrieve her property."

"Where's the watch?" The officer holds out his hand.

I take it from my pocket and hand it to him. "It was on the workbench downstairs."

"It's mine," says Wilson, rising. His voice is strident with outrage. A very good act. Or maybe he's the crazy one, really believes it's his. "That watch is *my* property. They were trying to steal it."

"I have the paperwork," I say. "Somewhere in my parents' documents."

"If you do have papers," he blusters. "They're forged."

He is very good at this. Even I almost believe him. But I stay calm. Something about finding the watch working and nestled in its box makes me feel solid, sure of myself in a way I haven't been since the accident. Dr. Black said that sometimes healing seems elusive, like we'll never be whole again. And then all of a sudden, you realize you're well. Or more well than you were. Or well enough for now.

"HRM," I say. "Those are my grandfather's initials."

Officer Merle looks back and forth between us, then

hands the watch to me. For whatever reason, he believes me.

"What are you doing?" shouts Wilson. "I'll have your badge."

Which seems like a funny, old-timey thing to say. But he does the whole indignant thing really well. He's an accomplished liar.

Then it's a screaming match, with Ralph trying to tell Officer Merle about Sandy, how she was dating Wilson, and now she's missing, what we found online about the missing woman in Cleveland, the emerald brooch. Wilson saying that we're both crazy, that I'm mentally unstable and Ralph is a stalker. Officer Merle trying to mediate. And I stay quiet, feeling the measured ticking of the pocket watch.

Officer Merle calls for backup.

We all wind up down at the police station. I have no idea what Ralph did with the gun. But when they asked him if he was armed before he got in the squad car, he said no. When they frisked him to be sure, they came back empty-handed. No one asked me if I had a gun. I didn't get a pat down. Sexism, right?

We all tell our stories to different people, the night winds on. I worry about Scout.

Finally, Officer Merle escorts me out. I wonder if they'll want to keep the watch, until all of this is settled. But no one tries to take it from me. It's been deep in the pocket of my sweater all this time.

"You believe me?" I ask Officer Merle on the station steps.

"I do." He has heavily lidded, kind eyes. "Mr. Wilson has a history of wrongdoing, as you found online. I think he tried to take advantage of you, steal your watch and then use your accident to make us question your sanity. That's pretty low."

He's right. That is pretty low.

"So what happens to him?"

Officer Merle shrugs. "I don't know. Depends on whether you press charges, what other investigations are open on him, what the DA wants. Lots of things."

"And what about Sandy? And that woman in Cleveland?"

We both turn toward the voice. Ralph seems to have come from nowhere, but I guess he was sitting on the outside bench waiting for me. They must have let him go, too.

"There will be an investigation," says Officer Merle. "A detective will be in touch. I'm sure they'll connect with the Cleveland officers investigating that open case."

It all seems very vague and anticlimactic. A stolen watch, a break-in, two women missing. Shouldn't there be some urgency? But life's not like that, is it? Sandy's not necessarily "missing." Gayle Marin has been gone too long. My stolen watch has been retrieved. The wheels of justice turn slowly, if at all.

"Do you need a ride?" asks Officer Merle.

I look at Ralph, who seems exhausted, beaten.

"We do," I say. Officer Merle drives us home, me in the passenger seat. Ralph in the back behind the grating, like a perp. No one says anything.

As I exit the car: "Thanks for the ride."

"I'm sure I don't have to tell you not to go back near that house. Or Wilson."

"You don't. I won't."

"Good night."

Ralph is silent as Officer Merle opens the door for him.

Scout is hysterical with happiness to see us, wagging his tail, whining desperately. I reach down for him and he smothers me with wet, stinky kisses. Ralph takes him for a walk around the block, then returns.

"I'm sleeping here on the couch tonight," says Ralph, shutting and locking the front door. "In case they let him go and he comes home."

He seems tense and worried. Sandy on his mind, no doubt. I'm not going to argue. I don't want to be alone either.

"Where's the gun?" I ask.

"I left it in the basement."

I see the way his mouth presses into a thin line, the quick wringing of his hands. He's just lied to me and I don't know why.

I guess I want to think this is over. I have my watch. And with it, some part of *me* is restored. But there's still Sandy. The woman from Cleveland.

"Ralph."

"Just get some rest. Okay?"

When I creep down later to check on him, I see him on the porch, chair turned to watch Carlton Wilson's house.

I go back to bed, lie awake, worrying, the pocket watch ticking softly on the bedside table.

I have no clue what to do.

XII.

"Jay."

The voice leaks through layers of sleep and I swim up toward it.

"Jay, wake up."

"What?"

"He's back. Wilson."

I fell asleep in my clothes. So when Ralph and I get

to the window in time to see Wilson backing out of his driveway, it doesn't take us long to run downstairs and get in my car to follow. Scout trots after us, taking his place on the folded blanket I keep for him in the backseat. I don't have the heart to tell him he can't come along.

We catch up with Wilson just as he makes a turn onto the road that leads out of town. Ralph is at the wheel. Why do men always think it's their place to drive? But the truth is I don't like to drive anymore. I do it as little as possible. Ralph hangs back, letting the other vehicle almost out of sight before he follows.

"What are we doing?"

We haven't discussed this. It seemed like a foregone conclusion when we saw Wilson leaving that we would follow him. But it's really stupid; we're following a potentially dangerous person into the woods. What do we think we're going to do, a math teacher and borderline stalker, a moderately damaged semirecluse and her dog? I can't help but think if we were normal, established people we wouldn't be in this situation.

Oh, well, here we are.

"Shit," says Ralph. "Where did he go?"

The road ahead of us, winding and surrounded by trees, has gone dark. As we move forward, I catch a glimpse of taillights disappearing down a hidden drive to our right. I almost don't say anything. Maybe he'll just turn around and take us home. But what if Ralph is right? What if cackling Sandy *is* missing? Dead or abducted? And Wilson is responsible. We should just call Officer Merle. I have his card in my pocket. Oh, I forgot my cell phone.

Shit.

"Back there," I say finally.

"Where?"

"Make a U-turn."

He does and drives slowly until we come back to the gravel drive.

"There."

He turns the car and kills the lights. The glow of the full moon is enough to cast the road ahead in a silvery light. Leaves drift around us. I roll down the window for some air and it washes in cold, bringing with it the smell of autumn. Scout whines in the back, picking up our nervous energy. We drive and drive, the road uneven and rocky, the car pitching and tilting.

"Are you sure this is where he turned?" asks Ralph.

"Yes. Well, no not really. I think so. Sorry."

He looks at me, then reaches over to pat me on the leg. "It's okay. I'm sorry. I shouldn't have dragged you into this."

I sense that he's about to turn back when around the bend we see the van. It's parked, dark, in front of a broad tilting structure, an old barn. The door stands ajar, revealing only black within. The moon drifts behind the clouds and the world turns midnight blue. A finger of fear presses into my belly.

"Now what?" I ask.

"Stay here."

"What? No."

A heavy hand on my shoulder. "Jay, stay here."

And then he's gone, jogging toward the barn. I look back at Scout, who offers a big yawn and curls up on his blanket, watches me with big eyes.

"Stay here," I tell him. "Don't bark. Don't howl."

I reviewed a book once, written by a so-called pet psychic. She claimed that animals understood a lot more than we knew, that they were tuned in to our thoughts and feelings. Looking into Scout's worried face, I believe it. He's quiet as I exit the car, leaving the windows open for air, but not low enough for him to get out and chase me. When I turn back to look at him, he has hopped into the passenger seat, watching me go.

It's so quiet. Now that the moonlight is dulled by cloud cover, the stars visible in the sky are brighter. I see Orion's Belt and the Big Dipper. Mars is a fiery red dot. Venus the brightest point in the sky. I hear something, though I'm not sure what. The quiet, the trees, the wind in the leaves seems to absorb all sound.

When I get to the barn door, I pause, heart thumping, hands shaking. I step inside the darkness.

At first it looks like a crowd—an audience, or a dance floor, a hundred bodies.

I almost let out a scream, but swallow it back with a hand to my mouth.

Each figure is white and rigid, arms posed—up, extended, waving. As my vision adjusts to the darkness, I see heads of waxen hair and glassy eyes. Smiling mouths with painted white teeth. It's a field of mannequins, some in costume—a flapper, a hippie, a rocker, a schoolgirl. Some are bare with black seams at their arms and legs, their necks.

My throat is dry as I work my way through the lifeless mob, careful not to knock one over. They're so close together that they'll tip like dominoes.

Voices, raised, angry, echo off the walls, the tall ceiling. I move in that direction until I see them: Ralph and Wilson in some kind of standoff. Someone else, tied to a chair, limp and lifeless.

Sandy.

Is this happening?

It feels like a dream and I will myself to wake up, back in my own bed with Scout on top of my legs. It's too strange, this moment. Like when I woke up from my coma and found my brother slumped in the chair by my bed where apparently he'd been every day, except for the day he had to bury our parents without me. My memories then of the crash were vague, my time unconscious a blur of dream images and strange sounds, muffled voices.

It's my fault. That was the first thing my brother said to me. *I'm sorry. I should have been there.*

It was just an accident. I tried to tell him, but there was a tube in my throat.

Oh, God, I think now, a new clarity burning through the fog of my memory.

"Just let her go," Ralph says. I see the gun in his hand. His voice is steady and reasonable. "You don't have to do this. You don't *want* to do this."

Wilson has a knife to Sandy's throat, his face a mask of menace. And Sandy already looks dead, pale and small, helpless. I feel bad. I have been so mean to her. I am part of the reason she and Ralph broke up. I know that. No one wants to be with a man who has to take care of his crazy sister, maybe forever.

A sister who most of the time doesn't even remember who he is, and when she does, blames him for his parents' death, even though she really blames herself. Even though she knows there's no one to blame.

Ralph. My landlord. My friend. My brother.

The moment swells and expands and my mind clears.

I see Ralph's trembling hands, and Wilson's malicious intent, the knife pressing into the delicate skin of Sandy's throat.

There is just a breath before something awful happens. Just like when that deer bounded into the road. There was a breath, a second when anything else could have happened.

But this time, there is something I can do.

I give the mannequins behind me and next to me a hard push. In a terrible clatter, they do in fact tumble like dominoes, one knocking the other, arms snapping off, hands falling lifeless, heads rolling in a bizarre mimicry of carnage.

Then I lunge, screaming, for Wilson.

The gun goes off.

Wilson is falling before I reach him but I career into him anyway, taking us both to the floor. The sound of the gun rings in my ears. Wilson is white and still beneath me, blood pooling a viscous black. Ralph's hands on me, pulling me.

The blood. It's mine.

Are you okay? Jay, are you all right? Oh my God, Jay.

I hear Scout barking far away. Then howling.

There are sirens then, I think. A white-hot pain in my side. Ralph's face over mine. "Jay, stay with me."

And then, though the world around me is fading, I see Officer Merle approaching us, gun drawn and yelling. Ralph puts up his hands and I close my eyes.

When I open them again, my brother, Ralph, is sitting in a chair beside my hospital bed.

"I'm sorry," he says when he sees my eyes open. "This was all my fault."

"Sandy," I say.

"She's alive," he says, rubbing at his eyes. "She'll be okay, I think. In time."

I am groggy, head throbbing, eyes heavy. "Then you're a hero, right? You knew something was wrong."

He blows out a breath. "You always thought more of me than I deserved."

I remember suddenly, panic rising. "Where's my stuff?"

He sits up, digs into his pocket. "You're worried about this?"

Ralph holds out the pocket watch, rises to hand it to me.

"No," I say. "It's for you. I had it fixed for you."

He looks down at it, blinking. "What happens when you don't know me again later? Will you think I stole it?"

"I won't forget. I think I'm getting better." I'm really not sure that it's true. But I hope it is. Dr. Black says I'll be whole again someday.

"I think you are, too," he says, still looking at the watch. We both know how much it meant to our dad. He'd want Ralph to have it; I know that.

"Scout? Where's Scout?"

"I took him home. He's okay. Mrs. Miller from across the street is looking in on him."

I try to sit, but pain keeps me down. I want to go home. Scout doesn't like to be alone.

"Oh my God," I say, reality dawning. "Did you *shoot* me?"

He closes his eyes and shakes his head.

"I did, yes," he says. "I'm really sorry. I was aiming for Wilson and you just kind of ran in there. A flesh wound, I'm told. You'll live."

He's making light, but I can tell by his pale face and the line of his mouth that he feels bad.

"Can I press charges?" I ask.

"Who's going to take out the recycling?"

"And Wilson?"

"In custody," he says. "The police were following him, that's how they knew where we were. They're going to search the property. He's apparently connected to several missing people. Officer Merle says they found what they think might be grave sites."

I remember Wilson's boyish smile when I brought him my watch. A liar. A thief. Maybe a murderer. All bad qualities in a neighbor. A tingle of dread travels through my body.

"Oh my God," I say. All of it. What a mess.

Ralph sits on the bed next to me, takes my hand.

"I'm so sorry." A tear trails down his cheek. My eyes go hot, too, throat constricting. "For not being there for Mom and Dad, for everything that's happened to you, for all of this."

"You've been there," I tell him, my voice raspy. "In every way, as a brother and a friend."

"Too late." His voice is just a rasp. He hangs his head. I think of the epigraph on Wilson's site. *I can turn back time.* If only.

"No such thing," I say, putting my hand over the palm where he holds the watch. "Time only moves forward. Not back."

He offers a mirthless laugh. "You have all the answers, don't you?" he says.

"Not by a long shot."

He reaches over to wipe my eyes with the rough skin of his thumb. We sit awhile, each of us quiet, my heart monitor beeping, the sound of a radio somewhere, two voices in low conversation.

"Hey," he says. "What's a six-letter word for neighbor?"

I think about it. *Brother*? No, that's seven.

Oh, I get it. That's dark.

We both say it at exactly the same time: *"Killer."*

* * * * *

HOWARD'S HEART

BY BRYON QUERTERMOUS

Howard told me three things before he died:

1. His last name was also Howard
2. The love of his life was a Ukrainian chat girl named Elsa
3. He was psychic

The first two turned out to be true, but I had my doubts about the third one.

I picked Howard up in front of the arrivals area at Detroit Metro Airport a few minutes after 1 a.m., and he was in a chatty mood. It wasn't particularly hot, we were coming off a nasty two-week heat wave, but he was sweating profusely and looked like a raw ham squeezed into a sausage casing.

"You seem like you're a good listener," Howard said as we left the buzzing, lighted area of the airport.

With an undergraduate degree in theology, one failed year as a pastor and four more years as a parole agent, you could definitely say I like to listen. Now I was a part-time rideshare driver, part-time private detective and part-time parent wondering if anyone was ever going to listen to me.

My normal route didn't usually include the airport because everything about it was overly complicated and I didn't need the money enough to deal with the hassle, but picking up rideshares was a nice way to pass the time.

"This would be a terrible job if I didn't," was all I said.

He seemed willing to fill in the conversational void, and I was thankful for the distraction. "Today's my birthday, and I'm here to meet my girlfriend after her show tomorrow night. She told me if I get here in time tonight, I should stop by and say hello."

He droned on from there and wanted my advice on whether he was being scammed. At first, I found myself internally mocking him for being so naive and a bit of a pervert, but eventually I started feeling bad for him and then wanting to protect him.

"I've been sending her money, not a lot, but, you know, a few hundred bucks here and there, and all I want is to see a photo of her that isn't, you know, staged or whatever. Because it's my birthday."

"It doesn't sound great for you," I said, trying to keep my eyes on the road while also trying to convey through eye contact how important it was that he not go to that club tonight. "Not only do I think you're being scammed, I think they might try to set you up when you meet her and try to rob you…or worse."

"I thought the same thing, too, and thank you for being honest, but you have to see some of these texts she sent me. They're not, you know, they're not just sexy. She tells me about her day and her family and…

Elsa, she's the love of my life, she's seen some of my other girlfriends and tried to talk me out of it, but this one, she thinks this one is the real deal."

"The love of your life isn't your girlfriend?"

"She lives in the Ukraine and can't really ever leave, so she encourages me to...jeez... I mean you've probably...have you heard this stuff before?"

"Not in this job, no," I said. "But before this, I—"

"You were a pastor. Is that what this is all about? You think I'm some kind of—"

I slowed down the car just as we were getting onto the expressway and had to merge into the fastest lane and almost got rear-ended before I regrouped my thoughts.

"How did you know I used to be a pastor?"

"I'm kind of psychic," he said. "That's why—"

"Are you trying to scam *me*? Because you picked the wrong guy."

"I know exactly who I picked," he said.

I didn't like the way he said that, but he didn't say anything else, and we drove the rest of the way to his hotel in silence. When I pulled up to the hotel, he didn't get out.

"Happy birthday, Howard. Enjoy your time in—"

"We've still got half an hour or so before the club closes," he said, "and it's just down the road there a bit."

"I, ah, that's fine, I don't have a problem taking you there, but I don't know how to make it work in the app. You could—"

"I don't care about the app. I can give you cash. We can do this under the table or whatever."

"Okay. Are you hungry or anything? We could—"

"Are you worried about me?"

"I just have a bad feeling about all of this," I said. "I really don't think you should go to that club tonight."

Howard handed me a wad of cash and smiled. "You're a good man, Casey, but I have to see her. I have to know."

I didn't say anything, but I could see in his face that he was waiting for me to make one more move. A move both of us knew I would make. Howard knew more about me than he had any business knowing, but all I could think about was how guilty I would feel if I heard later he'd been hurt at the club and I didn't try to stop him.

"I'll go with you," I said.

He didn't say anything as we drove down Middlebelt toward the Mile High Club, but he seemed relieved rather than smug that he'd manipulated me into doing his bidding.

When we pulled into the club, there were more cars in the parking lot than I would have expected that close to closing.

"You ever been to a place like this?"

"Jesus hung out with whores and tax collectors," I said, getting out of the car and going around the back to the trunk. "God finds us where we need Him."

"That's not really an answer. I just want to make sure you're not going to stick out and make this harder on both of us."

I opened the trunk and pulled a handgun and magazine out of a hard case, loaded it and clipped it to my pants under my shirt.

"I'll be fine."

We headed inside the club and I was pleased to see a friendly face at the door.

Dezzie Kline left the parole division a year or so before I did so he could become a PI and have a more flexible schedule for his kids. When my marriage finally fell apart for good, he helped me make the same transition. With him working security here, I felt more comfortable about Howard's chances.

"My buddy Howard here is supposed to meet a friend of his after the show, one of the girls," I said, handing him the flyer Howard had given me along with enough cash to cover our admission and a generous tip. "Could you let her know we're here?"

Dezzie looked at me for a second, I assumed, trying to figure out if I had an angle on this or if it was really as dumb as it sounded. He was taller than me by several inches and had the hardened stare that came with years of cop work before his parole job instead of my years of spiritual wandering. Finally, he smiled tightly and waved us in.

"Grab a drink and I'll send her over when she's free."

The next half hour was more enjoyable than I could have imagined, with Howard throwing money around to any girl who passed our way, interested more in finding out about them and their lives than seeing them dance. He drank from a massive pink cup refilled twice with some swirling booze concoction, and I nursed a surprisingly good old-fashioned and watched.

Between flirts, Howard told me about his life and how he made his money and why he felt the need to fall in love with exotic dancers and foreign chat girls rather than the sorts of women other men fell in love with.

"I like to make people happy," he said, minutes before the lights came up at closing, "and it always seems like once a guy gets married, he stops trying to make other people happy. I like meeting new people and selling them a car if they need one, buying them a ticket home if they need one, or helping a girl in trouble make a new life for herself."

I finished the last of my drink and looked around to see if I could spot Dezzie anywhere. Howard had the giddy smile of a kid at a birthday party waiting for the clown to show up.

"Does it ever go to the next level though with these girls?" I asked. "Or is it always on a stage or in a chat room or whatever? Sorry if I'm getting too personal. I don't drink very often."

"I was never good with the ladies, and never really got around to doing what boys are supposed to do in college. The summer after my senior year I came home from school early to surprise my family, but instead I surprised an intruder who was attacking my sister."

Before he could finish his story, a leggy woman with more grace than beauty materialized in our booth.

"Howard," she said, "happy birthday, and you brought a friend. Is it his birthday, too?"

"He's here to make sure you don't have some goon in the bushes to knock me on the head and steal my money."

"Casey Carlisle," I said, extending my hand across Howard's ample chest toward her.

"Misty Maize," she said. "And I would never hurt Howard. I love Howard."

Howard. Not Howie or H&H or any other kind of nickname. She sounded genuinely happy to be with him, but I also realized we were in a strip club where her livelihood depended on guys like Howard believing that.

"That's her real name, too," Howard said. "She showed me her birth certificate and everything because I was sure it was a made-up name."

"You really didn't stand a chance, then, did you?" I asked, immediately regretting how petty it sounded.

Misty frowned and hung a suspicious gaze on me, but Howard took the bullet and tried to defend me. "Casey here used to be a pastor, so he thinks this stuff is icky or whatever, but he's a good guy. Real worried about me."

"Pastor to protector?" Misty asked.

"Long story," I said, "but you'd be surprised what comes up in a search for 'what to do with a theology degree if you don't believe in God.'"

"Well, I'm starving," Misty said, standing and pulling Howard by the arm out of the booth. "Let's go over to the Ram's Horn for some pancakes."

Howard nodded and looked over at me. I shrugged. Dezzie escorted us out and locked the door behind us. I wanted to see if he was up for catching lunch in the next few days, but he seemed eager to get us out of there, probably so he could get back to his kids before he had to pay the nanny or babysitter overnight rates.

"You have a car?" I asked.

She shook her head. "Had a friend drop me off. Something with my transmission or whatever."

Howard's eyes lit up. "You need a new car? I can get you anything you need."

"Right now, I need something starchy in my stomach and a giant cup of coffee," Misty said. "We can talk cars later."

I drove them the three blocks to the Ram's Horn and offered to stay in the car while they went in and ate, but they insisted I join them. We all had pancakes and shared from a plate of mixed breakfast meats. Misty and Howard had coffee; I had Diet Coke.

An hour later, I dropped them off at the hotel, convinced not only that Howard was safe with her, but that she really was one of the loves of his life.

The next day was a Thursday, and it was raining heavily when I woke up. I figured I'd stay in bed all day watching movies and trying to enjoy my new bachelor life, but that plan went out the door when a pair of cops knocked on my door asking me about Howard. One of the cops was in uniform and the other was wearing black cargo pants and a polo shirt with an embroidered badge on one side and the name Wilson on the other.

"You drove Mr. Howard to a hotel and then to a strip club," Wilson said. "But only the trip to the hotel showed up in the app Mr. Howard used."

I wanted to know how they knew that so quickly. There was no way they got a warrant for the phone that quickly, so somebody must have told them. But I also wanted to help, for the time being, so I told them what I knew and gave them a full recap of the night's events.

"What time was it when you dropped them off at the hotel?" Wilson asked.

"I wasn't really paying attention to the clock," I said, "but it was late. Maybe 3 a.m.?"

"Maybe?"

"I wasn't keeping a journal or anything. Didn't think it would be important. Why are you asking?"

"Did you talk to Mr. Howard at all after you dropped him off at the hotel?"

"No. Why are you asking me these questions?"

Wilson looked at the uniformed officer, who gave no response at all.

"Mr. Howard killed a stripper named Misty Maize in his hotel room this morning after what appears to be a lovers' quarrel and then killed himself. We're trying to tie up any loose ends that might be—"

"Misty was the love of his life. He wouldn't kill her. It was his birthday." Even as I said it, I knew how naive I sounded, but I was trying to justify my involvement and pretend like I hadn't been absolutely played by Howard.

The cops nodded condescendingly and left their

cards so I could call if I thought of anything important. I threw the cards in a bowl by the door where I kept my keys and loose change and went back to bed. My body wasn't used to staying out that late, and the rain made it easy to justify trying to catch up on those missed hours of sleep, but every time I closed my eyes, my imagination tried to reconstruct the scene in Howard's hotel room and see if there was a way I could have stopped it.

My phone buzzed several times, but I ignored it and tried to watch TV instead. A few minutes into a Hallmark mystery movie, my cable went out. When I reached for my phone, I saw two missed calls and a text message from Howard, plus two more missed calls from a number I didn't recognize. I'd put Howard's number in my phone before going to pick him up in case he tried to contact me, and I hadn't gotten around to deleting it yet. Had the cops misidentified the body in his room and Howard was still alive?

My phone buzzed again, and I hesitated briefly before finally answering.

"Howard didn't kill that girl," a woman with a vaguely Russian-sounding accent said. "He's being set up, and you need to stop it."

I initially wondered how she got my phone number, then I realized that I had given it to Howard as part of the rideshare app, so we could keep in contact for the pickup, and he must have given it to her so she could check up on me if anything happened.

"Elsa?" I asked.

"You were to protect him. That's why we… I'm sending you link to a secure video line. Check your email."

She hung up, and I tossed my phone next to me on the bed. It seemed Howard had been a bit modest about his love's computer skills when he called her a chat girl. Part of me wanted to go and grab one of those business cards from the bowl out front and call the cops and tell them what just happened, but I knew that would only make me look crazy and there was no reason for them to believe anything other than a lovers' quarrel gone wrong between a stripper and a creeper in from out of town at a sketchy airport hotel. Except I spent my entire adult life trusting my instincts on when to believe the best in people, and I had every belief that Howard and Misty were good for each other.

I went to my computer, signed into my email and found the message Elsa sent me from Howard's account. The link took me through a number of authentication hoops before finally dumping me to a video site that looked like every porn site I'd ever seen. A second or two later, a woman wearing jeans and a flannel shirt with her blond hair tied up in a messy ponytail entered the screen.

"Casey?"

"You were feeding Howard information about me in the car, weren't you?"

"I wanted to make sure he was safe. Most drivers we scanned seemed fine, but it was a lucky stroke to find a God man who also worked in social services and carries a gun."

"Who are you? *Where* are you?"

"I am a matchmaker, from a long family line of matchmakers, like in your *Hello, Dolly!*, right?"

"That's not quite the way Howard described you."

"We're not a small village now. I'm not matching men with women for goats. Your American men are coming to my country and taking our women and many men here arrange that without tradition and the women…"

Her accent was thicker now, with hints of German as she described this, and her facial expressions tightened into a fierce pinch in her brow.

"My mother is traditional. My father is technical. I am best of both worlds, and I protect my loves. Howard was my love."

"You seem to know everything going on over here. Can't you check the security footage at the club and the hotel and figure out who killed him?"

"I saw the same things you saw," Elsa said. "Someone needs to ask the people around the cameras what they saw and heard."

I crossed my arms and leaned back in my bed against the headboard. Nothing about this sounded right, but I knew myself well enough to know that I wouldn't let this be. I was going to go asking around anyway, so why not be in good with someone who might be able to help me.

"Okay," I said. "I'll talk to some people."

I had Elsa send me over everything she had on Howard and Misty—friends, family, possible enemies, travel itineraries, text messages, voice mail transcripts—and printed it out and took the stack of pages to my couch to read. I sifted through as much as I could before I was overwhelmed; I was going to have to leave my apartment to make any further progress.

The Skyway Suites looked like a botched copy of a Vegas hotel from the 1980s with four stories of gold-tinted glass that formed a lopsided pyramid without the pointy cap at the top. I didn't see any police vehicles as I pulled up to the front entrance where I dropped Howard and Misty off less than eight hours ago, but it didn't look like the place was reopened for guests either. The automatic doors slid open as I approached, and I headed to the front desk to see if anyone would talk to me.

A lumpy old white man with wispy hair and yellowed features appeared from an office to my left and stepped in front of me. "We're not taking any guests right now." He coughed. "Sorry." He held his arm over his mouth as he unloaded a robust wave of coughing.

"I'm here about the shooting," I said.

"Cops already came and went, so you're a weirdo or a reporter and I ain't talking to either, so—"

"I was their driver," I said. "I took them out to breakfast and then I brought them back here and they ended up dead and I can't help but wonder what I could have done differently."

The man softened his posture and waved for me to follow him back into the office. "Can't tell you nothin' I didn't already tell the cops, but if it'll make you feel better to talk about it, I won't turn you away."

"I drive a car part-time, but I'm also a private investigator, and I just can't match up the two people I hung out with and dropped off here with a murder-suicide."

He drooped the right side of his head into his chest and rolled his shoulders. "Didn't sound right to me either, but I can't see in no man's heart, and it wouldn't be the first time a nice man killed a nice woman over sex."

I followed up with a few more rote questions to justify my effort coming to the hotel, but I was already resigning myself to the fact that I was chasing a dead end and the simplest answer was the only answer. Then he said something that poked at my brain.

"Go back," I said. "What did you say about the gunshots?"

"They're gonna haunt the place and drive me out of business."

"You said you just heard one shot the first time though, and then you heard another one later, right?"

"Probably gonna hear one every hour from here to eternity."

I thanked him for the help and went back to my car where I scrolled through my missed calls to the number I hadn't recognized and dialed. Dezzie Kline answered.

"She tried to call you first," Dezzie said, taking a bite of his omelet at the same Ram's Horn I'd been to with Howard and Misty, "but you didn't answer, so she called me."

"I'm not used to staying out that late and passed out when I got home. What happened?"

"I don't know the specifics, but she said they were fooling around, even though he said he couldn't do the deed because of his heart, and she kept pushing him and pushing him…"

"He had a heart attack."

Dezzie nodded. "She's a good girl," he said, "but she's not the most stable dancer at our club, and she's been known to get into trouble with the guests once in a while."

"Then why'd you let her go home with my guy?"

"He had you."

"I wasn't going to stay in the room with them."

"By the time I got to her she'd already shot herself in the heart…she had a gun in her purse and…"

"That was the first shot the manager heard. What was the second?"

Dezzie sighed deeply and moved some of his omelet around on his plate without taking a bite.

"She has a family, they're good people, and they tried to help her and now they don't have anyone. If they found out she went out like that…that guy didn't

have a family, nobody who loved him, and I figured
I'd—"

"Make her the victim?"

Dezzie shrugged.

I told all of this to Elsa later that day over a secure
line and she cried.

"*I* loved him," she said. "I didn't have to meet him to
love him, and she didn't have to push him. They didn't
need to be physical for it to be love either. We've got
this whole thing all messed up and everybody thinks it
has to be physical and we've lost the beauty of chaste
love."

"I'm sorry for your loss."

"His killer has to pay for this."

"Misty already took care of that herself, and I don't
think Dezzie—"

"Not them. Didn't you read papers I sent?"

"There was a lot."

I heard her sigh, and then she disappeared from the
screen. A few seconds later the background changed
and then I was looking at a newspaper archive site. The
story was about the attack on Howard's sister.

"He told me about this when I asked him why he was
attracted to girls he couldn't touch," I said.

"He told you everything?"

I read through the entire story and got to the part
Howard hadn't told me about. "He had a bullet in his
chest. From the person who shot his sister."

"From the person who *killed* his sister."

"So the killer's in jail, then?"

The background changed again to a different story.

"He was a child, and was only in a child's jail until
twenty-one," Elsa said. "He's man of God now, like
you."

Ronald Depp, the man who killed Holly Howard and shot her brother, leaving a bullet in his heart, had been seventeen years old and was sentenced to a juvenile facility until he turned twenty-one, when he was released. He was now known as the reverend Gabriel Justice of Metro Triumphant Tabernacle Ministries in Detroit.

"I'm no man of God," I said.

"Goodbye, Casey Carlisle."

The next day, I received $5,000 in my online wallet account from Heart&Soul, Inc.

A week later I received an email link to a newspaper story about a one-car accident on the Davison Expressway that killed Reverend Gabriel Justice. Alcohol didn't appear to be a factor, but police were looking at a possible glitch in the operating system of the electric vehicle the reverend had been driving. At the end of the story was a link to an online fundraising site for funeral expenses, and I clicked through and donated $5,000.

* * * * *

PERFECT STRANGERS

BY TILIA KLEBENOV JACOBS

I am not good at armed robbery, but when Dougal told me about the new cannabis dispensaries, I figured third time was the charm.

Dougal Henshaw was my cellmate at MCI-Norfolk, where he was doing ten to fifteen for marijuana distribution, and I was keeping him company for reasons already stated. Dougal is an interesting case. He's not a nice guy, but he's smart. The reason I say he's not nice is that he killed his wife, his girlfriend, and his mother-in-law, who happened to be his girlfriend's drug dealer. (Whole story there.) He told me once that between the time he killed them and the time he got caught, he found out that a tree makes enough oxygen for two people for their whole lives, so he planted a tree and a bush to make up for the three folks who'd stopped breathing because of him. However, I do not believe this was a sincere attempt at atonement, which is usually bullshit anyway in my experience.

Dougal was not in for triple murder. Nope, he's too

smart for that, and made sure to dispose of the bodies such that he could never be connected to the tragic disappearance of three people who all happened to know him real well. However, he is not so smart that the cops didn't know about it. They just couldn't prove it. But they could prove that he had a hundred pounds of marijuana in his garden shed, and that's an automatic two and a half to fifteen, with a likely slant to the top of the scale if they actually want you for something else.

Dougal never got over the unfairness of it, especially since truthfully he was not a drug dealer. The stash actually belonged to his mother-in-law, who, unbeknownst to him, had been using his premises as a business location shortly before he whacked her. Which made the Massachusetts state cops very happy, but was not so convenient for Dougal.

"Her final revenge," he used to groan. "Don't ever get married, Gershom. It ain't worth it."

My first armed robbery did not end well, in that the cops caught me twenty minutes later at my aunt Junie's Labor Day barbecue, which made for some real distinctive family photos that year. The cameras in the store had got a very clear picture of me, and so had a couple customers. When I told Dougal about it, he was sympathetic. "You were just a kid," he said. "Next time, wear a disguise. Glasses, wig. You can ditch them easy."

"Armed robbery while disguised is a five-year minimum," I said. I am not smart, but I do know how to read, and like they say, reading's free in the DOC.

Dougal shrugged. "I always wear a disguise, and they never got me for that shit."

Now, we were having this conversation in the prison exercise yard where we were so bored we had just spent an hour looking at puddles and trying to decide if worms can breathe in the rain, which might have indicated to anyone except Dougal that he wasn't such a success after all, but I decided not to mention it.

"And don't skimp on the wig," said Dougal. "Spend the extra coin for a classy one."

"Why? You can get one from a costume shop for, like, five bucks."

"Yeah, and it looks like it, too. Use your head, McKnight. In our line of business it's real important not to draw attention to yourself until you're handing someone a bag and telling them to empty the cash register into it."

I did my time for that first armed robbery at MCI-Shirley, which is a big brick pile close by a quaint New England town, although to be candid MCI-Shirley is not the quaint part, what with the guard towers and razor wire and all. Five years went by like a snail with a hangover, and upon my release I took a gig with a home security company. They knew I was an ex-con, and they paid me under the table. I couldn't get any other job, and the amount they gave me was about three rent checks short of what I needed to get by.

Now, it is a fact that a certain percentage of the houses where I helped install burglar alarms were subsequently robbed. It is also a fact that the person or persons who robbed the houses seemed to know a lot about how to bypass their security systems. But I want to be clear about one thing: I was never the guy on the inside. I just passed along useful information to interested parties for a percentage of the take. I truly wanted to keep my hands clean.

So it was just really shitty luck that one of the houses where I happened to be working belonged to a corrections officer who came home from an early shift and recognized me from Shirley. Sonofabitch told my boss, who acted real shocked and fired me on the spot.

Assholes.

As soon as I got back to my car, I texted someone I knew and told him to call off the job on that house, which was scheduled for that night. Which he did not. He also did not delete his text messages, which turned out to be a real hitch for me, as the judge was not moved by my argument that I was telling that individual *not* to rob the house. Which should have counted for something, in my opinion.

It also turns out that courts have no sense of humor whatsoever on occasions like this, and they say a lot of stuff about "abetting" and "conspiracy" and how it's people like me who make life hard for honest ex-cons who are trying to go straight. The judge explained all this to me while also explaining that I was going to go away for the next ten years, give or take. Which is how I ended up at Norfolk, which is where I met Dougal.

Now believe me, when you spend most of a decade sharing a very compact concrete box with a guy, you end up knowing each other real well. And since Dougal was a lot older than me and more experienced, he had some trenchant insights into where I had gone wrong.

"Too complicated," he said when I told him about the burglar alarm thing.

"It worked."

"Yeah, and then what happened? Listen, McKnight," he says, very sincere. "Life's not a fucking heist movie. Forget the safecracker and the bomb expert and the goddamn Chinese contortionist."

"What Chinese—"

Dougal held up a hand. "Stop. Listen. *K-I-S-S.*" He ticked off a finger for each letter.

"Say what now?"

"Keep it simple, stupid."

I scowled. "Thanks a lot."

"Gershom, I ain't trying to hurt your feelings. I'm just telling you a basic truth." Dougal put his hand on my shoulder and looked at me with his squinty little eyes as big and earnest as he could make them. "You don't need a complicated setup. You just need a kick-ass plan and the balls to carry it out."

I ended up getting released a little early, thanks to good behavior and a decent understanding of what a parole board likes to hear. (Pro tips: use the word "remorse" a lot. Also, brush your teeth.) Naturally, Dougal was eager to share his wisdom and know-how with me even in the waning hours of my incarceration.

"Don't fuck up," he said as I packed my stuff in the cardboard box that the Commonwealth of Massachusetts had generously given me to transport the crap I'd accumulated during my time.

"Course not." I couldn't afford to be a three-time loser.

"Remember how to tie your shoes?"

"Nope." That was kind of a joke we had, since the shoes they give you in prison don't have laces.

Dougal gave a big sigh. "I just hope whoever they put in here isn't a total ass-wipe like you."

"I'll miss you, too." I was trying to get my books to lie flat, but I had read them pretty much to death. The spines were U-shaped, the pages were soft as felt, and the covers curled like wood shavings.

"Yeah, well. Go celebrate. Get high as a kite and think of the friends you left behind."

"Good idea. I'll invite my parole officer." I shoved the books around and put one upright to hold the others in place.

"Might as well. Weed's legal now."

"So I hear." We don't get cable on the inside, but

we do get TV, and the local news had recently done a special on cannabis. A lot of the guys were talking about nothing else, especially some who were hoping the decriminalization of weed might mean a commutation of their sentences. Which did happen sometimes, but not a lot.

"That stash they pinned on me is probably some guy's pot shop inventory now," grumbled my cellmate.

The thing is, Dougal thinks he is the original No-J, which is the opposite of an OJ. You may recall that OJ Simpson snuffed two people but went free. By contrast, a No-J is a guy who is convicted despite being as innocent as Ivory soap. That was Dougal, or so he'd have you believe.

I lifted the box to see if the bottom would hold. It did, so I put it down again. "Okay, Henshaw. I'll celebrate my reentry into society by lighting up just for you." I pantomimed making a purchase. "Do you take American Express? Or wait—where *is* my platinum digital Apple device?"

"They don't take credit cards, you ignorant fuck."

"Who?"

"Pot shops. Feds won't let them. Far as they're concerned, weed's still a crime."

I stopped, invisible credit card still in my hand. "So it's all…*cash*?"

"Yeah." Dougal turned to look at me. He has kind of a doughy face, and this mop of gray hair that's all wild and curly. His eyes were hard and shiny, like granite in the sun. "I'm telling you, Gershom, an enterprising guy could clean up in one of those places."

Later that day, I walked out of MCI-Norfolk. It was nine years, three blurry tattoos, and two nicely healed stab wounds since I walked in. I was carrying my box, wearing lace-up shoes for the first time in nearly a decade, and thinking hard. I knew Dougal's words were his parting gift to me. Mulling them over, I realized I had to restructure my entire way of doing business, because if I got busted again, I was going away for good.

Maybe you heard of this old-timey bank robber named Willie Sutton. A lot of people had him pegged as a Robin Hood kind of guy, robbing from the rich and giving to the poor. But when they asked him why he robbed banks—figuring he would say they were the Man or something—he said, "Because that's where the money is."

Well, the banks noticed, and now they hardly keep any cash on hand. These days, the average bank robbery only nets you four or five grand. What banks do have plenty of, though, is cameras and guards. Plus, they generally aren't anywhere near a highway, meaning that your getaway is severely compromised. Willie Sutton may have made his pile bank-robbing back then, but those days are gone.

Mind you, cash pops up in unexpected places. There's a Stop & Shop on Cape Cod that used to need a Brink's truck every two or three hours. You may not think of a grocery store as being that flush, but imagine a holiday weekend or a big football game, and everyone's stocking up before they head to their beach house. Ten thousand people drop three hundred bucks apiece, and you see what I'm getting at.

Another place is jewelry stores. Best approach there is arrive at opening, when they're setting out the cases, or better yet, at closing, when they're putting stuff away and also the cash register is full. Standard procedure is to come in with several people and have one pretend to be shopping for an engagement ring while the others lift stuff on the sly. These stores are insured, so really it's a victimless crime.

However, I was not interested in hitting a Brink's truck or a Stop & Shop or a jewelry store. For jobs like that you need a gang, and now that I was a sadder and wiser man, I knew that a gang was a bunch of guys who would roll on you when convenient.

This time, I would be my own gang.

Keep it simple, stupid.

I went to my DOC-mandated halfway house, dropped my box in the dorm, and agreed with the on-site social worker that this was the dawning of a bright new day for me. I checked in with my PO, and we had a real chummy talk about curfews and urine tests. On my way back from his office, I stopped off at my local public library, sat down at a computer and googled "legal marijuana." This time, the only part of me that was gonna get dirty was the tips of my fingers where they hit the keyboard.

I found out quickly that Dougal was right, and also that he didn't know the half of it. They say by 2021, legal marijuana will be a $21 billion industry in this country. Also, it is true that pot shops can't take credit cards, so the sales are all debit cards or cash. The average customer spends one or two hundred dollars per visit to a pot shop. So if a shop has, say, three hundred visitors a day, and half of them pay in cash…

That's where the money is.

At first I wondered why pot shops don't do like Stop & Shop, and have an armored truck pull up every few hours. Well, turns out those same banks that won't let the shops take credit cards also won't let them open business accounts. The feds can shut down a bank that takes profits from the dread dope, and they can send the bankers to prison, with the result that most banks won't touch a pot shop with a sterilized bargepole.

So what do the shop owners do with all that cash?

Well, sometimes they open accounts at places like Wells Fargo or Chase, but they get shut down when the banks find out it's a pot shop. Sometimes they drop it in their personal account and transfer the funds to a business account, but legally speaking that is money laundering, so usually they stop pretty quick. And sometimes they neglect to fully describe the nature of their business to their bank, which can lead to sticky situations like when one entrepreneur took $30,000 cash to Middlesex Savings Bank after spraying it with Febreze so it wouldn't smell like marijuana. Kind of to everyone's embarrassment, the money-brick smelled like Febreze *and* marijuana, which signaled the end of that particular entrepreneur's association with Middlesex Savings Bank. Honest to God, you gotta feel for these folks.

The only financial institution in Massachusetts that will do business with cannabis dispensaries is Century Bank, and they have a team of lawyers working round the clock to make sure everyone stays legit. I made a note of that, and kept clicking.

PotGuide.com is a very handy way to find a marijuana dispensary, and thankfully for the public safety, they have stringent security measures in place, in that they ask you if you have a medical marijuana card. I clicked "Yes," and a map of Massachusetts popped up, spiked with little blue markers showing shops with cute names like ChemiHerb and High Priority. They were also listed alphabetically by town. The first one was in Amherst, which is scenic and touristy and too far away.

The second one was in Brookline, and although it got mostly very salutary reviews on Yelp, several people noted that there was a cop to help with traffic. Scratch Brookline.

Next was CannaBliss, in Framingham, a small city west of Boston. Google Maps showed that CannaBliss was conveniently located by a highway exit, with a Red Roof Inn directly across the street. Customers noted that it had ample parking and polite staff. No cop.

Third time's the charm.

I spent a few months at the halfway house, working at the job they found me and coming in by nine thirty every night (lights out at ten). I cashed my paychecks, got my driver's license, and went to group therapy on Tuesdays and Thursdays. The day I left, I thanked the social worker and told him he'd never see me again. It made us both happy.

My first investment was a Buick clunker that I'd seen on the side of the road. I drove it to a strip mall where I got a used computer and a brand-new, top-of-the-line printer and scanner. Then I went straight to the Red Roof Inn in Framingham.

I loved it. The room was spotless, with a huge window and a big bed, all for me. No dorm-style sleeping like at the halfway house, and no Dougal snoring a few feet away. I mean, when I felt that carpet underfoot I felt like landed gentry, man.

Now I just needed two other guys to complete my gang.

The first one would be Anthony Harrison, because I liked the name. Anthony was going to rob CannaBliss.

The second was called Michael Johnson. After the robbery, he would deposit the funds in his bank account.

And the third guy? That was me, Gershom, sitting on top of the triangle like an invisible god. The excitement was like bubbles fizzing in my veins.

That night, I allowed myself three hours of sleep. The next night I did six, but I set an alarm every two hours and walked around for forty minutes each time. By the time the sun came up, I could barely see straight. The nearest Social Security office, a big brick-and-concrete block with an American flag out front, was a ten-minute drive. I got there at eight thirty, at which time there were already half a dozen people in line. By the time the doors opened at nine o'clock, there were maybe twenty-five, mostly behind me. I got to the clerk and started apologizing like crazy.

"My son was born at home ten months ago with a doula, and the pediatrician never filled out the paperwork for his Social Security card," I said. "Man, I am *so sorry*. But I have his birth certificate and immunization record." Which I did, and they looked really good. Like I said, I hadn't skimped on the printer.

The clerk scowled, and I saw her eyes flick to the line behind me. I clutched the counter. "I'm telling you, my wife deserves a superhero cape. She was in labor for—" shit, how long are people in labor? "—eighteen hours. No drugs, no nothing."

There was this superlong pause. Like, about a year. Then the clerk looked at me and my bloodshot eyes and my two-day scruff, and her face got all soft. "Bet she won't be so eager for a home birth next time," she said as she reached for my papers.

I kept her entertained while she filled out the forms. "God knew what he was doing when he made women, 'cause if us men had to give birth, the species would go extinct, like, tomorrow. Guys would be all, 'I have to do *what*?'"

That made her laugh. By the time we were done, she was my best friend. "Now go home and get some rest," she said, handing me my son's Social Security card. "It gets easier, I promise."

Which it did. I got back to the Red Roof Inn and slept for nine hours solid. Kids are exhausting, man.

When I woke up, I hopped online and signed up for credit cards with my new Social Security number. Pretty soon Michael Johnson had two Mastercards and a Visa on the way.

While that was percolating, I went to a nearby Staples with my temporary driver's license. This is the paper the DMV gives you while you wait for the permanent card to come in the mail. I had kept mine, and pasted "Michael Johnson" over my name in the same font as the original. Once I photocopied it, it looked very convincing.

The next morning, I drove to Wellesley to open a Century Bank account.

Wellesley is a couple towns over from Framingham, and I didn't want Michael banking too close to CannaBliss. Mainly, though, I appreciated the irony that Century was the only bank in Massachusetts that would do business with marijuana dispensaries, because they were about to get a ton of money from one such establishment.

Century Bank in Wellesley is an old-timey building with big trees out front. Opening Michael's account was a piece of cake, what with his temporary driver's license and Social Security card. A guy named William Edwards set up the account. He showed me how online banking and bill pay worked, and how I was eligible for benefits like EZ Pay Protection. When we were done, he handed me his card and said to ask for him if I ever had any questions. I put it in my pocket and walked out the door, feeling so excited my feet tingled with every step. The thrill was unbelievable.

Here I was, setting up the biggest score of my life, and the bank was *helping* me.

There's a Dunkin' Donuts directly next door to the Red Roof Inn. I got a Caramel Craze Signature Latte and half a dozen crullers, put a Do Not Disturb sign on my door, pulled up a chair and a pair of binoculars, and planted myself at my nice, bright window with its unobstructed view of CannaBliss.

Foot traffic was light but steady. Customers came to the door and flashed an ID, which I figured had to be a medical marijuana card. A few seconds later, they'd open the door and go in. This meant the door was locked from the inside, and someone was using a camera to check IDs. Probably bulletproof, too. So either I had to start ordering dynamite and anvils from Acme, or I needed a medical marijuana card.

This was where Anthony Harrison came into play.

Getting a medical marijuana card is a pain in the ass. First of all, you have to be sick. Mind you, here the state is very generous, and you can have anything from cancer to insomnia to AIDS.

Next, you need to exhaust all non-cannabis treatment options. Now that you've had plenty of time to get sicker, you ask your doctor to write a letter explaining that no known medicine has worked for you. If the first doctor won't do it, which is at best a fifty-fifty shot, you find one who will. Then you take the letter and your driver's license and $200 in, of course, cash, and go to *another* doctor and explain that you have cancer or insomnia or AIDS or maybe PTSD. If the doctor agrees with you—and honest to God, how do you prove that you have insomnia?—they give you a personal identification number. Now you hop onto the Cannabis Control Commission website, where you punch in your shiny new PIN and your Social Security

number, and pay another fifty dollars. Then you wait
a week or two till they mail you your card. By which
time if you have cancer instead of insomnia, you are
probably dead.

Fortunately, however, the Cannabis Commission is
much like the DMV, in that they will email you a temporary card as soon as you register. It's a piece of paper
with your picture and their logo on it.

I finished the crullers and drove to Newbury Street,
which is the part of Boston that shows up on postcards
and calendars. Half a block from the Public Garden
is a salon called Hair for You. It's brick, with a plate
glass window reflecting a stone church across the way.
A bell on the door dinged when I went in, and a lady
with wrinkly skin and a lot of scarves wafted over to
ask if she could help me.

"Oh, God, I hope so," I said. "I have cancer."

Her eyes got big and shiny, and for a second I was
afraid she was gonna cry. "Oh, no. I'm so sorry."

"Yeah, thanks. I start treatment next week, and they
say I'm likely gonna lose my hair. So…you got any
wigs?"

She blinked a few times and nodded. "Follow me."

Scarf Lady was very apologetic about the fact that
most of their wigs were for women, but hey, it's a sexist
world, right? I found one that was a mess of gray curls,
and tried it on in front of a mirror. I almost busted out
laughing, because for half a second I looked just like
Dougal. "This one's perfect," I said.

Scarf Lady was doubtful. "Really? It's nothing like
your natural hair."

True enough, since my hair is short and straight.
The wig made for a very different effect, which was
the point. In fact, given what I was going to use it for,

looking like Dougal seemed right on target, like giving credit where it's due.

I handed Scarf Lady the wig. "Well, ma'am," I said, trying to look noble, "I didn't ask for this disease, but I got it. This is a whole new part of my life, so I might as well embrace that with a whole new look."

Scarf Lady pressed her lips together, and her chin got all wobbly. "You are so *brave*," she whispered.

An hour later, after she and her staff showed me how to wear and style and wash my wig, and they'd packed it in a stripy box with lots of tissue paper and made me promise to stay in touch and let them know how treatment went, I got back in my car.

I stopped in West Newton and put on the wig before going into a CVS just off the highway. A few minutes later, I walked out with a bunch of ID pictures, since my wife and I were taking a second honeymoon in Tuscany and I needed a new passport.

Back at the Red Roof Inn, I got to work. Like I said, the printer was top-notch, and inside an hour I had a temporary medical marijuana card featuring the Cannabis Commission logo, a picture of me in the wig and the name Anthony Harrison. I'm telling you, the Commission itself wouldn't have known it from the real thing.

And yet, holding that flawless card, I felt a flash of fear. What if someone figured it out? If this went sideways, they'd lock me up and melt down the warden.

No. Couldn't happen. I'd created the perfect gang.

I put the card down, and took a deep breath. It was time for Anthony to stomp all over the Internet.

First off, I gave him an Amazon account and had him eyeball half a dozen books on marijuana and PTSD. He left some pretty snarky reviews. I reposted those on Goodreads, where Anthony created a page so he could follow his favorite authors, who mainly wrote military thrillers. I set up a Twitter account, which is wicked convenient for following the news and checking up on Kardashians. I also created a Facebook page with one of the extra CVS pictures, which I pasted against a backdrop of red maple leaves because New England is so beautiful in the fall. I sent out a couple dozen friend requests to people with lots of followers, figuring they'd automatically hit yes when they got Anthony's request. About fifteen did. Anthony was real pleased to meet them. He made a few political comments, and shared a picture of his birthday cake, which I copied from Pinterest. I gave him nephews in Florida, two kids with a golden retriever from a clipart site. Anthony was looking forward to seeing them over Thanksgiving. He even mentioned them by name, but they never responded. The little bastards.

I leaned back in my chair and smiled at the night sky outside my window. The next day, all my hard work was going to pay off.

CannaBliss is sandwiched between a dentist and a RE/MAX. It opens at 10 a.m. At 9:57 I parked facing the exit and got out. One other guy was in line, poking his phone.

Remember Willie Sutton, the guy who robbed banks because that was where the money was? Well, that's not what he really said. What he actually said was, "Why did I rob banks? Because I enjoyed it. I loved it. I was more alive when I was inside a bank, robbing it, than at any other time in my life." I tell you, on that bright, clear morning with the sound of the highway close by, the weight of a gun tucked at the small of my back, and that dispensary in front of me just about smoking with cash, I knew exactly how Sutton felt. Electricity surged through my bones, and I thrilled all over. I had a kick-ass plan and the balls to carry it out. I would never see the inside of a prison again. My old, loser self was dead.

"Gershom?" said a voice. "What the hell're you doing here?"

The other guy was staring at me. He was wearing a hat and cheap glasses, but I knew those squinty eyes and paunchy cheeks in a heartbeat.

"Dougal?" I gasped. "What the hell? You have, like, five more years." My head was spinning. "Holy shit—did you bust out?"

He grinned and punched my arm. "Me? Never. I wrote to my judge and said he should commute my sentence since marijuana's legal now. And damned if he didn't!"

I wished I had a wall to lean against, because the parking lot was starting to pitch and roll under my feet. So Dougal writes a letter, and the judge does an evidentiary hearing that consists of giving his butt a really lengthy scratch, and the next thing you know this dangerous criminal is out on the streets? My God, they will release *anyone* these days.

Dougal squinted at me. "What's with the wig? You look like a fucking idiot, I swear."

"Dougal, I'll tell you the truth." I put my hands on his shoulders. "I…got cancer, man."

Dougal stared at me. His piggy little eyes got hard. "Bullshit."

"Hell of a way to talk to a sick person," I said indignantly.

Dougal swatted my hands away and stepped too close, glaring through his drugstore glasses. "You don't have cancer. You have a plan. Gonna rob this place, aren't you? Bet you're packing."

"Hell, no." I was shocked at his attitude. And glad

my jacket hid the gun. "I'm a regular customer here. Weed helps with the chemo."

"Liar. You remembered what I said about disguises, and now you think you're going to hit this place. Well, guess what? This was *my* idea, this is *my* score, and you back—the fuck—off." He shoved my chest.

I stumbled. Anger rose in me, thick and hot. "Make me."

Dougal grinned and lifted his phone. "Hey, Siri. Call 911. Yeah, I'm at CannaBliss—"

I swatted the phone out of his hand, sending it spinning across the asphalt. Dougal laughed at me as he picked it up. "Relax, jackass. I was just fucking with you. Now piss off, or I'll tell your PO how you've been using your parole."

The speaker by the door chirped. "Good morning."

Dougal thrust a paper at it. The door opened, and suddenly I was alone in the parking lot.

"Sonofa—"

I whipped my card at the camera. The door clicked. I yanked it open. At the counter, Dougal was holding a gun on a scared-looking girl. "It's a beautiful day for a holdup, darlin'. Open the register and empty it into this bag."

I jumped across the room and grabbed Dougal's arm. I was going to kill him till he was dead. He spun around, face all twisted, and smashed the gun across my jaw. I fell on my ass. Dougal raised the gun again, and—

"Freeze!"

About fifty cops spewed through the door. Half of them jumped Dougal. The other half yelled at everyone to get their hands up. Boots thumped. Radios blared. Voices barked. A cop helped me to my feet. "Are you all right?"

You know that feeling when it's like someone shoved a stick of dynamite into your ear and blew your brain into a hundred thousand little gray chunks, and now they're all buzzing around inside your fractured skull trying to find each other? Well, until that moment, neither did I. My hands, which had shot into the air entirely of their own volition, lowered, trembling. "Yeah. I'm good."

"You shouldn't have tried to stop him on your own, sir. That's what we're for."

"Didn't know you were on your way," I mumbled. My jaw hurt like hellfire.

I looked around. The fifty cops turned out to be four. Two of them were squishing Dougal against a wall and cuffing him. One was talking to the girl. "Did you make the 911 call?"

"What 911 call?" she said.

"I'm going to need to see some ID," said the cop who'd helped me up.

"Ah…sure." I felt sick. There was no way out of this one. I didn't know how many laws I'd broken putting this job together, but if puking on a cop was a felony, they were about to add that to the list. Gershom McKnight, three-time loser, was about to go away forever. I put my hand in my pocket and felt a card.

A banking card.

Inspiration boiled up inside me like storm clouds ablaze with lightning. As smooth as my shaking hands would let me, I pulled the card out of my pocket and handed it to the cop.

"Edwards," I said. "William Edwards, Century Bank. These people have an account with us."

The cop turned to the girl at the desk. "Is that right, ma'am?"

"We do. Yes." She looked queasy. I knew the feeling.

I pointed at Dougal. "What's that knucklehead calling himself these days?"

The cop picked up the marijuana card Dougal had dropped in the excitement. "Gershom McKnight."

Son of a *bitch*. "Cute. His real name's Dougal Henshaw, late of MCI-Norfolk."

"Seriously?" The cop shook his head in disgust. "I swear, sometimes I wonder why we even bother arresting them."

I chuckled in sympathy. "There's more. This—McKnight, is it?—is registered at the hotel across the street. Check his computer. Looks like he was planning a string of these robberies. Our investigation indicates he has several false identities."

Dougal's jaw dropped.

The cop's eyes narrowed. "Investigation?"

I waved an airy hand. "Bank security. We've been keeping an eye on him for a while."

"You goddamn *motherf*—" began Dougal, which is when the two cops took him by the elbows and frogged him out of the room.

When finally they all left, I leaned against the counter, totally spent. The girl and I looked at each other. I could see the gleam of sweat on her forehead, and I could feel the cold from the evaporation of droplets on mine.

"That was too close for comfort," she whispered.

"No kidding." I pushed myself up. "What was it that guy said to you?"

She half laughed. "'It's a good day for a robbery.'"

"That's right." I pulled my gun and a bag from the small of my back. "Now just open the register and empty it into this bag, okay, darlin'?"

* * * * *

DO YOU REMEMBER

BY LORI ROY

You must be wondering why, after all these years, I decided to reach out. The short answer, the easy answer, is a new family moved into our old house. The Williamsons, who lived there for twenty-five years, never mattered much to me. But last year, the Giffords moved in, and they're the reason I can finally write.

Plenty of times, I thought to reach out, even sat down with pen and paper. When Grandma died, I considered it. You probably don't know she died. It's been a few years now. I wonder if it brings you joy to know she's dead. You probably hope it was a painful death, but it wasn't. She went peacefully in her sleep, though it was four days before anyone found her. A neighbor called about the smell. I suppose that gives you some pleasure.

We had a lovely funeral for her. My husband planned the entire thing, insisted, though I told him it wasn't necessary. I think he was afraid of the memories that might rattle loose if I had to select the casket or order a spray of flowers. I told him once I remembered lilies at Mama's funeral. They were her favorite. Do you remember? My husband made certain…no lilies at Grandma's funeral. He's thoughtful that way. He even managed to track down all her friends. I was her only family. And you, I guess, by marriage.

Did you know I got married? Oddly enough, you probably remember him. Harmond Bails. He grew up on Locust Street, lived a few houses down from us. He's a couple of years older than me and was all legs and arms back then and had a mop of dark hair that always hung in his face. Still does. He and I live in that house, the one where he grew up. Do you remember it? A two-story Craftsman. Nice lot. Good shade trees. Live oaks. Not laurels. If I walk onto the front porch and stand on the top step, I can see our old house. It still has a blue door, just like it had back then. It was nice to have the Giffords living there, even if only for a short time. Especially sweet Gabby Anne Gifford with her dark brown braids, milky skin and icy blue eyes. What happened to that family…a terrible shame.

The backyard was dark before, dark like everyone should be sleeping, but now it's light. Gabby Anne Gifford sits tall in bed to get a good look out her doors—Mama calls them French doors—but the drapes are closed. She sees only the fuzzy shadows of patio furniture and Daddy's grill. Soon after they moved into their new house on Locust Street, Daddy said raccoons were coming in the night to dig through their garbage, so he put up a security light to scare them away, but Gabby Anne doesn't think raccoons turned on the lights this time.

The French doors in Gabby Anne's room lead to the backyard and are always supposed to be locked—always, always, always—because there is a swimming pool back there. The first Saturday after they moved in, Gabby Anne began going to swim lessons because, in Florida, even the babies know how to swim. Daddy sometimes fusses at Mama because she opens those French doors to let in the fresh air and Florida sunshine and doesn't always remember to lock them again. Gabby Anne doesn't like it when Mama forgets, either. On Gabby Anne's second day at her new school, Arabella Hollingsworth told her a woman drowned in the swimming pool at Gabby Anne's new house. The woman's lungs puffed up and burst, squirting bloody guts into the water, and now, most likely, she is a ghost who lives in Gabby Anne's backyard.

As long as Daddy's security light is shining, Gabby Anne is safe. It will keep the raccoons away, but it will also keep the woman who died and squirted bloody guts from creeping through the backyard and rattling the knobs on Gabby Anne's French doors. She grabs hold of the yellow glow shining through the curtains by squeezing tight with all her fingers and toes, squeezing tight as she can. She waits, waits, waits but still, the light switches off. As her room tumbles from light to dark, she slides deep into her bed and closes her eyes.

A click makes her open them again. A puff of air chills her cheeks and ruffles her eyelashes. Next, the bed shakes, something bumping against it. Like a hip or a knee. Gabby Anne's heart pounds in her chest. Her throat turns dry. The tips of her fingers tingle. Fresh air, filled with the smells of outside, rushes into her room. The fluffy white gardenias that grow on the side of the house. The neighbor's grass he cut that morning. The chlorine Daddy pours in the pool. Gabby Anne tries to pull her knees to her chest, slowly at first, one at a time, but the sheets coil around her ankles and her bed won't let go. She wants to jump up and run as fast as she can to Mama's room. But the more she kicks, the tighter the sheets hold on. And then something tugs at her quilt.

Her legs stop moving. Her arms, too. Her breath catches in her throat and sticks there as the quilt falls away. Off Gabby Anne's shoulder, down her arm, across her waist. She grabs at it, gives a yank, and it stops. She gasps, air rushing in. Now someone is patting her quilt. Pat, pat, pat like when Mama loses the TV remote in her bed and pats her fluffy comforter until she finds it. The patting stops. The mattress dips. Gabby Anne tries to call Mama's name, but her voice is wedged deep down inside and can't get out. The patting is closer. Closer. Something brushes against her foot, disappears and comes back again. It stops. That same something lands on Gabby Anne's foot, her left foot. It tightens, slowly, slowly and then it grabs hold of Gabby Anne.

Tugging on a T-shirt as he fumbles with his glasses, Harmond Bails tiptoes from his bed to the window and pushes aside the drapes. Down below, Locust Street is dark except for the red and blue lights of a police siren flashing beneath a canopy of oak leaves. With each pulse of light, the moss dripping from the twisted branches shimmers. The eerie scene, so familiar, tugs at a memory. It tugs so hard that when Truvy switches on her bedside lamp, Harmond startles.

"What are you doing?" Truvy whispers, her voice raspy because she snores. Harmond teases her about it because it's cute, isn't it, when a beautiful woman with large blue eyes and glittery blond hair does it?

"It's nothing," Harmond says, hoping she stays in bed. He waves at her to turn off the light. "Really. Go back to sleep."

A click and the room falls dark again. Harmond

lets out a sigh of relief, and that's his mistake. Truvy knows. The mattress creaks as she crawls from the bed.

"What are you looking at out there?" she says, her tiny feet padding across the floor.

Harmond turns to her. With each splash of light from down below, she's one step closer. Her face is scrubbed clean, her yellow hair hangs loose and she wears one of Harmond's T-shirts. It dangles to her knees. She looks young, helpless, about to be broken. My God, he loves her, and Harmond's job, his most important job, is to protect her, something he can do only with the truth. He presses his shoulders back and puffs out his chest.

"I'm sorry," he says. "But it's the police. They're outside your old house. You probably shouldn't look."

"You're sweet to be concerned," Truvy says, the lights making her eyelashes flutter. "But it's never really felt like my house. Heck, I don't even remember living there."

Truvy was too young, or maybe too traumatized, to remember when she first lived on Locust Street, but Harmond remembers. He grew up in this house, and except for a few years away at college, he's always lived here. It's no wonder Truvy is fiercely independent and struggles to let Harmond in. She was only seven years old when police officers and reporters descended on her old house. Her grandma whisked her away as quickly as she could, but Truvy still saw the stretcher that rolled out the front door, her dead mother on board. No telling what something like that does to a person.

This might be the moment Truvy finally remembers. The scene is almost the same as it was all those years ago. The play of the lights on the oaks. The shuffle of dark silhouettes in and out of her old house. The yellow glow in every window as if all that warmth can smother the darkness of whatever has happened. Be-

cause Harmond knows these things, he extends a hand
to Truvy. With a deep, fortifying breath because maybe
she does realize how difficult this will be, she takes
it and huddles at his side. Through a web of sparkling
branches, they lean left and right, and look down on
the house Truvy lived in until she was seven years old.

On the Giffords' first night living in our old house,
I walked down the block with Harmond to greet them.
I took a peach pie with me because Harmond told me
they had a daughter. Seven years old, he said and stared
at me hard to see if her being seven troubled me. I
smiled. He was obviously worried about me being at
the old house again, even though I've told him on several occasions that I don't remember living there. I've
told him I don't remember him from those days, either.
And he believes me.

When I went to the store to pick out the peaches for
my pie, I spent fifteen minutes in the produce section.
I cupped each peach in my hand, gave it a toss, rolled
it side to side. It's what Mama always did. I didn't remember until I stood in front of the bin, the nearby re-
frigerated storage chilling my bare arms and legs. After
Mama filled a bag with a dozen or so, she'd always pick
one peach that was spongy, almost brown and hold it for
me to smell. I did the same when I bought my peaches,
and the light sweetness, something I hadn't smelled for
over twenty years, was like a fist to the gut. When I got
home, I let my peaches ripen in a paper bag and then
cut them into chunks. Not slices. That's how Mama always did it. Do you remember?

The pie pan was still warm when I carried it down
the block that night, and as we stood on the Giffords'
porch, I stared at the blue door. The gardenias were in
bloom. I smelled them. Crisp. Clean. Do you remem-

ber? Though I couldn't see them from the porch, I knew they were there, growing alongside the house, white blooms dripping from waxy green bushes. Out in the darkness, the cicadas hummed and clicked. Overhead, beetles bounced off the inside of the light shining down on us. And then the door opened, and I wavered, almost stumbled.

You must remember how the neighbors here cling to everything original in their 1920s Craftsman homes. So, when the door opened onto the Giffords' living room, the floors were the same as they were when we lived there. Strip pine that creaked when Harmond and I stepped inside. The same baseboards, so thick Mama dusted them every week, ran across every wall. The same Cuban tile stretched across the sunroom. Even the same hardware hung on every door—glass knobs with bronze backplates. The same glass knobs Mama touched. You touched. I wanted to feel that cool glass, ached to touch one of the knobs, but I knew doing that would give me away. Instead, I passed off the pie plate and shoved my hands in my pockets, and when a little girl bounded into the room, two braided ponytails bouncing off her shoulders, I smiled.

"You must be Gabby Anne," I said.

Harmond fumbles with the latch on the bedroom window and when it won't slide open, pounds on the frame. Truvy nudges him, and they sidestep to the next window where they have a better view. Across the street and two houses down, the door at the Giffords' place stands open, the light from inside draining out onto their sidewalk. Neil Gifford leans in the doorway with the same relaxed stance he strikes when smoking a cigarette. Neil's a smug son of a bitch and Harmond has known it since the Giffords first moved

in. But tonight, instead of sucking on the end of a Marl-
boro Light, Neil has one hand pressed to his forehead,
not watching as people come and go. Not so smug now.

Harmond flips the latch on the second window, and
this time it slides open a few inches. The cool, damp
air of dawn rushes in as he presses his ear to the opening. Something squawks, faint but unmistakable. Truvy
startles at the familiar sound of a police radio, and Harmond quickly closes the window.

"Sorry," he says.

Truvy stumbles away, the memory having tugged
at her like it tugged at Harmond.

"It really is the police," she says. "How long have
they been down there?"

"Don't know."

"It's familiar, isn't it?" she says, turning her back
on the window. "The radio, I mean. Am I right? Am I
remembering it from that night?"

"Can't say for sure," Harmond says. "But yeah, I
remember the radios. The lights, too."

Fighting the smile that wants to erupt across his
face, Harmond slides up behind Truvy, draws her into
his arms and buries his face in her hair. She smells
of soap and fresh sheets. He hates to admit it, even to
himself, but he waits every day for one of these rare
moments. There was the time she got the flu, the days
after her grandma died and the day more recently when
she learned her father was to be executed. She's always
first out of bed in the morning, runs three miles before
he's had his first cup of coffee and recently passed him
in the moneymaking department. Truvy says wanting
a man is better than needing one, but that's hard for
Harmond to believe. It's ingrained probably, the need
to be needed, so he can't stop the smile that wins out.
It spreads wide because despite what terrible thing may

be going on down at the Giffords' house, this is what Harmond needs.

"Better?" he asks, pushing her hair aside to rub his stubble against her neck.

Truvy nods. "Better." And this time, instead of a whisper, her voice is a purr.

Leading Truvy back to the bed, Harmond helps her to sit, but before he can climb on top of her, she presses a hand to his chest.

"You better go see what's going on," she says.

Linda Gifford and I became friends instantly. The day after Harmond and I took the peach pie to her family, she returned the plate. I knew she would. She had that look about her. Rosy skin. Blue eyes. Smooth, brown hair. Perfectly drawn pink lips. She was a woman who couldn't rest until a borrowed pie plate was washed, dried and returned. Gabby Anne tagged along, those same braided ponytails frayed and fuzzy one day later. After we enjoyed homemade chocolate chip cookies and sweet tea, I dug paint and poster paper out of the closet as if it had always been there and wasn't something I bought that same day. We spread it out on a plastic tablecloth, and Gabby Anne painted while Linda and I talked. Linda told stories of Gabby Anne's tantrums, funny now that she'd outgrown them. She talked about how she loved being pregnant and that she couldn't wait to have another baby. I told her I was hoping to get pregnant soon and that I'd be lucky to have a little girl as sweet as Gabby Anne. I went to bed happy that night, maybe for the first time. Ever. At least since the night Mama died.

Grandma carried me from our old house that night, did you know? She draped her sweater over my head so I wouldn't see everything going on around me. But it was a loose knit, so I could still see the flashing lights of the patrol cars and the people coming and going. Radios squawked, cameras snapped, car doors opened and slammed closed. Neighbors, too, had gathered on the street, all of them with hands pressed to their mouths because they'd heard by then. Mama had been found dead in the pool and you, Daddy, had been taken away in the back of a patrol car.

As Grandma carried me from the house, me seeing the outside through a web of white, wooly yarn, she whispered in my ear. "You'll be all right," she said. "I'm so sorry you had to see that. I'm so sorry you had to see what your father did." When we reached her car, Grandma slipped her sweater from my head and my view turned sharp and clear. Straight ahead, Harmond, my future husband, stood with his mother and father. They were a warm, happy family. Harmond looked at me, and I looked at him, looping myself around him so that eventually, one day, he'd pull me back. He tells me he remembers that moment and that maybe he's loved me ever since.

The damp morning air surprises Harmond when he throws open the front door. He shivers, glad he rarely sees this soggy time of day. Life's tough enough in the daylight. Slipping on a jacket, he pulls the door closed, hard. He wants Truvy to hear it up on the second story. Truth is, he's angry. No, he's pissed. This is how it always ends with her lately, although it isn't usually the flashing lights of a few patrol cars that derail his advances. It's Truvy jumping out of bed to strap on her running shoes or being too exhausted by a long afternoon spent with Linda and Gabby Anne. She's practically a single mother, Truvy is always saying of Linda. Even on the weekends, Truvy is up and out of the house before Harmond rolls over to discover her side of the bed empty. At this rate, they'll never get pregnant.

It wasn't always this way for Harmond. He had his share of women before Truvy. Sure, he wasn't what you'd call a ladies' man, but he was better than that. He was a catch. Taller than average. A head full of dark, floppy hair. And he was an educated man with a bright future. He was all those things when he and Truvy reunited on the University of Florida campus, and he's done all right for himself in the years since and has even better years ahead. Any woman would be happy to have Harmond. He needs to remember that, especially in times like this. He'll hustle down to the Giffords' to find out what's going on and then hurry back to bed before Truvy falls asleep. She'll be grateful, feel safe because of him, and she needs that. Needs it more than anything. And just as he thinks he might still have a chance with her, the lights at the Stratton house pop on across the street, and he's not in such a hurry.

Wearing a silky white robe, Julia Stratton sweeps out her front door. Her long blond hair glows under the porch lights that have started to turn on, and as she drifts weightlessly across her lawn, Harmond wonders if she dresses that way every night. Yes, he decides. Most definitely, yes. Maybe he'll buy Truvy a night-gown like Julia's. Yes, he thinks again. He steps off the curb and follows Julia toward the Giffords' house.

"Can you believe it?" Julia whispers when Harmond slides up alongside her. She looks a good bit like Truvy but is…what…softer. Yes, her voice is softer, and her hand, when she brushes it across Harmond's forearm, is warmer. She's easier, too. Always smiling.

"What happened?" he asks. "Do you know?"

Julia smells nice, like a flower. He inhales and

thinks he might ask what kind of perfume she's wearing so he can buy some of that for Truvy, too.

"Don't know yet," Julia says, not looking his way but instead lifting onto her toes for a better view of the Giffords' house. "There's Neil."

Stretching higher, she grabs Harmond's shoulder for balance and reaches one arm overhead, the sleeve of her white, silky robe slipping down as she waves at Neil.

"He sees us," she says. "Yes, he's coming over."

Neil Gifford, wearing basketball shorts and a white T-shirt walks toward them. It's what he normally wears, but something is different. It's his eyes. They aren't focusing and his movements are slow, as if his arms and legs are too heavy for him to maneuver.

"Jesus Christ," Neil says. He blows out a long breath that smells of whiskey and falls into Julia's arms.

Julia cups his head with one hand and lays the other on his chest. This isn't the first time they've embraced. She knows exactly how to slip into the crook of his arm, and he knows exactly how to burrow into her silky hair. All the rumors are true. Harmond has heard them from a few of the neighbors, even told Truvy about them. After all, Neil's wife is Truvy's best friend. Men like Neil, they shouldn't get away with it, and if he's gotten himself into some trouble, well, he deserves it.

"What is it?" Julia says. "Dear God, Neil. What's happened?"

When I first learned of the new family, the strangers, who would move into our old house, I was worried. Before they came along, the house was always quiet, kept to itself because an old couple with no children lived there. I never had to think about it. But as the Giffords toted boxes and tubs from the moving van to our old house, I knew it would begin to breathe again.

We'd hear splashing from the swimming pool, bicycles creaking, little girls giggling. But within a few months of the Giffords' arrival, my worries disappeared. Yes, things changed. They planted flowers, replaced the concrete sidewalk with pavers, rolled out new sod. But what I hadn't expected…the house's quickened pulse was contagious. The hustle and bustle of the Gifford family crowded out the heavy past that had been allowed to fester in our old house and inside me for more than twenty years.

I began to think of Linda and Gabby Anne first thing every morning. The plans I made with them shaped my days, weeks and months. I'd hurry home from work to meet them at the park, spent evenings at soccer games and dance recitals, and on Tuesdays, I ducked out early to pick up Gabby Anne from school as a favor to Linda. Those Tuesdays were most precious to me. When I would lean over Gabby Anne to buckle her in my backseat, I'd feel her warm skin. I'd smell Chapstick and sunscreen and the grass she'd run through and the pages of the workbooks she'd written in. I'd close my eyes as all the makings of Gabby Anne's childhood leached into mine, replacing all my bad with her good.

I was inside our old house almost every day, and inside my old room at least once a week when, on date night, I babysat Gabby Anne. I stopped thinking of it as our old house, and it became the Giffords' house. I even found the courage to tell Linda what happened to me as a child. She hugged me, said she already knew and insisted I throw open the French doors in Gabby Anne's room that had been locked up tight the night Mama drowned. Back then, I couldn't reach to unlock them, couldn't reach to unlock any of the doors. They were designed that way to keep me safe from the pool. Instead, they meant I couldn't save Mama. Linda thought by my throwing open those doors, I would regain the control I lost that night, the control you took from me. And then...

"Too bad Neil is such an ass," Harmond said one night when we lay in bed.

Even before he said anything else or explained anything more, my happy world, the one I'd wrapped myself in for a few short months, collapsed.

"He's screwing around. Poor Linda. Doesn't suspect a thing."

Staring at Julia as she strokes Neil's hair, Harmond wishes he were the one Julia held in her arms and that it was his hair she stroked. As much as he needs to be needed, he needs that, too. To be loved and touched. But the squawk of a police radio snaps him out of it and regret takes over. He regrets thinking he might buy Truvy a white nightgown. Regrets thinking he might ask Julia the name of her perfume. That's not who Harmond is. He's one of the good guys. Not perfect, sure, but good. In case any of the neighbors are watching, he shakes his head as a sign of his disapproval and when he turns to walk away, Neil glances up from his cozy spot in Julia's arms.

"Gabby Anne's gone," he says.

"Gone?" Julia says. "Gone where?"

"No," Neil says. "She's...gone."

"You don't mean?" Julia asks.

"The pool," Neil whispers. "God damn Linda. She leaves that door open. All the fucking time, I'm telling her to quit leaving it unlocked."

"The French doors?" Julia says. "Is that what you mean?"

Neil nods. It's something they've talked about before, and if they've talked about Gabby Anne's doors, they've talked about other inside moments from the Giffords' marriage.

"She left them open again?" Julia asks. "Oh, my God. Neil, no."

"Jesus," Harmond says. "Right out of her bedroom?"

Julia swings around. "What do you mean?"

"I'm just shocked, is all," Harmond says. "This happening right here on our own street. Someone taking her from her own bedroom?"

Without any warning, Neil's knees give out beneath him. Harmond lunges, catches him by one arm and softens his landing on the curb.

"Jesus," Neil says. "You think someone did this? Went in her room? Why? Who would…"

"I… I don't know," Harmond says, his eyes jumping between Julia and Neil, both staring at him. "You said it. You said her door was left unlocked. I just thought you meant…"

"He meant, with the door unlocked, Gabby Anne could get to the pool. She's not a strong swimmer, isn't allowed." Julia peels herself from Neil and steps toward Harmond. "Do you know something, Harmond? Was someone in her room?"

"What," Harmond says. "No. You're twisting my words. I just misunderstood."

"What do you know?" Julia says.

"I don't know anything. Jesus. I'm… I'm just so sorry, Neil." Harmond continues to back away. "You said the door was unlocked. Jesus, I'm so sorry."

Julia leans in to get a good look into Harmond's eyes.

"I've heard about you, Harmond Bails," Julia says, backing away.

"Heard what about you?"

Harmond turns. It's Truvy. She's wearing a sweat-shirt and a pair of jeans. Her hair has been brushed out and tied back, making her look like a college student again.

"What's Julia talking about?" she says. "And where's she going?"

Julia now stands at the barricade of yellow tape and is talking to a police officer. Scanning the crowd of neighbors, she points a finger directly at Harmond.

"I don't know," Harmond says to Truvy. "It's Gabby Anne. I think she's... I think she drowned."

"Well, whatever it is," Truvy says, taking Harmond's hand, "she's talking to the police, and she's talking to them about you."

Neil Gifford meant nothing to me before I found out about his affair. He wasn't part of what was wonderful about the Gifford house. He was the property you never buy, the piece on the board you never move. And yet he was able to so quickly ruin everything. Our old house sank back into the past once I knew Neil was a cheat and a liar. Because you, Daddy, were a cheat and a liar. And as the house sank, it became our house again, not theirs. It became my bedroom and not Gabby Anne's. I could feel the weight of the drapes on the French doors when I pushed them aside the night Mama died. I was too young to know why you were never home and why I'd see Mama crying by the pool and drinking red wine. But all those things were true that night. I was too young to know about loneliness and sorrow. I was too young to know Mama needed you, but I was old enough to know you weren't there.

I never liked when Mama turned on the pool lights after dark. They made the water glow and the pool bottom disappear, and when Mama stripped down to nothing and dove in, the water cracking open and sucking her under, I worried she'd never come back. So many nights, I watched as she did just that. I'd wait at my French doors, forcing my eyes to stay open, until she climbed out, wrapped herself in a towel and went inside. But that night, something was different. I wasn't sure at first what I saw outside the French doors. I stood on my tiptoes and rattled the knobs, but Mama, unlike Gabby Anne's mother, was always careful to keep the doors locked. I was never allowed outside by myself because the pool was dangerous. I hopped up and down to get a better look. Something was floating, the lights from beneath making its underside glow.

I snuck out of my room even though I wasn't allowed. That's how scared I was. I tried every door, but they were all locked. I couldn't get outside, not even when I stood on a chair and knew it was Mama floating out there in the pool. I rattled knobs, banged on doors. There were no glittery ripples in the water. Her arms didn't sway in circles like they did when she glided from one end of the pool to the other. Her feet didn't flutter like they did when she kicked down to the bottom and exploded back to the top. She was still. The water's surface, lifeless.

Harmond trails Truvy toward Julia and the police officer.

"Here," Julia says, as Harmond and Truvy approach. "Look how brazen."

The officer is young, and his eyes are red, as if he's not yet accustomed to these long nights and early mornings.

"What is it you're telling me, ma'am?" the officer says.

"I'm telling you I think this man knows something

about what happened to Gabby Anne," Julia says, jabbing a finger at Harmond.

"That's not true," Harmond says.

"Even his own wife is afraid of him," Julia says. "Just ask her."

Harmond swings around to face Truvy. "Afraid of me? What…"

"Oh, Harmond," Truvy says. She steps away from Harmond and toward Julia. "Is that where you went? Why you weren't in bed?"

"What?" Harmond says as neighbors begin to close in on the conversation. "What do you mean, where I went?"

"He wasn't in bed," Truvy says to the officer. "For the longest time. And then I must have fallen asleep. I don't know. But when I woke, he was back and looking out the window. And there are clothes, wet clothes and shoes, too, in our shower."

"Do you hear this?" Julia says to the officer, slipping an arm around Truvy's shoulders. "Are you going to do something? Anything? My God, he took Gabby Anne. Drowned her."

"That's not true," Harmond says. "None of that."

Truvy clings to Julia. "What will I tell Linda?" Truvy says. "I should have known, should have seen this coming. I should have warned her."

Harmond backs away, keeping his eyes on Truvy. She's coiling up, preparing to strike again.

"That's not true." Harmond shakes his head and jabs a finger at Truvy. "Truvy, she's the one. There's something wrong with her. She didn't even care when her grandmother died. I did everything for the funeral. She didn't even want to go. And when her own father died…"

"Do you see?" Truvy says to the officer. "He's come

unhinged. I've been telling Linda for weeks now. Linda, that's poor little Gabby Anne's mother. I've been telling her something wasn't right. I've been afraid even. Afraid of Harmond. He's obsessed with me, my past. My mother, she died in this house, did you know? My father killed her. It's been the most horrible thing. My father was executed for it. And ever since, Harmond, he's been...well...troubled. Ask Linda. I've been telling her for weeks."

That's where you found me, standing on a chair, looking out onto the pool, banging on the glass. Do you remember? I was screaming. My hair hung in my face, wet, matted. My cheeks were streaked with tears. You grabbed me, frightened just to see me like that, and then you saw Mama. And then Grandma was whispering in my ear.

"I'm so sorry you had to see your daddy do that," Grandma whispered as she tucked me in the backseat of her car.

She knew the same as me. She knew all the nights you left Mama home alone. All the lies. All the excuses. She knew about the yelling and drinking and sadness. She knew how the sneaking and lying dirtied up everything. You made us all sticky to the touch. Made us want to wipe our hands of each other. But mostly, the loneliness. We both knew you should have been there to save Mama.

"Yes," I whispered back. "I saw what Daddy did."

"He was terrible to her," Grandma said once we were in the car, cushioned from the outside noises. "He was never home for you. He was never home for her. That's why she's dead. You saw him hold her under. That's what you saw, yes?"

I nodded and blinked as the red and blue lights spun past. "Yes, Grandma. I saw."

"Show me how again," she whispered.

I stretched out my fingers as wide as they would go and touched my hand to my face. I did the same for the judge in a courtroom. Do you remember?

"And he held her down," I whispered back. "All the way under."

I thought I was done punishing you and that the Gifford family was the thing to finally cure me of my past. I was happy again because Gabby Anne was happy. But that changed when I learned about Neil. I realized you hadn't suffered enough. Not nearly enough. Gabby Anne died because her daddy was just like you.

I wonder sometimes…who will next move into our old house. They'll be strangers for sure, at least when they first arrive on Locust Street. Linda and Neil are getting a divorce, or so I hear. I live alone now. The house is far too big for one person. Harmond won't ever be coming back. But I'll stay because I can step onto the front porch and see the door at our old house. It's still blue. Do you remember?

* * * * *

ASSIGNMENT: SHEEPSHEAD BAY

BY PAUL A. BARRA

Percy Fletcher let the lines go just before noon and watched the falling tide ease *Double Tap* into the stream. He inched the throttles forward, beginning his voyage down the coast to a place in New York called Sheepshead Bay.

The big Hatteras was an easy handling boat built for blue water sailing, with more power than anyone could ever need. She was Fletcher's home, facilitating his peripatetic life as an assassin for hire. Registered in Beaufort, where he was born, the sport fisherman berthed in ports large and small, up and down the eastern seaboard, sometimes for a day, other times overwintering, and was now maneuvering through an anchorage in Gloucester, Massachusetts, before settling in for a run through light seas at twenty knots.

Sitting next to him, Ethyl was nearly as tall in the seat as her master. Trained as a guard dog, the giant schnauzer seemed to be enjoying the sea time, scenting the air and tracking birds.

Fletcher sailed due east across deep shoals and then south to skirt the Cape and Nantucket Island. At this comfortable speed, he figured she sucked in sixty-five gallons of diesel an hour. He had a contract with a man named Smirnov that would make the trip worthwhile. Smirnov wanted an operative from out of town, and was willing to pay for the advantage. Percy Fletcher was from out of town, no matter where the town was located.

The *Double Tap* roared south, ducking in to come up under Montauk. He slowed her after dark and cruised the ocean shore of Long Island westward into Brooklyn.

By midmorning they made the city piers in Sheepshead Bay where he had a reservation. He parked her and went ashore to take Ethyl for a walk. A misty rain had started by the time they got back to the marina. A man in a yellow slicker was standing by his boat.

Cognizant of the size of his dog, Fletcher stopped without getting close. The visitor was a big-chested guy, not too tall, not too young. He needed a shave and his face glistened in the weather.

He pointed a stubby finger at Ethyl. "What's that?"

"A dog."

"Funny man. You own this boat?"

"Yes, sir, I do. You want to buy her?"

"Not me, but maybe my friend. Can I see it?"

"I just now got in and haven't cleaned up yet, but you're welcome aboard."

"Don't worry. We ain't buying clean."

Fletcher sat Ethyl in the stern sheets and took the man for a tour. He asked a few questions about the boat, looked in cupboards, ran the sink water, flushed the toilets. He did not ask for a test run. After maybe fifteen minutes, they sat in the cabin and drank bottled water. Offering the *Double Tap* for sale was the gambit Fletcher and Smirnov had agreed on to establish their mutual bona fides. He just had to find out if this man was the contact he was looking for or some guy wanting to actually buy a luxury open-water boat.

"This is a nice boat, Mr…?"

"Fletcher. Percy Fletcher."

"Percy, huh? Never knew a guy by that name before. Your mother musta had a sense of humor. Or maybe she knew you'd grow into a big fella."

Fletcher said nothing.

The man cleared his throat. "I'm Peter Rossman. My boss is interested in buying a boat, for fishing and, er, whatever. We saw your ad in the *Eagle* yesterday."

"Why doesn't your boss come by and see it for himself? This here's a big investment."

"He's a very busy man. I'm like his first line of defense, y'know? I see it and like it, he comes to take a look too. If it was junk, he doesn't have to bother himself."

When Rossman left, Fletcher went out to Ethyl, who was still sitting in the mist, water droplets on her dense coat blinking in the hazy light like sea sparkle in the night off Bimini. He rubbed her down with a towel and brought her inside. She stayed in the cabin while he went to dinner in the early twilight.

Some of the restaurants along Neptune Avenue had Cyrillic letters on their signs, but he chose one called The Silk Road Inn because it offered lamb. Unlike most Southerners, he liked the meat.

It was fragrant inside. Icons edged in gold paint decorated the walls and a sort of tinkling Asian-Fusion music, lutes and flutes with violin background, drifted through the place, along with the smells of cumin and other spices he couldn't identify. He stood on the mosaic tiles of the foyer until a girl came out of a back room and saw him. Her pleasant face burst into a smile.

"Hi, there. Sorry I didn't notice you."

"Is it too early to eat, ma'am?"

"Around here, mister, it's never too early to eat."

The place filled slowly, so the noise level had risen above the music by the time he was finishing his *lagman*, a noodle dish with carrots and onions floating in broth, and a crispy lamb roll. His waitress had a distinctively flat Turkic cast to her features, as did many of the customers.

"You like your food, big man?"

"I did. It's delicious, and cooked to perfection."

"So how come you don't finish?"

"I got to save some for my dog."

She laughed. "Okay. Maybe you will have a midnight snack, yes? I'll put the rest in a box for you."

He was counting out money for his bill when the restaurant quieted suddenly. He looked up and saw what had caused the chatter to diminish. Two men walked in, pushing chairs aside and scowling at the people. A slim waiter moved to greet them, but the man in front put up a meaty palm. The waiter stopped and stepped back. They came to Fletcher's table and stood there, looking down on him. The waiter watched them.

The man who led the invasion—if that was what it was—looked decidedly unfriendly. His bowling ball head was welded to a neck as thick as the bollard to which the Hatteras was tied. Muscled arms jutted from his chest, ending in hands like welding gloves. Huge slabs of more muscle ran down his front. The man's black eyes looked hard at Fletcher, not blinking. He began flexing his fingers.

But it was the man with him who spoke. His voice

was quietly modulated. "Mr. Smirnov wants to see you, pal."

This one had black hair, slicked back and curling around the collar of a cashmere suit jacket. Fletcher thought he looked like Billy Martin, the Yankee second baseman who had been Mickey Mantle's best friend. He nodded at Billy and followed him out. Bowling Ball went behind them. Fletcher saw him glance at the bills he'd left on the table, but he didn't reach for them.

The Brooklyn evening had gotten cool, but neither of his escorts seemed to notice. "We walking?"

Billy said, "Yeah. It's not far."

They started off, but spun around like tap dancers when the restaurant door banged open. The waitress rushed out, holding something in her hand.

"You forgot your—"

Bowling Ball slapped Fletcher's doggie bag from her and shoved her back toward the door. The waitress squealed in surprise. He snarled, "Get back in your cave, you weegee cunt."

Fletcher didn't like his action or the slur, and said so. He didn't know what a weegee was, except that it was some sort of insult the way the goliath spit it out. Before he could engage with the bald mountain, Billy Martin jumped between them.

"No, no, Yuri, let it go. This is Mr. Smirnov's guest."

Yuri swept the smaller man aside as if he were a bothersome horsefly. Martin stumbled, looked as if he was about to go down; Fletcher caught his arm and held him up.

As he was saving Billy Martin from a fall, Yuri swung at his face. It was as if he'd been waiting for the opportunity to wreak some damage; or maybe he just didn't like Fletcher calling him chowderhead after he'd assaulted the waitress. Either way, he was going to pound this tall dink-lover with the fancy boat.

Yuri moved with surprising quickness, punching as if he were in a shot-putting event. The punch bounced off Fletcher's shoulder as he was turned toward Billy Martin. Even the poorly aimed blow rocked Fletcher and brought him up to his toes. He came down, set his feet.

The Russian bore in, but his aggression didn't get any further. Fletcher confronted him quickly, snapping a straight left to the end of the wide man's nose. Fast hands are more important than bulk in a street fight, and Percy's hands could fly. Yuri roared as his fleshy nose turned sideways to his face with the sound of cartilage rupturing. He was momentarily blinded by pain. Fletcher twisted his weight into a right cross through the blindness that dropped the hefty Russian.

It felt like hitting a fastball on the sweet spot, but the sound of the punch was the wet thwack of a cannonball thudding into a fibrous palmetto log. As Bowling Ball fell, Fletcher whirled to Billy Martin. The smaller man had made no move to interfere. His hands were open in front of him, a peace sign. Yuri was down, mouth open and eyes rolled up in his head.

Fletcher stepped toward the storefront and picked up the cardboard container. He brushed it off and spoke to the waitress, now flat against the door.

"Thanks for bringing this out to me. My pooch will appreciate it."

He smiled at her. She stood flat against the door of The Silk Road Inn with her eyes wide and her mouth open. She nodded and darted back inside. Bowling Ball was still on the sidewalk; one foot was twitching and blood ran from his nose. Fletcher and Billy left him there and walked on. An older couple coming from the other direction went out on the street to avoid the human lump on the sidewalk. The husband raised his smartphone and took a picture of BB's downfall.

Fletcher asked Billy, "What was that all about? She's a weegee?"

"Yuri Vasilek doesn't like anyone who is not a white Russian. The girl is a Uighur, from central Asia. He hates them even more if he cannot pronounce their name."

They walked a few minutes longer, Billy Martin looking back twice at the heap that was his earlier companion. The street turned to Emmons Avenue, and the bay appeared on their right. Billy's heels clicked on the concrete.

They came to a restaurant across the road from the water. It was called the Ekaterina, and was so garish Fletcher wondered if it had been designed in Bollywood, all reds and golds and flashing colored lights, picture windows with brightly painted figures of Cossacks on white horses and women in silk robes to either side of a double door made to look like a gilded gate. In front stood a junior Bowling Ball in pantaloons and a bright blue vest. His arms were folded in front of him, but he opened the gate smoothly when he saw Billy.

Inside was an oasis. The decor was as ugly as the frontage, but the interior was otherwise calm, with textured walls and thick red carpeting. Classical music played.

They walked past full tables to a circular booth in the back. Billy slid into the booth and spoke in Russian to a thin man in a suit who sat with Peter Rossman. The thin man's eyebrows went up as he listened.

The thin man gestured to Fletcher and said, "Please have a seat."

Fletcher pulled a chair from a nearby table and sat,

putting his go-box in front of him. The thin man looked at the container as if Fletcher had spit on the tablecloth, but said nothing. He pulled the last clam from a silver salver of shells and sucked it down. A waiter in black with gold braids on his sleeves nipped in and removed the tray.

"I am Andrey Smirnov. I am interested in your boat, but I did not expect to have my associate assaulted when he came to invite you to dinner."

"I've eaten already, thanks."

"You are not going to assault me?"

Smirnov looked unconcerned when he spoke. Fletcher thought he probably had a few more Bowling Balls watching his table.

"I reckon a man with enough class to play ol' Rimsky-Korsakov in his restaurant can't have violence on his mind."

Smirnov smiled and moved his chin toward the speakers. "Nikolai and I share the same patronymic, Andreyevich. I'm happy you appreciate Russian music. Maybe you and I can be friends, after all. Eh, what do you think?"

"That would be fine with me, but we don't have to be friends to do business. That's why God made lawyers."

Smirnov laughed. He patted his lips with a cloth napkin. Dropping the napkin, he waved a hand, and the four men were suddenly alone in the table's alcove.

Nevertheless, the host spoke in a lowered voice. "I hope the incident tonight does not compromise your, er, mission. Yuri won't bother you again, believe me."

"I hope he does."

Smirnov and his two associates looked at each other. When they turned back to Fletcher, their smiles looked tentative. Was this stranger more than they had bargained for?

Fletcher spoke to Smirnov. "We have a contract and I intend to fulfill it."

Smirnov nodded. Peter Rossman and Billy Martin left them. Alone with the assassin, the Russian man told him about his target, a man Fletcher would recognize. They agreed to a financial arrangement: $100,000 for the hit, a Zelle transfer as soon as Smirnov had verification he was dead. Their contract was verbal only, first communicated with temporary phones that had since been disposed of, and finalized now with no witnesses. The names Percy Fletcher and Andrey Smirnov may even have been aliases, for all the other man knew.

Fletcher left him and returned to his boat. Ethyl liked the lamb leftovers Fletcher brought for her. He didn't tell her how much trouble they had initiated.

The next morning, he put the leash on Ethyl and walked down the pier and along the bay. Small groups of men wearing yarmulkes and speaking a guttural language walked uptown and crossed under the elevated subway tracks. Fletcher followed one group into a diner called Linda's.

The dog sat close to his chair in her sphinx pose. A waitress came over to the side away from Ethyl and placed a plastic menu on the table.

"You want I should read it to you?"

"I'm sorry now?"

"You must be a blind man, seeing's you brought a dog into an eating establishment. I figure you can't see the menu, I could read it to you."

She was a heavyset woman with a shiny forehead and her hair pulled into a kind of black bandana. She wore a short apron over jeans. The way she pronounced *dog* made it sound like a French vulgarity, but her attitude was friendly so Fletcher smiled at her.

"Thank you, ma'am, but I don't need a menu. I'd like four eggs, scrambled, with sausage, a double order of corned beef hash and cheese grits."

That brought a big grin to her round face.

"This may be South Brooklyn, buddy, but it ain't hardly the South. Not a grit in the joint. I can give you toast. White, wheat or rye. A bagel with seeds or no. Or maybe a bialy with a schmear? You'd probably like that. Coffee?"

"Please."

The bialy turned out to be a sort of bagel with chopped onions where the hole should have been. The schmear was cream cheese. He liked it; so did Ethyl. The woman came back to clear his table. The men he had followed in were speaking loudly enough to be overheard. Fletcher thought New Yorkers talked as if everyone wanted to hear their conversations.

"What're those fellas speaking?"

She looked at the corner table over her shoulder. "Russian with some Yiddish thrown in, I think. They're Russian Jews. Come in here every Saturday morning before temple."

"You think they know a guy named Yuri Vasilek?"

She glanced at him quickly and looked away. "Maybe you should ask them."

She went over to the men and spoke to them, pointing at Fletcher. One of them waved him over.

"Funny thing," he said, "we were just talking about Yuri. You know him?"

"I met him last night."

Another man sat up straight. He had an idea. "Where you staying?"

"I'm living aboard my boat."

"Hey! That flashy white one?"

He nodded.

"We seen it there. What a beauty. Peter Rossman told me some guy come down in that big-ass boat, gonna sell it to the boss. That true?"

That was the cover story he and Smirnov had concocted, so Fletcher admitted to it. The speaker snapped his mouth shut and widened his eyes as the link between the out-of-town boat arriving and Yuri being beaten by a stranger occurred to him. The table grew quiet. Fletcher looked at the men and could see fear on their faces. One of them spoke in a low voice.

"You decked Yuri last night?"

Fletcher nodded as the waitress came by to heat up their coffee, unaware of the tension at the table. She patted Fletcher on the back, happy he had made some friends. They waited until she left to mention Yuri again.

The first man, Georgy Petrov, looked at his two friends and apparently received some sort of silent permission. He spoke quietly.

"We have a major problem with Yuri Vasilek."

"I imagine you do," Fletcher replied. "I got the impression he's a bully."

"He's more than that. He's a fucking terrorist." Petrov growled when he said that, his face red and spittle flecking his lips. He took a breath and went on.

"He'll come in here to eat, staring at us, like. Daring us to even look back at him. Then he walks by and drops his check in front of us."

"You pay it?"

"Got to. We don't, and next thing you know something bad happens to one of us. A car gets broken into. A fire on a front stoop. One time, Sammy Mirzayanov's son finds his bedroom window open and a rat sitting on his bed eating a raw chicken neck. Sammy goes to talk to Yuri and gets two teeth knocked out.

"And that ain't all. He walks down the avenue and we got to step out of his way. We don't, he claims assault and pushes us around. Russian men don't like that kind of shit, y'know?"

"I can't think anyone would like it."

The men looked at their table, brooding. Petrov spoke again.

"We're happy you beat Yuri up, but I'm afraid we're going to pay for it. He's going to be ramming around here like a maniac after being embarrassed."

"I'm sorry for your troubles. If you do see the mutt, tell him I'm looking for him."

Fletcher left and walked down Emmons again.

Billy Martin was waiting by the gilded gate of the Ekaterina. "You got time for a quick ride, *bolshoy chelovek*? Something I want to talk to you about."

He blinked a new Buick to life. It was an aerodynamic station wagon the Russian drove like an Italian rally racer. Seven minutes after dropping the dog off at the boat, they stopped by the aquarium in Coney Island and the two men got out. They walked past a long concrete wall that Fletcher realized was actually a sculpture depicting the evolution of the sea or something. They sat on a bench in the sun and watched some folks making the most of an early ocean-side visit, sitting in the sun, walking in the shallows. One potbellied man was working a metal detector along the high tide line.

"It seems so peaceful out here, doesn't it?" Fletcher detected pessimism in the man's voice.

"You saying things are not as they seem?"

"Yeah. I'm afraid that's just what I'm saying."

The man resembled Billy Martin even more in the mood that had taken him. Martin, for all his brilliance as a manager of major league teams, was often beset with nihilism, doubt. Fletcher hoped this Russian wasn't going to react as violently as the real Martin often had when he was in the grip of his anxieties. He sat and waited.

"It's Yuri."

"Yuri? The ape-man with the bowling ball for a head?"

Martin allowed himself a smile, but his heart wasn't in it. "I'm afraid he's gone rogue, Percy. You must take care."

"What has he done?"

"Well, first off, someone reports him lying on the sidewalk last night, thinking maybe he's dead. By the time the cops arrive he's awake, screaming, throwing punches and everything. He's covered in blood, so the cops arrest him. I hear that wasn't easy. He spends the night in the drunk tank up on Ocean Avenue, but he never had even one drink. He was so frustrated by you ruining his reputation, in his mind, that he lost it. His mind."

"That's bad, Billy."

The man didn't react to the name.

"It gets worse. This morning, they set his nose, which you broke. So he's running around with a big metal brace or something, black eyes, swollen face. Not a happy Rooski."

Fletcher had learned that some people turn inward after getting hurt for acting uncivilized; others plot revenge. According to Billy Martin, Bowling Ball wanted only to get back at Fletcher.

"This fella works with you?"

"Not really. Andrey—Mr. Smirnov—hires him once in a while, for guard duty, like. I'm sure he now wishes he never had."

Yuri's conversations with the normal associates of Smirnov were brutally brief, he said, and rarely refined. Yuri had seen Fletcher arrive in the Hatteras and go into the Uighur restaurant, and had led the way to summon him to dinner at the Ekaterina in order to point out the place.

"He claimed he didn't know the name of the restaurant where you were eating, so he was my guide. I now think he went looking for trouble."

"With the Uighurs, or with me?"

"Could be either one. Like I told you, he doesn't care much for Asians—or African Americans or the Spanish, for that matter. But he also doesn't like big guys walking around his neighborhood, thinks he needs to be the toughest guy on the block. That sort of thing."

"Sounds like a plague on y'all."

"You got that right. Yuri has been banned from The Russian Weight Room, where some men go to beast it up, because he was seen injecting himself in the locker room. Steroids, likely. The cops know him, but they don't get many complaints. Russian men are macho guys, y'know what I mean? But I think they're all afraid of Yuri. He goes around like he owns the town, taking things from stores, breaking into lines… Stuff like that. It's easier just to let these things go by. Then you got less trouble. Andrey probably fired him after the incident with you and the waitress at the Silk Road, but someone saw him a little while ago, outside the Uighur restaurant."

"He looking for me, you think?"

"I think so. He gets his confidence back, he could come to the Ekaterina thinking he can push other people around. Then we're going to have trouble once he finds out he's been fired."

"That's the problem with having a mad dog in your house—sooner or later it's going to attack its master."

"True," Billy Martin said. "Funny you should say

that, because Yuri is supposedly deathly afraid of dogs. He probably won't bother you when you have Ethyl with you."

They walked up the boardwalk to Paul's Daughter and ate hot dogs and sauerkraut while standing in the sun and the salted onshore breeze. The sausages popped when they bit into them, a burst of simple pleasure. It was too cool for the beach, but people walked and waded anyway, taking their simple pleasures where and when they could get them. He had heard that some of the Russians in Little Odessa, as Brighton Beach is sometimes called, actually swam this time of year. He shivered at the very idea.

"You cold, Percy?"

"No. I'm just amazed at you Russian guys. Tough like that—and putting up with a bully like Yuri."

"Yeah. Life is complicated."

Only he and Smirnov knew his target, so Fletcher figured he better get the job done and kill the guy before Yuri could blunder into his way and interfere with his assignment.

Later that night, Fletcher tracked his target to the vicinity of the city pier where the *Double Tap* was berthed. In another month, the docks would begin to get active, but for now everything was tranquil. The stays of an empty flagpole chimed faintly. The bay sloshed against pilings; gulls fluttered their feathers as they slept in the cold night air. He could smell the harbor vapors, rich and muddy, hovering above the surface of the black and sluggish water.

As Fletcher came down the dock he saw Ethyl on the fantail. She was looking at the marina office. A low growl made his neck hairs bristle. He quickly stepped into the shadow of a deck lamp and drew his CZ-75, a

Czech 9mm semiautomatic that never failed to operate. The pistol felt natural in his hand, even with his thin leather gloves on.

A small intermittent light in the marina office looked like someone using a flashlight. There was nothing valuable in the office, but Fletcher's reservation data were in a file cabinet. He had paid his berthing fee to a clerk somewhere in the bowels of the NYC Parks Department, but a copy of his application was kept on-site. Could someone be trying to find out about him? Could that someone be his target, hoping for a preemptive strike at him? The Hatteras was the only boat docked in Sheepshead Bay that early in the year except for the permanent charter boats.

Fletcher called quietly to Ethyl. She leaped to the pier and ran to his left side. She stood there, vibrating with restrained curiosity, staring at the office and the moving light. As one, man and dog crept to within five feet of the front door, both all in black. They stood in the shadow of the flagpole, still and invisible. Three minutes later, the doorknob turned slowly.

When a figure in a hoodie crouched out, Fletcher assumed a shooting stance and spoke loudly, "Stand fast. Don't move!"

The figure jumped, fired his handgun high and in Fletcher's general direction. The muzzle flash blinded Fletcher momentarily.

The intruder took off running. Fletcher sent Ethyl after him. She caught him in four long bounds, jumped on the figure's back and knocked him to the deck concrete. The hood shifted in the collision, revealing a shining brace on his nose.

Yuri screamed and threw the dog off him with an enormous burst of strength. Ethyl rolled away from the Russian, yelping and scrabbling to regain her footing, unable to stop her momentum. She skidded to the edge of the pier and dropped off into the blackness.

Vasilek regained his feet before Fletcher reached him. Yuri was snarling and keening like a crazed man. He fired three times into the bay, flame spurting from his gun, stopping only when Fletcher shot him in his big round head.

Ethyl was splashing wildly, whining piteously, swimming in frothy circles.

Another figure appeared, darting from behind the office. Fletcher pivoted to him, but before he could take aim the man jumped into the bay as a bloom of color appeared around the dog. The frigid seawater brought a loud gasp from the man as he swam into the blood, grabbed Ethyl's skin and dragged her to his body.

Grunting with effort, he held the dog tight to him and sidestroked to the pier. Twice the water lapped over their heads. The man spluttered each time. Fletcher could hear the man's ragged breathing as he made it to a ladder, straining to carry the dog. Fletcher pulled them up; the man would not have made it otherwise. Ethyl weighed nearly ninety pounds.

The man sat down hard on the dock. It was Billy Martin.

The schnauzer came to Fletcher, still whining softly but walking without a limp. He could see a furrow torn out of her right shoulder; a bloody wound, but treatable.

Billy Martin slumped on the deck, panting harder than Ethyl, his chest heaving and his legs splayed out in front of him. The combination of the icy water and the exertion required to rescue the big, panicked animal had exhausted him. He looked at Yuri's body, watched listlessly as Fletcher walked over and picked up the bully's gun. He pointed it at Billy Martin—his target.

"Thanks for saving my dog."

He pulled the trigger. Billy Martin flopped backward with a hole between his eyes. Fletcher fitted his own gun into the corpse's hand and threw Yuri's back to him. He yanked Billy's Glock from the holster at the small of the dead man's back and put it in his own. The marina was deathly silent.

Percy Fletcher and his dog walked over to the *Double Tap* and boarded. He cranked the diesels, cast off from her berth. They motored slowly through Sheepshead Bay and out to sea.

He sent a single-word text to Andrey Smirnov: Done.

* * * * *

P.F.A.

BY MICHAEL KORYTA

The couple from Florida moved in on the Fourth of July, and the first time Janice Jardine saw either of them was when their pug ran into her yard and took a dump not ten feet away from the grill where her barbecued chicken was cooking.

Janice lifted a spatula and prepared to utter a creative oath that her grandfather had perfected back in the days when Port Hope, Maine, was still a shipbuilder's town, but before she could let it fly a petite blonde woman stepped between the birch trees and entered Janice's yard with a smile and an apology.

Janice matched the smile. Janice was swell at putting on a smiling mask when her heart was a cold black fist and her mind a whirlpool of red tides.

"I'm *so* sorry!" the blonde said, showing white teeth against her tan, unlined skin. She was wearing white capri pants and a pink tank top and probably weighed little more than the spatula in Janice's upraised hand.

"Adam John!" the blonde hissed at the pug, snapping her fingers. "Come here, right *now*!"

The canine kettlebell straightened from his hunker and galloped across the yard toward her, but not before scratching a couple swaths of soil over his mess. Janice had just cut the grass for the holiday, and now there were ruts and dog turds in it.

"Well, this is no way to meet a neighbor," the blonde said, laughing and gathering the dog into her arms. Good thing she was a nimble little thing; you could throw your back out, hoisting that pug. "I apologize. Let me get him home and I'll be right back with a poop bag."

"Don't be ridiculous," Janice said, still with the smile plastered across her broad face. She didn't see much to like about the dog or the woman, but what Janice *did* like was intel, as she had always called it despite her husband's exasperated sighs in the days before he died of a heart attack.

It's gossip, Steve would say. *It's yapping over the back fence about somebody else's business. It's a lot of things, but it sure isn't intel, intelligence or intelligent. Quit trying to dignify it.*

But Steve benefitted from Janice's intel. Most of the neighbors did. The Jardine family didn't run Happy Hills without Janice's intel-gathering ways, and somebody had to keep an eye on the neighborhood or it would go straight to hell.

You gathered intel best when you offered kindness, Janice knew, and so she bustled her bulk down the steps from the deck and served a handshake alongside the smile.

"Don't you ever worry about letting that little cutie into my yard," she said.

"I've got to clean up his—"

"Oh, please." Janice waved her off. "I'm a pet person, honey."

She was a cat person, truth be told. She didn't care for dogs and she despised small dogs especially, and purebred small dogs with flat faces? Oh, they were just the worst. All five of Janice's cats knew how to use a darned litter box, but this curly-tailed mongrel had sashayed into her immaculate yard and crapped while looking her dead in the eye.

Janice smiled and reached out to pet the ugly thing. He grunted in that way that pugs did and then shoved his face forward and licked barbecue sauce off the spatula.

Janice's forced laugh came out high and shrill, but the blonde didn't know how unnatural that sound was. The blonde nymph was new in the neighborhood.

"Adorable," Janice said. "Isn't he just precious? And he knows good sauce!"

"I'm so sorry," the nymph said, pulling the grunting little cur back. "We were unloading the U-Haul and I thought the front door was closed but he snuck right—"

"You need to learn how to stop apologizing if you're living in Port Hope, Maine!" Janice said, laughing again and extending the spatula to the dog. "Welcome to Happy Hills. The name may seem silly, but it really *is* happy up here. I'm Janice Jardine."

The nymph put her child-sized hand into Janice's palm and said, "Lily Goodwin. My husband, Riley, is still unloading."

Janice had a niece named Riley. She'd never cared for it as a man's name. Well, you met all kinds these days. Janice had noticed plenty of liberal bumper stickers in town of late. Election years had a way of grinding her gears. At least she didn't need to worry about the political yard signs anymore. She'd fixed that with a few trips to the town office, clutching copies of the subdivision covenants in her hand.

"Well, it is so good to meet you—*and* to have the chance to send you home with some barbecued chicken!" Janice told the nymph, beaming.

"We couldn't possibly—"

"You can and you will. I cook so darn much, if you guys don't take it, I just wouldn't know what to do with the leftovers!"

The nymph smiled. "You're very kind. That's a relief because we're strangers in town. You never know how that will go until you move in, right?"

"You never do," Janice agreed, watching the ugly dog nuzzle up against the nymph's neck, leaving a smear of sauce on her suntanned skin. Janice did not tan, she either burned or freckled, but Janice was also smart enough to wear some gosh-darned deet in the summertime in Maine, and a layer of deet would teach a dog not to lick your neck.

"I was planning to come over and greet you," she told the nymph, "but I didn't know when exactly you'd be arriving, and I hadn't counted on it being right on the holiday. I saw the For Sale sign come down a couple weeks back, but I never did get a chance to talk to the Realtor."

In truth, the Realtor refused to speak to Janice. They'd had a few standoffs over the years, and that was just fine. If it was up to Janice, nobody would sell a house in Happy Hills without checking in with the neighbors first. It was the respectful thing to do. Janice also avoided the Realtor's recent trips because he'd wanted the spare keys back. Janice had a way of acquiring keys. Everyone needed the occasional favor done, and if you were the first one to offer, you were usually on the receiving end of an in-case-of-emergency key.

Janice didn't mind doing the favors. Feed a cat or water a plant, fine, happy to do it, because you never got a better intel-gathering opportunity than from a few precious unmonitored minutes in someone else's home. Why, she hadn't even known Sherrie Holmes was allergic to gluten until she had the chance to go through her pantry and review some recipe cards, and there wasn't a soul in the neighborhood who'd known about Bob Louden's depression until Janice got a glimpse of the medicine cabinet in the master bathroom.

"It seems like a very peaceful neighborhood," the nymph said, admiring the towering pines and birches and taking a deep breath of air that had been tinged with the scent of freshly cut grass right up until the pug poop wafted into the wind.

"It brings your blood pressure down, living here," Janice said. "You guys will be so happy here. Lily and Riley Goodwin, of Port Hope, Maine." She put a cheerful lilt into it. "That does have a nice sound. Now, did I hear you call that dog Adam John?"

The nymph laughed. "It's a strange name for a dog, right? He was called Bosco when we got him from the breeder, but we were watching him as a puppy, joking about the dumb things he'd do that reminded us of my brothers, and so we just started blending their names." She shrugged. "It stuck with me."

It stuck with you because it's stupid, Janice thought while she put on a show of hearty laughter. *It stuck with you because you've got no brains, little missy, and now you're my neighbor, a brainless blonde with an ugly little dog who poops in my lawn. Happy Fourth of July, Janice Jardine!*

"Well, isn't that adorable," Janice said. "Where are you all from, anyhow?"

"Florida," the nymph said.

"Florida! How *lovely*!" Janice lied with gusto. "All that sunshine and the palm trees."

Oh, heaven help her, they were From Away. In Maine, there were two kinds of people: natives, and People From Away, the dreaded P.F.A.s, as she and Steve had always called them.

"Palm trees, yes, but I sure don't miss the humidity," the nymph said. Janice could picture her doing yoga on some beach while a stereo blared unholy hip-hop music and muscle-bound millennials spent their parent's hard-earned money on cocktails with umbrellas but declined the bread before dinner because they were counting carbs. Oh, she could see it, no trouble at all.

"I bet you'll miss that humidity in February," she said. "When the first nor'easter blows in, you'll miss Florida plenty!"

She was still laughing when the nymph said, "Well, we're actually going to have to head back down for the winter. Riley can work from home year-round, but I've got to be back in the office for the academic year."

Heaven help me, they're not just from away, they're seasonal*!* Janice realized with mounting horror.

She swallowed, got the smile back, and then said, "Lucky ducks! What I wouldn't give for that chance. Maine and Florida. That's a good combination, right there."

Janice didn't like leaving the neighborhood for long stretches, even on vacation. Anything could happen if you weren't watching. Anything at all.

"Do you have kids?" she asked.

"Not just yet." Lily smiled a tight smile, the kind that might have meant *a little privacy, please* to some folks, but Janice had never been bothered by social cues.

"When the time is right," she assured the nymph, and then said, "Let me get you that plate of chicken.

You all have been moving furniture, you guys must be famished."

"You really don't need to—"

"It's what I *want* to do that matters," Janice warned her. "Not what I need to do."

That, as the residents of Happy Hills had learned, was the gospel truth.

She turned and heaved her prodigious hips back through the open gate at the base of the deck steps. She went inside and got two foil pans and came back out to check the chicken. When she was sure that Lily Goodwin wasn't looking, Janice used the spatula that the dog had licked to move three lovely pieces of barbecued chicken into one of the foil pans. Those she brought down to Lily with a smile.

"You're too kind," the nymph said. "Really."

"It's called being neighborly. I look forward to getting to know you guys. You'll have to bring your husband by sometime."

She gave the nymph a little wave and a cheerful goodbye and then she stood on the deck and watched her disappear through the trees toward the old Thomas house. The Thomases had been good people, good Mainers who made maple syrup and gave out their house keys without hesitation. Left the doors unlocked, most times. You could trust a person who left their doors unlocked.

Janice turned off the propane and used clean tongs to move the remains of the chicken into a fresh pan, gave the dog turd in the lawn one last glare, and then went inside. The cats swarmed at her feet.

"I met the neighbor," she told them. "Got a chance to chat when her silly dog waddled right into our yard and took a dump."

The cats yowled in commiseration. Janice took five

cans of Fancy Feast out of the pantry and went for the can opener. The cats trailed at her heels.

"P.F.A.s," Janice announced grimly. Out-of-staters. Pains in the behind, you could count on it.

The cats meowed, and Janice nodded as if they'd spoken.

"Ayuh. Florida. Little blonde thing looks like she just got blown in from the beach. Only be here for the summer, she says. Acted like she's got a job, but she doesn't seem like the working type to me."

She fed the cats and then set to work fixing salad and corn on the cob to pair with the chicken. She was alone on a holiday, but that was the way it had been since Steve died. He'd had a heart attack one day when she was explaining a utility easement concern to him, just up and died on her. Her son didn't come back to visit his mother the way he should, but that was his wife's fault, and Janice had a plan to fix it.

The Thomas family who lived next door had been part of the plan, but then they'd sold their house without so much as a word to her, almost as if to spite her, all because of a little dustup over the green space on the other side of their property. Foolish, when you considered that she'd set out to help *them*. The pond in that green space was a gosh-darned liability, and she was willing to move it out of neighborhood care and convert it into a private lot.

One for her son, Bobby. Bring the family back to the neighborhood. That way Janice could keep an eye on them. The green space was a prime building lot but for some reason the Thomases hadn't seen it that way. Well, the blonde nymph from Florida was good news in this respect. She and her husband would understand the situation once Janice explained it properly.

She could be convincing. Or exhausting. Either way, what Janice Jardine wanted, she got.

She ate her Fourth of July barbecue alone, gazing out the window. In the yard, Adam John's offering still sat, steaming. Apparently, the nymph had taken Janice seriously about it being no big deal.

P.F.A.s from Florida. Couldn't be too surprised at anything they did. The good news, though, was that they were bound to be stupid. And that was important because the green space conversion required their signed letter of assent. The Thomases, for all of their maple-syrup making, hadn't been good neighbors when it came to signing that simple letter. If you believed the gossip, Janice's efforts to claim the green space were actually one of the reasons they'd moved. But Janice knew better than to believe gossip. She dealt in the realities of legal research, and her legal research said that property could be converted once she had the approval of the abutters. There was some other legalese in there, sure, but most of Janice's enemies at the town hall had died and now she'd hectored old Sam Jones, the town planner, into consenting to rezone it as a building lot—provided Janice could get signatures of approval from each resident in Happy Hills, including the abutters. She could count on twelve of them, but the new neighbors were unlucky number thirteen. She'd been concerned about that until she'd seen the blonde with the pug.

Janice smiled and licked barbecue sauce off the fuzz above her upper lip. P.F.A.s. This would be easy. The nymph would sign, and once the lot was rezoned as a buildable property, Janice could claim it for nothing more than the tax bill. She'd worked that out with Sam Jones. Once it was hers? Well, a house would go up for

Bobby then. He was married now and had two kids of his own and that little shrew of a—

Stop it, Janice, that's your daughter-in-law, the mother of your grandchildren.

That lovely little *lady* of his was strangely averse to visiting. Ever since the ridiculous argument about Janice perusing their check register—an entirely innocent mistake because what was it doing in the top drawer of the breakfast nook, anyhow, where any stranger in the house was likely to find it?—her son and his family had kept their distance.

But Janice knew what they were saving their money for: a building lot. Bobby had told her that plenty of times. They wanted a few acres in a nice, peaceful neighborhood with old-growth trees. Janice had those requirements on the record, from Bobby and Sarah both. Well...

Merry Christmas, kids.

The nymph would sign. Oh, yes, she would.

Janice waited a week before she arrived at their door with the pie and the paperwork.

The Goodwins seemed pleased to see her, even if the husband, Riley, looked a bit perplexed at her unannounced arrival. *Get used to it, folks; you're not in Florida anymore.* People in Port Hope were neighborly. You shared pies. And house keys.

"The secret to the crust is adding just a pinch of sea salt," Janice said, and then she launched into the recipe while she slid the letter of assent onto their kitchen counter. The letter was partially obscured with a large Post-it Note with Janice's phone number and the words: "Call anytime, for anything! Welcome, welcome, welcome!!"

She stayed on the subject of pies for most of the conversation cyclone that she blew through the Goodwins' kitchen. She got all the way through the history of the farm out in Union where she'd gotten the blueberries before she even mentioned the paperwork. Then, she treated it as if it was an afterthought.

"Oh—and this. Ugh. You guys, you don't know how lucky you are to be arriving *now*, after this headache is done."

Riley cocked an eyebrow that arched up over his glasses. He was a bookish-looking man who'd probably never had a callus in his life.

"What headache?"

Janice gave a dismissive wave. "Oh, you don't even want to hear about it, trust me! Just one of those neighborhood things, someone has to take charge, and *I* was drafted!" She gave her most put-upon sigh. "But I got it handled."

"Got what handled?" Riley asked.

"The green space," she said, pointing in the general direction of the vacant wooded lot beside them where Bobby would soon live. "There's a stormwater pond back there, though you'd hardly know it, the thing is so small and overgrown. But it is a liability. There's a drain pipe that must be three feet in diameter, and it goes all the way under the pines and down to the river at the back of the property. There's not so much as a grate over it to keep the debris out. If you two had little ones, I'd be worried sick just thinking about what might happen if they fell in." She shuddered. "But you *don't* need to be worried about it, because we finally got that white elephant out of the collective hair of Happy Hills."

"How's that?" Riley said. He was looking at Janice, but Lily, the nymph, was reading the signature page. Janice had whited-out the page number when she made the copy, so they wouldn't know that there were five pages prior to this one.

"The county's going to convert it, some sort of annexation thing, I don't need to bore you with it all, but the good news is, it is done and you guys won't have to worry about it, thank goodness, it was all done before you even moved in! But you'll have to sign to show you're aware, that's all."

"It needs to be notarized," the nymph said.

Janice smiled. "Good news," she said, and took her notary stamp out of her purse. "I actually am a notary."

This was true; she'd had to take the course and pay the fee to expedite some paperwork on a little easement dispute with the Abel family who'd lived up the road until a few years ago, when they moved out in a huff.

"Where's the rest of the document?" the nymph asked.

Janice's smile faltered. "Pardon?"

The nymph lifted the signature page. "This would be the last page of the document. It would follow the text that we have supposedly read and understood and agreed to."

"There's really not much else but a parcel map, but I'll see that you get a copy," Janice said, uncapping her pen. "You guys really are lucky, you know. You got here at the right time. Won't have to sit in any of those *endless* zoning board meetings!"

She offered the nymph the pen and a 100-watt smile.

The nymph returned the smile but didn't take the pen.

"It's a protected green space," the nymph said. "That's in the deed and covenants. So what would it be *converted* into?"

Well, well, the little P.F.A. could read. Good for her.

"Converted into a taxable parcel," Janice said. "That

means it's no longer part of the subdivision, which means it's no longer your headache. The liability insurance on that pond won't cost you one thin dime."

"Who's paying the tax?" the nymph asked.

Janice wet her lips, trying to keep the smile in place.

"It's not something I'm advertising, because I don't want people to feel bad for me, but… I agreed to pay it. You know, it isn't so much, and I've got some savings, so I just figured, if I can remove this problem from everyone else, well, that's what my mother would've called *the neighborly thing* and I want to live like my—"

"So you'd own the property." The nymph stated this flatly and without much warmth. Riley blinked behind his bifocals, clueless.

"*Technically*, I guess." Janice pursed her lips, as if this notion of ownership had just occurred to her. "The way to look at it is, I would own the *liability*, really. When you two have little ones, you won't have to worry about that pond. I'll make sure there's fencing put in."

"It's a green space," the nymph said. "It belongs to all of us. That's in the covenants."

She must have run out of issues of *O* magazine to read on the drive up from Florida if she'd spent this much time perusing the gosh-darned covenants.

Janice said, "It *used* to be. But we all agreed to convert it, so the liability issues wouldn't be hanging over everyone's head all the time."

The nymph said, "This is not something we can support."

The smile returned to Janice's face, but it was a different smile, not the mask, oh, no, this time it was the real deal. It was cold and it was unyielding. Janice Jardine had been playing the long game in this neighborhood since before the nymph hit puberty. She'd run into a few folks who cared to read legalese before. Most of them had moved out. All of them had signed.

"I'm sorry to hear that," she said with a sigh, "but the problem, you guys, is that all of this is already done. See, there are thirteen lot owners that make up the neighborhood, and a majority of Happy Hills' residents agreed long ago that the best thing was—"

"Majority doesn't matter," the nymph said.

Her husband made a soft sigh, the sort of sound a downtrodden man makes without being aware of it, and wandered off to the fridge, opened it and got out a beer. Of course, he was a drinker. Janice Jardine didn't touch alcohol. It dulled the mind.

Drink up, buddy, she thought, and then returned her focus to the nymph.

"I'm not sure how it worked in Florida," she said patiently, "but you guys are in Maine now. We have a different legal system. Trust me, it is one ugly mess. I was a paralegal for twenty-five years, and I spent a *lot* of time unwinding big balls of messy knots. Up here in Maine it's all about town ordinances and planning boards and then you've got the county to deal with, and then there's the state, because the DEP has an interest in that stormwater pond, so it's a very different process from the nice and polite little HOAs you guys probably had down in—"

"Majority doesn't matter," the nymph said again. "It's a shared asset. It belongs to all of the homeowners. That means all of the homeowners have to agree."

"And all of them have agreed," Janice said. "It's already been decided."

The nymph showed her perfect little white teeth. "Not all of them."

Janice wanted to smack those teeth into the back of her little blond head.

"Look," she said, "I don't want to see you guys get off on the wrong foot in this town. It's a welcoming place but I'll be honest, some folks don't exactly love the snowbirds, okay? People from away can get on the wrong side pretty easily here, and I would hate to see that happen for you over something so silly as a—"

"It's not silly," the nymph said. "It's privacy. We chose this house because it is private. We will not sign anything that removes that privacy. We like to be left alone."

Oh, did they now? Did they come north in search of a little *privacy* in Vacationland? Wasn't that sweet. Wasn't that just the sweetest thing Janice Jardine had ever heard!

"See," Janice said, "the only thing that really matters is what the *law* says. That's all I'm doing here—explaining what the law says. Don't shoot the messenger! But Mr. Jones with the town planning board can explain that—"

"I'll give him a call."

Janice took a deep breath. Watched the husband drink his beer. He gave her a little shrug, like, *My wife, what can I tell ya?*

"It's the law," Janice repeated. "So it's not really a matter of opinion, or what you were hoping the place would be like, okay? This all began a long time ago, and it is something for lawyers to argue about, not neighbors."

The nymph showed her teeth again. "Good news," she said. "I'm a law professor."

For a moment, it was silent. Janice looked down at the pen in her hand, and at the pie she'd spent the morning on, and then she capped the pen and put it back in her purse with her notary stamp.

"Well," she said, "I can see it will take a day or two to sort this out."

She smiled. The nymph smiled. The husband drank his beer and looked from one of them to the other as if tumbleweeds were blowing between them and they each had hands floating just above their gun belts.

"Enjoy that pie," Janice told them, and then she left the house.

So the nymph was a law professor. Wasn't that cute? A law professor who lived in Florida. Not licensed in the great state of Maine. Janice Jardine knew quite a few attorneys in Maine. She needed to bake a few more blueberry pies, she decided. One for each of the lawyers.

And one for Adam John, the pug.

The dog died that night, and Janice sat on the deck beneath the citronella torches and sipped iced tea and listened to the sobs. The husband, Riley, was talking about heart attacks and strokes. Lily the Nymph Law Professor kept saying she wanted to go to a veterinarian.

Little late for that, Janice thought, but then she heard the nymph's faint voice add an interesting word: *necropsy.*

Janice stopped swinging on the porch glider so that the yard was completely quiet and listened for more.

"That's not necessary," Riley was saying, and oh, how Janice agreed with him. It was absolutely not necessary. Dogs with flat faces had breathing defects; tragedies happened to those breeds all the time. They didn't have the longevity of a cat.

The nymph was still talking and still crying but Janice could no longer make out the words. She heard a screen door open and close and then the woods were quiet. After a long time, she returned to swinging in the glider.

Necropsy. That wasn't a word most people threw around. What kind of law did the Florida nymph teach, exactly?

Janice took out her iPhone and entered "Lily Goodwin" into a search. Scrolled through the options and didn't find the right match. She returned to the search page and put in "Lily Goodwin" and "Florida." Still no matches. "Lily Goodwin" and "Florida" and "law professor." Nothing.

Must be a diploma mill she teaches at, Janice thought with pleasure. *I knew there were no brains to her. I knew exactly who she was the first time I laid eyes on her.*

Surely, there was an online directory for the Florida State Bar Association.

Janice stood up from the swing and went inside. She wanted to use the desktop computer. Outside, the mosquitoes were beginning to buzz and soon would bite.

She sat at the computer for two hours. At first, she was incredulous, but then that morphed into delight. Pure, unadulterated delight.

P.F.A. indeed. A Person From Away, yes, but also a *phony fraud attorney!*

There was no Lily Goodwin licensed to practice law in the state of Florida. There was no Lily Goodwin on the faculty of any of the colleges in Florida that had a law school. In fact, there was no Lily on any law school faculty, *period,* so even if she used her maiden name professionally, Janice would have found her.

She thought of that smug little white-toothed smile and heard the little chipmunk voice saying, *Majority doesn't matter* and *Good news—I'm a law professor.*

The little liar. That filthy little bleached-blonde *liar*!

In the morning, Janice would pay a visit. She would bring the signature sheet again, and her notary stamp, and this time she would not bring a pie.

"We'll get to thirteen signatures," Janice told the cats. "Oh, ayuh. We will most certainly get to thirteen."

She took her time the next morning, savoring her coffee and watching the cats watch the birds. It was a beautiful day. Cobalt sky and a light breeze off the sea that had the birch leaves shimmering. Maine. A good place to be from. A tough place to barge into when you didn't know how a small Yankee town worked.

She heard a car engine start next door and went to the window in time to see Riley Goodwin drive off in his Jeep, alone. Wonderful. It would be just Janice and the nymph, as it should be. The husband had never been anything more than a bit player in this brief little neighborhood drama. Husbands rarely were, in Janice's experience.

She hadn't even had a chance to knock on the door when it swung open. The nymph stood there, staring at her with red-rimmed eyes. It had been a long and emotional night for the poor thing.

"Good morning," Janice said. "May I speak to you and Riley for a moment?"

"Riley is gone," the nymph said tonelessly. Her eyes seared Janice like hot daggers. "He is taking Adam John to the vet for a necropsy."

Janice put a hand to her breast.

"Do you know what a necropsy is?" the nymph asked, still in that empty voice.

"Of course. To determine cause of death. Oh, no. Oh, dear. Oh, I'm so—"

"Shut up," the nymph said. "I don't want to hear it.

The only thing I want to hear is the result of that necropsy. If it's what I think it is, then you'll be hearing from me soon enough. They can put old ladies in jail, you know. Yes, they can."

Janice Jardine smiled. The little lady from Florida thought she had some leverage here. Oh, how much she needed to learn about Port Hope, Maine.

"Where is it that you teach law?" Janice asked.

The nymph tried to hide the flicker of apprehension, but Janice saw it, and her smile widened.

"Where?" Janice repeated.

The nymph tried to gather herself. Gripped the door frame and said, "The University of Southern Florida. Now get the hell off my—"

"Under what name?"

Pause. A blink. "I am telling you to get off—"

"You don't teach law. Not at USF or anywhere else. You don't practice law. You never passed the bar in Florida. You're a fraud and a liar and I think people around here will be very interested to learn a little about you. I don't know it all yet. But I will, honey. You rest assured. I will."

She turned and walked away then, calling out over her shoulder, "You just give me a ring when you're ready to sign. I left my phone number with the paperwork."

She didn't even have time to sit down. The phone was ringing almost before she'd closed her front door. She stood in the center of the living room and listened to it ring and she smiled. Then she picked it up.

"Yes, dear?"

"Come back, please."

"What's that?"

"Please. I will sign it. I will sign whatever you want."

"I know you will, dear," Janice said kindly. "I'll be right over."

Janice Jardine hung up the phone, sat on her rocking chair and lit a cigarette. She allowed herself six per year, on special occasions.

Victory, she told the cats, was a special friggin' occasion.

When the cigarette was gone, she flicked the butt into the sink, washed it down the garbage disposal, gathered her notary supplies and returned to her new neighbors' home.

The nymph who called herself Lily Goodwin was waiting on the front porch, sitting on the step. She wore sweatpants and an oversize hooded sweatshirt and her hair was a mess. Those red-rimmed eyes appeared to have fresh tears in them, poor thing.

"We didn't have to do it the hard way," Janice told her. "I hated to do that to you guys. But…" She gave a sad sigh. "You kinda forced my hand there, you know?"

The nymph nodded. Looked up at Janice and spoke in a soft, thick voice. "Will you show me the pond? I'd like to take a walk and…" She swallowed with an effort. "Tell you a few things about us. About me."

"Oh, hon," Janice said. "You can trust me. Really, you can. I don't want to be the bad guy. I just want to look after all of my neighbors, okay?"

"Okay."

So they left the yard and walked through the pines together, into the five-acre, wedge-shaped lot where soon Bobby and Sarah and the grandkids would live, right down the road, under Janice's watchful eye, as it always should have been. For once, Janice let silence linger. She rarely favored this approach, but she knew a broken woman when she saw one, and Lily Goodwin was toast.

"Do you know my real name yet?" the nymph finally asked.

"No," Janice said. "But you should tell me. Because I will find out, hon. Trust me on that."

"I do." The nymph made a sad, choked laugh in the back of her throat. "That's the problem. I really don't think you'd *ever* stop, would you?"

Janice just smiled. They were headed downhill now, stepping over the snaking roots that interrupted the pine needle–strewn ground like miniature mountain ranges. Janice knew every step. She'd been scouting this property since long before the "Goodwin" family first crossed the Piscataqua River. The stormwater drainage flowed beside them, riding a natural ridge of granite on its way down to the retention pond. When the water was high—and it was now, after an unusually wet spring with a lot of snowmelt—the water in the pond poured into a massive drainpipe and vanished below ground, funneled deep beneath the hill, and emptied out into the river below. From there, the water drifted on to Bell Pond, where soon Janice would teach her grandchildren to swim while they watched their new house go up.

Long game. You had to play it ruthlessly to win, but it was all worth it in the end.

"Do you have your phone?" the nymph said.

"What?"

"Your phone. Did you bring it?"

"Yes."

The nymph stopped walking above the pond and sighed. Wiped at her nose with the sleeve of her sweatshirt.

"Google the name Robin Ross," she said.

"Why don't you just tell me, dear?"

But the nymph shook her head, and Janice could tell

she was in no condition to speak. If she parted those foolish lips again all that was going to come out was a lot of blubbering and tears. A shame, and so unnecessary. Janice Jardine wasn't hard to get along with. All she'd needed was a silly signature.

"I'll look it up," she said, "but first? You really do need to sign my paper."

The nymph nodded. Janice offered her the signature page and a pen.

"Put down whatever name you'd like," she said. "But ideally it would match the name on the deed."

She laughed at that, but the nymph didn't join in. She just rested the paper against a tree trunk so she could scribble her name on it.

"That's the last of them?" she asked. "Now it's just a matter of paying the tax bill and it's free and clear?"

"That's right," Janice said, taking the signature sheet back. She almost felt bad for the silly little thing. "People from away don't understand our little towns, you know. It's so much better to learn how things already work in a place than to come in and try to change them."

Lucky number thirteen was in the bag. Janice would call the excavator tomorrow. The excavator would do his work cheap because Janice happened to know a few things about his son's heroin habit that the man would rather not have shared around town.

"Put the name in on your phone, please," the nymph said. "Robin Ross."

Now that the long game was won, Janice had only passing interest in whatever foolishness the little twit had gotten caught up in back in Florida, but she was always willing to gather more intel, so she humored her, and took out her phone.

"You were right about me," the nymph said.

"Of course, I was." Janice opened the web browser.

"I don't teach law."

"Of course, you don't." Janice put "Robin Ross" into the search bar.

"I haven't passed the bar."

"Of course, you haven't." Janice pressed Enter.

"But, in the immortal words of Jay-Z, 'I know a little bit.'"

Janice didn't know what that meant, but her attention was on the screen, anyhow. It had just refreshed, and there was a picture of the woman who now stood in front of her. In the photo, she was much paler and had brown hair, but the face was undeniable, and so was the caption beneath it, from a newspaper in Billings, Montana.

Accused Murderers Robin and James Ross Still Missing.

Janice looked up from the phone and into the nymph's bright smile and the muzzle of the gun in her hand.

"As I think I told you," the nymph said, "we picked this house because we wanted privacy."

Janice dropped the phone and the signature page. Took one step backward. Began to say, *You guys don't need to worry about me, I will never tell a soul, I promise*, but got only as far as "You guys—" before the first bullet punched between her eyes.

The second blew through her heart. The gunshots were loud, but the sound faded into the pines without drawing any attention. The best thing about Happy Hills was its solitude.

Robin Ross put the gun back into the pocket of her hoodie. She knew she hadn't needed the second shot, but her dog had demanded she take it. One bullet for business, one bullet for vengeance.

She threw Janice Jardine's phone into the pond. Watched the current tug it toward that fat, gaping drain-pipe as it sank.

"That thing *is* a liability," she said aloud.

She reached for Janice's purse next but stopped herself before throwing it in. She removed a sheaf of paperwork and flipped through it. Twelve signed letters of assent to convert the designated green space property into a building lot. Lily Goodwin's made thirteen.

She thought it would be wise to wait a few weeks before she called the town planner to discuss the property, but in time, that was the thing to do.

The more privacy, the better.

She set the letters aside and rolled Janice Jardine into the pond. Even rolling her downhill, it wasn't easy. Janice was a sizable presence, dead or alive. Once she was in the water, the current helped. It took a few minutes of guiding the corpse with a long branch, but eventually, water and gravity conspired together, and Janice Jardine was gone.

Robin climbed back up the hill, gathered the letters of assent and started home. She figured it would be a few days before anyone dropped by with questions. Janice Jardine had seemed like a lonely lady. Her absence might be noted, but she wouldn't be *missed*, exactly. Janice Jardine, she thought, might have an enemy or two in Port Hope.

She looked forward to hearing some of the theories. She thought that people would share them happily and without much restraint.

Nothing brought strangers together faster than a good murder story.

* * * * *

GENIUS

BY ELAINE TOGNERI

How smart do you have to be to kill a genius? I'm about to find out.

I'm not sure if a musician actually counts as a genius. It's not like David Leefield is good at math or science or anything real. Playing a sax shouldn't count. So he can write songs and play anything after hearing it once. Big deal. Clearwater's Ruth Eckerd Hall might call him a musical genius. I call him dead.

As I drive into the parking lot of Brimm's Funeral Home, I turn my head to the left so I don't have to see the landscaping any more than I need to. Even though Brimm's is located amid the urban decay of US 19, every blade of grass is a vivid green and the same exact height. Shrubs appear annoyingly hand trimmed into perfect leafy balls. Undertakers always purvey the greatest pretense on the newly bereaved, as if bodily fluids aren't being drained away in the basement and corpses aren't pumped full of preservatives before being dressed like mannequins and put on display. A total ruse denying how messy death is. I know the reality firsthand.

I'm a stranger to Florida. Two years ago, the fire I couldn't beat back with my gloved hands roasted my brother alive in the bowels of the earth. I still hear the pop as stirred-up coal dust ignited him into a ball of flame. His skin melted and left his body raw. He died three long, horrible days later. It destroyed our family. Mom didn't last another four weeks. Six months later, I left the Leefield coal mines and Tennessee far behind. Another reason I hate the green. It reminds me too much of home.

The Genius's wife died three years ago. Now her aunt Tilly has fallen to the Grim Reaper's scythe. David is in Brimm's to say his final goodbye, giving me my best chance to observe and evaluate his strengths and weaknesses. If only I could park my rented black SUV with my eyes closed to avoid the grounds' false perfection, but I can't take the risk.

I pull into an open spot and hurry toward the white entrance door. Even that short walk in Florida's heat beads sweat on my forehead and dampness under my armpits. Life is as disgusting as death. Per Brimm's website, Tilly's service will start in five minutes. Time enough to fake signing the guest book and take a seat in the rear of the room, preferably under an air-conditioning vent.

I fade into the crowd of forty-plus mourners, the back of the Genius's head barely in sight. He's shorter than he looks onstage, and I shift to keep his blond-streaked hair in sight. He bears little resemblance to his brother Steven. A minister stands and mumbles through a litany of prayers and readings before asking family and friends to speak on behalf of Aunt Tilly.

When David takes his turn, I settle into my seat. His

neck bends slightly and his hands rise in front of him as if he's holding his alto saxophone. All the years of playing and wearing the strap that secures the weight of the instrument have bent his neck, but built up his finger muscles. I won't underestimate his grasp. He's of average weight for his height and has no advantage there. Dimples appear and disappear on his face as he blah blahs about Aunt Tilly. I've seen him perform and he frequently dips and moves around the stage, demonstrating strong balance and leg strength. For this speech, he stays in place, looking like a viper coiled, ready to pounce. More formidable than one would suppose for someone who has spurned the family business to spend his time playing music.

He returns to his chair and after a final long-droned prayer, the service ends. People form a receiving line, and I join it to satisfy my cameo conceit. He doesn't know me, but he will. At the end, it gives me a charge to see a flicker of recognition, often mixed with a hint of question or confusion. A perk of the job.

When I reach David, I grasp his hand and confirm my evaluation. Quite a grip. "So sorry for your loss," I say.

David nods. "How did you know Aunt Tilly?"

I'm not impressed. Too simple a question for a so-called genius, and one I'm obviously prepared for. Tilly's obituary stated she taught English at Pasco-Hernando State College for many years. "One of her students," I say. "She helped me a lot."

He nods again, watching me closely before a young woman behind me rushes forward to kiss him, grabbing both his hands. Strong hands that will soon be stilled and cold.

It's then I decide a close encounter is contraindicated. I nod to the funeral director on my way out the door and reach a hand into my pocket. Extracting a simple pushpin, I pause by David's celebrated yellow BMW. Like I said, I do my research.

I bend as if to tie my shoe and press the pin between two worn treads. When he pulls out, the pin will pierce even farther into the tire's skin. Between the heat and rainy season's unrepaired potholes in Pasco, a blowout is inevitable. He'll be doing seventy on the Suncoast as he returns to Tampa and careens out of control. Goodbye, David. Say hello to Aunt Tilly.

I drive to the combo gas station–convenience store close to the parkway to wait. Time for a bathroom break and ham sandwich. No fried pickles available at a place like this, not that I'd trust any Florida cook to make them right, other than the one at Ron's BBQ. I walk around the store for a bit, buy some pork rinds, then sit in my SUV with the air running.

Another half hour passes. Seems like the wait has been far too long, and I'm considering retracing my route, when I finally see David's BMW pull into the parking lot. Thankful for the SUV's tinted windows, I watch as instead of parking next to the gas pump, he ends up right next to me. I clasp my phone to my ear in a phantom phone call. He exits the car and walks around the vehicle, pressing and prodding the tires. He glances at the building. No mechanics at gas stations in Florida because they're all self-serve, just like Tennessee.

A tall man in a greasy uniform comes out of the store. David calls to him. "Are you a mechanic?"

"Air-conditioning installer. What's up?"

"My tires don't sound right."

"Not sure what you mean."

"The hum is off."

The man shrugs and says, "Maybe you got a stone in

the treads or a slow leak." He jumps into a van labeled Keep Your Cool Air-Conditioning ending the conversation with, "Take it easy, buddy."

David bends down and inspects the tires, one at a time.

Damn. I don't wait for him to find the culprit. My opportunity's blown by his super sense of hearing. A mistake. I don't like making mistakes. I'm too smart for that.

I slam my SUV into Reverse and roar away, heading for the Tampa airport. I'll put on my old man outfit and change rental companies to pick up a different car, maybe a Caddy. I'll catch up with David tomorrow. In the meantime, I already have plan B, a murderous alternative that can't be blown by a sound. I flip on my favorite internet station and listen to Appalachian balladry, the one thing I still like about Tennessee.

David charged four new tires yesterday. I know because I have access to his credit card account. One of the pieces of information I hacked from his insecure online presence. Once I was an uneducated coal miner, a sucker for a company that didn't do crap to protect employees. The owner, Steven Leefield, even denied my brother's family settlement claim, saying he should have known to clear coal dust before mining. They had no inspection or dust collection program to avoid an explosion. I don't know how I managed to get out as the mine collapsed. Afterward, all Steven Leefield did was close up shop.

The government sent us to a coding school as part of a transition program to convert us into computer geeks. That joke of a program didn't lead to a job, but it did give me knowledge of the dark side of tech. I know David's hotel. I know his schedule. I know where he keeps the reeds for his prized instruments. I know his secrets. He can't hide and soon, Steven Leefield is going to know what it feels like to lose a brother.

Tonight David and his band play Ruth Eckerd Hall. A not-to-be-missed opportunity. I hack the hotel registration file and locate the band's rooms. They have several, but I'm only looking for one. Hunched over and walking feebly through the hotel dragging a bag, I ape the cadence of an elderly man and ask for a room on the fourteenth floor, the same as David's. I take the elevator up.

As soon as I arrive in my room, I order room service: two bottles of beer and a shrimp cocktail. The room has a black-and-white-striped rug, heavy curtains over white sheers and a king-size bed with a burgundy duvet. Nice but I won't be sleeping here. It's early afternoon, and I've got plan B tonight.

I throw my bag on the bed and head to the glitzy bathroom. It's all gold-dotted wallpaper and gold fixtures. The sink appears clean, but I run hot water to rinse it anyway. I towel dry and push the stopper to plug it. Never hurts to be careful. I toss the towel into the tub and return to the bedroom.

A tap sounds on the door and a voice calls, "Room service."

I open the door and point at the desk. "Over there, please." After he places the platter there, he heads out the door and I hand him a couple of bucks. Can't tip too much or too little. I must estimate the "just right" Goldilocks amount. My brother used to joke and say that from the fairy tale his daughter requested every night before the mining company stole him from her life. Enough. I need to get to work.

The tray. I open a beer and pour a glass for me. I walk everything into the bathroom and drain the other bottle into the sink. The damn plug isn't flush, and some beer goes down the drain until I press to seal it securely. I sacrifice some liquid from my glass and add the shrimp, tails and all. I mash the shrimp with my hands until the foam dissipates, and the resulting stew is pulpy and amber. My plan is to soak his reeds so they absorb the essence of shellfish and the odor of beer. I know David's habits. He drinks a couple of brewskis before each performance to relax. More importantly, he has a deadly allergy to shellfish.

Now for the dangerous part. At the last Black Hat USA convention, I picked up a microcontroller that when plugged into the DC port under the lock, reads a hotel room's key code and transmits it back. Open sesame.

I call David's room. No answer. I check the hall through the peephole. No one around. I make my way down the hall, keeping up my old man act. I tap at David's door. No answer. Without wasting time, I hack the lock. I'm in.

The room is dark, and it takes a second for my eyes to adjust. Along the far wall past the two beds, I see sax cases and next to them is his reed storage container that's shaped like a small hard briefcase. I have to use his reeds, as I've read he spends hours perfecting them, whittling and licking until they suit him. He would notice replacements. Being a musical perfectionist, he changes reeds when his perfect pitch hearing catches a minor off note, normally every time he plays. I grab the case and return to my room. I take a picture of the contents before I plop all the reeds into the beer-shrimp stew.

I wait an hour and extract one. Holding it close to my nose, I take a big sniff of ale. Any shrimp odor is masked by the strong bitter scent of the beer. I drain the sink and allow the reeds to dry on a cheap towel I picked up at the dollar store, one I'll be sure to toss in an anonymous gas station bathroom during my travels. I can't wait too long to return the reeds, so I grab the hair dryer and use the cool setting to hasten the drying process. After a while I replace them in the case, taking care to match the picture I took.

With a plastic bag, I scoop the shrimp remains out of the sink and flush them down the toilet. I clean the sink, counter and toilet with a spray bottle of bleach. Several careful swipes and I'm done. Then I'm back down the hall with the reed case, finessing my way into David's room again.

This time when I open the door, a man's voice calls with a British accent, "Is that you, Dave?" One of the queen-size beds has a form under the covers.

I freeze. The guitar player. David's reed case was on the other side of the room. I need to replace it there. I stand in the slight hall by the bathroom, out of view.

"I'm sick. Stay away so you don't get this. Wake me up when it's time to go." The form rolls over away from me.

There's no closet, just a bar to hang clothes on. A suitcase sits nearby. I set the reed storage container on top and back out of the room, easing the door open and closed. The situation is not ideal. I could have killed David's roommate to get the reeds placed properly. But finding the guitar player dead would probably have canceled tonight's concert.

I return to my room and mess up the bedcovers. I sweep the place, putting all my things and the trash into my bag. Laying the room key on the desk, I grab my suitcase. A peek through the hole shows the hall's empty. I exit the room and return to my car. Having signed up for express checkout will make it look like

I left early in the morning. I go back to the airport and turn in my Caddy with regret. But I'm careful. I change into my cool guy clothes, jeans, a T-shirt with a picture of David's band on it and a long-haired wig. I rent a scratched-up Ford Fiesta from another vendor. I've got a couple of hours to kill. On my way to Ruth Eckerd, I stop at a restaurant and order dry rub ribs and corn bread. I arrive early to pick up my ticket at the will-call window.

My seat is toward the front but all the way on the edge with a view behind the curtain when it's open. The band's instruments are sitting waiting for musicians as am I. The woman next to me has drowned herself in a sickeningly sweet perfume, the kind morticians use to cover body rot. Her hair is long and she finger-combs it incessantly. Thankfully before I yank her hand off her head, the lights dim and the band is onstage. David introduces the players and they start with a crowd fa-vorite to oohs of recognition. The woman next to me hums along, shaking her head. My eyes are only on the Genius. He's quite good, maybe excellent. Too bad. But his death will be good for album sales and for me.

I wait for him to choke or miss a note through the whole first set. Nothing. Not even when he switches to a soprano sax. When the intermission comes, I stand and rejoice as the woman beside me rushes off with her friends to get drinks or use the restroom. Who cares? As long as she's gone. Stretching my legs, I wander along the edge for a look in a gap between the cur-tains at the side stage. No one around for the first five minutes, but then I see David with his reed case. He removes the mouthpiece of the sax and the used reed. He pulls one out of the case, considers it, then tosses it and does the same two more times. He seems to like the next one. He twirls it around in his hands, decides he doesn't like that one either. What is he looking for?

Finally, he finds one to his liking, but puts it in the smaller instrument that's only used on a couple of songs. He pulls a reed from his pocket, inserts it in the alto sax and then he's gone.

The second set starts, and I take my seat. I wonder how long it will take for him to choke to death once he uses the soprano sax. David plays a couple of songs, and then with a nod to the band goes offstage, rubbing his fingertips. He must have more than a food allergy if they are swelling. A contact allergy too. Almost there. This is going to work. I can't wait.

The band highlights each of its members with the drummer announcing their names. I lean forward to look to the side stage. David's drinking water. Someone throws him a tube of something and he rubs it on his hands. He drifts back onstage and plays his heart out on that sax.

I wait and wait, but he's not picking up the smaller one. Instead he comes down the stairs into the audience and plays right next to the first row, then up the aisle to the last row in the front section, down my side. He never misses a note. But those eyes aren't closed in the ecstasy of the song, they're peering into our faces.

My cool guy hair is a wig he hasn't seen. I grin like I'm into the music and point with both thumbs at my shirt. I don't dare talk in case he recognizes my voice. But the woman next to me outdoes me. She is shouting, tossing her hair and throwing kisses. Finally she comes in handy as a distraction. The Genius plays on by and returns to the stage.

"Is that part of the act?" I ask the woman.

"He does it all the time," she squeals. "That's why I got these seats. He is so cute."

I nod, unconvinced. How far does his genius go? Could he have recognized me? I don't mind if he does at the end, but not until I finish my job. Plan B is evidently a bust.

I'm tired of waiting. No more making it look like an accident. Hey, aren't we in the "Gunshine State"? Gun shows everywhere, and private owners who believe in everybody's Second Amendment rights. No problem. I won't get caught, but if I do, I'll just claim I'm standing my ground, a convenient Florida law.

I slip out of my seat never to return. It's too late for a gun show, but the darknet is always open for a visit. I'm sure I can find local black markets for guns and make a connection. If I'm lucky and David isn't, by the time he returns to the hotel, I'll be in the parking lot, armed and ready.

I find a Starbucks and order a ristretto on ice, purely for the caffeine jolt. Lots of open space, so I grab a table where no one can look over my shoulder. In spite of the innate slowness of anonymity, I find what I'm looking for and arrange a meet before I can finish my drink, which barely covers the bottom of a small paper cup.

The transaction works out well, and I drive to the hotel, apprehensive about doing this at night. But the dark of night is nowhere near the darkness of the mines. When your headlamp goes out, you can't see your own hand in front of your face. I have moonlight and time to let my eyes adjust to the dark.

I turn off the Ford's courtesy lamp and am cast into darkness. My plan isn't genius. Just watching for David's car. Positioning myself. Shooting him as he gets out. I fill two clips and snap one into the gun, the other in my pocket.

I'm glad this job's coming to an end. Success will taste sweet.

Cars come and go less and less frequently. My head leans against the headrest and my eyelids forget I'm loaded with caffeine.

An engine purrs. I jerk up. It's the BMW. I grab the gun and ease the door open. I'm out into the cool night air, crouching behind vehicles as I follow his quest for a parking spot. He finds one and I position myself perfectly.

His door opens. I shoot. A grunt, and the body falls.

But then the passenger door opens. I see David. He scoots down. Footsteps scrabble. The man I hit is too tall to be the Genius.

I dodge between two SUVs, dive to the pavement and look both ways for feet. Nothing.

But I hear pounding to my right. I run toward the sound and it stops.

I ease around the front of a Jeep and see brown loafers in front of me.

Hands grip my neck. Strong hands. I jerk around, shooting all the way. Headlights shatter, but David presses harder. He's tough. As mean as his brother Steven.

"I know you," he says. His eyes harden. "Your brother burned up back home."

I can't talk. My windpipe is collapsing. I thought I was a stranger. Another mistake.

I remember the gun and shoot him directly in the chest. But his hands keep strangling. Those strong, strong finger muscles.

I'm falling right into the bowels of the earth, bringing him along with me. The lyrics of the last ballad I heard mock me. "Poor boy, you're bound to die."

I'm smart enough to kill a genius, but not smart enough to survive.

* * * * *

RUSSKIES

BY JONATHAN STONE

Now I'm just gonna start up this here machine, okay? Tap the microphone, make sure it's running, and ask you some questions. My partner Detective Anderson over there in the corner, he's gonna sit quietly and take some notes, and you just answer truthfully, just say what happened. Name?

But you know my name.

I know, son, but we have to get it officially. So, name?

Owen James Ames.

Age?

Twelve. Are Mike and me in trouble?

No, son, you're not in trouble. Now, tell us where you live.

Edson Farm, rural route 3. Where you came to get us at.

Okay.

I'm scared.

(PAUSE. SLIGHT WHIMPERING.)

Now, now, calm down. We'll take good care of you and your brother, okay? So you just tell us what happened.

Starting when?

Well…why don't you tell me first how you happened to be there in the bomb shelter?

Well, we'd go play in there.

Really?

Well yeah, see 'cause our farm's got no good climbing trees, and the driveway's dirt so's our bikes is no good on it, so we'd go play in it. It was fun in there.

Didn't your dad lock it?

(PAUSE. SLIGHT WHIMPERING.)

Son, it's okay. Just answer and everything will be all right. So, did your dad lock it?

Not at first, no. He said it was so hidden, there in the high grass, that no one would know where it is, and he said as long as we swore not to tell anyone at school about it, he'd leave it open and we could play in it. But we had to keep it neat and promise not to touch any of the supplies or nothin'.

(MORE WHIMPERING.)

Now, Owen, I'm sure he wouldn't be mad about that. I'm sure it was okay.

But then I told him how I'd told Becka at school about it, and he thought she might tell her folks, and he said it was important that no one else know, because we wouldn't have the room or supplies to save our neighbors, so then he started locking it.

So then what?

Well he kept the key on the Frigidaire, so we would just open it up anyway and play there, and when he found us in there we was plenty scared, but he just laughed and walked away.

And tell me about yesterday.

The Russkie attack?

Uh, yes, the Russkie attack.

Well, you know, our pop said they could come any-time, they were learnin' to disguise theirselves, and speak American and such. So we was gettin' ready for 'em. We'd pretend Emma was a Russkie, and Leo.

Emma?

You know—our cow. And Leo's our rooster. There weren't no one else to play it with. We'd push Emma over and declare victory. Anyway, when we went in there, we'd lock the door from the inside.

And what'd you do in there?

Turn on the lamp. Lie on the couch. Turn on the radio, mostly. Pop said we could fool with that. We'd lie there in the dark and listen to the Cardinals. It was cool.

Did your dad seem worried about the Russians? Here in Indiana?

He talked about 'em a lot. How evil they are. How Communism is the devil's faith and such. He'd tell us stories at bedtime, and the Russkies was always the bad guys. He said our family and our farm was about the last people the Russkies would get to. We'd have the longest experience of American freedom. He said that was the good news. He said the bad news was by the time they got to us, they'd have already overrun everywhere else, New York and Chicago and Atlanta and all the cities, and we'd be the last defenders of freedom, the last to fall.

Overrun, huh? The Russians here in Indiana?

On weekends, he drove us to some of the missile silos, way up to Gary and Wheeler. Talked about how missiles would come from Russia straight to Gary and Wheeler and hit our missiles before they launched— unlessen we launched ours first.

You want a glass of water, Owen?

No, sir, I'm okay.

Okay, so back to yesterday. Tell me everything you can about what happened yesterday.

We finished our farm chores, me and Mike, and we was playin' in the shelter, and we had it locked like always...

Like always, what does that mean?

You know, bolted from the inside, like our dad showed us to keep out the Russkies. And then we heard a car engine and tires on the driveway, and we was gonna open the shelter and see who it was, but right away there's yellin', bunch of voices hollerin' and whoopin' and my pop yellin' "Hey! Hey!" real angry, and then we hear like a pop, pop, pop...and someone scream out and then a loud moanin' like some animal in pain, moanin' like I never heard before, I figured it must be Emma our cow, but see it can't be because I hear Emma bellowin' at the same time, frightened-like... And we didn't know what was going on, and we was real scared, so we turned out the light, and listened... And then got even scareder 'cause we heard footsteps runnin' toward us, and someone pullin' on the shelter door real hard, just pullin' and pullin' and pullin', and then there's a big loud crash against the door. And then it's real quiet, and we stay real quiet, and I'm listening for Russian, and there's more pop pop pop, which I figured out by now is shootin', and then laughin', and then they're talkin'—

They?

The Russkies... Male and female, sir. They got this bad laugh.

Can you hear any words?

No, just laughin' and screamin' like they was drunk or somethin', like they was at a carnival and ridin' a carnival ride, that kind of wild fun screamin'... I heard 'em makin' cow sounds over by the barn, and then three shots, and I hear Emma our cow moan and go quiet, and that's when I know it's Russkies.

How do you know?

Takin' our milk supply. Pop said they'd do that. Said they're all starvin' over there. We're real quiet, and I can hear the kitchen screen door slammin', and their voices.

Then?

Then a minute later, I hear 'em again in the yard, and they're calmer now, and I got my ear pressed up against the shelter door, and I can hear what they're sayin, and they say it in English, which I figure they musta been practicin' and trainin' on for the attack.

What did they say?

They said, "There's a boys' bedroom," and then they're quiet. If they seen our bedroom, I know'd they musta been in the house.

Good thinking, son. Go on.

I move back—into the back of the shelter. I don't hear 'em comin' over. But next thing I hear, they's outside the shelter door. Still usin' their English. To sound like they're from around here, but I can tell they ain't.

What are they saying?

They say, "I ain't touchin that," and then, "Well, you got to," and then there's a scrapin' on the door. And then there's pullin' on the door, more pullin', just like before, and then more talk. One goes, "It's locked." Other one goes, "Yeah. From the inside." And then it's quiet. And then...

(PAUSE. CRYING.)

Take it easy, son. Just go nice and slow.

Then they shot out the lock, sir. So loud. Me and my

brother, Mike, jumped. And they come down the bulk-head steps, and into the shelter.

And then?

· *Well, when they gone in the house, that's when me and Mike got the shelter all ready.*

Meaning?

We know where Pop keeps the gun, and we know where the shells are, but he thinks we don't. So we got the gun—which we NEVER touched in the shelter before, I swear to you, sir—and we put the shells in...

How'd you know how to do that?

Why, we shoot squirrels and varmints and such all the time with our .22s, so we know how to work Pop's gun no problem. And we had it all set up. The chair pulled over, Pop's gun propped nice and steady on top of it, some shells lined up on the seat and Mike holdin' the rest of 'em. And they come into the shelter, and course it's all dark on 'em, suddenly comin' straight out of the sunshine like that, just like for us when we come in here playin', so we shot the Russkies, the both of 'em. Shot both shells at 'em, put more shells in real quick, and shot again, we was so scared.

And then?

Then we stayed right there in the shelter. We was too scared to go out and find more of 'em. I jus' ran over to the shelter door and pulled it closed.

And you and Mike sat in there with the...the dead Russkies?

We sat in there and I turned on the Cardinals game, sir, to get us to not think about it, and then you came. We looked at 'em, lyin' there. Russkies all right, like Pop warned. Beards and weird clothes and funny boots and such. Are we in trouble, sir?

No, you're not.

Can we see our parents now? Are they mad at us?
Is that why they haven't come to git us yet?

(PAUSE.)

Sir?

Sorry. Yes, son?

Are they mad at us?

No, they're…(PAUSE.)…they're proud of you.
You're good boys. They'll always be proud of you.

Sir?

Yes, son.

Sir, did…did the Russkies get 'em?

(PAUSE.)

Yes, son.

The…the Russkies got 'em?

Yes. That's right. The Russkies. Your parents died
defending our country.

Defending…defending the United States of Amer-
ica…?

Yes. They're heroes, your mom and dad. And you
boys are heroes, too. You hear me? Heroes, okay?
Don't you ever forget that. Now we're gonna bring your
brother, Mike, in here, so you can be with him. We were
talking to him in the next room, so he could tell us what
happened, too. And now, some nice people are gonna
come take care of you both. They're with the state of
Indiana. And you'll be safe from the Russkies, safe
from everyone, from now on. Come on in here, Mike.
You just sit down here next to your brother, Owen, for
a spell. That's it. Now you got to be nice to each other,
you hear? Be real nice to each other, from now on.

And now, fifty-five years later, Owen James Ames
turns off the recording once again. Presses the button on his computer. That's how it is now. He had the
old reel-to-reel recording transferred to a cassette tape

years ago, and the cassette tape to a CD after that, and he recently had the CD digitized and backed up on the cloud, whatever that is exactly. He'd been able to get hold of the tape originally because of the FOI Act. He'd been able to locate it in the first place, because of who he is. Because of his authority and influence. He's listened to it occasionally, now and again, over the years.

He turns to Detective Bowman. Good man. Taking over the division. Just as Owen James Ames, former chief of detectives, is finally retiring. He shifted to a consulting arrangement a few years ago so local law enforcement could still tap his long, unparalleled expertise. But now, at long last, Ames is stepping away.

"Spree killers," says Ames. "Started the night before at a gas station outside Terre Haute, killed an older couple in Evansville, stopped for food or fuel or thrills or God knows why at an isolated family farm." He smiles tightly. "Ours."

He squints out the window. "That was the enemy, Bowman. Not some frozen, starving, struggling peasants six thousand miles away. Benign-looking everyday kids from just up the highway, kids whose brains got scrambled up by who knows what, a father's drunken intimidation, or a mother's sexual advances, or relentless humiliation, or rape or incest at their own isolated family farm, or else they were just bored crazy, and something snapped in them."

He leans back in the big leather chair, swivels a little, drums its arms with the fingers of both hands. "That's your enemy. Homegrown, home-sprung violence bred right there in Indiana. Violence the local cops tried to comprehend, reconstructing it for weeks, months, I'm sure, and in the end, nobody knew any more than we do right now, a half-century later.

"Spree killers, Bowman. Stopped by a twelve- and

ten-year-old who thought they were Russians." Ames shakes his head, smiles again, more wistful now. "My pop was paranoid about a Russian invasion. Hardworking farmer, eighth-grade dropout, mule of a man, never touched the sauce, but all caught up in what he saw in the newspaper and on our grainy, fuzzy TV. Paranoid—but as it turned out, not paranoid enough."

Bowman is smart enough to stay silent. To know he is hearing something significant. A confession from fifty-five years ago, and a confession now. Was Ames playing it now, for Bowman, to guide him somehow in his new role? To offer a lesson, a cautionary tale, about the rush to judgment? About the true nature of bravery? About humility?

Former chief of detectives Ames is sure Detective Bowman has heard some version of this story before—through hearsay, or seeing old news clippings, or offhand gossip from chatty detectives at adjacent desks. Some version of the story has inevitably made its way around every police force where Ames has ever worked—Philadelphia, Baltimore, DC. Decades on the toughest urban forces. A long way from a farm in Indiana.

Most cops, after all, don't have a defining moment like this. A moment of terror, a sharp crack of gunshots that have shaped a life. But it's always been a version of his story, Ames has discovered, filled with inaccuracies, drifting into myth. So every so often over the past fifty-five years, Detective Ames has shared the tape. To correct the version. To set the record straight.

What former chief of detectives Owen James Ames *doesn't* say to Bowman, because it's trickier, more complicated...

How, yes, he's clarifying the record—but not quite setting it straight.

How his confession as a twelve-year-old boy in Indiana has forever given him extra intuition into the other side of the interrogation table. How it has endowed him early with special insight into the subtleties of the truth.

How, yes, the events of that Indiana morning steered him somehow inevitably, inexorably into this career. Gave him a lifetime of trying to repair that day. To see what went on, on the other side of the bomb shelter door. To see what goes on on the other side of locked doors ever since.

How a bomb doesn't necessarily fall from a Russian plane. A bomb can be hiding anywhere, take any form, detonate anytime—from right beside us, or even from within us.

How when he plays a certain section of that tape, the words of his twelve-year-old self still reverberate—across the decades—with fresh pain:

—And then got even scareder 'cause we heard footsteps runnin' toward us, and someone pullin' on the shelter door real hard, just pullin' and pullin' and pullin'—

How it had been his father, it turned out. His poor father. Trying to get to the gun in the bomb shelter. To protect his family. To defend them. A father's protective instinct. Not knowing, of course, that the boys had been playing in the bomb shelter.

Not knowing he was inadvertently leading the killers right to the boys. Did his father realize all of this in his last moments, pulling frantically at the shelter door? That his two boys were in there? That the killers would now look to see what was behind that bolted door?

—And then there's a big loud crash against the door.—

His father's body, blasted, hitting the door.

—And then it's real quiet, and we stay real quiet, and I'm listening for Russian, and there's more shooting, and laughing—

Now Detective Bowman will understand for sure, beyond the myth and hearsay, the ancient prairie rifle that hangs on the wall behind Ames, amid all the plaques and citations. Most assume it's just a memento of his rural upbringing, shooting rabbits, squirrels, other varmints, but Bowman will know now, for certain, it is much more than that. He'll know exactly what gun it is.

"Russkies," says Ames, shaking his head once more. "Good Lord. Seems like another lifetime."

And yet, it is this one.

Ames smiles wistfully, ruefully. "To a twelve-year-old farm boy, it was the Russians. But it was never really the Russians, was it?" He cocks his head, looks at Bowman, assuming that Bowman will see the point: It was people who talked like us. Looked like us. Could *be* us. Until suddenly, they weren't.

Ames sits up suddenly in the big leather chair, stands up sharply, reaches out to shake Bowman's hand. "You'll make a terrific chief of detectives, Bowman. You'll do great."

He places his left hand over their handshake. As if confirming it. Cementing it. Blessing it with a big, warm smile.

It was never really the Russians, was it?

That was enough, right? That should serve as enough of a useful lesson, a cautionary tale for Bowman, right?

Bowman didn't need to know the rest. No one needed to.

Especially Mike.

He'd never been able to find his brother's confession tape. His ten-year-old brother, Mike, interviewed in the next room. He didn't know exactly what was on the tape, or exactly what Mike had said. He'd always been curious.

He'd learned early—real early—not to trust confessions.

Because twelve-year-old Owen James Ames had known right off it wasn't Russkies.

He'd known it was crazy people. He'd known by the voices, by the accents, it was someone from around here. Who sounded like they were from just down the road. He could tell by the sounds. He could tell by the snippets of crazed conversation. He could tell by the screaming. He could even tell by his father's confused, "Hey! Hey!" that it was someone that his father—for a moment—thought he knew.

Just as Owen James Ames knew—had always known—that it was their father pulling on the shelter door.

Knew it immediately. As it was happening.

He hadn't let his father in because if he opened the door, he knew the killers would get in, too.

He hadn't let his father in because he was protecting Mike.

Letting his father die. To protect his kid brother. To protect himself.

—*We was too scared to go out and find more of 'em. I jus' ran over to the shelter door and pulled it closed.*—

Closing the shelter door quickly behind the two dead "Russians" to keep his brother from seeing their father's body. The body Owen knew was lying out there.

You boys are heroes, the Indiana sheriff had said.

Really? Leaving their own father to die? Heroes?

His brother, Mike, would be at the retirement dinner next month.

He'd never shared with Mike that he knew it wasn't Russians. The convenient, well-turned lie his paranoid father had armed him with. His lie to the police, to protect his brother and himself. His lie to let them be seen as simple, deluded twelve- and ten-year-old farm boys.

It was never really the Russians, was it?

As it was never simply the Blacks or the Latinos or the skinheads, in his intervening lifetime on the chaotic, drug-infested, crime-ridden streets of Philly and Baltimore and DC. It was never simply the Other.

It was, instead, how you *reacted* to the Other. The Other being the stress of the moment. The angry crowd that gathered spontaneously. The incendiary situation. The Other being what you caught yourself thinking. The surprising emotions and reactions and versions of events that rushed at you. What you said in the moment, what you chose not to. The Other was yourself, and you had to discover it for yourself, by yourself, and preaching it to Bowman would do no good.

It was never simply the stranger on the other side of the door. It was the stranger on this side.

The one who, fifty-five years later, was still keeping it to himself.

Telling himself once more the truth in the lie, the lie in the truth—that he was still protecting Mike.

He'd always protected Mike.

He was a born protector. He was a born cop.

Who had learned so early…

There is no shelter.

* * * * *

A DIFFERENT KIND OF HEALING

BY STEVE HAMILTON

It's a cold night in February and Charlotte is about to see her first snowfall.

And her first gunshot wound.

It's the night shift. Her first week in the city. Sixteen hundred miles from home, and she's still feeling every mile. The call comes in from EMS on the special red trauma phone. GSW, the shorthand for gunshot wound. Nonresponsive, palpable pulse at the neck, patient bagged, twelve minutes out.

By the time the stretcher bangs through the doors, the attending physician and three nurses, including Charlotte, are already gowned and masked. The airway tray and the blood are ready. Charlotte cuts away the man's shirt, revealing a single ragged entry wound to the chest. Right center, between ribs two and three. They can't find an exit wound, which means a bullet inside that bounced around God knows where. The bright red blood bubbling from the mouth signals a damaged lung.

Rapid intubation. Large bore IVs. Prep for immediate surgery. But then the blood pressure crashes. The pulse skyrockets one second, flatlines the next. It's all slipping away, within a matter of seconds.

Charlotte watches the man's face. He's white, unshaven, with hard lines on his face. But his bare chest is pale and smooth in the harsh fluorescent light, like an alabaster statue. He's not much older than she is.

The doctor charges the paddles and hits him with a jolt. The line stays flat. Hits him again. It's a waste of time and electricity.

The doctor takes a long beat and then calls it. Takes off his gloves and walks away. Charlotte keeps looking at the man's face. She wonders what kind of man he is. She wonders if he has a family somewhere, wife or children who even now are wondering why he hasn't come home. But the hard street-lines on his face suggest he doesn't, which if nothing else might make this night a little easier. Because nobody will show up here looking for him.

An hour later, she's outside the hospital, walking down a block to stand on the edge of Prospect Park. The snow is coming down hard now. Some of the snowflakes hit the street in suicide missions, immediately turning into gray slush. But out on the level ground of the park there's a smooth white blanket building, one inch on top of another. You'll get a dusting of snow in South Texas some winters, but nothing like this.

Charlotte watches her own breath as it hits the cold air. Wonders again how she got here. But she doesn't have time to dwell on it. She turns around and goes back to work, ready to face whatever new trauma this night will bring to her.

Three time zones away, the virus is spreading. It's twenty days away from the city.

* * *

This is not how she thought her life would go. Valedictorian of her high school. Center on the girls' basketball team, first team all-county. Top 5 percent in her nursing school, a few months away from her degree and an open door to just about any hospital in the country. A boyfriend at that time, the two of them unofficially engaged to be engaged. He wanted them to stay in Texas. She was warming up to the idea, to stay close to both families, have that support system when they started having kids of their own.

Three years later, after everything that happened, it's like she's finally come back into her own life. She found out how much they needed qualified nurses here in the city, bad enough to move you here from anywhere in the country, pay for your last semester, let you do it online, whatever the hell it takes to get you on three twelve-hour shifts per week, plus on call for three more.

So she left it all behind her, as much as she ever could, and now she's living in a tiny one-bedroom on Seventh Avenue. Not the Manhattan version of Seventh Avenue, but a world apart here in Brooklyn. The Borough of Immigrants, they call it. There's a Vietnamese restaurant just below her apartment, Malaysian across the street. Indian, Pakistani, Ethiopian. So many languages, and everyone talking so loud that most days her own Texas drawl barely seems to register.

It all moves in a blur. The traffic, the people, the way they walk, the way they talk, in whatever language. But nowhere does it move faster than here at the hospital.

She's trying to settle into the rhythm. Everything she learned from a book, everything she observed on her rotations, it all feels inadequate here, under the bright lights of big-city medicine. But she's determined to learn the rules, one more piece of the puzzle every day.

It's the Emergency Room to most people. Some of the doctors and nurses call it ED. Emergency *Department*. Sometimes it's just Trauma. Or, unofficially, the Grinder or the Pit—although you never let an administrator hear you call it that.

The consistent first priority is triage. A French word for *sorting*. Obviously if you're rolled in on a stretcher, clinging to life, you move to the head of the line. Among the walk-ins, it's the chest pain, the suspected stroke, the acute appendicitis that gets you a golden ticket. Otherwise, if you're stable, even if you're holding a towel against your wound to control the bleeding, you sit in the waiting room. Some nights, when the trauma room is rocking and all of the beds are full, when you finally get seen by someone it'll happen right in your waiting room chair.

By the end of the first week, Charlotte realizes that she's going to be seeing a lot of children with sore throats, mild fevers, persistent coughs, upset stomachs. The parents don't have insurance, so there's nowhere else to go. Here, nobody gets turned away.

She learns that it always gets busy right after 11 p.m. because that's when prime-time television is over.

She learns that anytime she sees a foreign object stuck in a patient's body—just name the orifice and she'll eventually see something that went in but won't come out—there's a 99 percent chance the patient will claim to have no idea how it got there.

And she learns that, contrary to urban legend, a full moon doesn't mean a busier night. Truth is, you never know when things will go from quiet to insane.

"It takes a special breed of person to work in this department," the head nurse tells her. "Most nurses don't stay here…and that's okay. If it's too much, you just tell me."

The head nurse is named Maguire, and she reminds Charlotte of Major Houlihan from the old *M*A*S*H* reruns she used to watch. Blond hair pulled back tight, just turned forty but still kicking ass. Maguire has seen it all, in EDs across the city, and now she's watching Charlotte every night to see if she's that one in a thousand: a natural-born trauma nurse.

In her second week, there's a multicar accident that brings four broken bodies through the door. They all get examined, x-rayed, reexamined. Concussions, broken ribs, broken collar bones, a compound fracture of one arm. Two of the patients get sent to Surgery. Charlotte catches her breath as she sits in front of the computer screen. She didn't realize she'd spend so much time sitting in this chair, entering data.

A man comes to the desk, stands over her and asks her how much longer it's going to be before his father gets some attention. Just as Charlotte looks up, she hears the doors open, feels the cold blast of air from the February night. A young woman is standing there, like she can't take another step forward. Alone, lost and unsure, her arms folded across her chest.

In one-tenth of a second, Charlotte knows exactly what this look means.

Everything else fades into the background as she gets up and goes over to the young woman. She's eighteen years old, nineteen, twenty. Can't be any older than that. "What's your name?" Charlotte asks.

"Stephanie," the young woman says, meeting Charlotte's eyes for one instant and then looking back at the floor.

"You've been assaulted," Charlotte says. Not a question.

Stephanie doesn't respond to that. There's no surprise that this stranger has just divined her secret.

"Everything's going to be okay," Charlotte says. "Why don't you come with me…"

She takes Stephanie out of the main room, doesn't want to put her in a bay with just a sliding curtain for privacy. Down the hall there are stand-alone examination rooms.

As soon as Stephanie sits down on the exam table, she already wants to leave. "I'm sorry," she says, "this was a mistake."

"You're safe here," Charlotte says. "I promise you. Now, can you tell me what happened?"

Stephanie doesn't say anything, keeps staring at the floor. Charlotte waits. And waits.

Until it finally comes out. A professor at the college. She accepted an invitation to his private residence, after a long series of texts back and forth on their phones. Charlotte's mind races ahead of the story, is already seeing how it could be interpreted by a skeptical outsider. Or a defense attorney.

But not by Charlotte. She knows that none of these things matter. They are weightless when compared to the iron meteor of the crime itself.

"Do you have someone who can come get you?" Charlotte asks.

Stephanie shakes her head.

"There must be someone," Charlotte says. "It doesn't have to be family. It can be a friend."

Stephanie thinks about it, finally gives Charlotte a name and phone number. Charlotte sticks her head out the door, catches the eye of another nurse and gestures for her to come into the room. She is not going to leave Stephanie alone, not for a second.

When the other nurse comes in, Charlotte tells

Stephanie she'll be right back, goes to call the friend, asks her to bring Stephanie a new change of clothing. Everything, down to the underwear.

Charlotte's next call is something she would have done anyway, even if it wasn't mandated by state law. She calls the police, asks the dispatcher to send over a female detective.

"I'll see what I can do, ma'am," the dispatcher says. A heavy *New Yawker* voice, right out of a black–and–white movie.

"It has to be a woman," Charlotte says, all Southern politeness gone. "Do not send a man over here."

An hour later, Charlotte is back with Stephanie, sitting in silence. The detective finally shows up, a Black woman in an all-business pantsuit. Charlotte never gets her name. She's asked to leave the room, doesn't hear the questions, doesn't take part in the physical examination although she's glad to see it's one of the female doctors who goes into the room.

The detective takes Stephanie's clothes away in a brown paper bag. The rape kit will be sent wherever they go to await processing.

Charlotte doesn't even see Stephanie leave the hospital. But the young woman's face is still in her mind when she ends her shift. When she goes out into the cold night and walks home. Even hours later as she lies awake in her bed, listening to the never-ending sounds of the city.

As the sun comes up the next morning, the virus is thirteen days away.

In the hospital, a low-level hum is starting to build. There are fifteen known cases now, all in the state of Washington. On most days it would be hard to worry about something happening on the other side of the country when there is so much pain and injury and sickness right in front of you. But this thing that's coming isn't a flu bug. It's a new strain of virus and you don't have to know anything about "R-zero reproduction numbers" to know that this will be a tsunami.

Everyone in the hospital can feel it in the air. A basic, primal awareness, like animals sensing a great storm moving across the open plain. It spreads from doctors to nurses to technicians to patients.

The hospital administrators are busy counting supplies while the daily work goes on. Charlotte has been dealing with a run of heart trouble on this shift, fortunately nothing more serious than A-fib and one mild heart attack. She's sitting at the same workstation when the same doors open. It's the lady detective who walks in again.

Charlotte gets up and intercepts her in the hallway. "Detective," she says, "excuse me, I'm the nurse who helped with Stephanie last night."

It takes a beat for the detective to make the connection, then she remembers. "Oh, yes," she says. "No, I'm not here about that. There's someone else I need to see about—"

"Can you tell me what's happening with her, at least?"

The detective just looks at her.

"The man who assaulted her," Charlotte says. "Did you arrest him?"

The detective looks down at Charlotte's name tag. "Look, Charlotte," she says, lowering her voice. "I appreciate you being concerned about her, but you've got rules here at the hospital about what kind of information you can share with other people, right?"

"Of course, but—"

"And we've got rules, too. I'm doing what I can for

her. And that's all I can say about it. So if you'll excuse me…"

The detective gives Charlotte a squeeze on her arm,
keeps walking down the hallway.

Two hours later, Charlotte is still trying to let it go.
She's about to take her meal break, glances over at the
blank computer screen.

She's right, Charlotte says to herself. *We both have
our rules.*

And I'm about to break mine.

Charlotte doesn't even know her last name. But she
cross-checks the daily logbook and quickly narrows it
down to get the contact information.

Staten Island. She doesn't know how to get there,
how far the subway goes, then how you buy a ticket for
the ferry. *Wait, isn't there a bridge?*

But then she pictures herself showing up at the front
door, ringing the bell, and then what? Someone in her
family answers the door, what does Charlotte say?

In the end, she decides to call her on the phone,
finds a lonely corner in the hospital cafeteria and dials
the number, hoping it's a cell phone so she can reach
Stephanie directly.

"Hello?" The voice that answers is so quiet, so flat,
Charlotte has to cover one ear and listen hard with
the other.

"This is Charlotte," she says. "I was the first nurse
you saw last night."

A long beat, until: "Yes?"

"I just wanted to see how you're doing."

Another beat. "I'm fine."

"Listen, Stephanie… I just want you to know… If
there's anything I can do… Like if you need someone
to help you through this. I can—"

"No," Stephanie says, cutting her off. "I don't need anything. Thank you. I have to go."

"Stephanie, wait." Charlotte closes her eyes, takes a breath. "I know how this works, all right? As soon as they charge him, he's going to come after you."

"They're not going to charge him."

Charlotte tries to process the words. "What are you saying?"

"The detective told me how this would go. What I'd have to do. Testify in court. Face-to-face. Answer anything his lawyer asks me. I'm just… I don't want to do any of that."

"I know," Charlotte says, "but you have to. If you don't…"

Don't say it, Charlotte tells herself. *Don't make this worse and tell her he'll do it to someone else. She knows that better than anyone else right now.*

"I have to go." The line goes dead.

Charlotte puts the phone down, stays there for a long time, replaying the conversation, over and over, thinking about what else she could have said to make it turn out differently.

There's nothing you can say, she finally tells herself. *And you're the last person in the world to be saying it to her, anyway.*

Because you know how this goes.

Different city, different time.

But it's the same crime. And the same system.

What makes you think this one will be any different?

When Charlotte walks home late that night, she hugs her coat around herself with every step. Wonders how long she'll have to live here before she stops feeling like she's going to freeze to death.

She tries to sleep, finally sits up and grabs her phone.

She hits the redial button before she can talk herself out of it.

The phone rings four times. Then the sleepy voice on the other end: "Hello?"

"I promise you, I'll never call you again," Charlotte says. "Just tell me two things."

"What?"

"Tell me his name," Charlotte says. "And where he lives."

The next day, Charlotte rides the subway for the first time. It's much easier, much cleaner than her Texas imagination had told her it would be. She looks out at the East River as the train goes across the bridge. But she doesn't understand the difference between the express 4 train and the local 6 train and ends up riding all the way up to Harlem, has to double back at 125th Street and get on the local coming back so she can get off at Eighty-Sixth Street.

She finds the brownstone on Ninety-First, walks by it a few times, finally finds a coffee shop a half block away where she can keep an eye on the front door. She looks at her watch, wonders how long she's going to have to wait.

The minutes pass by slowly. She keeps buying more coffee, uses the bathroom and prays that she doesn't miss her chance to see him.

Finally, just as the sun is going down, she sees a car stopping in front of the house. Charlotte leaves the coffee shop, quickly crosses the street. As she gets closer, she sees the lighted Lyft sign in the car's windshield. The passenger gets out of the car, slams the door with unnecessary force. He's in his fifties, solidly built, like a man who played football back in his day. He's wearing a long coat with a fur collar, his reading glasses in one gloved hand, the handle of a leather messenger bag in the other. He looks preoccupied, mildly irritated by something or someone. But as Charlotte gets closer, the man stops dead in the middle of the sidewalk. She feels herself being scanned from top to bottom. Appraised. Cataloged.

He doesn't move. He's blocking her way, so she has to step around him. He nods to her with a slight smile.

She nods back. *Hello, rapist.*

Ten yards past him, she can still feel his eyes on her back. She turns the corner, doesn't stop walking until she knows she's out of sight. She's breathing hard in the cold air, not even sure why. Her heart is racing.

Charlotte's never seen Central Park before, so she takes a quick detour, walks down the pathway between bare trees.

I just had to see him, she tells herself. And the lie is born.

The lie grows for two more weeks.

Charlotte has the routine down now as she rides the express to Grand Central, switches to the local and gets off at Eighty-Sixth Street. Like a New York City professional. She knows the coffee shop, the pizzeria, the diner, the Dunkin' Donuts. Most importantly, she's starting to learn his schedule. He's a creature of habit, like most people. He takes a car from the brownstone to his teaching job at the college. Charlotte doesn't know what he teaches, and doesn't care. What matters is that he comes home somewhere between five and six o'clock on Monday, Wednesday and Friday. After six on Tuesday and Thursday. Most nights he has food delivered. So he almost certainly lives alone. One of those single men who can afford a home with a nice kitchen, but never has to actually use it.

She makes this trip to the Upper East Side as often as her work schedule allows. On the first day of March, she's in the hospital and Head Nurse Maguire wants to see her.

"I just wanted to see how you're doing," Maguire says. The exact same words Charlotte said to Stephanie on the phone.

Charlotte gives the same answer: "I'm fine."

"You seem…preoccupied lately."

"I'm good. Really."

Maguire holds on to the question for another beat, then lets it go. "I don't know if you heard," she says, "but we have a positive diagnosis in New Rochelle. That's fifteen miles north of the city."

She doesn't have to say anything else, because this means two things:

The virus has arrived.

Life in the hospital is about to be turned upside down.

And for Charlotte, it also means one more thing:

It's time to stop lying to herself, and to admit what she's really been doing.

What did you think you were going to do? Catch him in the act of raping someone else? Call the cops and send him to prison?

Is that how you think this story ends?

The next morning, she wakes up knowing that her work life is about to change. Everything in the city is about to change. She doesn't know how bad it's going to get. She doesn't know how long it's going to last. But she knows she can't be so far away from the hospital anymore. Not if her team needs her.

Which leaves today. But there are cameras all over

the city. Nobody moves anywhere without it being recorded, probably a hundred times over.

So I have to do something about that.

As she gets ready, she thinks back to the Halloween night when she was fourteen years old. Her sister Emily was twelve. Her sister Anne was nine.

That's right: Charlotte, Emily and Anne. Because her mother was an English professor who happened to have three daughters and who happened to revere the Brontë sisters. The original badass riot grrrls of the nineteenth century. They dared to write novels at a time when many women weren't even allowed to *read* them. So the inside joke this one Halloween would be that the three sisters would dress as the three male pseudonyms that the Brontë sisters had to assume in order to have their books published. Wearing men's clothing purchased from the Goodwill shop and with beards and moustaches drawn on with eyebrow pencils, young Anne became Acton Bell, Emily became Ellis Bell and Charlotte became Currer Bell. Which wasn't nearly as cool a name as Acton or Ellis, so she just had everyone call her "Charlie" that night.

Ten years later, Charlotte once again puts on men's clothing. She pencils in a faint beard and moustache with her eyebrow pencil. She's already tall enough to pull this off, but now she puts two hand towels over her shoulders to make them a little bigger before she slips on the varsity jacket. Then she tucks her hair underneath the baseball cap.

She looks at herself in the mirror and says, "Hello, Charlie."

She's dead calm on the subway. Head down, not looking at anybody. A lone male rider keeping to himself.

The gym bag is on the seat next to her, holding the tools she will need. And as the train rumbles across the bridge, she lets her mind go back to three years ago.

She's in her final year of nursing school. Emily's in her first year of law school. Anne is a sophomore at Baylor. A visiting professor, a longtime friend of their father's, has rented a house nearby for the school year. He's far from home, with no other friends nearby, so he spends a lot of time at the house. Sometimes, he helps Anne with her studies.

Charlotte has just come home for winter break. Emily is not home yet. Anne is locked in her room. She won't come out. Charlotte remembers the trick with the door, slides the pin inside the knob to poke the lock open.

Anne is curled up in a ball on her bed. She won't talk.

It goes on for three days, until the visiting professor comes to dinner. Emily is home now. Charlotte and Emily both go up to check on Anne. This time, it all comes out. The professor had come over when nobody else was here. Anne was upstairs, taking a shower. When she stepped out, the professor was there in the bathroom.

Waiting for her.

It's three years later now, and everything that came after that is still a sick blur. Anne is past the seventy-two-hour window for an effective rape kit. She's always been the troubled child of the three, with a history of depression, anxiety, occasionally irrational behavior. The professor meanwhile has every legal tool, every legal connection to draw upon. He's questioned, but never charged.

A year later, he will attack another young woman. A half dozen more crimes will emerge when this one is fully investigated. He will finally be convicted and go to prison.

But Anne won't be there to see it, because she has already ended her own suffering in the only way she knows how, while playing her favorite music and sitting in a warm candlelit bathtub, just a few feet away from where she was attacked.

Their mother is broken, never to be repaired. She is watched over by Charlotte for three years, until Emily steps up to take her turn. Their father is gone, last spotted somewhere in Arizona, drinking himself into oblivion.

As the train pulls into Grand Central, Charlotte wipes a tear from her face. Lone male subway riders don't cry. Not if they want to remain unnoticed.

As she switches to the local train, she passes a transit authority cop. She holds her breath as she walks past him, starts breathing again when she gets on the next train.

Ten minutes later, she comes up the stairs on Eighty-Sixth Street. Just in time to hit the dinner hour. She doesn't want to go into the coffee shop to wait, wants to avoid as much human contact as possible.

She walks slowly down the block, keeping an eye on the brownstone. *Don't walk back and forth too much. Don't just stand in one place, either.* She's watching for the dinner delivery. It's going on seven o'clock. The streetlights are on. Medium traffic. Just another night on the Upper East Side.

Then she sees the deliveryman walking up the street, carrying the white bag. From the diner, a block away. The deliveryman goes to the front door, rings the buzzer, waits a moment and then goes through the door.

He'll be back down in a minute.

I'm really doing this.

Charlotte feels her stomach turning, has to remind herself that she already knows how to handle this. Because there's always that moment in the hospital when she has to acknowledge her own fear, then put it in a box in the corner of her mind so that she can do what she needs to do.

She's jarred by the sound of her phone ringing. She looks at the caller ID. It's Maguire. Must be calling her to come in. For the first time since coming to New York, she lets the call go to voice mail.

A few seconds later, she sees the deliveryman come back through the door, empty-handed. He heads down the street, back to the diner. Charlotte waits one more beat, goes to the door, takes out an empty white package from her gym bag.

She takes a breath. Presses the buzzer.

"Who's there?" the voice says.

She glances up at the little camera above the call box. Somewhere inside, the man is watching her.

"From the diner," she says. "We forgot to deliver your special dessert."

She doesn't bother to disguise her voice. Let him think it's a woman outside, or a man with a feminine voice. What he thinks right now is not going to matter. All that needs to happen right now is that the man who's conditioned to buzz in food deliveries every night does it one more time.

"What are you talking about?" the voice says. "I didn't order any dessert."

There's irritation in his voice. Maybe even suspicion. Charlotte glances down at the street, wondering how fast she can get away if she has to.

"It's something special for our best customers. It should have come with your order, I apologize."

Another agonizing moment passes. Then the door buzzes. Charlotte pushes it open and steps inside.

As she closes the door behind her, the noise from the street is gone. It's suddenly so quiet that she can hear a clock ticking in another room. She stands before a great staircase with a polished banister.

"Up here!" the voice says. More irritation. Impatience. Charlotte welcomes it. She wants this man to meet her worst expectations right now, in every possible way.

She pauses one moment to take one of her tools out of the gym bag. The bag stays slung over her shoulder as she goes up the stairs. When she gets to the top, she's not sure which direction to turn. But then the man surprises her as he appears in the doorway on her right.

He's wearing his reading glasses and holding a book. "So what is this?" he says, looking at the white package in her left hand. He doesn't notice the tool in her right hand. Not yet.

But then it all hits him at once. The voice he heard on the intercom doesn't match the person he's seeing now. And why does this man's face not look quite right?

Charlotte hands him the white package. He takes it from her, an automatic reaction when someone hands you what you assume is a bag of food. It takes another second for him to realize the bag is too light. Is this empty? But now, with the man's hands occupied, Charlotte is free to take one more step forward and press the cattle prod firmly between his legs.

A regular stun gun is designed to send a jolt of electricity through the body of an average-size man. A cattle prod is designed to do the same thing, but through the body of a sixteen hundred–pound animal. Both weapons are strictly illegal in the state of New York, but this cattle prod came from a ranch in Texas, stored in Charlotte's suitcase against imagined big-city dangers. She's seen a cattle prod like this applied to a man's genitals one other time in her life, on a drunken bet at a party, and the effect it has now when she turns it on is just as spectacular. The rapist lets out an inhuman scream of pain as his body slams to the floor. He curls up into a fetal position, both hands clutching at his groin. Charlotte kneels down next to him, the cattle prod poised in case she has to apply another dose. But the man has his eyes closed tight and he's lost somewhere in his own private world of pain.

Charlotte has been trained her whole life to treat other people, to ease pain, to lessen misery, to find the humanity in every human being and to help that person heal in any way she can.

But not this time.

This time, it's a different kind of healing. At least that's what she's telling herself. She's healing the world itself by removing this sickness, the same way you'd cut out a cancer from a patient's body and never feel one moment of remorse for the tumor once it's thrown in the medical waste bin.

Charlotte takes out the last tool from her gym bag. It's a syringe and a vial of succinylcholine. *Sux*, as the doctors and nurses call it. One injection and it circulates quickly, depolarizing every muscle in your body.

You can't move. You can't breathe. You can't even blink.

It's normally used on a patient when a ventilator is going to do his breathing for him, but here, injected into this man on the floor... It means he's going to stay fully awake as he realizes that he's lost all control of his own body.

As he realizes that he's about to die a slow death.

Just like you did to Stephanie, Charlotte thinks.

The exact same thing.

The man is rocking gently on the floor, making a low humming noise in his throat, his hands still clutching at his groin. Charlotte actually wants him to open up his eyes right now. She wants him to see her as she takes off her hat and lets down her hair.

This is a woman doing this to you, my friend. No testosterone needed for this particular brand of Texas-style justice.

Charlotte hears the chirping of a text on her phone. She ignores it, plunges the tip of the needle into the vial.

The phone chirps with another text. She takes out her phone and looks at the screen. It's Maguire.

Charlotte, please call me.

And then the second text.

We need you.

A fresh tear runs down her face. She wipes it away.

I've been carrying this around for three years, she tells herself. *I couldn't do anything for Annie. But this time, I can.*

She taps the syringe, a force of habit. Clearing any air bubbles because God forbid you inject one into the bloodstream and cause an embolism. The thought is almost laughable right now.

We need you.

No, Charlotte thinks. *Be quiet.*

We need you.

As soon as this is done, she thinks, *I'm all yours. My mind will be free.*

No, the voice says. *The detective knows who this man is, what he's accused of doing. She'll remember you asking about Stephanie. And she'll know, as soon as she sees the forensics, that you have access to a medical murder weapon like this.*

She won't come after me, Charlotte says. *Not if she knows that he was going to get away with it.*

You think she'll violate her oath as a police officer, just like you're violating your oath as a nurse?

Then I'll use something else, Charlotte says. *I'll just beat his brains out. Trash the place, make it look like a break-in.*

You're not going to crush a man's skull, the voice says. *You're not capable of doing that. And even if you were... What happens the next time you see a rape victim in the hospital? And then the time after that?*

Charlotte doesn't even know where this voice is coming from.

But she knows, deep down, that everything it's saying to her is right.

"But I miss her," she says out loud, more tears streaming down her face. "I miss Annie so much."

She cries for a full minute. Then she puts the syringe back in the bag.

Charlotte stands up and looks down at the man still writhing on the floor. She knows that she has to go back, *right now*, because they need her at the hospital. Because a single strand of RNA from the other side of the world is mindlessly replicating itself over and over again, in people of every age and color, man or woman, good or evil.

Because the virus has come to town and it's Charlotte's job right now, above anything else, to help fight it.

She's about to put the cattle prod into the bag. But then she stops, comes back over to the man, who has now rocked over onto his back. She leans over and gives him one more long shot to the groin, making him scream so loud they can probably hear him in the Bronx.

"That one's for Annie," she says. And then she's gone.

* * * * *

TOKYO STRANGER

BY TINA DEBELLEGARDE

Mr. Sasaki gets into his car, his pressed uniform sliding easily on the leather seats. The muted thump of the Mercedes door's closing signals the start of his shift. He turns the ignition and gently the engine comes to life, quietly, almost imperceptibly, but his practiced senses can feel the hum as it idles. He tunes the radio, searching for the classical music program scheduled to begin at midnight. He pauses to admire his gloved hand on the dial. The gloves, a gift from his wife, his name stitched inside so they would never be lost at the station.

He glides the car into Drive and pulls into the colorful streets of Tokyo. The time on the dashboard shows twelve o'clock just as he arrives at the old apartment building.

She steps out as he pulls up. Tonight she wears a fuchsia dress riding high on her thighs, stiletto heels and a silk wrap of emerald green thrown over her shoulder against the chilly breeze. She carries a small umbrella.

He presses a button, and the left rear passenger door opens automatically. She slips in and unwraps her shawl in the cozy interior.

"*Konbanwa*, Sasaki-san."

"*Konbanwa*, Yuki-chan."

Good evening, they greet each other, despite the late hour.

He puts the car in gear, and they start their weekly trip across town.

Friday night is his favorite fare. He peeks in his mirror and watches this young girl, so much like his daughter except for the startling slash of bloodred lipstick. He can't resist watching her fiddle with her mirror and her complicated clothes. He observes quietly as Yuki reapplies her lipstick. He can almost believe it is his daughter. Not only does she wear her hair in the same bob as Haru but the color is exactly the same. With hints of red or purple, magenta maybe. And like his daughter, she chews her lip as she thinks.

What is on her mind? Is she thinking about her upcoming evening or her life outside these midnight trysts? Does she have a family she is working to care for? Sasaki doubts it, she is so young. Or does she just look young? He has never seen her in the light of day, only embellished with the blues and reds of the late-night city lights.

Twenty minutes into his reverie he pulls into a silent street, the large homes on each side hidden by walls. He slows down as he approaches and inches his car close to the gate. From her purse she pulls out a tiny remote. He looks back through his mirror again; she is furiously chewing on the edge of her lip.

He puts the car in gear, but stops when he hears her catch her breath, as if startled. Once again, his eyes find her reflection. A tiny drop of blood emerges from her lip as if her lipstick had come to life. He passes her his linen handkerchief. She takes it from him with a slight bow of her head and dabs at the blood. Once, twice, but the droplet reappears. The third time the blood stops. She passes the handkerchief back. He glances at the blood and lipstick, the linen permanently damaged. He lays it carefully on the seat next to him so as not to stain his gloves.

The gate opens, he pulls in and parks. Sasaki releases her door and it quietly opens to the cool night air, but he tells her to wait, for the rain has already started, earlier than expected. He runs around the car and pushes open a wide golf umbrella. With this protection he escorts her to the door. She lets herself in, offers him a shallow bow in thanks and closes the door.

He has over two hours until he must return to pick her up. Tanaka pays him for the entire three hours, doesn't want him picking up any other fares between eleven thirty and two thirty. He wants Sasaki at his disposal. For what Tanaka pays him, Sasaki doesn't mind as long as he is able to keep his mind occupied.

He drives away, dreading the idle time ahead of him. Guilt rushes in to fill the void. Guilt over his wife, over his daughter. And tonight, guilt over delivering this young girl to a yakuza boss or worse. Tanaka has a "business associate" visiting from out of town who specifically requested Yuki. She is Tanaka's personal favorite. This stranger must be pretty powerful if Tanaka agreed.

Sasaki circles the block looking for a spot. He parks around the corner from the Black Cat Jazz Club and walks the half block in the misty rain.

He enters the smoky haze and sits at his usual corner seat by the bar. The bartender pours him a shot of whiskey on two cubes of ice. Sasaki removes his gloves before lighting up a cigarette and swirling the drink. He prefers his whiskey neat, but on Friday nights he allows himself one shot on some ice. It is his habit to nurse it slowly and allow the ice to melt, a diluted drink is better than none. He needs to have his wits about him to drive.

The cigarette, the drink and the alto sax smooth over his tension and guilt. They are his only remaining vices. Sasaki lights another cigarette and closes his eyes to listen.

When the musician finishes his set, he takes the stool next to him. "Very nicely done."

The musician motions to the bartender. "Tengo, refill his drink on me."

Sasaki pauses, thinking how pleasant it would be to sit here for another drink and chat with this musician, but comes to his senses. "Thank you, no. I'm done drinking for tonight." He turns his wrist. Two fifteen. He empties his glass and puts on his gloves after saying his goodbyes.

Outside, he lights his last cigarette of the evening and smokes it under the black awning.

The rain is heavier now. He pulls up the collar of his uniform jacket and heads for his car.

The gate is closed when he arrives. Usually Yuki opens the gate once he pulls up. He sits in the drive, the car idling, a Mendelssohn violin concerto gently playing on the radio. The rain beating on the window almost drowns out the soft music.

He glances at his watch, two forty-five. He gets out of the car, pulls up his collar once again and looks around.

The rain suddenly lets up. In the silence he hears a tiny crack, like a squirrel walking on the autumn leaves. Then a little cry. Again, louder this time, more like a child. He walks along the path, tracking the sound.

It's a steady cry. Then a hiccup and another whimper. He stands still to quiet his footsteps.

"Yuki, is that you?"

"Sasaki-san?"

He spots an opening where the gate meets the wall and squeezes himself through.

He follows the noise until he finds her. Yuki is crouched behind the hydrangea bush, barefoot, one shoe in her hand, her fuchsia dress darker in some spots. Her hair clings to her face, the obvious tears lost in the rain.

"Are you hurt?"

She shivers, but doesn't answer.

When he gets closer, he realizes the spots on her dress are blood.

He looks her over, but decides she is uninjured. He scoops her up, she doesn't protest.

Tiny as she is, he hardly has to exert any effort at all. He presses the button to open the gate, then places her gently in the back of the taxi. The car is still idling and the warmth engulfs them both.

"You have to tell me what happened."

"I… I wouldn't let him… I couldn't let him." But Yuki gives him nothing more.

"I will be right back."

As he turns to close the door, she puts a hand on his arm. "Please don't leave me."

He is torn. He looks at her, so small in the car. Wet and still shivering. It reminds him of the times he took his daughter to the ocean. She would erupt from the water with her hair hugging her chin. Shivering, her arms crossed until he wrapped her in a towel.

He gently pries Yuki's hand from his jacket.

"I promise. I will be right back."

She shakes her head and grabs his arm. "I promise." She closes her eyes and lets go.

He finds the front door ajar. He stops to listen. There is only silence. He looks toward the stairway and sees a streak of blood along the bannister. At the top he stops again. Complete stillness. The door at the end of the hall is the only one open. He approaches it slowly.

In the bedroom, he finds the stranger facedown on the bed on blood-soaked sheets. Yuki's green shawl sprawled along the foot of the bed is like a winding mossy trail leading to her purse, the contents spilled on the bed. Her missing shoe, along with a knife covered in blood, are on the floor beside a pair of men's slippers.

Sasaki turns to run. But in the hallway he stops.

He returns to the bedroom. He removes his gloves, then retrieves the shawl and the shoe. He grabs Yuki's lipstick and keys along with the rest of her belongings and shoves them back in the purse.

He grabs a towel from the bathroom and wipes down every surface, the headboard, the doorknob, the side table, anything Yuki might have touched. Then he gingerly picks up the knife and wraps it in the towel.

Down the boulevard, his temples pound as he forces himself to drive within the speed limit back to Yuki's house.

He rummages around in her purse until he finds the key, then picks her up and carries her into the building.

He tries to avert his eyes while he strips off her clothes and leans her in the shower. He searches for the warmest clothes in her closet and helps her dress. He dumps out the contents of a shopping bag and fills it with more clothes and toiletries. He finds ten thousand yen on her dresser and adds it to the rest.

Back in the car, he puts the bag on her lap and closes the door.

"Sasaki-san, where are you taking me?" she asks, but doesn't wait for the answer. She leans her head on the doorjamb and falls asleep.

Forty-five minutes north of the city, he pulls up to a deserted train station and buys a ticket at the kiosk. The sun is just peeking up over the tracks. The train is due in twelve minutes. He waits ten minutes, then goes to get her.

"Take this." He hands her all his money. Combined with her own money, enough to last a while if she is careful. "I bought you a ticket to Aomori. Do not come back here. Ever. Do you understand?"

The rumble of the train drowns out his last few words.

She nods and steps into the open door. The doors close behind her. She leans her head on the glass and the last he sees of Yuki is her dazed eyes staring out over the platform as the train pulls away.

Sasaki drives his car onto the bridge behind the train station. He grabs the package in the trunk and scrambles down the embankment to the riverbed. He finds the largest stone he can handle, adds it to the towel and ties a sturdy knot. Then throws it into the river. He watches it sink before he leaves.

Sasaki enters his apartment. Dog-tired. More tired than he has ever been in his life. He walks to the far corner, taps the bell and tilts his head in prayer, then looks up at the picture of his wife and daughter on the altar. How many years has it been?

He closes his eyes again. Nineteen years, and he has

finally redeemed himself. Nineteen years since they took that fatal drive, when he wasn't there to protect them. Nineteen years of aging alone. All that remains is his job. Driving to numb the pain.

He strips, one piece of clothing at a time. Slowly, deliberately. First his hat. He places it carefully on the dresser. Then he removes his jacket and slides it onto the hanger, buttoning the first and last buttons. His pants, he picks up by the crease and clips to the wooden hanger. He does not rush. With the same reverence as every other day, he hangs his uniform in its proper place.

After he showers, he sits on the bed. Usually he sleeps for eight hours before getting up to start his day shift.

Today he will have to settle for less sleep, but he needs to be refreshed when they come for him. He must be sure he isn't too tired, that he will be clearheaded. He needs to be completely convincing, so the search will stop at him.

He gently swings his legs up on the bed and rests his head on the pillow, contemplating the ceiling. If he sleeps until noon, he can get enough rest before they come for him. It will take them about that long to find the gloves. It will take them about that long to track him down at work and then show up at his door.

He closes his eyes.

* * * * *

LAST FARE

BY JOE HILL

He couldn't look her in the face, not the whole last day she was in the house. When her suitcase was packed Gene stood by the door. A part of her wanted Walter to look at her and a part of her was afraid of what she would see in his eyes if he did.

"I'm going!" she said, in a falsely cheery voice. "I don't think the train is due into Vilmos until after eleven, but you'll be awake won't you? To watch the returns?"

He nodded. He sat on the ottoman, in the blue shirt he had worn to the party the evening before. It was wrinkled from a night on the couch. He sawed his index finger back and forth over his upper lip, a thing he did when he was struggling to clamp down on his anger. She had never once seen this gesture in the first five years they were married. She had seen quite a bit of it in the last five months.

"I'll call when I get in, if you'd like that," she said.

"No, I don't think I would. Because you'll be drunk

by then and I can't stand to hear it in your voice. But it hardly matters what I want, because you'll be drunk, and you'll do what you like."

"I'm not going to show up there drunk," Gene said, and she wanted with all her heart for that to be true. She was surprised by the choke in her voice. "I don't want to live like this anymore."

"That makes two of us," he said. He laughed without humor. "I don't want to drive home from work at five in the afternoon, wondering if I'll find you passed out. Or dead. I don't want to be standing next to you at the party when you insult our friends. I don't want to go get you a cup of punch and walk back and find you in Don Treadaway's lap—"

"Okay."

He went on as if she hadn't spoken "—the both of you crocked and his hand rubbing your hip. I don't want to have to smile like it's all very funny when he tells me to collect you in the morning."

She stood with her hand on the doorknob and the suitcase at her feet, beginning to shiver.

"I guess I won't be home in time for Thanksgiving. What will you tell your parents?" she asked.

"I'll tell them you went to a clinic to dry out."

"You want them to know I'm a drunk?" she asked.

"They already know."

She nodded, absorbed this as her due. Walter told his parents everything. Well—almost everything. He hadn't mentioned the miscarriages. When the second sent her to the hospital, Walter told his mother she was being treated for a uterine cyst, which Gene supposed came in at least breathing distance of the truth.

"Will you be here when I get back?" she asked.

That finger stopped moving back and forth across his mouth and at last he lifted his gaze. He stared past her, at a point just beyond her left ear. His eyes were veiled and faraway.

"Why wouldn't I be here? Who do you think paid for this house?"

Whether she was welcome in it anymore was apparently a subject better left for a later date.

When Gene called ahead, they said the Sunset Limited was due in at 4:15 p.m., but when she got to Union Station it had been pushed back an hour. The lobby was a stone oven and it seemed every other woman was jiggling a crying baby. The air reeked of pissy diapers. An old Black man paced between the benches, holding a battered Bible aloft, promising that neither idolaters nor adulterers nor the covetous nor drunkards would inherit the Kingdom of God. For Gene MacMurray that was all a little too on the nose. It seemed like the whole list had been drawn up with her in mind.

She found a place on a pew, put her suitcase down between her feet. She had hardly sat before an obese old woman, fragrant as a boiled cabbage, squeezed in beside her. The old girl had a fuzzy white moustache and a brown wart the size of a housefly on her right eyelid.

"I hope my train isn't late! I have to get home and vote. I haven't cast my ballot yet."

"No. Me neither," Gene said. The election had seemed so important just a few weeks ago. Now the thought of exercising the franchise was about as inviting as picking a crushed cigarette off the floor and smoking it.

"You will, though?" the old biddy asked, patting Gene's hand. "We have to stop Kennedy. He has two Black babies in Georgia. It's a great crime it hasn't been more widely reported. Two chocolate babies. The *New York Times* knows but won't write about it."

"I campaigned for Kennedy."

The old lady blinked and pulled her hand back. "He's a fornicator. A Catholic fornicator."

"I know. Me too. That's why I campaigned for him." Gene glanced at her sidelong and said, "What's that thing on your eyelid? It looks like cancer. Have you had it checked out?"

The old lady heaved herself up to a bench across from Gene, where she could fix her with a furious glare. It nauseated Gene, the way the wart on the old woman's eyelid quivered every time she blinked, like it was about to fall off. Or maybe it was the hangover turning Gene's stomach sour. Either way, she ached for fresh air, needed it almost as badly as a free diver surfacing from a long plunge in the depths.

It was better outside, pacing back and forth in the last of the day, the air so clear and sharp it almost stung her nostrils, and the sunset painting the adobe a shade of cherry blossom. Her circuit took her past a taco cart, a Mexican in a serape dishing out beans and beef into flour tortillas. There was a cooler built into one end of his cart and when he lifted the steel lid, Gene saw beers buried in crushed ice. Thirst clicked in her throat and she wanted to cry. She went straight back inside and leaned against the wall, her shoulders pressed to the cool plaster.

The train would be there at five fifteen and she would get on sober. The lay preacher shouted that you could not drink the cup of the Lord *and* the cup of devils. Gene said "Amen," but under her breath. She was watching the clock over the ticket windows so intently that she missed it, at first, when they moved her train back to 7 p.m.

Gene went out again to watch the sun bury itself in the west. A star—or maybe it was Venus—gleamed all alone in the navy blue sky. She inhaled the fragrance of spicy stewed beef and her stomach responded with a comic rumble of hunger. She hadn't eaten all day and for the first time since waking her insides weren't knotted up with sick.

She was going to have to be strong. Sooner or later, Gene reminded herself, she was going to need to eat, and where there was food there would also be alcohol. She got in line.

There was a guy buying tacos ahead of her, a tall man in a powder blue suit, pale yellow tie and meringue-colored fedora. He smiled at her when she appeared beside him and unapologetically looked her up and down before turning back to the cook.

"One for me and one for her," he said.

"You don't have to do that," Gene told him.

"Are you kidding?" he said. "I'm on a train to Houston all night. Seven hours. I'm going to be imagining the life we *aren't* going to have the whole way. The house, the kids, the sunburn I got on our fifth anniversary in Cancun." He shook his head and clucked his tongue. "Good memories of all the stuff that didn't happen."

At that moment, a kid in a white linen suit dashed out of the lobby. "We gotta scram, Mr. Beaufort. Last call on our train!"

The romantic grabbed his suitcase, nudged Gene's elbow and winked. "Ah, well. Catch you in the next life."

"Plan on it," she said and smiled as he grabbed a bottle and a grease-spotted bag and squeezed away into the crowd, following his junior partner.

Gene turned back to the cook, a man with the long lashes of a Hollywood ingenue and the broad, imperial features of an Aztec. He popped the cap of a Lone

Star with his church key and set it down on the counter. Little flecks of ice slipped down the sides of the wet bottle. When the romantic said *one for me and one for her*, Gene had thought he was talking about tacos. She stared at the beer as if it were a tarantula.

"You don' wan it?" asked the cook. "Z'cold. Z'pate for."

Her throat clicked with thirst once more.

"Can I ask you something?"

"Sure," he said.

She took the beer by the neck. "Do you know if there's a bar car on the Sunset Limited?"

The Sunset Limited didn't roll out of Phoenix until after eight and by the time she climbed aboard, Gene was three beers in. She felt that all her good intentions had been overruled by forces greater than herself. The hand of fate had pushed aside her well-meaning goals and handed her a tall cold one instead. Anyway, it seemed a shame not to have a drink on election night.

And the bar car was so lovely. Just sitting there made her feel sexy. She was a woman alone in a long car with mahogany-paneled walls and a lot of brass fittings. The mirror behind the counter would've looked just fine in a grand hotel and she was conscious of men watching her in it. She paid for her first gin and tonic. A tall olive-skinned man with bristly silver hair paid for her second. But when he started over to sit across from her, she lifted her left hand and wiggled her rings at him. He laughed and shrugged and turned back to the bar and she liked him tremendously. After that, though, she paid for her own G&Ts.

At some point she found a Southerner sitting across from her, a man with a bald head like a peeled hard-boiled egg. His boulder-like chest strained at the buttons of his wine-red silk shirt. He reminded her of an actor she knew from the horror films Walter liked, a monstrous ex-wrestler with tree trunk legs and blunt fingers. Had a name like a stone. Rock Johnson? Tor Cragson? Somehow she was holding Crag Rockstone's fat, pasty hand and pleading with him to tell her when they got to Vilmos.

"What's in Vilmos, darlin'?" he asked, in that syrupy voice of his, watching her with unblinking eyes.

"There's a clinic for people like me."

"You mean drunks?"

"Yes."

"Now, why would you wan' a stop drinkin'? I'm goin' a Fort Worth. Come on with me. I'll give you five hunnert dollars a month to be my Fort Worth girl-frien'. I'm meetin' some Jap businessmen wanna sell me components for radios. Five hunnert to be my girl-frien' and five hunnert more to be theirs."

"I'm a drunk," Gene said. "Not a whore."

"Don' sell yourself short, hunny. People'n be more than one thing."

She rested her forehead on his big knuckles. "Just tell me. When we're at Vilmos."

He patted her head and called her his good drowsy girl. He said if she needed to doze he had a sleeper unit. She *did* need to doze. She felt leaden with tiredness. She also thought if she went to his sleeper car with him then, when she woke, she'd exit the train while it was still moving. She'd throw herself at the first telegraph pole she saw. In fact, she might not wait for morning. She might leap on the walk to his cabin. It would be less painful for her, she felt, in the long run.

"Did you say you're getting off at Vilmos?" said someone else.

It was hard to lift her head. It was like it had tripled

in weight, was too much for the slender stem of her neck. When she looked up, the olive-skinned man with hair like silver shavings was standing over her table. His gaze shifted rapidly from her to Block Johnson.

"Mmm," she said.

"That's this stop. We're there *now*. You're about to miss it."

The Southerner rolled his eyes. Gene looked through the window and saw a concrete platform and a dainty brick station. She struggled to her feet and fell into the silver-haired man, who caught and steadied her.

The Southerner still had her other hand. "Someday you'll remember ma offer with a real sense of pride, peach. How many women can say they know the 'zact moment they were at their peak worth?"

"Tor Johnson," she said, suddenly, and took her hand back. "That's who you look like. You don't want to date me, darling. Go make out with a giant ape who's got a TV set for a head. That's more your speed."

Three deep furrows appeared across the smooth egg of his forehead.

She weaved down the length of the car, descended two steps, and inhaled a deep breath of the high desert air in Vilmos, New Mexico. It smelled of blazing hot iron: a frying pan left to heat on the stove. Someone caught her elbow. It was the silver-haired man. He had come down off the train with her suitcase, which she had forgotten. He handed it to her and squeezed her arm.

"I hope you're on your way somewhere safe," he said. "I hope there's someone to take care of you."

He let go and climbed back onto the train and a moment later it shuffled out of the station in a series of jolting hisses and clanks. She watched it go. Windows flickered by. The same person stared back at her from each one: an uncanny figure wearing the mask of a girl, someone with plastic expressionless features and black holes where the eyes belonged. It took her a while to realize she was looking up at her own reflection.

A lone taxi idled in the brick turnaround, a yellow Studebaker Starlight with a round silver grille that brought to mind an airplane's propeller. It was the past's idea of what the future would look like, had to be ten years old…although there wasn't a speck of road dust on it. It could've just rolled off the showroom floor.

The driver bent toward his radio, a guy in a satiny windbreaker the same color as his cab, an Irish flat cap on his head. He didn't notice her swaying by the car so she hunched to rap her knuckles on the glass. He lifted his head and he had a gold coin over each eye, an image so bizarre and terrible she overbalanced and had to grab the Starlight to keep from going down.

He jumped out and hurried to her side. She searched his face with alarm—if there were coins where his eyes belonged she was going to scream. But no. His eyes were brown and friendly and gentle. She looked into the car again. The coins were still there. They hung from the rearview mirror by a delicate chain. Only a trick of *her* eyes had made them appear to be *his*. It occurred to her that she was very drunk.

The wheelman opened the rear door for her. Gene didn't know he was helping her in until he closed the door. He carried her suitcase to the trunk for her.

News announcers spoke in news announcer voices. They were so toneless, as they discussed the election returns, it was hard to follow them. Ev e r y th i n g c a m e s o s l o w l y.

Her driver eased behind the wheel and put the flag

down on the meter. It began to tick like a Geiger counter searching for radiation in a Tor Johnson movie.

"Can you take me to feels bar?" she tried, then shook her head. Her tongue was heavy and clumsy.

"Fields Bar? Is that the new place just opened in Elephant Butte?"

"No. Feels. *Far*. SPAR. Fees spark." The harder she tried to say it the worse it got.

"Fieldspar!"

"That's it. It's a hos. Per. Tull." Words with multiple syllables were difficult.

"Yes, ma'am," he said. "I know it."

They pulled away from the curb and glided through a charming little downtown, where the roads were brick not blacktop. The barbershop was closed for the night but the striped pole glowed merrily by the frosted glass door. They passed a darkened Texaco that looked like a whitewashed Spanish chapel.

"Truth or Consequences, straight ahead." He pointed through the windshield.

"S'true," she agreed. She felt he had said something very profound. "Been heading toward them for a long time. S'my appoinment in Samarra." She pronounced *Samarra* just right on the first try and was very pleased with herself.

He politely drove to the end of the block before he said, "Truth or Consequences…it's a town. Fieldspar Hospital is out that way."

"Oh. Right." She let the car carry her along for a bit, then felt the need to offer some clarifications of her own. "I played it. When I was a kid. Truth and consaquenches. I always chose the consaquenches, never the truth. Took my underwear off and tucked it into a Coke bottle in front of the other kids. Wasn't very ladylike but it caught my hushbin's eye. He wasn't my hushbin then. And he didn't care if I was drunk. He got drunk too! He kept that Coke bottle on a windowshill in his dorm room for a long time."

"Things go better with Coke!" her driver said, and she had to laugh. He was a clever little elf. "So what's happening in the world? Besides the election?" He smiled at her in the rearview. "I want to know everything about everything."

"Trains are running late. Babies have been scrying. Crying. Lone Star beer is cold. Until you drink it. Then it's stomack tempa-sure." She frowned and said, "Are you asking about *me*? What shappening to me sper-cif…sperf…spessifcally? I dropped an A-bomb on my marriage and now I'm radioactive. I'm aglow." She considered for a time. "Din't they drop the A-bomb shout here?"

"Near here. In Alamogordo."

"I know Allama-gorgo," she cried. "Hungeback of No-der-Dame, right? Nice guy. Bit of a limp. Great kisher."

"That's the very man. He moved out here for the sun. Not much sun in the belfry of Notre-Dame."

She narrowed one eye to a squint. "Now you're teasing."

"It's our company motto, ma'am. We aim to tease."

When she looked out the window, the little town was gone, and the star-drowned night was wheeling over the cinder-colored desert, over the sharp peaks in the north. She had a sense not of driving, but of flight.

"I saw it," he told her, in a tone of voice that was almost shy.

"What'dya see?"

"The A-bomb."

"You're skidding."

He shook his head. "It flashed like someone took

a picture with the world's biggest camera. Like someone was trying to take a snapshot of God's face. That's
how we said hello to the universe, after four and a half
billion years of keeping to ourselves. I saw it from ten
miles away, saw the sun coming up on the wrong side
of the sky, and I knew right away we couldn't un-ring
that bell. No, ma'am. I knew right away it would bring
folks around to check on us." There was an update on
the election. The driver cocked his head to listen. They
called Louisiana for Kennedy. The driver clucked his
tongue. "Seems like a nice guy—Kennedy—and I wish
him all the best, but what I'd really like is if they'd say
something about the World Series."

"Why would they menjin that?" she asked. "It was
last momfh. *Mumth.*"

"They wouldn't mention it," he agreed sadly. "They
never mention it in November." He looked at her in the
rearview, his eyes bright as coins. "Do *you* remember
who won? Was it Brooklyn?"

"No," she said, with a certainty that surprised her.
She couldn't remember who won. She had been drunk
most of the last few weeks of baseball season. But she
was *sure* it hadn't been Brooklyn, although she couldn't
have said *why* she was sure. They had won just a few
years before, hadn't they? Couldn't they have won
again?

The time bomb tick-tick-tick of the meter gave her
a queer feeling in the head. She reached for the crank
and lowered her window halfway, feeling a sudden urgency for fresh air. The night smelled of baked clay,
the still-hot kiln of the painted desert. The stone-oven
heat rushed in and dried the bad sweat on her forehead.

"We're goin fash," she said.

"This old taxi can just about go faster than light," he

said. "But not this evening. We'll be at Fieldspar before you know it. Twenty minutes maybe?"

Twenty minutes. A dreadful number. Twenty minutes was so soon. She made a pitiful little sound in her throat, somewhere between gag and sob.

"I don't want to go to Fieldspar." She only realized it as she said it aloud.

"Hmm?" he asked. "Oh, ma'am."

"I mean like this. Like I am. Like, all drunk." Just the thought made her want to cry.

Her driver paused for a delicate moment. Then he said, "Miss? They've been there since before the war. They've seen it all. The important thing is, you're going."

"And I'll take the cure."

"That's right."

"I hadda idea for another kinda cure. I was goin' jump off the train earlier. Cure for all that ails."

The driver said, "And ruin that dress?"

She didn't expect to laugh and was surprised when she did. "It's my hushbin's favorite. Was. Is. Our relationship hasn't settled on a tense. The only thing we settled on is it's tense."

"Maybe you need space from each other. There's nothing but space out here! You've never seen so much space." He leaned his head to the left to look up into the vast expanse of the star-choked night. He smiled, as if he had caught sight of an old friend. Then he peeked at her in the rearview again. "What's your name?"

"Gene. MacMurray. To whom do I have the pleasure?"

He told her.

"Wha' kinder name is Whit Lemon? Sounds like a dessert."

"I go down just as sweet with a black coffee."

"Shoulda got a coffee while we were in town. Then I wouldn't show up there drunk off my ash." She paused, then said, "I guess you've probably seen a lodda folks who were drunk off their ash."

"I've had all kinds in this car," he said. "All kinds. A couple years before they dropped the bomb, I drove two men with white eyes. No pupils. No irises. Thin men in white suits. They asked me to leave them in the desert. I stopped the car in the middle of nothing and nowhere, five miles from Caddyhenge, and they got out with their briefcases and walked into the heat haze. They wobbled a bit in the melty heat coming off the desert and then they were gone."

"Caddyhenge?"

"It's on the way. You'll see it. Past the drive-in. You'll see that too. They're having a special screening tonight. Invitation only. A political thing, actually." He reached out and flicked one finger against the gold coins hanging from the rearview to make them dance. There was something odd about those coins. They burned and flashed as if the sun was glaring off them, even though the sun had been down for hours. "One of them—one of the thin men—paid with two silver dollars, which was about thirty-seven cents more than they owed. Only when I checked the cashbox they were these instead."

"What a rip. Goddamn fare jumpers."

"Not quite," he said, fondly. "They're worth more than you'd think. They're better than gold, these honeys! You could pay the fare to just about anywhere with one of these coins."

"S'right? Why, are they rare?"

"You've never seen any like them! Here. Take a look." He slipped one off the chain—it happened so quickly she didn't see how he did it—and offered it to her.

She took it from him, a gold disc big enough to almost fill the cup of her palm. It was light, as light as foil, so light she was worried she would crush it. It was deliciously cool to the touch and she shivered. It was like reaching into ice water to grasp a bottle of beer—it felt that good. There was nothing printed on either side of it, but when she closed her eyes, the gold coin left an afterimage burned on her retina, as if she had been staring directly into a lightbulb: and there *did* seem to be a picture in the afterimage, a sphere with needles of light jabbed through it. The sphere rotated in the darkness behind her eyes for a moment before it faded.

"What's it made of?" she asked.

"Compressed light, I believe," he said.

"Ha. That's funny," she said and tried to hand it back.

"Hold on to it, Gene," he said. "Isn't it nice? Like if someone minted a coin out of a mountain stream."

"Yes," she said.

She squeezed it a little. It felt so light, it should've crumpled in her hand, but it didn't flex in the slightest. She turned it over to look at the other side—also blank—and when she shut her eyes she saw a glowing afterimage of three suns (old suns, old and red and friendly). She almost laughed again. It was the most delightful and peculiar thing, the way the coin seemed to be inscribed, but one could only see the images stamped into it when they closed their eyes.

"But you were going to tell me about what's happening now!" he said. "I want to know everything. What are people watching on TV?"

She opened her eyes and inhaled deeply, breathing in the desert sweetness, feeling better, feeling *clearer*.

"The debates. Nixon looked like he'd mug you in an alley." She thought about what Walter liked to put on. "*Bonanza. Gunsmoke*. Shoot-'em-ups."

"What about girls? What are they wearing?"

She laughed. "You got eyes, don't you?"

"Only for the road, darling."

She said, "Mohair. Doesn't that sound dirty? Just saying it makes me want to blush. And bikinis."

"The hell's that?" he licked his lips, then gave the word a try, as if saying it for the first time. "Bee-keen-ee?"

"It's a little two-piece swimsuit. Models wear them. I'd be too shy myself. I think they look, well, like something from a grubby men's magazine. You know what they named them after? Bikini Atoll. They're the atom bomb of fashion."

She shut her eyes and saw that line of old, venerable suns again. Opened them and shook herself like a dog trying to dry off. The fresh air really was helping with her head. "How come you don't know about bikinis? They're the biggest turn-on since Marilyn Monroe stood over a subway grate. Everyone knows bikinis. Unless you spent the last year stranded on a desert island, cut off from civilization?"

"That's one way to describe this part of New Mexico," he said. "Far as that goes, you could describe the whole planet the same way. What about kids? What do kids play with these days?"

"I don't have kids," she said and her insides clenched up and a wave of sick feeling broke over her. She put her head back against the leather seat and thoughtlessly pressed the coin to her forehead. It felt as good as her mother's cool hand pressed to her brow during a fever. "Tried. Second one put me in the hospital. They couldn't stop the bleeding."

"Oh, my dear."

"Scared my husband. Said we couldn't try again." Then she said, "Do you know what a rubber johnny is?" If she was sober, just the thought of asking such a question would've made her stiff with mortification, would've made her face burn.

"Yes, ma'am," he said. "Say no more."

She had been raised Catholic and knew well the gloomy security of the confessional. A late-night taxi was much the same. Here, with Whit Lemon—a man she was sure she would never see again after tonight— she felt she was permitted to speak truths she could hardly permit *herself* to consider by the sober light of day. It helped that he was a good man. She was certain of this, had known it when he said it would be all right to arrive at Fieldspar in her current state, that they had seen it all there. And what *was* her current state? She was losing her good drunk feeling, couldn't hold on to it. The taste of her own mouth made her want to brush her teeth. The feel of her dress sticking to her thighs made her want to shower.

"I hate them," she said, but she said it softly, and after it was out of her mouth, she hoped he hadn't heard.

He had. Whit said, "He doesn't want to be the reason his wife drops dead."

"It's not fun anymore. For either of us. He's just pretending to like it." It astounded her, the things that kept coming out of her mouth. She couldn't seem to stop herself. She would not even have said such a thing to a priest, would not have alluded so directly to the sexual act.

It was the coin, she thought, irrationally. It had been a mistake to accept his coin. It was like in a fairy tale— you had to beware of taking beans or a goose or an apple from the old woman in the deep, dark woods. She had not understood, when Whit offered it to her, that he was purchasing her honesty. This was a child-ish, absurd idea that also felt somehow incontrovert-ible and true. "It's all ruined. I ruined it."

"You're just about to see something beautiful," he said. "Hang on a little longer." She thought he was talking about the marriage, but then he pointed his finger out the passenger side window. "There. Isn't that a doozy?"

An enormous rectangle of light floated over the hardpan to the right of the car, at the base of the foot-hills. For a moment, Gene had the dizzying sensation of looking into a window in the side of a mountain...a window into an ashy brilliance. A flying saucer, big as a jet, hovered in place behind that window. Rows of cars were arrayed below it, radiating spokes of vehicles organized in a way that made her think of a thousand worshippers bowing to Mecca. She waited for the mo-tion picture to cut to a new shot, but it didn't. The UFO remained suspended over the viewers for one minute and then two, as Whit's cab approached, drew along-side the drive-in, and went past.

TONITE, read the unlit sign in front of the dirt road into the Galaxy Drive-In: WE GATHER TO HONOR AND REMEMBER LEMMINGS! UFSP MEM-BERS ONLY! TONITE'S THE NITE! WHO KNOWS WHO'LL BE NEXT 2 RISE???

She turned in her seat to watch the screen as it dis-appeared behind them. There was never anything on it except that single pie-pan flying saucer. She thought-lessly turned the coin over and over in her hand. It never warmed up, remained that same perfect sliver of cool-ness, a slice of ice, a spoonful of moon.

"Didn't you say they're having a political thing at the drive-in?" Gene asked. "I thought I saw a spaceship."

"Yes, ma'am. That's a meeting of the Universal

Flying Saucer Party, headed by presidential candidate Gabriel Green. He is addressing some of his most committed supporters with a prerecorded film reel."

She laughed. Whit didn't laugh with her.

"Is that a real party?" she asked.

"It is," he said. "I was an early member."

"Oh."

"Don't feel bad," he said. "You don't join the Universal Flying Saucer Party if you don't have a sense of humor! I admit I had hoped Mr. Green would pull off an upset this evening—or at least win New Hampshire, where there was an all-out attempt this year to raise awareness. The skies over Merrimack County were lit up every night for almost a week. Hundreds of sightings. A Super Sabre jet fighter chased half a dozen of what the air force calls 'foo fighters' over northern New Hampshire. The pilot lost them when they went orbital. Still," he sighed. "It wasn't enough. It will be Mr. Kennedy or Mr. Nixon. Hard to say which yet. They are running neck and neck, aren't they?"

"I've never seen a UFO."

"And yet, you are only too familiar with their technologies! We would not have Styrofoam, the integrated circuit or contact lenses, if not for the wisdom of the Seti-Taurans, who have been visiting these hills—these very hills!—to trade with the Pima peoples for millennia."

"I did not know that," she said, wanting to be kind to him, as kind as he had been to her. "What's a contact lens, anyway?"

Whit didn't reply, not at first. He cocked his head to one side, as if paying close attention to the radio once more. Then, abruptly, he said, "Not yet? Oh. Later, then. That will be later." She opened her mouth to reply, then shut it. She didn't think he had been talking to her. She wasn't sure who he had been talking to. Himself, maybe.

"And what about the Lemmings? Isn't that a kind of mouse?"

"Yes, ma'am," he said. "A quite friendly and harmless kind of mouse, I'd like to think."

"Why would a political party honor Lemmings? Is that, I don't know—a mascot for the Flying Saucer Party? Or is it a joke?"

"Probably a bit of both," he said.

"And what does it mean—who will be the next to rise?"

"Many hope to make direct contact with the Seti-Taurans and someday travel with them."

"Have *you* made direct contact with the Seti-Taurans, Whit?" she asked, as gently as she could. Something had shifted between them—she was not sure when it had happened—and she felt a tremendous tenderness for the little man in the flat cap. Also, she was more clearheaded now then she had been for hours…or maybe weeks. It was like waking after a long bout of fever to a crisp, bright autumn morning, the shadows of leaves rippling across the ceiling. She could feel every part of her body, the sweet ache in every joint, the tight knit of muscles. She turned that splendid gold coin in her right hand, again and again, without thought, hardly aware she was doing it.

"I came out here looking for them! I was living in Brooklyn, with my friend Bill Tate who I met in the navy. Bill had the cancer." Whit tapped one temple. "In his head. He had it so bad, he could hardly stand up. I was just about out of my mind with worry, I was so sure I was going to lose my best amigo. I fell to studying at the library, trying to find something the doctors had missed…which is how I learned about the ley lines. Do you know about the ley lines?"

"I'm not up on them, no. Please tell me."

"Well, they are like the magnetic bands that encircle the earth. Did you know that geese follow magnetic lines when they migrate? The geese can feel those beams of energy in their wingtips. Ley lines are bands of energy too. The places where they cross are full of charge, like enormous batteries. Two such lines meet in the Bermuda Triangle of course. *Three* cross in Jerusalem, very close to the most likely candidate for Golgotha. And a pair cross here, in New Mexico." He nodded to himself. "I had many encounters with the inexplicable, almost from the day we arrived. Quite often, driving at night, I would see streaks of red and green fire blaze across the sky. I'd chase 'em out into the desert, get up to seventy, eighty miles an hour, trying to keep them in sight. The next morning my whole face would be sunburned. Other times, I'd be out driving in the early hours, and I'd pass myself going the other way! And of course there were the thin men who paid me in Seti-Tauran coin. I have mentioned them already."

"What happened to your friend Bill, Whit?"

"Well, the coins happened to him! Bill would put them over his eyes at night, like he was already in his coffin. He'd sleep sixteen, seventeen hours! But when he woke he was his old self. He could even do crosswords again! Sometimes he had no pain at all. Those coins made Bill's cancer regress and bought him another nine months, when all of the doctors agreed he'd be lucky to get three." Whit smiled to himself, seemed for a moment almost overcome with the sweetness of memory. "The ley lines worked their wonders too. The scars from his first two operations vanished. The big scar on his biceps that he picked up in Guadalcanal, that disappeared too. He was as smooth and flawless as a young man after a few months here. At the end even the lines on his hands were vanishing! Everything except his love line. Everything except that." He sighed a little shakily. "I don't like to think that he might've been saved outright, if only we came out here a few years earlier. Bill and I had been best mates for years and years. We bunked together in the navy. Sometimes he'd talk about cars in his sleep. He'd say, 'A car at night stitches the darkness with brilliance.' Or, 'Get me a taxi, I want to drive to the end of pain.' I thought we'd have the rest of our lives together. I'd drive the cab and he'd be my dispatcher. His voice keeping me company all night. That good, kind, warm voice telling me where to go next." He squeezed the wheel so tightly his knuckles whitened.

"I'm so sorry you lost him," she said.

Whit's hands loosened and relaxed. "Well. He's not really lost. His energy joined the energy of the ley lines. That packet of information and power has been to one end of our universe and back a hundred times in the decades since."

"I suppose it's lucky for me that this clinic I'm going to is so close to where the ley lines cross!" she said. "I can use all the help I can get."

"It isn't an accident. One often finds places of healing and worship along the path of the beams."

"I didn't know there was a place of worship out here in the painted desert."

"But there it is! Right here. It's coming up on the left now!"

When she craned her head, she saw a shape like Stonehenge, a football-shaped oval about eighty yards from end to end. She was looking at thirty cars, their front ends buried in the red clay, the back ends aiming like artillery at the stars. The taillights had been rigged to blink and flash like someone's Christmas decorations. They stammered and flashed an irregular message to the cosmos.

"Isn't it something?" Whit Lemon asked, slowing so she could take it in.

"What *is* it?"

"It's a marker! Like the Nazca Lines in the high desert plains of Peru. Or like a sign you can see from the highway that says Texaco, so you know to pull over and gas up." He took a last lingering look at the half-buried Fords and Caddys and then began to accelerate again, following the road as it wound into the foothills. "Those cars belong to men who are no longer with us." He stroked the steering wheel. "This car belongs there too."

"After you're done with it," Gene said.

"After I'm done with it," he agreed, and he gaily flicked one finger against the coin that still hung from the rearview mirror. It chimed softly and spun, flashing.

And she could not help it, she was quite fond of Whit Lemon, with his eager voice and cosmic certainties. She wondered if he had always been this way—sweetly deluded—or if it had happened to him after his beloved Bill Tate had been taken from him. Whit was like a yard sale teddy bear with a missing eye and popped stitches. Free to a good home, not even worth twenty-five cents. He was an adorable discard. She thought there was a chance she might be on the verge of becoming an adorable discard herself. The next month would tell.

She supposed she ought to give his special coin back and she reached it over the seat to him. He slung it on the chain beside its twin. Two venerable old suns that jiggled and flashed. Gene slumped back into the dark leather of her seat as the car banked into the first rise, climbing the hills for Fieldspar. Something tickled unpleasantly in her temples. She closed her eyes—a part of her hoping to see that starscape again, that bright afterimage— but instead there was only a painful throb of pressure and she looked up again. Something about the coins hanging from the rearview troubled her. Trying to figure them out made the whole inside of her head feel ill.

"Hey!" she said. "The coin you ga'me. It didn't have a hole in it! Where'd at hole come from?" Her tongue felt heavy and strange. She clutched the armrest molded into the door, felt that if she let go of it, she would begin sliding this way and that across the backseat like luggage.

"Sure it did, Gene," Whit said. "You just didn't notice."

"I did too! Notice. No hole." She narrowed her eyes. "I am beginnin' to thing that is a strick coin." God, she was so drunk.

She ached with remorse, hated herself for every gin and tonic. The cab climbed higher and higher and at each switchback they had a better view of the floodplains below. Caddyhenge appeared as a crimson wheel, flickering and stammering in an idiot's idea of Morse code. Farther back down the highway, she saw the still brightly lit rectangle of the Galaxy Drive-In's movie screen, now an impossibly vivid postage stamp on a black sheet of paper. Beyond that was a cobweb of light: downtown Vilmos. The sprawl of the stars made it all look very small.

Fieldspar came into view just after the fourth switchback: a building in the style of a Spanish mission, with a brick courtyard before it, and a spouting fountain in the center of the yard. Palms towered over the entrance. It had the look of a luxury resort, which it was, in a way. But instead of the Gideon Bible in the nightstand, one would find a copy of the AA big book, and instead of shuffleboard in the morning, one was expected to attend classes about the twelve traditions. A nurse would show her to her room. An orderly would search her bag for liquor.

Out here she had that sky of bottomless mystery, those thousands of stars, those thousands of possibilities. It was a scattering of unbearable riches, so close she could almost touch them. But it would be morning soon enough and the sun would take it all away from her. She could hardly bear the thought of pulling up in front of Fieldspar and getting out. It sickened her, the idea of going in like she was. The idea of going in at all. The moment she stepped through the door, she would leave the splendid night behind. Every inch of road they traveled brought her a little closer to tomorrow and tomorrow was a place she didn't want to go.

"I don't wan' go," she said and was surprised at the breathless panic in her voice. "Whit? Whit, pull over."

He was silent and at first she thought he wasn't going to do as she asked, was instead, absurdly and honorably, determined to do what was *best* for her instead, and what kind of cabby listened to his conscience instead of the client? Whit Lemon, of course, that was who.

But he touched his blinker and they glided to the dusty margin of the lane. He turned to look at her, elbow up on the back of his seat.

"You don't have to be afraid of them, Gene. There's help for you here. Just up the road from us. Just a few hundred feet away now."

"Wasn' I bedder?" she asked and disliked the pleading whine she heard in her voice. "Wasn' I bedder on the ride? I am very confused." She really was. It was getting hard, already, to remember what they talked about on the ride. She had the terrible idea she had said the words *rubber johnny*. She swayed toward him. "For a minute I feel like I was a pretty okay person."

"You're still a pretty okay person, Gene," he promised her.

She wasn't mollified. She flopped back against the seat.

"What about the Seti-Taurans?" she asked. "They invenned Styrofoam, din't they? Don' they have something for us shitty drunks? Sommin' easier?" She blushed and looked away and wanted to cry. "'Pologize for my mouth, Whit. You deserve bedder."

At first he didn't reply. He looked wistfully out at the night and its harvest of stars.

"They can fix it," he told her at last. "They could even make it so you can still drink! An alcoholic is like a car going downhill with severed brakes. They can repair the lines and more. They can give you better to drink than you'd ever find in the bar car of the Sunset Limited. They can give you a golden wine, made from the crushed leaves of a plant so vast, it covers an entire world in orbit around a dwarf star. Get drunk on that and you can see the tunnel your own life has made through time itself. You can walk through that you-shaped tunnel of light and slip out into the best and happiest moments of your own life." He took a deep breath. "But you'd have to go a lot farther than Fieldspar and you can't come back. Not really. Not to stay. They can project your consciousness back into the world—maybe once every few years—to wander around and see what's happening. But it's a long transmission, Gene, and you can't stray too far from the ley lines. To go with the Seti-Taurans is like dying in a way.

A human body is like a rocket ship—it can only take you so far. To go farther, you have to get out."

"Where d'ya learn so much, Whit? About the Titty-Saurans?"

"I learned about them after the bomb," he said. He lifted his chin and his eyes were as bright as gold coins. "A few hours after it burned up the sky. I had got out of my car—pulled off into the desert to pray—and they came along while I was still on my knees. By then it was raining burnt crickets. Fried crickets fell like confetti after a great parade and it smelled like the end of the world."

"An' they tolt you all this stuff? 'Bout goin' away an' not comin' back?"

"They didn't tell me. They showed me."

She looked out at the stars herself, considering what might be up there. The constellations seemed to wheel gently above her, as if she were on a slowing carousel. Even that small sensation of motion nauseated her. She shut her eyes.

"Coul' we juss park here for a bit? You'n let the meter run. I have money. Maybe we could jus lissen to the elec-shun. Maybe if we sit a while, I can hear who won before I hafta…" Her voice trailed off.

He lowered the flag. The Geiger counter stopped ticking.

"No charge. You were my last fare tonight. There won't be another train this evening and the bars closed five minutes ago." He sighed. "And I still don't know how far Brooklyn went this year."

Even dazed with gin and tiredness, she registered the puzzle at the center of this question all over again. How come he *didn't* know? How exactly had Whit Lemon contrived to miss out on the whole baseball season? She opened her mouth to ask, but what came

out instead was "All the way to Los Angeles." She remembered as she spoke: "Dodgers moved to the West
Coats. *Coats.* Coast."

"What? No. Come on. Are you pulling my leg?"

She laughed. "Where you been living, you don'
know they're in Los Angeles now? The moon?"

"Farther than that."

"Oh. Right. Where everyone dring golden wine an'
no buddies a alcoholig. But there's no baseball season."

"Do you want to go, Gene?" he asked, in a light
tone of voice.

She put her head against the edge of her window.

"So much. I messt everything up, Whit. My whole
life. I'm married to a man is never goin' see me like he
usta. I lost his respect and I deserved to lose it. I'd like
to go so far away, I can't even find this planet on a tele-
scope. I screwed up my shot in this world and even if
I get sober s'gonna be awful. Soon as my head is clear
I'mma have to take account of everyone I hurt, everythin' I broke, everythin' I can't fix, every good thin' I
throwed away. I could use a whole new world. Really
any world but this is okay with me."

A cool breeze whisked through the car. Once these
mountains had been in a basin at the bottom of an
ocean and now, in the small hours of the night, they
were remembering their deep water chill. The night
lay upon them, as deep as a sea.

"Do you want to go, Gene?" he asked again. When
she opened her eyes he was looking over the seat at her
and he had one of those gold coins in his hand. There
was no hole through it anymore, no possible way to
hang it from a chain. She looked at it in his calloused,
blunt fingers and remembered how good it had felt to
press it to her forehead, as good as Mother kissing her
brow. "If you want to go, I'll make sure you can cover

the fare." The coin flashed as he turned it in his fingers, shone like a sun.

On the radio they were saying that Illinois was still too close to call. They were saying Nixon might make a statement soon.

Gene rested her head on the window. "I really, really like John Kennedy and I really, *really* don't like sweaty Dick Nixon. I campaigned for Jack. Let's see if he wins. If Kennedy wins, maybe the planet Earth isn't a total waste. Maybe it's worth stickin' around a little longer, see what happens."

"All right," Whit Lemon told her. "It's a deal, Mrs. MacMurray."

Later, when she was sweating out the DT's—vomiting every fifteen minutes, crawling back to bed on all fours while she trembled helplessly, a feeling like her skin was coated in cobwebs—she told one of the orderlies about driving to Fieldspar with Whit Lemon, and how if Nixon'd won she'd be drinking golden wine with the Seti-Taurans now, and the orderly laughed and said, "Whit Lemmings drove you, sure. Santy Claus is pickin' me up after my shift is over, we're goin' up to the North Pole to make a snow fort." The orderly was a big Black woman with sleepy eyes. Fieldspar was full of Black men and women in nurse scrubs, looking after wealthy white women who could not look after themselves, who needed to pay other people to do it. The orderlies looked on their wards with a kind of weary pity, which was, Gene felt, exactly what they deserved.

She was there thirty days. In December, a couple weeks after Thanksgiving, Walter made the six-hour drive to collect her. He hugged her when she came down the front steps with her suitcase, but it was a stiff, gentle, formal hug. She was so grateful for it she nearly burst into sobs. He looked ten years older and had nicked himself several times shaving.

On the drive back east, they glided past Caddyhenge in their Pontiac. Until then their conversation had been awkward, uncertain, the verbal equivalent of tenderly probing a wound to see how it was healing. But when Caddyhenge came into sight—a dozen cars pointing toward the sky, the sun dancing off the chrome, the flaking rust the rich orange of the hills—a smile touched Walter's lips, the first she had seen since his arrival.

"Isn't that a crazy thing," he said. "A guy at the Texaco in town told me sometimes empty cars turn up at the local drive-in. Like, men have just left their cars and walked away from them. Disappeared into the desert or something. If the cars aren't claimed after three years, they put them out in Caddyhenge. How's that for spooky? It really is like a graveyard for robots or something. Those cars are like headstones."

The Studebaker Starlight was there, among the others, although the doors were brittle with rust, and the back windshield was missing, and it had been scoured by years of blowing sand. She would've known Whit Lemon's ride anywhere—or Lemmings, as it turned out. She had been sitting in that car when Richard Nixon conceded to Kennedy and it had come to her she was going to have to live here in the world after all.

The older staff at Fieldspar remembered him, the local taximan who had seen the A-bomb ignite the western horizon, and had left the keys in his car and walked away into the desert, never to be seen again. Lemmings had a reputation for queer ideas, probably thought it was the end of the world. He had started the local chapter of the Universal Flying Saucer Party, he said Styrofoam was an alien vegetable and claimed to have sometimes given rides to ghosts. Maybe he was a swish too—that was the rumor—but in that part of New Mexico, you didn't poke your nose into other people's bedrooms unless you were looking for a horsewhipping. And, anyway, the Universal Flying Saucer Party had loved him and still celebrated his memory. They'd had a particularly large remembrance for him the very night Gene had arrived at Fieldspar.

Gene almost told Walter to stop…and then thought better of it and let Caddyhenge slip by without a sound. She did not want to take the smile from her husband's face.

After they called it for Kennedy, Whit had rolled the last quarter of a mile into the brick turnaround in front of Fieldspar, and the two of them had sat in the warm, idling car.

"Guess I'm stuck here," she said.

"Guess so," he told her, twisted around in his seat to smile at her. He offered her his hand—an odd gesture from a cabby driver—and she reached to take it, only he flicked his wrist and suddenly was holding one of those big golden discs. Pennies for the ferryman, she thought.

"If you ever change your mind, though," he said, "you can always come back out here. Where the ley lines cross. You can come to Caddyhenge with one of these. You don't know who might stop by to give you a ride…or how far they can take you. And if they do, you'll need to be able to pay your way."

"Thank you, Whit," Gene said, in a tone of voice that she hoped let him know how much she liked him, how glad she had been to spend time with him. "I'll hang on to it."

Only she couldn't hang on to it, lost it not forty-eight hours after she got to Fieldspar. She lost a lot in those two days: ten pounds, her self-respect and her sanity.

It was possible she had tried to bribe an orderly with Whit's coin for a bottle of gin and when he wouldn't take it, she had thrown it at him in anger and lost it then. She didn't want to think that was true and later another possibility occurred to her: there had never been a Whit Lemon. Lemming. Whatever.

Three years later she was on Monroe Street, in the shadow of the Valley National Bank, when she learned John F. Kennedy was dead. People were running past her, some of them in tears. A young lady in cat-eye glasses ran straight into her, and Gene caught her and steadied her and asked what was wrong, and that was how she found out. She learned more from a Panasonic TV playing in the window of the Woolworths. Kennedy's brains had gone all over his wife, who had tried to escape the shots by climbing across the trunk of the moving car. They didn't show that—there was no film of the incident, not then—and they didn't say it either, but somehow that information was everywhere, on everyone's lips.

At last she picked herself out of the crowd gathered around the window to watch the TV and by then she was crying herself. Her left hand was in her purse. Her right was squeezing her daughter's hand. Her daughter was crying too. The girl didn't know what she was crying about, didn't understand what had happened, but she was two, she didn't need a reason. It was enough that her mother was weeping.

Gene was fumbling in the depths of her bag when her fingers found Whit's coin: that blank golden disc that had secret designs sketched across its surface in light, pictures you could only see as afterimages burned upon your retinas when you closed your eyes. Her hand closed upon it, that smooth impossibly cool wafer of alien metal, and in that instant she saw an old yellow cab approaching through the dusk, and her heart lunged with a fierce relief, and she thought, *Come get me, Whit, come get me and my girl and my good Walter, and get us off this awful murderous planet before it can hurt us anymore. I've got the fare. Come take us away, old friend.*

Only it wasn't Whit and it wasn't Whit's Studebaker, it was a 1957 yellow Checker, and when she plucked the coin out of her purse, it was the chip she had earned for thirty days of sobriety almost three years before. It had been drifting in the bottom of her purse, largely forgotten and unnoticed, ever since. Her hand had already flapped up to catch the taxi driver's attention. He swung to the curb and, moving automatically, hardly thinking, Gene opened the rear door. Her daughter scrambled into the back ahead of her.

"Is it gold?" her little girl asked her, wiping her cheeks and staring at the coin in wonder. Jackie's face was swollen and there was a gleam of snot on her upper lip, but her eyes had lit up with inspiration at the sight of the bright, brassy medal in Gene's left hand.

"*Better* than gold," Gene said, and gave it to her, then picked her up and set her in her lap. She held her daughter to her chest all the way home.

Author's note: Gabriel Green's Universal Flying Saucer Party was real, although Mr. Green withdrew from the race in October of 1960 and endorsed John F. Kennedy.

For Charles Portis, Rest in Poetry.

Joe Hill
Exeter, NH
May 2020

* * * * *

ABOUT THE AUTHORS

Paul A. Barra is a former Naval officer (Bronze Star with valor "V," Combat Action Medal), reporter for local newspapers in South Carolina and senior staff writer for the diocese of Charleston. He is also a chemistry teacher. His last novel, *Westfarrow Island*, was called "exciting" by Publisher's Weekly: "The relentless action in the dual story lines keeps the reader engrossed. Barra offers it all: murder, smuggling, chase scenes, romance, and international intrigue." He has published four other novels and a nonfiction book about the creation of a private Catholic high school without diocesan support. He is married to the former Joni Lee; they have eight children and live in Columbia, SC. His website is www.paulbarra.com. His edress is: paulalfredbarra@gmail.com.

Alafair Burke is the Edgar-nominated, *New York Times* bestselling author of thirteen novels, including *The Better Sister*, *The Wife*, *The Ex* and the Ellie Hatcher series. She is also the co-author of the Under Suspicion series with Mary Higgins Clark. A former prosecutor, she remains a professor of criminal law and lives in New York City.

Michael Connelly is the bestselling author of thirty-five novels and one work of nonfiction. With over eighty million copies of his books sold worldwide and translated into forty foreign languages, he is one of the most successful writers working today. His very first novel, *The Black Echo*, won the prestigious Mystery Writers of America Edgar Award for Best First Novel in 1992. In 2002, Clint Eastwood directed and starred in the movie adaptation of Connelly's 1998 novel, *Blood Work*. In March 2011, the movie adaptation of his #1 bestselling novel, *The Lincoln Lawyer*, starring Matthew McConaughey as Mickey Haller, hit theaters worldwide. His most recent #1 *New York Times* bestsellers include *Dark Sacred Night*, *Two Kinds of Truth*, *The Late Show*, *The Wrong Side of Goodbye*, *The Crossing*, *The Burning Room*, *The Gods of Guilt* and *The Black Box*. Michael's crime fiction career was honored with the Diamond Dagger from the CWA in 2018.

S.A. Cosby is an Anthony Award–winning writer from Southeastern Virginia. He is the bestselling author of *Blacktop Wasteland*, Amazon's #1 Mystery and Thriller of the Year and #3 Best Book of 2020 overall, a *New York Times* Notable Book of the Year, a *New York Times* Book Review Editors' Choice, and a Goodreads Choice Awards Semifinalist. He is also the author of the upcoming *Razorblade Tears*. His short fiction has appeared in numerous anthologies and magazines, and his story "Slant-Six" was selected as a Distinguished Story in Best American Mystery Stories for 2016. His short story "The Grass Beneath My Feet" won the Anthony Award for Best Short Story in 2019.

Tina deBellegarde writes the Batavia-on-Hudson Mysteries for Level Best Books. *Winter Witness*, the first book in the series, was published in September 2020. Her short stories appear in the *Seascape* and the *Masthead* editions of *The Best New England Crime Stories*. Find her flash fiction in *Palm Sized Press Vol. 2* and online at Retreat West, Ad Hoc Fiction and Reflex Press. Tina lives and writes in Catskill, New York. Visit her website at tinadebellegarde.com.

In 1995, **Jacqueline Freimor** won first prize in the unpublished writers category of the Mystery Writers of America's 50th Anniversary Short Story Competition. Since then, her stories have been published in *Ellery Queen Mystery Magazine*, *Alfred Hitchcock Mystery Magazine*, *Rock and a Hard Place Magazine*, *Red Herring Mystery Magazine* and *Murderous Intent*, among others, as well as in the e-zine *Blue Murder* and at akashicbooks.com. Two of the stories received Honorable Mention in *The Best American Mystery Stories*, the first in 1997 and the second in 2000. Jacqueline's most recent story is forthcoming in *The Best Mystery Stories of 2021*, edited by Lee Child. She lives in Westchester County, New York, and is a musician and music teacher.

Steve Hamilton is one of the most acclaimed mystery writers in the world, and one of only two authors (along with Ross Thomas) to win Edgars for both Best First Novel and Best Novel. His Alex McKnight series includes two *New York Times* notable books, and he's put two recent titles on the *New York Times* bestseller list. He's either won or received multiple nominations for virtually every other crime fiction award in the business, from the Private Eye Writers of America Shamus Award to the Anthony to the Barry to the Gumshoe. His first book, *A Cold Day in Paradise*, won the Private Eye Writers of America/St. Martin's Press Award for Best First Mystery by an Unpublished Writer. After it was published, the novel went on to win the Mystery Writers of America Edgar Award for Best First Novel and the Private Eye Writers of America Shamus Award for Best First Novel, the only first novel to win both awards. His second novel, *Winter of the Wolf Moon*, was named one of the year's Notable Books by the *New York Times* Book Review and received a starred review from *Publishers Weekly*, as did his next three novels. In 2006, Hamilton won the Michigan Author Award for his body of work. He lives in upstate New York with his wife Julia and their two children.

Joe Hill is the #1 *New York Times* bestselling author of *The Fireman* and *Heart-Shaped Box*. His second novel, *Horns*, was made into a feature film starring Daniel Radcliffe; his third, *NOS4A2*, was filmed as a television series on AMC. His book of short stories, *20th Century Ghosts*, won the Bram Stoker Award and

British Fantasy Award for Best Collection. He earned the Eisner Award for Best Writer for his long-running comic book series, *Locke & Key*, featuring the eye-popping art of Gabriel Rodriguez, and which became a Netflix show in 2020. Among his recent works is *Full Throttle*, another collection of short stories, and the hardcover omnibus of his comic books series *A Basketful of Heads*, both published in the autumn of 2020.

Tilia Klebenov Jacobs is the bestselling author of two crime novels, one middle-grade fantasy book and numerous short stories. She is a judge in San Francisco's Soul-Making Keats Literary Competition, and a board member of Mystery Writers of America-New England. Tilia has taught middle school, high school and college; she also teaches writing classes for prison inmates. She lives near Boston with her husband, two children, and a pleasantly neurotic poodle.

Smita Harish Jain has published several short stories in a variety of anthologies, including *Mumbai Noir*. Her next four stories will appear in *Ellery Queen Mystery Magazine*, Malice Domestic's *Mystery Most Diabolical* and two Sisters in Crime anthologies. Even though she has lived in an airpark, a red-light district (not on purpose) and on a boat in the Bahamas, her writing often brings her back to her first home, Mumbai, India, where her story, "Kohinoor," is set.

Michael Koryta is the *New York Times*–bestselling author of eighteen novels, including *Those Who Wish Me Dead*, which was made into a feature film starring Angelina Jolie and directed by Taylor Sheridan. A former private investigator and newspaper reporter, he lives in Maine and Indiana.

Joe R. Lansdale is the author of forty-five novels and four hundred shorter works, including stories, essays, reviews, film and TV scripts, introductions and magazine articles. His work has been made into films such as *Bubba Hotep* and *Cold in July*, as well as the acclaimed TV show *Hap and Leonard*. He has received numerous recognitions for his work, including the Edgar Award, the Spur Award, the British Fantasy Award, ten Bram Stoker Awards, the Grandmaster Award and Lifetime Achievement Award from the Horror Writers Association, an American Mystery Award, the Horror Critics Award, and the Shot in the Dark International Crime Writers' Award. His books and stories have been translated into a number of languages, and many of them are under option for film. His novel *The Thicket*, selected by *Library Journal* as one of the Best Historical Novels of the Year, is set to film in the near future, and will star Peter Dinklage.

Emilya Naymark is the author of the novel *Hide in Place*. Her short stories appear in *Secrets in the Water, After Midnight: Tales from the Graveyard Shift, River River Journal, Snowbound: Best New England Crime Stories 2017* and *1+30: The Best of Mystory*. She has a degree in fine art, and her artworks have been published in numerous magazines and books, earning her a reputation as a creator of dark, psychological pieces. When not writing, Emilya works as a visual artist and reads massive quantities of thrillers and crime fiction. She lives in the Hudson Valley with her family.

Bryon Quertermous is the author of the novels *Murder Boy*, *Riot Load*, *Trigger Switch*, and co-author of *Jackpot* with Stuart Woods. Visit him online at bryonquertermous.com and on Twitter @bryonq.

Lori Roy is the two-time Edgar Award–winning author of five novels, the most recent of which is *Gone Too Long*. Her work has been named a *New York Times* Notable Crime Book twice, a *New York Times* Editors' Choice, and included on numerous "Best of" lists. Her novels have been published in several languages and her debut, *Bent Road*, was named a Notable Book by the state of Kansas. Lori lives with her family in Florida.

Jonathan Stone has published nine mystery and suspense novels, including *Die Next*, *Days of Night*, *The Teller*, *Parting Shot* and the bestseller *Moving Day*. His short stories have appeared in *Best American Mystery Stories 2016*, *New Haven Noir*, and two previous MWA anthologies, *The Mystery Box* (ed. Brad Meltzer) and *Ice Cold: Tales of Intrigue from the Cold War* (ed. Jeffery Deaver). He is married, with a son and daughter. Learn more at jonathanstonebooks.com.

Elaine Togneri's mysteries have also appeared in MWA Anthologies *Blood on Their Hands* and *The Rich and the Dead*. Her story "Five Words" is in *Malice Domestic 15: Murder Most Theatrical*. Elaine holds an MA in English from Rutgers University and is a member of MWA and SinC. She is the founder and a past president of Sisters in Crime: Central New Jersey Chapter.

She lives in Florida with her husband and their rescued Labrador retriever.

Lisa Unger is a *New York Times* and internationally bestselling author. With books published in twenty-six languages and millions of copies sold worldwide, she is widely regarded as a master of suspense. Her new release is *Confessions on the 7:45*. Her critically acclaimed books have been named on "Best Book" lists from the *Today* show, *Good Morning America*, *Entertainment Weekly*, *People*, *Amazon*, *Goodreads* and many others. She has been nominated for or won numerous awards including the Hammett Prize, Macavity, Thriller Award and Goodreads Choice. In 2019, she received two Edgar Award nominations, an honor held by only a few authors, including Agatha Christie. Her writing has appeared in the *New York Times*, *Wall Street Journal*, *NPR* and *Travel+Leisure*. She lives on the west coast of Florida with her family.

Amanda Witt's short stories have appeared in several MWA anthologies and in *Alfred Hitchcock's Mystery Magazine*. She's also the author of four dystopian novels (The Red Series). She lives in Texas with her husband and the thousands of books their adult children promise to come back for someday.

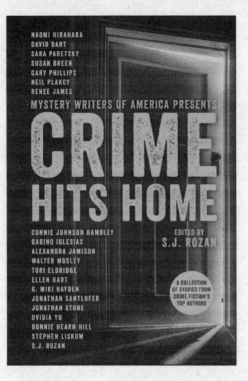